PRAISE FOR FARRAH ROCHON

"Everything Farrah Rochon writes is an utter joy to read!"
—Ali Hazelwood, *New York Times* bestselling author

"Rochon is a romance master." —*Kirkus*

"Farrah Rochon is one of the absolute best romance writers today. Period."
—Kristan Higgins, *New York Times* bestselling author

"Rochon's books are always witty, hot, and engaging."
—BuzzFeed

"Rochon is incisively funny, gifted at winging between laugh-out-loud scenarios, crackling banter, and pointed social commentary." —*Entertainment Weekly*

"Rochon woos readers with ample wit and charm."
—*Publishers Weekly*

"Farrah Rochon writes intensely real characters with flaws and gifts in equal measure."
—Nalini Singh, *New York Times* bestselling author

ALSO BY FARRAH ROCHON

The Boyfriend Project
The Dating Playbook
The Hookup Plan

PARDON my FRENCHIE

FARRAH ROCHON

FOREVER

NEW YORK BOSTON

Forever
Hachette Book Group
1290 Avenue of the Americas, New York, NY 10104
read-forever.com
@readforeverpub

First Edition: June 2024

Forever is an imprint of Grand Central Publishing. The Forever name and logo are registered trademarks of Hachette Book Group, Inc.

The publisher is not responsible for websites (or their content) that are not owned by the publisher.

Forever books may be purchased in bulk for business, educational, or promotional use. For information, please contact your local bookseller or the Hachette Book Group Special Markets Department at special.markets@ hbgusa.com.

Library of Congress Cataloging-in-Publication Data
Names: Rochon, Farrah, author.
Title: Pardon my Frenchie / Farrah Rochon.
Description: First Edition. | New York : Forever, 2024.
Identifiers: LCCN 2023051330 | ISBN 9781538739143 (trade paperback) | ISBN 9781538739150 (ebook)
Subjects: LCGFT: Romance fiction. | Novels.
Classification: LCC PS3618.O346 P37 2024 | DDC 813/.6—dc23/eng/20231103
LC record available at https://lccn.loc.gov/2023051330

ISBN: 9781538739143 (trade paperback), 9781538739150 (ebook)

Printed in the United States of America

LSC

Printing 1, 2024

Dedicated to the memory of Chermaine Roybiskie, the best mama a girl could ever ask for. Your work here was done.

Well done, good and faithful servant. —Matthew 25:21

1

Crouching near the start line, Ashanti Wright peered up at the white board on the judges' table, examining the rankings for today's event.

She stooped low and whispered into her French bulldog's pointed ear.

"Listen to me, baby. This title is ours for the taking. Just run your race and don't let these other doggies distract you."

She glanced over at the Pekingese who posed the biggest threat to Duchess winning Best in Show. The other pup had been quick through the obstacle course, but Ashanti's Frenchie was quicker. More agile. And cuter. Plus, she rocked a hot pink faux pearl tiara while zipping through the weave poles. Could the Pekingese do that?

Nope. Don't think so.

A shadow fell upon Ashanti a second before she heard, "Uh-oh. I know that competitive look. You're trying to *win* customers, not scare them off."

Her younger sister Kara stood above her, licking a popsicle shaped like a dog bone.

"No reason Duchess can't win too," Ashanti countered. "And why are you eating a popsicle made for dogs?"

"The vendor said the ingredients are all natural. It's not bad." Kara shrugged as she bit off one end.

"Get back to the booth. You're supposed to be taking orders for *our* dog treats, remember?"

"Is the French bulldog ready?" the head judge asked.

"You were born ready," Ashanti murmured softly as she gave Duchess a final head scratch. She stood and, in a louder voice, said, "Yes, she is."

This wasn't exactly Westminster. It wasn't even an official AKC event. But Ashanti still wanted to win. When it came to Duchess, she had a fierce competitive streak.

The final event was a handler-free run through the seven-apparatus obstacle course. Duchess wasn't a show dog, but a course similar to this one was part of the regular exercise regimen Ashanti offered at Barkingham Palace, the doggy daycare she'd opened three years ago. A solid performance by Duchess was bound to draw interest from the dog lovers attending today's Geaux for Fi-Deaux Jamboree.

That was the real reason she was here. Business. Her homemade dog treats had sold out within a half hour, which was why she had Kara now taking orders to ship and helping to drum up new clients for the daycare. Having Duchess take home the Best in Show ribbon would be gravy.

"On your mark," the judge said. "And go!"

She gave Duchess's butt a firm pat, and the dog took off, racing through the crawl tunnel and catapulting over the jump bars. Her baby was *killing* it. Ashanti couldn't hide her ridiculously proud grin even if she tried.

She didn't try.

But her smile faded when she felt a low vibration thump in her chest.

"Oh no," Ashanti murmured.

The bass was coming from a vehicle that was still several blocks away.

"Not that," she whispered, her attention swinging from Duchess to the car. "Anything but that."

But it *was* that. Her stomach dropped at the unmistakable intro to Juvenile's "Back That Azz Up."

"Nooo," Ashanti cried. But it was too late.

Duchess stopped just before reaching the hoop jump and started wiggling her pudgy tail. Her hind legs pumped up and down in time with the music.

Ashanti closed her eyes, expelling a defeated moan.

The laughter that broke out among the onlookers was so loud it drew an even bigger crowd, including Kara, who'd jogged back to the obstacle course. Her younger sister put her hands on her knees and popped her back, mimicking Duchess.

Ashanti cut her eyes at her.

Kara raised both hands. "Don't blame me!"

"Oh, I am *absolutely* blaming you." Kara and their other sister, her identical twin, Kendra, were the ones who'd trained Duchess to drop it like it's hot to the late-nineties anthem that continued to be a source of pride for New Orleans.

The crowd laughed and cheered even louder when Duchess resumed the obstacle course once the car passed, as if nothing had happened.

Duchess's dance break had cost her the blue ribbon, but a line of festival-goers followed them back to the booth. It wasn't the kind of advertising Ashanti had intended, but now she wondered if she should rethink her marketing strategy.

She and Kara handed out the remaining bite-size samples of Duchess Delights' sweet potato and carob twists—her most popular flavor—while a parade of people took selfies with her ridiculously photogenic Frenchie.

She was encouraged by the enthusiasm emanating from the crowd as she answered questions about the daycare. The minute the line slowed down, Ashanti turned to Kara.

"Where's Kendra? She was supposed to be here an hour ago."

"Sorry, but our twin telepathy is kinda like the ice cream machine at McDonald's these days." Kara pressed her thumbs to both temples. "I think it's indefinitely incapacitated."

"Text her," Ashanti said before turning to a woman with two middle school–aged children and a collie in dire need of a brush. "Hello there," she said. She stooped to dog level and ran her fingers through the collie's mane, trying her best not to grimace at the tangles she found. "And who is this cutie?"

"This is Sadie. Where's Puddin'?" the girl with blond pigtails asked.

"My kids love Duchess and Puddin'," the mother said. "They made me play that Instagram Reel you posted last night ten times."

Ashanti laughed, even though she hadn't looked at their Instagram since last week. Between her one-woman treat-baking side hustle and supervising Barkingham Palace's staff, she couldn't afford to fall victim to the time suck that was social media. However, as a businesswoman, she understood the value of it. And she was grateful for the antics of Duchess and her standard poodle friend, Puddin', that were suddenly sweeping the Internet. Kara was more than happy to post silly videos and promotion specials across their online platforms.

"Puddin' is back at Barkingham Palace," Ashanti said. "Have you ever thought of sending Sadie to daycare?"

"Oh no. My husband works from home, so there's always someone there with her."

"Doggy daycare is more than just dog sitting. It's a way for Sadie to socialize with other pets in a fun, safe environment." She held up a placard with a QR code. "Scan the code. It will take you to our website where you can learn about all that we offer."

"Are there any more Duchess Delights?"

"I'm sorry, but we're sold out. And we just gave away the last of the samples. You can find them at our daycare, and also at Lana's Treasures in the French Quarter. And remember, your pet gets a free Duchess Delights treat every day when you book a seven-night or longer stay."

Ashanti leaned toward Kara and whispered through her smile, "Am I trying too hard?"

"Like a freshman without a date for homecoming," her sister whispered back.

Duchess and Sadie were still in the butt-sniffing stage of their getting-to-know-you meet and greet when, without warning, the collie snapped at Duchess. That ended Ashanti's quest to reel her in as a client. If a dog couldn't get along with *her* dog, they were not the right fit for Barkingham Palace.

Ashanti scooped Duchess into her arms.

"Bad girl, Sadie." The mother smiled at Ashanti, as if her demon dog hadn't just attempted to commit a felony against her Frenchie. "She does that every now and then."

"You may want to talk to her vet about it," Ashanti said. "I'm sorry, but it looks as if the fest is winding down. We need to start packing up our booth."

As she and Kara started to break down the booth, Ashanti considered calling Kendra to help, but they would probably be done by the time her sister made it here from their house in the St. Roch neighborhood.

"We have to change the labels on the treats," Kara announced as she rolled up the retractable banner. "I'm no longer happy with them."

"What are you talking about? People loved the labels."

"But I didn't get the 'wow' reaction I was hoping for. I want customers to be so overwhelmed by the sheer cuteness of the packaging that they fall to their knees in awe."

Ashanti rolled her eyes for what had to have been the hundredth time today. It was a common occurrence when dealing with her sister's drama.

"Take Duchess to potty while I finish up here," she told Kara. "I want to be back at the daycare in time to help Leslie with the evening feedings."

Twenty minutes later, after dropping Kara off at a friend's, Ashanti headed for Barkingham Palace. She tried to estimate how many of the people they talked to today could become potential customers. She wasn't desperate for business, but every night one of the doggy suites went empty, it was another night that she wasn't maximizing her profits.

The expansion plans she had in mind would require every cent she could make. She glanced at Duchess in the rearview mirror, sitting up high in her car seat.

"It'll be worth it in the end, won't it, baby?"

Ashanti pulled into her parking spot at the daycare. She

didn't bother with Duchess's leash, carrying her up the steps and into the daycare.

"How'd it go at Geaux for Fi-Deaux?" asked her receptionist, Deja Fontenot.

"Duchess didn't win Best in Show, but I sold out of the treats I made, and I wouldn't be surprised if we get some new customers," Ashanti said as she made a beeline to the smaller, inside play area. Duchess squirmed in anticipation. "Okay, okay. We're almost there."

The moment Duchess saw Puddin', she dove out of Ashanti's arms like Tom Daley off a ten-meter platform. She and the poodle danced around, behaving like long-lost friends who hadn't seen each other in ages. They had been together just a few hours ago.

"These two are ridiculous," said Leslie, Deja's cousin and Ashanti's second-in-command.

"At what point does their obsession with each other go from being cute to problematic?" Ashanti asked, observing the dogs as they wrestled with each other over Duchess's Peppa Pig plush. The moment one dog won the tug-of-war, it would immediately offer the plush to the loser.

Leslie shrugged. "It's still pretty cute to me."

Ashanti matched her shrug. "Let's get the rest of the dogs fed, and then Duchess and I are going home."

"I've already handled tonight's feeding," Leslie said. "And I brushed them all down."

"Even Lulu and Sparkle?" The Sanchezes' Pomeranians were notorious biters when it came to grooming.

"Done," Leslie said. "Mark will be here for the overnight shift in another twenty minutes, so you and Duchess can head out now if you want."

Barkingham Palace was the only boarding house in the city that offered staffed care onsite, twenty-four seven. They usually took turns doing overnights, but because of all the baking she had been doing lately, Ashanti had not worked one in more than a month.

"Okay, then," she said, excited at the prospect of an extra hour of free time she hadn't anticipated. Maybe she could catch up on an episode of *Bridgerton*. "Let's go, Duchess."

Her dog stopped in the middle of jostling with Puddin'. She looked from Ashanti to Leslie, then darted behind the play gym.

"Uh-oh. Looks like someone doesn't want to leave her boyfriend."

Ashanti sighed. "Not today, Duchess."

"Leave her," Leslie said. "She's fine. Mark won't mind her being here tonight."

She crossed her arms over her chest. "I must say, I feel some kind of way about my dog choosing a boy over her mama."

"Face it. Puddin' can do more for her than you can."

Ashanti narrowed her eyes as she pointed at the dogs. "You two better behave."

They both barked, then simultaneously converged on Peppa Pig.

2

Okay, Monday, I'm gonna need you to stop acting like a Monday."

Ashanti dropped to her knees and peered underneath her bedroom dresser, searching for her purple-and-white polka-dot ponytail holder. She spotted a hoop earring she hadn't seen in ages, a lone sock, and the plastic chew toy Duchess had rejected like a scorned girlfriend rejects excuses on Valentine's Day. But no ponytail holder.

She did not have time for this today.

The oven timer chimed with the distinctive tune that she had begun hearing in her sleep. She pushed up from the floor and darted down the short hallway, through the combined living room and dining room area, and into the kitchen. Even a minute longer in the oven would render the dog biscuits unsellable, and with the number of orders she had on her hands this week, there was zero margin for error. Geaux for Fi-Deaux had been extremely good for business.

Ashanti yanked open the oven door and retrieved two cookie sheets from inside, then searched in vain for somewhere to put them. It wasn't until she'd launched this unintended side hustle that she finally understood why her mother used to complain about the kitchen's lack of counter space. She was one big order away from this setup being unsustainable.

Who was she kidding? Her current situation had become unsustainable the morning she woke up with a silicone baking mat stuck to her face.

As she carried the cookie sheets to the dining room table, she spotted Kara bounding down the stairs with a sheaf of papers. The tips of her jet-black bob were aqua today to match her aqua Nikes.

"I can't come up with a label design that screams 'wow,'" Kara said. "And you need to invest in the next generation Cricut machine if you want me to take you seriously as an entrepreneur."

"I told you, I cannot afford to spend eight hundred dollars on a printer," Ashanti said.

"The newest model is a thousand now, and it is an *investment.*"

"Talk to me after I pay the rent on the daycare." Ashanti looked to the stairs. "Where's Kendra?" It felt as if she'd asked that question a thousand times this month. "And what time did she get home last night?"

"Umm…I'm not sure," Kara hedged.

Ashanti gave her a *don't play with me* stare.

"It is not fair of you to demand I rat out my twin," Kara said. "That goes against every sibling code there is. You've been a big sister long enough to know this. Frankly, I'm disappointed in you, Shanti."

Ashanti rolled her eyes. "Get to school."

She started up the stairs, nodding at her parents' wedding picture on the way. The practice had become as automatic as breathing. On most days it was to reassure them that she had things under control, but on days like today, the nod was her way of accepting the encouragement she knew Lincoln and Felicity Wright were sending her from the great beyond. She needed that encouragement more and more lately when it came to dealing with Kendra.

Before she reached the landing of the second floor of their compact two-story house in New Orleans's solidly gentrified St. Roch neighborhood, Kendra walked out of the bathroom wearing a plain black T-shirt and faded jeans.

"Hey, Ken, everything okay?"

"Fine."

The single word was as cold as a Mongolian winter.

"School starts in"—Ashanti looked down at her Apple Watch—"less than fifteen minutes."

"This is my third year there. I think I know by now what time school starts," Kendra said.

Ashanti sucked in a breath and counted to five. The therapist had told her a long time ago that addressing hostility with hostility would only lead to more hostility.

"It's been a rough morning, Ken. I don't need the attitude."

"You're the one who came up here to bother me," her sister said, edging past her.

"I came to check on you. Excuse me for being concerned, especially after finding your room empty at eleven last night," Ashanti shouted as she followed her down the stairs.

So much for their hostility-free environment.

She stopped at the base of the stairs, where Kendra sat

on the bench in their narrow foyer, pulling on a pair of tennis shoes that were as worn and dirty as Kara's were new and spotless.

"I know you girls are sixteen and deserve some space," Ashanti said. "But missing curfew on a school night is unacceptable."

Kara walked up to them with her hands held high. "I just want to point out that I was home before curfew."

"Oh, just get on your knees and lick her fucking boots," Kendra said.

"Hey!" Ashanti yelled. "That's the last time I hear that kind of language in this house, you hear me?"

Kendra stood and pulled the strap of her backpack over her shoulder. "Whatever," she mumbled.

"Hey," Ashanti said again. She grabbed her by the arm. "I don't know what's going on with you, and I am trying to be as patient as possible, but don't speak to me that way."

"Sorry," Kendra mumbled. In a louder voice, she said, "I'm going to be late for school."

Ashanti reluctantly let go of her arm. She looked to Kara, who hunched her shoulders as she followed her twin sister out the door.

Ashanti sucked in a breath and whispered the first line of the Serenity Prayer.

She couldn't spend her morning agonizing over whatever was eating at Kendra, not with her mile-long to-do list. But she and her sister would be having a heart-to-heart soon. This couldn't go on.

She went to her bedroom—formerly her parents' room—and changed out of the worn LSU Veterinary Medicine T-shirt she'd slept in last night and into a lilac Barkingham Palace polo shirt. After slipping on a pair of jeans and stuffing her feet into her favorite pair of Skechers, she gathered her micro-braids at the nape of her neck and secured them with her black hair tie.

She checked to make sure the oven was off, then gave the kitchen one last look. She had to get another space. If she had known three years ago when she'd found the building that currently housed Barkingham Palace that she would get into the dog treat–making business, she would have opted for a place with enough room to build an industrial kitchen. Duchess Delights had taken over their entire home.

She had her eye on two possible buildings for her new venture. The one she *really* wanted was in the city's Lower Garden District and so far beyond her price range that the James Webb telescope wouldn't be able to see it. She had settled on the two-story double-gallery house five blocks away from the daycare's current location. The place needed some work, so she was waiting for the asking price to go down before she made an offer.

Now that she was sure she wanted to take Duchess Delights to the next level, she would have to make a move soon.

"You *are* sure, right?" Ashanti whispered.

What was she talking about? Of course she was sure. The best way to capitalize on this newfound success and maximize profitability would be to invest back into her business.

As she made her way to the car, her phone buzzed. Ashanti pulled it from her pocket and glanced at the screen. It was a text from Kara.

Duchess and Puddin' are snuggled up again
on the doggy cam. Those two need to get a
room.

Ashanti grinned as she texted back. Tell me about it. I
couldn't get my own dog to come home last night. She
didn't want to be away from her boyfriend.

She slipped in behind the wheel. Put your phone away
and pay attention in class.

Kara responded with a thumbs-up emoji.

Ashanti took the longer way to work, traveling through
the half-dozen blocks of the Faubourg Marigny and into the
Bywater neighborhood, all so she could check in on the house
that had gone up for sale six weeks ago. It was so big that it
would allow her to double the size of the daycare and create a
storefront for Duchess Delights.

She stopped at the corner of Clouet and Royal Streets and
stared longingly at the yellow creole cottage with gray gin-
gerbread trim. To her disappointment, a sign proclaiming
NEW LOWER PRICE had not been added to the FOR SALE sign
overnight.

"That's okay, my beauty," Ashanti said. "I'll have you soon
enough. You will look stunning in purple."

Less than five minutes later, she pulled into the narrow
driveway between Barkingham Palace and the house belong-
ing to the daycare's neighbor, Mrs. Short. The retiree, who
owned more cats than Ashanti could keep count of, sat on the
top step leading to her house, drinking coffee and smoking a
cigarette.

"Morning, Mrs. Short," Ashanti called with a wave. Unlike

others in the neighborhood, Mrs. Short had never given her permission to address her by her first name.

"One of those dogs took a shit in front of my house," the woman called back.

Ashanti said the second line of the Serenity Prayer.

"I doubt it was one of the dogs at Barkingham Palace. Our dogs are only allowed to roam around the backyard, not on the street. And the staff cleans up after each dog. Always."

Mrs. Short huffed and went back to her cigarette.

Maybe Ashanti shouldn't wait for the price to drop on her new place in the Bywater after all. Her future neighbors had to be more amiable.

As she approached the daycare's front door, she was reminded to get in touch with the artist she'd commissioned to replicate the mural of the iconic wrought-iron gates that surrounded London's Buckingham Palace. She would need the same feature at her new place. Lately, it had become a sought-after background for the Instagram selfies of tourists.

The same artist who had painted the outside mural had painted the reception area to look like one of Buckingham Palace's staterooms, with faux columns on the walls and filigree in place of crown molding. A portrait of her favorite California-based royals hung on the wall above the chew toy display.

"Morning," Ashanti muttered as she approached the reception desk.

"Morning to you too," Deja said. She tipped her head out from behind the monitor. "You don't seem your usual chipper self. What's going on?"

"Monday is showing its ass."

"Yeah, well, brace yourself because you're about to see a bit more of Monday's ass."

"Not yet." Ashanti covered her ears with her palms. "Let me at least love on the dogs before giving me any bad news."

Deja wiggled her fingers toward the door that led to the rest of the daycare. "You get ten minutes. Then you can address this letter from the councilman's office. It looks as if our neighbor reported us."

"For what?" Ashanti snatched the letter Deja gestured to from the reception desk.

"She says the incessant barking has given her cats anxiety and she wants you to pay for their medication."

"She can kiss my—" Ashanti stopped herself before she could curse again. "What is it with this woman? I know a lot of the people here were against allowing businesses to open in residential areas—the same has happened on my street in St. Roch—but we go out of our way to be courteous neighbors."

"I think it's more the *type* of business you opened that Mrs. Short is against," Deja pointed out. "In case you hadn't noticed, she's a fan of cats."

"Whatever," Ashanti said. "I think she just likes being petty and vindictive." She tossed the letter back onto the desk. "Maybe I should report her for all the cigarette butts that mysteriously find their way onto our side of the fence. I picked up three in the exercise pen yesterday."

"Go for it," Deja encouraged.

Or, maybe this was a sign that she *should* finally go for that property in the Bywater. If anything qualified as the last straw, being reported to the city council because there was barking coming from a daycare center for *dogs* should be it.

"I need to hug my Duchess," Ashanti said.

She made her way to her favorite area of the daycare. The smaller of the two playrooms' aesthetic was a nod to her Frenchie's white-and-black piebald coat, with splashes of purple to add a royal flare. Portraits of Duchess hung on the walls in gilded frames. Was it a bit over the top? Absolutely. But when it came to her baby there was no top.

Seconds after she entered the room, Ashanti was bombarded by a cadre of feisty canines with Napoleon complexes. This is what she missed the most. Having to devote so much time to baking, she didn't get to play with the dogs nearly as much as she wanted to.

"Hey, Lulu and Sparkle," she greeted the Pomeranians, giving each dog one of the dime-sized treats from her pocket. "And how is my favorite Chihuahua," she called to Bingo, who had been coming to the daycare since the first week it opened. She followed the treats with quick head rubs for each dog, then went in search of Duchess.

"Where's my dog?" Ashanti asked Leslie, who was running the Parkers' Cavalier King Charles through the agility maze. Leslie gestured to cushioned mats in the corner.

Ashanti walked over and found Duchess hugged up next to Puddin'. The two lay in a yin-yang pattern, with Duchess's head nestled against Puddin's chest, and her squat legs arcing around the puffy topknot atop the poodle's head.

"Kara was right. You two really do need a room."

At the sound of her voice, Duchess's stubby tail started wagging like a windshield wiper gone haywire, but she still didn't move away from Puddin'.

"If you don't get over here," Ashanti said. She reached down and lifted Duchess into her arms. "Don't forget who keeps you in tiaras and rawhide," she said, nuzzling the dog's flat nose with her own.

Static crackled through the intercom system a second before Deja's uneasy voice came through the line. "Umm, Ashanti, can you come up to reception?"

Ashanti shut her eyes. If it was Mrs. Short lobbing another complaint about dog shit she was going to lose it.

"Lord, grant me the wisdom to know the difference," she said, setting Duchess on the mat. She quickly made her way through the maze of rooms and back up to reception. Her steps faltered when she slid open the pocket doors.

That was not Mrs. Short.

3

Ashanti took in the man waiting just to the right of the reception desk. He stood with arms crossed over a very nice, incredibly solid-looking chest. Sunglasses—seriously, dude, wearing sunglasses inside?—covered what appeared to be a very nice, incredibly chiseled, light brown face. He could cut steel with that jawline.

Several tattoos peeked out from the cuffs of his short-sleeved T-shirt, which strained around sinewy biceps. His sculpted muscles looked as if they had been carved out of the granite she wanted for her kitchen countertops.

He was average height, yet he took up too much space, standing there with his legs braced apart and an irritated look on his face. Guess she wasn't the only one having a sucky Monday.

"Can I help you?" she asked.

"This guy says he's here to pick up Puddin'," Deja offered.

Ashanti's forehead furrowed with instant skepticism.

Puddin' had been a round-the-clock boarder for the past five weeks, ever since her owner suffered a fall. Frances Sutherland had called Ashanti from the ambulance, asking her to go to her home in Tremé to retrieve her beloved poodle. Ashanti had made sure someone at the daycare texted her a daily photo ever since.

"How do you know Puddin'?" she asked, looking at the portrait of Harry and Meghan just above his shoulder instead of his appealing jawline. The Sussexes were safer.

"It's my grandmother's dog," he said. "She sent me to pick it up."

"Mrs. Frances is out of the hospital?" Ashanti asked, relief filling her chest. "That is so good to hear. I'm surprised she didn't call to tell me she was home. She knows I would have brought Puddin' to the house for her."

"She's not home," he said. "Well, not at her house, at least. Look, can you just get the dog?"

His brusque manner caught her off guard.

Mrs. Frances had often mentioned she had a grandson in the Army. His muscular build supported the idea of him being a soldier, but that didn't mean she would just hand the dog over to him without confirming his identity.

"Deja can check Puddin's profile, but I'm pretty certain the only other person authorized to pick him up is Mrs. Frances's neighbor, Tasha Jones. And Tasha is on a nursing assignment out of town." She wanted him to know that she knew her clients. "You will need to provide proof that you have permission to pick up Puddin' before we can release him to you, Mr. Sutherland."

"It's Sims," he said.

"Sorry. Mr. Sims," she corrected.

He continued to stand there with his arms crossed over his chest. Ashanti waited for him to say something else.

"Well?" Ashanti asked.

"You were serious." It was a statement more than a question, but she answered it anyway.

"Of course I'm serious. We do not allow people to just come in off the street and leave with a client's dog."

He released an exasperated sigh. "It's just a dog."

Just a dog?

"Do you have any idea how much a purebred standard poodle goes for? Puddin' is not just a dog. And if you were really related to Mrs. Frances, you would know that she does not consider Puddin' to be 'just a dog' either. He's her family."

Mr. Sims removed his sunglasses and hooked them on the front collar of his T-shirt like an extra straight out of an eighties movie. Ashanti had not been prepared for his eyes. They were gorgeous. Chocolate brown and *stunningly* gorgeous.

He retrieved a cell phone from his back pocket, swiped across the screen, then turned the phone to face Ashanti. A moment later, Frances Sutherland's kind face stared back at her.

"Mrs. Frances!" Ashanti said, unable to contain her glee at seeing one of her favorite people in the world. "How are you?"

"This hip has put me out of commission," Mrs. Frances replied. "How is my Puddin'? Is he giving Thad a hard time? Those two don't get along, but they're about to become the best of friends."

Ashanti glanced up at the woman's grandson long enough to notice how his already chiseled jaw became even more rigid.

"So, Mr. Sims here really is your grandson?"

"I told you that," he said.

"Yes, that's my grandson, Thaddeus," Mrs. Frances said at the same time. "His friends all call him Thad." Then she added, "He's single."

Another sigh from Sunglasses—aka Thaddeus. This sigh

was more irritated than exasperated. He turned the camera to face him. "Grams, can you just give her permission to release the dog to me?"

Surly. Single and surly.

As much as Ashanti wanted to say it, she abstained. "I can add Thaddeus as an authorized custodian if that's what you would like, Mrs. Frances."

"Please do. Thad will be picking Puddin' up from now on. This new place they put me in doesn't allow pets."

"You had to leave your home?" Ashanti's heart pulled. When she'd talked to her last week, Mrs. Frances was still in the rehabilitation facility but hoping to be released soon. "I'm so sorry. Maybe the new place would be willing to make an exception. I can vouch for Puddin' if you'd like."

Thaddeus turned the phone to his face again. "Grams, I need to go. You and your friend will have to pick up this conversation another time."

"Bring Puddin' to see me as soon as you leave Ashanti's," Mrs. Frances hollered before he disconnected the call.

He stuck the phone back into his pocket and said, "Can you get the dog now?"

"What's going on with Mrs. Frances? Why isn't she at her house? Did they extend her rehab? Is she in skilled nursing? How long before she gets to return home?"

Ashanti knew she'd gone overboard by the third question, but she couldn't help it. Frances Sutherland was truly one of her favorite people. She was the one who'd first encouraged Ashanti to sell the baked treats that she initially only gave out as a weekly gift to her regulars. She was also one of those older Black Southern women who constantly shared unsolicited advice, but who did so in such a subtle and polite way that you didn't mind.

"I'm just concerned," Ashanti said. "I've known your grandmother for years."

For a moment she thought he would ignore her barrage of questions, but then he said, "She had to move to an assisted living facility. She's doing better after hip surgery, but she needs to be in a place where there are people who can take care of her if something like this happens again."

That must have been a hard pill to swallow for such an independent woman.

"Is it the facility on Orleans Avenue or the one on Esplanade?" Ashanti asked.

He cocked his head to the side and stared at her, his expression the very definition of annoyance. "You're her dog sitter. Why do you need to know all of this?"

"Because I consider Mrs. Frances a friend," Ashanti said. She was beyond offended by his tone and by being relegated to the role of a simple dog sitter. She owned this business, and she did a hell of a lot more here than just dog sit.

"What is your problem?" she couldn't help but ask.

"My problem?" he asked as he reached into the pocket opposite where he'd put his phone and retrieved a wallet. "Let's see. Maybe it's that we're standing here playing twenty questions instead of you getting that dog so I can get on with the rest of my day." He slid out a credit card and handed it to Deja. "You can put the balance on this."

In the span of five seconds there were at least five inappropriate responses that nearly shot out of Ashanti's mouth. But he was a client. Well, client-adjacent. The first rule of being a good business owner was that you did not curse out your clients. No matter how much they deserved it.

Her eyes still trained on him, she sucked in a calming breath before she said, "Deja, please ask Leslie to bring Puddin' up to reception. He should have three containers of food in the refrigerator. Have her bring those too."

Thaddeus's bored look only agitated her more as they waited for the dog.

He must be adopted. Or maybe it was one of those situations where Mrs. Frances had taken him in as a kid and he'd started calling her his grandmother. There had to be some other explanation, because there was no way this cranky-ass man and that sweet, kind woman had the same blood running through their veins.

"Thanks," he said, taking the credit card and receipt Deja handed him. He looked at the printout then looked at Ashanti. "Are you serious?"

Before she could respond, the pocket doors slid open and Leslie came in with Puddin'. The poodle growled at Thaddeus before running to Ashanti's side.

Smart dog.

She dropped to one knee and rubbed his fluffy ears.

"It's okay, sweetie. I know you don't want to go with this"—she looked up at Thaddeus— "man. But it'll be okay." She stood. "He's had his morning meal. He eats again at six." She handed Thaddeus the containers with the homemade food that Leslie had brought up from the back, then walked over to the display rack and pulled a small bag of the hypoallergenic kibble from the shelf. "I'm not sure if Mrs. Frances has any of Puddin's food at home. He has strict dietary restrictions. Mix a half cup of the food in those containers with a half cup of the food in this bag."

Shaking his head again as he reached for the dog food, Thaddeus muttered, "It's a dog. He'll be happy with whatever I give him."

Ashanti pulled the bag away before he could grab it. "Why don't you just leave him here?" she suggested. "We've been taking care of Puddin' for the past two years. He knows and loves the entire staff."

"Lady, come on. I need to get going."

Lady?

She nearly broke the first rule of being a good business owner.

Holding back another barrage of swear words she rarely used, she finally handed him the food, then fluffed Puddin's topknot. "I'll see you tomorrow, sweetie."

"No, you won't," Thaddeus said as he wrapped Puddin's turquoise-and-black zebra-striped leash around his hand. "I'm not wasting money sending this dog to daycare."

"What?" Ashanti all but gasped. He could not be serious. "Where will he go during the day?"

"He will be at the house like a normal dog."

"Puddin' is not a normal dog! Wait, no. I mean, of course, he's a normal dog, but he needs social interaction. I told you, Mrs. Frances has been sending him here for two years."

"Have a nice day," he said, turning for the door.

"But our annual dog pageant is this weekend," Ashanti called. "Puddin' always takes part."

"Not this year," he said without bothering to look back.

She stared in dismay as he and Puddin' exited the lobby.

"What an ass," Ashanti said the minute the door closed behind him.

"With a very nice ass," Leslie added.

She wasn't lying.

4

Thad had reached the second-to-last step before he realized his grandmother's cantankerous poodle hadn't followed him off the daycare's front porch. He turned and gently, but firmly, tugged on the leash.

"I don't have time for this shit today, dog. Come on."

Puddin' plopped down and refused to move. The sun glinted off the absurd rhinestone collar wrapped around his pencil-thin neck.

For a hot minute, Thad considered bringing him back inside and washing his hands of this spoiled, stubborn pain in his ass. At least the one with the braids—he figured she was the owner—would be happy about that. But after seeing the charge to his credit card for the dog's five-week stay, he refused to pay that dog sitter a single extra cent. Who in the hell charged that kind of money to watch a dog?

Maybe if she got rid of some of that fake, gold-plated royal family crap she wouldn't have to charge her clients the equivalent of a monthly mortgage.

"Move." Thad tugged again.

Puddin' stretched his front legs out in front of him and went from sitting to lying flat on his stomach.

Thad dropped his head back and swore up at the sky. Eight months ago all he had to do was snap his fingers and a company of over one hundred soldiers would follow his orders to the letter. Now, he couldn't get a bare-assed poodle with a sparkly collar to show him respect. He'd left behind a fifteen-year military career for this?

He jutted his chin toward the door. "She the one give you that stupid haircut? And you still want to hang around here?"

Puddin' let out a doleful whine and wagged the pom-pom on the tip of his tail. It really was a stupid haircut.

"Look, we're not doing this today," Thad told him as he climbed back up the steps. He scooped the poodle into his arms and carried him to the Ford Maverick XLT he'd bought from a used-car dealer when he'd arrived in Louisiana a month ago. It took him two tries before he could get the door open while still cradling the dog.

He cursed again as he set Puddin' on the passenger's side. He should have thought to bring a towel or something for the seat. Now he'd have dog hair all over his new-to-him truck.

Did poodles even shed their fur? Maybe he could ask the dog sitter. She would know.

Thad shut the door and hauled it to the driver's side when he realized he was fishing for an excuse to go back inside.

He'd kept his sunshades on longer than necessary so that the one with the braids, Ashanti, wouldn't notice how he couldn't stop staring at her. It was the freckles. A smattering of freckles on a woman's nose and cheeks got him every damn time.

Nope. He was not stepping foot in Barkingham Palace—that name was as ridiculous as Puddin's haircut—again.

The dog let out another whine. Thad started the engine and turned up the radio to drown him out.

He'd just put the truck in drive when the purple-and-white front door opened and the woman he'd just convinced himself he wasn't making excuses to see came jogging down the steps.

"Wait!" she yelled while flagging him down.

Thad put the truck in park, turned down the radio, and lowered the window.

Before he could get a word in, she shoved a plastic chew toy shaped like an alligator inside the open window. "You forgot Ali. It's Puddin's favorite."

As if to put an exclamation point on her statement, Puddin' jumped up from the seat, climbed into Thad's lap, and clutched the chew toy between his teeth. He waved it around like a maniac, thwacking Thad in the jaw.

"Dog, get off me." Thad lifted him from his lap and set him back on the passenger side.

"I told you, it's his favorite," Ashanti said. She grabbed on to his door, making it so that he couldn't raise the window without smashing her fingers. "Can you please just let me take care of Puddin' until Mrs. Frances can find another caretaker?"

"My grandmother already told you, *I'm* the dog's new caretaker."

"But it's obvious that you don't want to be. And, to be honest, I'm not sure you wouldn't do something to hurt him just so that you wouldn't have to be bothered with him."

Thad cut off the engine and turned to face her.

"You met me, what, fifteen minutes ago? The only thing

you know about me is that I'm Frances Sutherland's grandson. Yet, you're gonna stand here and accuse me of being some kind of dog murderer?"

She looked contrite. Up close, Thad realized she had even more freckles than he'd first thought. Shit, she was cute.

"You're right," Ashanti said. "That was uncalled for. I apologize. But don't pretend you actually *want* to care for Puddin'. I can tell that you don't."

He would rather watch *Gilmore Girls* on repeat for the next month than take care of this dog. And after having done that exact thing the summer his sister broke up with her high school boyfriend, it said a lot about just how much he dreaded becoming Puddin's caretaker.

But his grandmother loved her poodle as much as she loved her grandchildren—possibly more. He would do as she'd asked.

"Let me give you a tip," Thad said. "If you're going to take care of other people's pets, it's best if you don't get so attached. It doesn't appear to be healthy." He gestured to her hand. "Can you move that? I have somewhere I need to be, and I've already wasted too much time here."

Her nose flared, but she didn't say anything, just backed away from his truck.

Thad glanced in his rearview mirror as he drove away, cursing himself for being so harsh. He had to remember that he was part of civilian society now. He couldn't talk to someone like Ashanti as if she were an infantry grunt. He guessed it was a good thing Puddin' wouldn't be going to her doggy daycare center anymore.

"It's a good thing for both of us," he muttered.

Thad used the truck's touchscreen to put a call in to his

best friend and—if things went according to plan—eventual business partner, Von Montgomery. Von picked up on the first ring.

"I won't be able to meet you at the barbecue place," Thad said. They had passed the point of requiring a greeting a long time ago. "My grandmother is demanding I bring her dog to see her ASAP."

"Aw, damn, that's too bad, man. The food here hits."

"I knew you would say that," Thad said. "Text me what's good and I'll order takeout."

He disconnected the call as he pulled up to the corner of Clouet and St. Claude, where he was met with a sea of red taillights. He looked right and saw a dump truck with its bed tilted up and a dusting of what he could only assume had been a dirt haul remaining on the floor of the bed.

"You gotta be kidding me," Thad said with a groan. He wasn't about to get snarled up in this mess.

Thad surveyed the cars idling perpendicular to him. He honked his horn and motioned for a black Mustang GT to back up so that he could drive across St. Claude. The driver looked annoyed, but Thad didn't give a shit.

It pissed him off that he even had to ask the guy to back up when there was a sign telling drivers not to block the intersection. What was so hard about following simple traffic rules? That's something else he didn't have to worry about eight months ago. He was used to operating in an environment where rules were followed or bad shit happened.

He had about six inches of clearance on either side, but he managed to squeeze through and make it to the other side of St. Claude Avenue. Once he reached Royal Street and could finally make a right turn, he looked to his left as he eased off the brake. Then slammed on it a second later.

Puddin' went tumbling toward the floorboard.

"Shit." Thad unhooked his seat belt and reached over for the dog. Puddin' growled and snapped at him. Thad held both hands up. "I was trying to help."

When he reached for him again, the poodle allowed him to pick him up. Thad placed him on the seat and pulled the seat belt across him. Puddin' immediately stepped out of it.

"Fine, break your neck then, you lil asshole."

Someone behind him honked.

Instead of turning right, Thad continued straight on Clouet and parked next to the gray-and-yellow house at the corner. That lacy trim would have to come down, but as for the rest of it?

He lowered the windows about two inches, enough to keep air circulating, then got out of the truck. For a second, he thought about not locking it. Maybe someone would come by and steal Puddin'.

They would probably return the damn dog after ten minutes and make off with his radio instead. He pressed the lock on the key fob.

Thad walked the length of the house, then backtracked so that he could check it out from the front. He glanced over at the truck to make sure the dog was okay before jogging up the steps so he could peek into the small window on one of two front doors. He liked what he saw inside.

He took out his phone and called Von.

"You decide to come to the restaurant after all?" Von asked. "I'm in the latrine. Let the server know you're with the handsome guy at the back table near the bar."

Thad rolled his eyes. "I told you Grams wants to see her dog. I'm..." He looked around. "I think this area is called the Bywater. There's a spot here that has potential. *Real* potential," Thad emphasized. "I'm going to send a few pics and the address so you can look it up on those real estate sites you've been searching."

"Snap a pick of the FOR SALE sign. I can search it by the MLS number," Von said. "Oh, and I talked to the manager here at the restaurant and he said they've done pop-ups before. They'll roll the smoker out and set up shop wherever you need them to."

"Based on the size, this property probably has a place for that in the back," Thad said. "I'll try to poke around the fenced-in area before I leave."

"Or you can just use Google Earth like every other nosy person in the world who wants to look into someone's backyard," Von said. "Damn, Sims. Not even a year out of the corps and you're already losing your touch."

"Fuck you," Thad said. Von's laugh came through the phone before Thad could disconnect the call.

He searched for Google Earth using his browser because he didn't trust the app enough to have it downloaded on his phone. Not that he couldn't be found by any entity who cared to look—no one could stay completely hidden these days—but why make it easy for them?

Thad plugged in the address for the property at Clouet and Royal Streets. The backyard was even better than he first thought.

"Yeah, this could work." He snapped a few more pictures and texted them to Von as he walked back to his truck.

Once there, he peered through the window and frowned

at the tufts of white cotton strewn about the seat. "What the hell is this?" Thad asked, opening the door.

That's when he saw the Puddin'-size bite marks on the center console.

"I know you didn't—"

Thad leaned over to see the passenger side. The little bastard had chewed up the console.

Puddin' lay on the seat, his chin resting on the alligator chew toy.

Thad snatched the alligator and wagged it in the dog's face. "This is what you're supposed to chew. The *chew* toy! It's in the fucking name!"

Puddin' looked up at him then turned his head.

Thad counted to ten before he slid behind the wheel. He started the truck, but left it idling while he tried to calm down. The urge to throw his grandmother's beloved poodle out of a moving vehicle was too strong to trust himself not to do it.

Puddin' let out a loud snore.

Thad looked down at the dog. "I hate you," he said as he drove off.

He parallel parked into a spot across from Chateau Esplanade Senior Living's front gates ten minutes later.

Thad hadn't been happy when the doctors recommended his grandmother transition to an assisted living facility. Knowing how much she valued her independence, and how much she loved the house she and his grandfather had lived in for more than fifty years, he feared the move would hit Grams the same way leaving the Army had hit him.

He could not have been more wrong.

For one thing, Chateau Esplanade was a hundred times

nicer than any place he had ever lived in. They'd leaned heavily into the French theme throughout the building and the grounds, and the staff kept the place immaculate. But it was the companionship of the other residents that gave him peace of mind. He didn't have to worry about Grams being lonely, which had been another of his concerns.

His phone rang. It was his grandmother.

"You didn't get in an accident on the way here, did you?" she asked. "Where's my dog? Is he hurt?"

"At least I know where *my* well-being lands on your priority list," Thad said. "We just pulled up. Give me a minute."

Thad clipped the leash onto Puddin's collar. "Come on before she sends a search squad out here for you."

His grandmother was waiting on the porch that spanned the length of the building's palatial façade. As usual, she was impeccably dressed in pressed slacks and a silk blouse. Not a single strand of her silver hair was out of place. Thad had never once seen her in polyester or hair curlers.

"There he is! Oh, my baby!" She yanked Puddin's leash from Thad's hand and settled into one of the rocking chairs on the porch. The dog immediately put his head in her lap. "There's my good boy. I've missed you so much, my Puddin'."

Thad didn't bother mentioning that he, her only grandson, was also present. His mild annoyance shifted to amusement as he observed their reunion. He couldn't tell who was more excited, Grams or the dog.

"Did you talk to the director about the loose handle on the shower door?" Thad asked as he perched against the porch railing. He'd offered to fix the handle when he visited her on Saturday, but she pointed out that maintenance was included in the facility's astronomical monthly fee.

"It was fixed this morning," she said. Without looking away from the dog, she asked, "So, what do you think about Ashanti?"

Thad's head snapped back at her quick subject change. "What do you mean what do I think about her?"

"Don't play with me, Thaddeus," his grandmother said. "You are not getting any younger, and Ashanti Wright is perfect for you."

"Don't do this, Grams." He dragged a palm down his face. "First of all, I'm only thirty-four, so don't go asking the staff here if there's a unit for your grandson. And I just moved back home. I already told you, the only thing I'm interested in right now is getting my business off the ground."

"She is *perfect* for you," she repeated in that stern voice she used on him when he was eight years old. Thad had to admit, all these years later and it still made him flinch.

"Still not interested," he said.

He had more pressing matters to attend to, like figuring out just who in the hell *retired* Major Thaddeus Sims was.

For the past eight months he'd suffered through an existence that made him feel as if he were walking around in a shirt that was two sizes too small. Nothing about his post-Army life seemed to fit. The therapist he'd started seeing soon after he retired suggested he make a clean break, which was why he'd decided to move forward with his plans to go into business with Von here in New Orleans instead of remaining in Colorado Springs and transitioning into a civilian job with the DOD.

But navigating this new, unfamiliar, uncomfortable stage in his life had proven more difficult than he anticipated. He didn't need the added torture of making small talk with a woman his grandmother set him up with. Especially a woman who clearly didn't like him.

"The two of you have a lot in common," Grams continued as if he hadn't spoken. "She started her own business, so she can give you pointers."

"I don't—"

"And she's one of those do-gooder types, just like you. Especially when it comes to kids. She's always participating in some kind of activity for youths around the city." She finally tore her attention away from Puddin'. "Over the summer, she held an event specifically for kids with a fear of dogs. They were encouraged to visit the daycare so they could be exposed to dogs in a safe environment. Isn't that a beautiful thing to do?"

He sighed. "Yeah, it's nice, but—"

"Oh, I have the best idea!" Her face lit up. "You should suggest an event for the children of deployed veterans. That's right up your alley."

It *was* right up his alley. He'd served as his base's youth activity coordinator for three years. He'd been influenced by his grandfather, who'd stepped up big-time after his parents divorced and his mother, Thad, and his sister, Nadia, came to live with them. Gramps had been everything from troop leader to PTA president to surrogate father to several of Thad's high school friends. He saw the difference his grandfather made simply by being there and had been inspired to do the same.

But that didn't mean he was going to coordinate anything with Ashanti Wright.

Maybe if he admitted to his grandmother that her dog sitter probably didn't want to see him ever again after the way he'd behaved this morning, she would pump the brakes on her obvious matchmaking.

"Oh, and I want Puddin' to wear his dark green collar with the bow tie for the pageant," she was saying.

"What was that?" Thad asked.

"The pageant at Barkingham Palace. It's this coming Saturday. I want Puddin' in green. His collars are in the chest in my closet."

"Grams, I—"

"And I want you to FaceTime me during the pageant. It's always so much fun, and the dogs are adorable. I hate that I can't be there in person, but those steps at the daycare are just too steep for me to climb." She returned her attention to the dog, but continued talking. "You'll need to upgrade that old iPhone now that you're taking care of Puddin'. Find out from Ashanti what kind she has. She sends beautiful pictures. Do you think you can get a new phone before the pageant?"

He searched his mind for a viable excuse to get out of spending his Saturday at a damn pageant for dogs, but one look at the excitement on his grandmother's face put an end to that.

"Yeah, I'll make sure to FaceTime you," Thad said.

Guess that meant he *would* be seeing Ashanti Wright again, whether she wanted to see him or not.

5

Here."

Thad shoved the bowl of high-priced kibble in front of Puddin' with his foot. It was a good thing Barkingham Palace's cute-as-hell owner had given him another bag because there had only been crumbs left in the one in his grandmother's pantry.

"I shouldn't feed you at all after what you did to my truck," Thad said.

Puddin' turned his bare ass to him as he leaned over his bowl and started in on his dinner.

Hate was a strong word, one he seldom used outside of spiders and people who preyed upon the vulnerable. But Thad could say without hesitation that he truly hated this dog. Less than a day into his new role as caretaker and he was tempted to call his sister and ask if she would be willing to take Puddin' to live with her family in Austin. His nieces would love it.

But before he left Chateau Esplanade, his grandmother made him promise that he would bring Puddin' to visit every Sunday. She had not verbalized that it was a condition of his being able to stay in her home rent-free, but Thad had the impression that it was absolutely a condition. Anything happened to Puddin' and his ass would be on the curb.

He carried the dog food back to the pantry and made a mental note to add plastic storage containers to the list of items he needed to pick up the next time he went to one of the big-box stores. Just looking at his grandmother's pantry shelves gave him anxiety. Everything was either in its original packaging or in unlabeled ziplock bags. Thad planned to get rid of all of it and start fresh.

He knew it was a carryover from his time in the Army, but he didn't care. He needed more order and fewer sugar ants.

He hadn't made any changes to the house in the weeks he'd spent relocating everything he owned from Colorado Springs back to New Orleans. He didn't have to change anything. His grandmother and sister had already taken care of that.

Frances Sutherland was seventy-eight years old with the style of someone half her age. Nadia, his older sibling by three years, had come to New Orleans last year and, with the help of HGTV's evening lineup, had assisted Grams in overhauling the double shotgun-style home's more traditional decor, which his grandfather had preferred. Now everything was clean lines and modern finishes done in varying shades of gray, white, and pale blue.

Apparently, Nadia had caught the home design bug. She'd volunteered to help with the interior of Thad and Von's new venture when she came down for her best friend from high school's wedding in about five weeks. The friend was, ironically, marrying the same guy Nadia had broken up with that long ago *Gilmore Girls* summer. Life was funny and strange like that sometimes.

Thad opened the refrigerator and studied the array of local beers he'd stocked. Just one of the sacrifices he had to make for the sake of inventory and market research for The PX, the sports bar, cigar bar, barbershop, and all-around hangout spot for active duty and veteran military he and Von were opening, hopefully by Veterans Day. They would sell national brands, of course, but he and Von had decided to support local breweries and distilleries as much as possible. And if those local businesses were owned by fellow veterans, all the better.

He grabbed an Abita Purple Haze, then walked over to the box his sister had mailed, picking out a container of wasabi-flavored snack mix. He'd been getting a box every other day with items Nadia suggested they serve at The PX once they finally opened it.

If they ever opened it.

They would. Between the bonuses he'd saved up over the years, the cash payout he'd received for unused sick and leave days, and the hundred grand Von was contributing, they had enough to make a cash offer on a building. The generous, no-interest loan from his grandmother would provide them with everything else they needed to get up and running by their target opening date.

The only thing left was finding the right venue, and Thad had a feeling he'd stumbled upon just that earlier today.

"Guess that lil asshole dog is good for something," he muttered, recognizing that it was his trip to Barkingham Palace that had led to his impromptu drive through the Bywater.

He had never considered that area for their bar, despite hearing about how the neighborhood had transitioned from residential to semi-residential with a sprinkling of somewhat funky, somewhat swanky restaurants and businesses over the years. He and Von would have to do a bit more research to make sure what they had in mind for The PX would vibe with the Bywater, but Thad had a feeling it would.

He brought his beer and the snack mix to the dining room table, where he'd set up his laptop. Without thinking, Thad logged into the message board for veterans.

"Shit." He set his elbows on the table and rubbed his temples.

It had been automatic, like stepping on the brake at a stop sign, or breathing. He'd made a vow to spend no more than twenty minutes on the site per day. He had already gone over his allotted time while having breakfast this morning.

Von was the one who'd made Thad realize that he had become addicted to the site. And who had made him question why it was so hard for him to let go.

Thad had initially called bullshit on Von's theory that he was using the message boards as a lifeline because he regretted retiring from the Army. He had put in fifteen years—eleven more than he had originally planned. The message boards were just a way for him to pass the time and keep up with fellow vets.

But it had become more than that. It had become a crutch.

Thad had been forced to admit it a couple of weeks ago when he'd hopped on with the intention of checking in with some of the recent retirees he had befriended on the site. A dozen DMs and several rabbit holes later, he discovered that three hours had sailed by.

When Von called to ask if he had finished up the marketing plan he'd promised to work on, Thad had made up an excuse. Of course, Von saw right through it. He'd sent several screenshots, showing Thad's time-stamped posts. Further evidence of how difficult it was for anyone to go completely underground.

He'd fessed up because he'd had no other choice. And he'd promised Von that he would wean himself off the message boards. But how did you step away from the only thing that brought you peace? He'd heard horror stories about veterans adjusting to civilian life, but he never thought he would experience it.

What had he told Ashanti about becoming too attached? Maybe he should take his own advice.

His phone buzzed. He read the text from Von just as a knock sounded at the front door.

Outside. Let me in.

Puddin' went into an instant frenzy, racing back through the kitchen and to the den at the front of the house. By the time Thad arrived at the door, the dog was howling like someone had set fire to that puff on the end of his tail.

"Move, dog," he said as he opened the door. "What's up?" Thad greeted.

Puddin' went into full-on attack mode, zeroing in on Von's shoelace.

"What the hell is that?" Von asked as he tried to shake the dog off his foot.

"Puddin', heel!" Thad barked. The poodle backed off the shoelace and huffed at Thad.

"Don't tell me this is your grams's dog?" Von asked.

"Von, meet Puddin'," Thad deadpanned.

"I know you're fucking lying." Von burst out laughing.

"I wish," Thad said, motioning for him to come inside.

"No way," Von said as he followed Thad into the kitchen. "No way your grams stuck you with a half-naked poodle named Puddin'."

"You bring any of that barbecue from earlier today?" Thad asked.

"No, but I did bring some good news," Von said, holding up his phone. "I checked out that place on Royal and Clouet, and it's perfect. There's a bar a few blocks away, but it has a completely different vibe. Caters more to the hippie crowd."

"I didn't know there was a hippie crowd in New Orleans," Thad said, taking a pull on his beer.

"Dude, this place is Hippie Central. I can't look out my window without seeing a skinny white guy with dreads riding a bicycle." He turned the phone to face Thad. "Here's what makes this place perfect for us. You cross St. Claude Avenue and five minutes later you're at Jackson Barracks. Head a little farther into Chalmette and you've got the National Guard and the Coast Guards all within ten minutes of it."

Thad squinted at the map Von had pulled up. New Orleans's neighborhoods were so distinct in their character and flavor that it was easy to forget just how compact the city was.

"It really is the perfect location," Thad mused. "Even if the jarheads decide to make the trip across the Mississippi from Federal City, it would only take them fifteen minutes, tops. And if we stick to our plan, The PX will become a destination spot. People will be willing to travel to hang out there." He looked up at Von. "You thinking what I'm thinking?"

Von held up his phone. "I already contacted the real estate agent. He can meet us there at six."

Thad gulped down the last of his beer as he shot out of his chair. He held up the bottle and said, "We need to have this one on tap," as he and Von made it through the kitchen and the den on their way out the door.

He'd reached the second step when he heard a godawful howl coming from the other side of the door.

"Shit," Thad said. He gestured for Von to continue. "Go, go. He'll be fine."

"Puddin' is a he? Whose idea was it to put that rhinestone collar on him?"

"Probably the damn dog sitter," Thad said.

He hopped into the passenger seat of Von's Dodge Challenger and closed the door. He could still hear the dog's howl.

Thad threw his head back and cursed at the car's low ceiling.

"I can't leave him here making all that noise," he said. "Someone's going to call animal control."

"That dog's not getting in this car," Von said. "We're going in your truck. Good thing it's a quad cab."

Five minutes later, he and Von were in his truck with Puddin's head resting between them on the center console that Thad had covered with duct tape.

Thad looked at Puddin', then at Von.

"I hate this fucking dog."

6

A little more to the left."

Ashanti tugged the ruffled skirt across the front of the ten-inch-high platform, then stopped when Kara yelled, "My left, not your left!"

"Really, Kara?"

"Just leave it where it is, Boss Lady," Deja said as she sailed past carrying an armful of crowns in various sizes and colors.

"Yeah, Deja's right. It's fine where it is," Kara said. "Besides, we have other things to do. People will start showing up soon. Did you decide if you're going to double the ticket price at the door?"

"We are not charging people twenty bucks to see a dog pageant, no matter how cute the dogs are," Ashanti said.

"It's for charity!"

"No, Kara. We have the silent auction. That will bring in extra money for Budd's Bed and Bark."

The last two years the proceeds from Barkingham Palace's Doggone Cute Pageant had been divided among the various animal rescues around the city, but this year Ashanti had turned it into a benefit for one of her competitors. The Mid-City boarding and grooming spot had suffered a devastating fire. She figured it was good karma, and hoped the same would be done for her business if she ever found herself in a similar situation.

She stepped up on the stage and surveyed the larger play area. She had done her best to achieve the look of the Throne Room at Buckingham Palace while staying within her fifty-dollar decorating budget. They'd covered the walls with red plastic tablecloths from the dollar store and borrowed gold brocade drapes from Deja and Leslie's great-aunt's formal living room. Posterboard cutouts of filigree spray-painted in gold completed the look.

"What about the seating for the kids from St. Peter Claver's Youth Choir?" Kara asked. "Should I rope it off?"

Another thing Ashanti did was pick a youth group to serve as special guests and judges for the pageant. This year's guest was the choir at the church she'd attended as a child. She hadn't been to Mass in years, but she still showed the congregation love when she could.

"Run to my office and print up three RESERVED signs. We'll tape them to the back of the chairs on the first three rows. That should be good enough."

Everything seemed to be falling into place. Mark and Colleen, the trainer and groomer on staff, were in the staging area with the dogs who would be taking part in today's pageant. The only thing missing was a certain poodle whose absence had been felt by the entire staff all week, but especially by her sweet Duchess.

It had taken a couple of days for Duchess to recognize something was wrong. She was used to Puddin' not being around over the weekend, which had been standard before Mrs. Frances went into the hospital, so Ashanti figured that's what accounted for her lack of concern Tuesday and Wednesday. However, by Thursday afternoon, Duchess wouldn't go more than ten minutes without running to the door of the small dog play area. At mealtime, she waited at Puddin's usual spot. Last night, she paced back and forth in Ashanti's room, a clear sign of anxiety. It was heartbreaking.

Duchess wasn't the only one missing Puddin'. Kara had sent screenshots of messages they'd received this week from loyal viewers of the webcam who had jumped to the awful conclusion that Puddin' had crossed over the Rainbow Bridge. When Kara responded that Puddin' was fine, but no longer attending the daycare, the responses had all been the same, disappointment. Some were even angry, as if they were paying Puddin's daycare bill and had a say in any of this. Entitlement ran rampant on social media.

Ashanti had considered calling Mrs. Frances and begging her to send Puddin' back to daycare, free of charge. But she knew it wasn't her place to get involved. Her grandson was Puddin's caretaker now, and she certainly would not beg him for anything.

Kara returned with the RESERVED signs and the fake gold and ruby scepter from the chew toy display in the lobby.

"You can't have a pageant without this," she said, handing it to Ashanti. "Now, are you sure you can handle going live on Instagram?" she asked.

Ashanti used the scepter to make a cross over her heart. "Promise. I practiced this morning while finishing up the latest order for Duchess Delights. One of the viewers suggested we add CBD oil to them."

"That's actually not a bad idea," Kara said. She pointed an accusatory finger at her. "But you didn't clear going live with me. Let's not make a habit of that."

"Let's remember who owns this business," Ashanti said.

"Touché." Kara taped the last sign to the back of a chair, then spun around to survey the room. "This doesn't look half bad. I'm sorry I'll miss it."

"You have more important things to do," Ashanti reminded her.

"I know." She rolled her eyes. "The SAT prep class ends at six, but I might go to the movies after."

"Is Kendra going with you?"

"Why are you asking when you already know the answer?"

"Invite her to go with you," Ashanti said.

"Look, I love my twin sister like I love my Nike Air Maxes with the magenta laces, but she is not the best company these days. Besides, even if I begged her to come, she would still blow me off." She shrugged. "She's just in a bad mood. She'll get over it."

Ashanti knew she was right. But Kendra's moodiness seemed more extreme these days. She'd been giving her this stank attitude for at least two weeks now, and Ashanti was over it.

"Fine," she said. "But text me when you get to the movie and when it lets out."

"Should I text you a pic of the candy I buy from the concession stand?"

"Smart-ass," Ashanti muttered under her breath.

Once Kara left, Ashanti took out her phone and shot Kendra a quick text.

Kara's going to the movies after SAT prep.
You should go with her. I'll CashApp you
popcorn money.

Her sister replied with the thumbs-down emoji.

Ashanti frowned at the phone. She was *so* over the mood-iness.

She shoved her issue with Kendra to the side and returned her focus to something she *could* control: today's pageant. The room had begun to fill with the families of most of their boarders, people from the neighborhood, and even a few she recognized from last weekend's Geaux for Fi-Deaux Jamboree.

Colleen poked her head out of the door to the tempera-ment testing room, where the dogs participating in the pag-eant were being held, and gestured for Ashanti to come over. The short brunette, who had always reminded her of Velma from *Scooby-Doo*, was a genius when it came to training large breeds.

"Are we almost ready?" Colleen asked.

"Almost." Ashanti peeked at her watch. It was ten min-utes to one. "We should be able to start on time. How are the dogs?"

"Mister Miyagi yanked off Chloe's tutu and tried to make a run for it, but Mark caught him. The rest are enjoying the extra treats they're getting for good behavior."

"Let's keep the Shiba Inu and the bichon frise separated," Ashanti said.

An uptick in chatter, accompanied by excited gasps and applause, grabbed her attention. Turning to see what had caused it, Ashanti parted her lips in stunned surprise as Thad walked toward her. Her heart did the slightest pitter patter at the sight of him—must be indigestion—but it was the bundle of adorableness at the end of the leash he held that made her spirits soar.

"Puddin'!" She rushed to meet the poodle, dropping to her knees and gathering the dog in her arms.

So maybe he had been right about her becoming too attached, but she couldn't help it.

"Oh, baby, we've missed you!" Ashanti said, pressing a kiss to the top of his head. "Thank you so much for bringing him."

"Give me that sweet boy," Colleen said. "We've got to get him ready for the pageant." She looked to Thad. "He is here to take part in the pageant, right?"

Thad nodded.

"Let the audience know we'll be another ten minutes," Colleen told Ashanti as she took Puddin's leash from Thad's fingers. "And he's wearing his green bow tie. Excellent choice. Come on, Puddin'. Duchess is going to go bananas when she sees you."

Ashanti so wanted to peek in on that reunion, but she had mistress of ceremony duties to attend to. She turned to Thad.

"Wait right here," she said. "Seriously, please don't leave yet."

"I'm not going anywhere," he said.

Her head popped back. Had his voice been this smooth and deep on Monday?

She dismissed her unexpected reaction and quickly made her way to the stage. She held her hands out to the crowd.

"Welcome to Barkingham Palace. We are so excited to

have you all here for our annual Doggone Cute Pageant. Three years in a row makes it an annual event, right?"

The crowd replied with more applause. She offered a special welcome to their guests of honor and reminded the audience that all proceeds would benefit the rebuild at Budd's Bed and Bark.

"The pageant will get on the way in another ten minutes. If you haven't done so yet, be sure to check out the silent auction items on the table to my left. We have custom crocheted sweaters, a gift certificate for a custom painting, and a free night's stay at Barkingham Palace. And, the best item in my opinion, a month's supply of Duchess Delights treats."

She left the stage and headed straight for Thad. He stood with his arms crossed over his chest, his back against the wall. She experienced that same feeling she'd had on Monday when he stood in the lobby, that he took up too much space. She sensed he was the type who would always take up too much space, no matter the size of the room he occupied.

"So," she said, leaning her back against the wall and matching his posture. "Do I have to ask the obvious question?"

"I prefer Coke products, but I'll drink a Pepsi if I'm desperate."

She hit him with the kind of side-eye she usually got from her sisters when she made a corny joke. His eyes crinkled, but she couldn't tell if it was the makings of a smile or if he'd gotten dust in them.

"I was told this pageant just wouldn't be the same if a certain poodle didn't participate," Thad answered, then held up his phone. "And my grandmother asked me to FaceTime her so she can see Puddin' strutting across the stage. I couldn't say no."

She was reluctant with her admission, but it had to be said. "That's actually very sweet," Ashanti told him.

"I'm not trying to be sweet. I really couldn't say no. She would probably kick me out of her house if I did."

A laugh escaped before she could suppress it.

Thad shrugged. "It's not too much to ask if it'll make my grandmother happy."

She found his commitment to Mrs. Frances endearing. It was no secret that he wasn't Puddin's biggest fan, yet he'd agreed to care for him because he knew what the dog meant to his grandmother.

Ashanti tipped her head to the side and studied him for a moment as an idea began to take shape.

"What if I offered you a way to make Mrs. Frances *really* happy?" she asked.

His forehead furrowed with his cautious frown. "How?"

"What would it take to get you on that stage?"

"Not for all the free Sprite in the world."

She plopped her hands on both hips. "Be serious. Do you know how much Sprite there is in this world? And we're talking five minutes onstage."

She didn't necessarily need him onstage. Honestly, it went against her own policy. After two owners nearly came to blows during their first pageant, she'd decided only Barkingham Palace employees would handle the dogs, but she was thinking as a business owner right now. The combination of a hot guy with a cute dog would do wonders for their social media numbers.

The more Ashanti thought about it, the more she wanted to make it happen.

"It wouldn't be difficult at all," she said. "Deja can Face-Time Mrs. Frances. All you would have to do is—"

"Not happening," he said.

"But—"

Her phone chimed with an incoming text message. Ashanti knew it was Kara before she looked at the screen.

Why haven't you gone live yet?

Because the pageant hasn't started yet, Ashanti replied.

WHY NOT?????

Colleen poked her head out of the door again and sent Ashanti a thumbs-up. She returned it before texting Kara back. We're starting now. Get off Instagram and pay attention to your instructor.

She turned to Thad. "All the Sprite in the universe."

"Nope."

He pulled his phone from his back pocket and raised it to eye level, then shook his head. His gaze spanned the room, then he nodded toward the opposite side of the stage. "I think I'll have a better vantage point over there."

That's where she'd planned to stand, so that she could catch both the stage and the kids from the youth choir in the frame.

"I'm not following you," Ashanti said, doing exactly that. "I have to go live on Instagram and had already planned to shoot from that side of the room."

He glanced over his shoulder, and she was almost certain she'd spotted a grin. So he *was* capable of smiling? Who would have thought?

Her elbow brushed against Thad's arm as she wedged herself between him and the plastic agility bridge. Ashanti refused to acknowledge the brief tingle she felt on her skin. It had nothing to do with him. She'd probably rubbed against poison ivy or something.

"This is why I'm getting a bigger place," she said. "There's just not enough room here."

"Why didn't you hold the pageant outside?" he asked.

"Because my next-door neighbor would have complained about the noise. It's starting," she said. She pulled up the Instagram app. "Have you gotten ahold of your grandmother?"

"Doing it now," Thad said.

The pageant kicked off with the dogs parading in formal wear. Ashanti's heart melted at the sight of Duchess and Puddin'. With Duchess in her pink ballgown and Puddin' in a vest and bow tie, they looked as if they were off to prom.

"I can't believe I'm standing here watching this," Thad muttered.

"How could you want to be anywhere else?" Ashanti asked. "They are adorable."

"Yes, they are," Mrs. Frances chimed in through his phone. "Thaddeus, you should have been on that stage with Puddin'. You two would have made a pair."

Told you, Ashanti mouthed. She looked down at her phone and noticed the bevy of translucent hearts fluttering across the livestream. Comments were scrolling up the screen.

"Instagram agrees that the dogs are absolutely adorable," Ashanti said. She could only imagine what their reaction would have been if Thad had served as Puddin's dog handler. Probably a lot more fire emojis than hearts.

"Dammit, that's my physical therapist," Ashanti heard Mrs. Frances say. "Thaddeus, record the rest of the pageant for me. Do not miss a thing."

"I'll make sure he doesn't, Mrs. Frances," Ashanti said.

They had moved to the talent portion of the pageant. Leslie stood in the center of the stage with Baguette and Cannoli, motioning for the dachshunds to twirl. The audience went wild. Little did they know, they too could get dogs to twirl if they hid a chicken-flavored dog biscuit in each hand.

Mark came out with a Hula-Hoop under one arm and Chi Chi, a Yorkie that had only started at the daycare a couple of weeks ago, under the other. He set the dog down in the middle of the stage and she immediately peed.

"Oh no," Ashanti muttered. She turned the camera to face her. "We'll have a brief pause in the live broadcast. I promise we'll be back."

"I've got it," Deja called, already making her way to the stage with the accident cleanup kit.

"Guess that's to be expected," Thad said.

"Probably nerves. This is Chi Chi's first time onstage," Ashanti said. She nodded toward the youth choir, who were all falling over themselves laughing. "But kids love gross stuff, so it's a win." She looked over at him. "So you're living in the house in Tremé? Not that I'm trying to get all up in your business," she quickly added. "But earlier you said your grandmother would kick you out if you hadn't come today."

Maybe she *was* trying to get all up in his business, but instead of calling her on it, he answered.

"Yeah," he said. "I just moved back to New Orleans and into my grandparents' house a few weeks ago. It's my house too. I grew up there." He glanced at her. "I didn't mean to be short with you on Monday."

Ashanti startled at the unexpected subject change. "Umm...okay," she said.

"I was irritated at having to deal with the dog, and..." He shook his head. "I just wasn't at my best."

"Is this your version of an apology?"

"Yes."

As far as apologies went, it was a two on a scale of one to ten, but at least he tried.

"Apology accepted," she said. "But I have to ask, is having to look after Puddin' really that bad? Everyone who has ever met him thinks he's a sweetheart."

"I hate that dog," he said so quickly that Ashanti knew it had to come from a place of deep truth. "We hate each other. It's been that way since he was a puppy. Whenever I came home on leave, he'd find a way to terrorize me. Piss in my shoes, chew up my phone case. Puddin' is a menace."

Ashanti pulled her bottom lip between her teeth to keep from laughing. After she'd collected herself, she said, "I'll bet it's a territory thing. You're the only other male in the family."

Thad shot her an incredulous frown. "You're not a dog psychologist or some shit like that, are you?"

She couldn't help it. She burst out laughing. The expression on his face made her want to lie to him, just to see his reaction.

"No, I'm not," she said. "But don't knock the discipline. Animal behaviorists play an important role in the relationship between pets and their owners. Maybe you and Puddin' should visit one."

This expression was so much better.

"Or...maybe not," she said, barely able to get the words out.

His brows drew inward as he stared at her with a perplexed frown.

She immediately sobered. "What's wrong?"

After several moments passed with that frown still marring his brow, he said, "I'm not used to people laughing at me. Other than my best friend, Von, but he doesn't count."

It took *her* a moment to realize that he was serious. She had to bite down on the inside of her cheek to stop herself from laughing again.

But then the unbelievable happened. The barely there smile she'd glimpsed earlier flourished into an all-out grin. It was beyond devastating.

"Laughing releases endorphins," she said. "Maybe you should try to do more of it."

"Is that why you're still laughing at me?" he asked. "Endorphin rush?"

"I was trying not to," Ashanti said.

He leaned over and, in a lowered voice, said, "You failed." The amusement dancing in his eyes softened the rest of his features.

Goodness.

Her phone dinged with a text, dragging her attention away from his intensely attractive face.

Kara: Why aren't you live? It doesn't take that long to clean Yorkie pee.

Ashanti startled. Onstage, Colleen was with Hercules, the English mastiff, who was trying to guess which cup she'd hid a rock under. She hadn't even realized the pageant had started again.

"I need to get back to Instagram," she said.

She pulled up the app, zeroed in on the stage, and tried her best to push the last five minutes out of her mind.

Thank goodness she had an iron-clad list of reasons why men were off the table, because Mrs. Frances's grandson had her reconsidering her life choices.

There wasn't a chance of it happening. Not even a small chance.

After an incident with her last boyfriend nearly jeopardized her guardianship of the girls, Ashanti had decided it wasn't worth it to get involved with anyone until Kara and Kendra were eighteen and no longer at risk of the courts handing them over to their aunt, her father's sister, Anita.

Anita was only part of the reason she planned to ignore the butterflies that took flight in her belly when Thad had laid that smile on her. She was just too darn busy to date right now. Raising teenaged twins, running two business, and being a devoted mother to a high-maintenance Frenchie didn't leave time for much else.

Of course, the most obvious reason she would not allow a nice smile and five minutes of surprisingly enjoyable conversation to affect her was that the man did not like dogs. If ever there was a red flag in her book, that was it.

7

"Hey, Boss Lady, you need help?"

Ashanti looked up to find Deja standing just over her shoulder, chomping on an apple.

"What are the chances that you've been hovering to the side, waiting until I was almost done cleaning up this mess before you came to offer help?" Ashanti asked.

"Very high," Deja said. "But at least I offered." She nodded to the elevated orthopedic bed that was standard in each of Barkingham Palace's four-by-six-foot pet suites. "Lil Lulu had a rough night, huh? The good news is Dr. Williams said it doesn't appear to be anything more than anxiety. She won't need to bring her into the clinic for bloodwork or further testing."

"I suspected that," Ashanti said. "Lulu does fine in daycare, but the moment she has to stay overnight we get, well, this." She gestured to the stained bed. It would likely have to be replaced. Ashanti had been scrubbing for at least fifteen minutes, but Lulu's little accident wasn't coming out.

She sat back on her heels and rested her gloved hands on her thighs. "I remember those early days when I naively thought running a doggy daycare would mean I get to play with dogs all day."

"Instead, you spend most of your day cleaning up poop," Deja said with a shrug. "By the way, Dr. Williams is checking on Sparkle, too, just to make sure everything is okay with her."

"Good. Tell Evie I'll be there in a few. I just need to finish disinfecting this suite."

Her former college roommate, Evie Williams, ran a veterinary practice with her longtime boyfriend, Cameron, who had also attended LSU School of Veterinary Medicine with them. She came in twice a week to examine the dogs and provide basic care where warranted. Having a board-certified veterinarian on staff, even part-time, was one of Barkingham Palace's biggest selling points.

Ashanti pushed up from the floor, picked up the empty spray bottle, and made her way to the supply room. She was refilling it with pet-safe disinfectant from a gallon jug when Leslie poked her head into the open doorway.

"We've got a situation," she said.

"What now?" Ashanti asked.

"Marcia Lewis is on the phone again about Buster. What should I tell her?"

Ashanti dropped her head back and sighed up at the ceiling. It was a Monday.

"Tell her that our policy has not changed. Buster cannot be boarded here unless he is current on all his vaccinations," she said. "And remind her that she did not have an issue with getting her previous dogs vaccinated."

"She also didn't have a problem with her dogs being microchipped, but she had Buster's removed," Leslie said. "Some people should not be allowed on the Internet."

Ashanti had to agree with her.

She returned to the suite Lulu shared with her sister and sprayed every surface with disinfectant. If history was anything to go on, now that she was over her initial jitters, the dog would do just fine for the rest of her five-night stay. Still, Ashanti was grateful Evie had agreed to come over on one of her unofficial workdays to give Lulu an exam.

Of course, Ashanti could have done the same exam, but her clients had been assured that any medical needs would be attended to by a board-certified veterinarian. She wasn't a board-certified veterinarian, even though she had almost finished her degree.

Brandy's "Almost Doesn't Count" began to play in her head, because her brain was her biggest troll. Ashanti headed for the temperament assessment room, which also doubled as an exam room on the days Evie worked at Barkingham Palace. Just as she arrived, she got a text.

"Gah. Gah. Gah," Ashanti said as she read over it.

"You know, you're the only person I ever hear using the word 'gah' in real life," Evie said from the other side of the exam table. "The rest of the world only uses it in texts or when posting live updates about the *Real Housewives*."

"But it captures what I'm feeling so well," Ashanti said, her fingers flying across the phone screen.

"What are you gahhing about?" Evie asked as she flashed a penlight in Sparkle's ears.

Ashanti sent off the text and re-pocketed her phone. "I just had to turn down an order for Duchess Delights treats from this boutique on Magazine Street," she said.

"Why'd you turn them down?"

"Because they wanted ten dozen by the weekend. I just

don't have the time to fill an order that big. I can barely fill the ones I have. And, in case you forgot, I have a daycare to run."

"Your staff can run this daycare without you," Evie said, scratching Sparkle's tummy as she checked her parathyroid glands.

"My staff is top-notch, but I'm not ready to give up the reins of this place in exchange for baking doggy cookies," Ashanti said. "Despite the occasional problematic owner or Pomeranian with explosive diarrhea, I actually enjoy my work." She pushed herself up on the exam table and pulled Lulu onto her lap while Evie continued examining her sister.

"The thing is, as much as I love the daycare, I can't ignore how quickly Duchess Delights has grown," Ashanti continued. "I just wish there was a way to continue the growth without having it take over my entire kitchen. More than three hours' sleep at night would be nice too."

"It sounds as if you need a second staff for Duchess Delights," Evie said.

"I do," she said. "Especially once I move into the new building and open a full-scale doggy bakery."

"You know what you need? An investor—a real one. You should try to get on that *Shark Tank* show."

"Uh, yeah." Ashanti rolled her eyes. "I can just imagine Mr. Wonderful's response when I ask him to invest a million bucks in my doggy cookies. I get enough sarcasm from the twins, thank you very much."

"What's going on here?" Evie asked, narrowing her eyes. "You're usually so annoyingly sweet and positive that I need a shot of insulin when I leave this place."

Ashanti hunched her shoulders and nuzzled Lulu's head. "I just have a lot I'm dealing with. Kendra's in full moody teenager mode, and I'm exhausted trying to run two businesses."

"Well, I stand by my statement. The pet industry makes tens of billions of dollars a year. Duchess Delights is a solid investment. You could be selling so many more of those treats if you had the money to scale up this business." She used a pen-light to check Sparkle's eyes. "I wish things weren't so tight at the practice. I would invest in Duchess Delights in a heartbeat."

"What's going on with the practice?" Ashanti asked, reaching over to rub Sparkle's head with her free hand.

Ashanti was ashamed to admit it, but it had taken a while before she could talk to Evie about her veterinary practice without feeling both jealousy and longing. The longing lingered a bit, but it had lessened over the years. The jealousy was gone completely.

She and Evie had met on the first day of organic chem during their junior year at LSU. Evie had been on track to become a family general practitioner, but by the time they finished undergrad, she was applying to the university's School of Veterinary Medicine along with Ashanti. The only difference between them was that Ashanti's life had imploded during their final year of vet school where Evie's had not.

"The practice is doing okay, but it would be doing even better if the Walmart of pet stores would stop taking huge chunks of our business," she said. "Remember Cassandra Dutton? She was in Systemic Pathology with us."

"Curly blond hair?" Ashanti asked.

"Yep. She runs the clinic at the new chain store that just opened."

"Traitor," Ashanti said.

"Yeah, well, if the landlord raises the rent on us one more time, Cameron and I may join the ranks of traitor," Evie said.

"Don't give in. That's what they want."

"I'll try not to." Evie examined Sparkle's teeth and gums. "This little one looks good, but she can stand to gain a pound or two. She weighs less than her sister."

"That's because Lulu steals all the treats," Ashanti said, nuzzling the dog again.

The door to the exam room swung open and Ridley King barged in wearing one of her signature Scanlan Theodore mid-calf skirts and mohair sweater combos, and looking like she owned the world.

"It's about time you got off the pot," Ridley announced. "Hey, Eve." She gave Evie a kiss on the cheek before coming over to the side where Ashanti sat. Lulu barked. Ridley pointed at her. "Shut up, Toto," she said, before planting a kiss on Ashanti's cheek.

Ridley had become their suite mate during their third year of undergrad. Despite not sharing their love of animals, she had agreed to move into an apartment with Ashanti and Evie while she pursued her MBA. A decade later and they were all still the closest of friends.

"It looks as if you finally took my advice." Ridley squeezed Ashanti's shoulders in a one-armed hug. "Congratulations on making the big move."

"What are you talking about?" Ashanti asked.

"That house in the Bywater. You bought it, right?"

Ashanti stiffened. It felt as if someone had shoved ice directly into her veins.

"Please, tell me you're the one who bought the house," Ridley said.

She shook her head, too stunned to speak.

"Oh no," Evie whispered.

"Dammit, Shanti. Didn't I tell you this would happen?"

Ridley pointed a stiletto French-manicured finger at her. "This is what they mean by fuck around and find out. You fucked around, dragging your little size-seven feet, and now you're finding out what happens when you don't pull the trigger fast enough."

"You just used like five different metaphors," Evie said. "Besides, what's the point of saying I told you so?"

"The point is I *did* tell her so! I've been telling her so for the past month. A building like that will not just linger on the market forever, especially in that neighborhood."

"But Lena Clark told me I didn't have anything to worry about," Ashanti said. Ridley had to be mistaken. There's no way someone had bought her house.

"Who is Lena Clark?" Ridley asked.

"Zuzu's mom. He's another Pomeranian that boards here. Lena is a real estate agent who specializes in commercial properties. She said the house was priced too high for the amount of work that had to be done in it. She told me to wait it out, that the seller would have to bring the price down."

"Well, I guess Lena was wrong, because there's a big, fat SOLD sign on it and a black pickup truck in the driveway," Ridley said.

"Right now?" Ashanti asked.

"As of five minutes ago when I drove past there."

Ashanti scooted off the exam table and sat Lulu next to her sister. "I'll tell Deja to bring the dogs back to their suite."

"You're not going there, are you?" Evie asked.

"Don't waste your time," Ridley said. "It's too late to do anything about the house now."

"Maybe," Ashanti said. "Or, maybe not. Only one way to find out."

8

Thad stood in the doorway of the downstairs bathroom at the house he and Von had purchased just one week after he'd first set eyes on it. When his sister called to congratulate him on the day he turned in his retirement paperwork, she'd encouraged him to become more spontaneous and less rigid. If this didn't qualify as less rigid, Thad didn't know what would.

He just wished Nadia had told him how nerve-racking this "being spontaneous" shit really was.

He reminded himself he had no reason to be nervous. It wasn't as if he hadn't played out every scenario that could go wrong—and right—with this new venture. The most significant item in the *goes wrong* column was the potential to lose his life's savings. It scared him, but he could always make more money.

It was the long list of things in the *goes right* column that had compelled Thad to make a cash offer after their second walk-through with the real estate agent. The PX would not be just a regular sports bar. It would be a place where people like him—vets who were feeling unmoored after the shock to the system that came with returning to civilian life—could find solidarity and camaraderie. Being able to provide that to his fellow brothers- and sisters-in-arms was as satisfying as getting a perfect score on the ACFT.

An involuntarily shudder raced down his spine. The Army Combat Fitness Test was one of the very few things about the Army he would never miss.

Thad took a couple more steps inside the bathroom and had to cover his nose and mouth with his arm. The stench of mildew was heavy, but after sending video of the green splotches covering the walls of the downstairs bathroom to Von's brother, Mitchell, who worked for the EPA, it was determined that the mildew wasn't harmful and could be killed with a bleach and water mixture. Buying enough bleach to fill the bed of his truck's cab was number one on his agenda.

"Hey, Thad, come get your dog! He keeps getting in my way."

Thad blew out a sigh of frustration as he backtracked to the front of the house. He laughed at the sight that greeted him.

Von held up one side of a wooden mantel that had fallen at the base of one of the home's six fireplaces. Puddin' stood between his spread feet, the pom-pom on the tip of his tail whisking back and forth across Von's leg.

"Making friends?" Thad asked.

"Can you get him to move?" Von pleaded.

"Come over here, Puddin'," Thad commanded. The dog didn't budge. "Stubborn little bastard," Thad muttered as he went over and tugged Puddin' by his rhinestone collar.

Von set the mantel on the floor and dusted his hands on

his jeans. "You're going to have to leave him home when we start the real demo. He's going to get hurt."

"I can't leave him home," Thad said. "I went to the grocery store Friday evening and the neighbor told me he barked the entire time I was gone. She said that's why Grams had him in daycare, because he barks constantly when he's alone."

"Well, bring him back to the dog sitter. Or hire one to take care of him at the house. He won't be able to stay here all day."

Thad had considered it after seeing Puddin' engaging with the dogs and staff at Barkingham Palace on Saturday, but there was something about spending that ridiculous amount of money on this dog that just didn't sit right with him.

"He's fine. It'll be okay," Thad said.

"Easy for you to say. He hates your ass. I'm the one he's following around."

Thad grinned. "What do you always say? You've got a magnetic personality? Guess it works on both women and poodles."

Von responded with a string of expletives that would make even a seasoned soldier blush.

"Help me move this," he said.

Thad picked up the other end of the mantel and, together, they carried it to the opposite side of the room and placed it with the other reclaimed items they had found. Their plan was to reuse whatever they could in the house. Of course, it would all have to undergo a thorough inspection before they included it in The PX's rebuild.

Mitchell had come through for them again last week when he'd asked a contractor friend who lived in Mississippi to take the hour-long drive to look over the house. The contractor's assessment had been enough for Thad and Von to determine that the house was a solid buy. The seller had knocked another 5 percent off the asking price because of their willingness to forgo an official inspection.

Thad tried to convince himself that the awkward weight in his belly was from excitement and not fear.

"This is a good thing, Thad. Don't be scared," Von said.

Thad shrugged off the arm Von had draped over his shoulder. "Stop reading me like a damn book. That shit creeps me out."

"Stop being so transparent then," Von said. "I don't want you getting any ideas, like heading back to Colorado."

"I can't. I've got a dog to look after, remember?"

"Yeah, that dog is another reason I can see you packing up and leaving."

Von knocked on the wall that divided the living room and what the real estate agent had explained was a formal parlor. It would have to come down. They wanted to use this entire space for the sports bar. "Sounds hollow enough to me," Von said.

"Yeah, but that doesn't mean it isn't a support wall. We're going to have to hire Freddy to do a more thorough assessment and give us some direction," he said.

"But we're still doing the work ourselves," Von said. "I promised the guys that we would have some construction work lined up for them."

"I know," Thad said. "I made promises too."

He and Von had pledged to hire only military vets to work at The PX once it opened. But then they decided to bring in military—both vets and active duty—to work at every stage of the process, including any renovations that had to be done.

Based on the state of this place, they would need all the help they could get.

Thad picked out the broom from the supplies they'd brought with them and began sweeping the hardwood floors. They were beautiful even with the layer of dust and grime covering them. He could only imagine how good they would look after being sanded and polished.

The sound of feet stomping up the front steps was quickly followed by a knock on the open door. A second later, Ashanti Wright stuck her head in and said, "Hello?"

A jolt of awareness flashed through him at the sight of her. It dimmed when she locked eyes with him and came charging into the front parlor.

"I knew it!" she said. "I knew it was you the moment I saw that truck."

Puddin' ran to her and started jumping around like fire ants were attacking his paws.

"I knew it was you the moment I saw you too," Von said as he dusted his hands on the front of his T-shirt. He held one out to her. "Von Montgomery. And you are?"

"She's the dog sitter," Thad answered for her. He fought the instinct to push Von out of the room.

"Ah! Puddin's favorite person," Von said. "That would explain his excitement."

Ashanti dropped down to one knee and rubbed the poodle behind the ears while nuzzling his nose.

It would be stupid and immature to admit he was jealous of a dog, and yet...

"Tell me you're a contractor," Ashanti said, still fussing over Puddin'. She looked up at him and that headiness he'd felt as he stood next to her on Saturday returned. He tried to ignore it.

"Are you?" she asked. "A contractor?"

It took him a moment to find his voice. "I'm not, but if that's what you want me to tell you, then sure, I'm a contractor."

She closed her eyes and muttered what sounded like the Serenity Prayer under her breath. "Just...please, tell me that you did not buy this house."

"Again, if that's what you want me to tell you—"

"Did you buy this house!" she snapped. Her freckles had turned from light brown to a deep red.

"We did," Von said, gesturing between the two of them. "We're business partners. And friends. And fellow vets," he finished. "And your name is?"

"Ashanti Wright," she answered. "And I'm not a dog sitter, I own a dog daycare and boarding facility."

"That she named Barkingham Palace," Thad said.

"Aw, that's cute," Von said. "Do you speak in a British accent while at work?"

She looked around. "Do you plan to live here?"

"No, no, no," Von said. "I'm single. This is way too much house for me."

Thad frowned at him. Was this motherfucker flirting?

"We're opening a sports bar," Thad interjected.

"A sports bar!"

Based on her tone one would think he'd said they were starting up an operation to torture newborn puppies.

"Sports bar, cigar bar, and a barbershop on the top floor, to be more specific," Thad said, resting his chin on the broom handle. "A one-stop shop for all your entertainment and grooming needs."

"One thing this city does *not* need is another bar," she said. "There's already one on every corner."

"Not like the one we're opening," Thad said.

"Everyone thinks their idea is different and special. This house deserves more than to become a random bar."

The light suddenly went on in Thad's head as he remembered what she'd said on Saturday about wishing she had more space at the daycare.

"You wanted this building for your dog sitter business, didn't you?"

"I am not a dog sitter!"

"Sorry, I thought that's what they called people who looked after dogs." He tipped his head to the side. "Are there really enough folks in this city willing to pay sixty bucks a night for your fancy dog hotel to warrant an expansion?"

"Damn. Sixty a night?" Von said. "That sounds like a good side hustle. I did canine training for a few years, back when I was enlisted. You offer training there?"

Thad sent him the kind of look that did not need further explanation. Of course, the asshole ignored it.

"Where is—what's it called?" Von asked. "Barkingham Palace? I really love that name, by the way. Where's it located? Maybe I can come check it out."

That was enough of this shit.

"We have a lot of work to do," Thad said. "I'm sorry if you wanted this place, but it became ours as of nine this morning. Cash sale. The paperwork will probably be filed with the clerk of court's office by the end of the week."

"I can't believe this," Ashanti said. Her shoulders dropped in the most melodramatic display Thad had seen since he was forced to be in a production of *Macbeth* in high school. "This is a tragedy. That's the only way I can describe it."

She knelt again to love on Puddin'. Thad could do nothing but watch as the lucky bastard ate it up, that stupid pom-pom wagging back and forth like a metronome. When Ashanti rose to face him her expression was lethal, yet when she spoke, both her words and tone were the exact opposite of what he'd expected.

"Tell your grandmother that I was able to save the entire recording of our Instagram Live from Saturday. I'll be sure to get her a copy of it." She looked to Von. "It was nice meeting you."

Her lack of a smile proved that all Von's flirting had gone to waste. Good.

But it also confirmed that the flicker of interest Thad thought he'd sensed coming from her on Saturday had been doused. Thoroughly.

He wouldn't deny that he was disappointed. Was he surprised? Not really. He was lucky she'd given him the time of day after their encounter last Monday.

Grams would be disappointed that her matchmaking plans had no chance of working, but Thad wasn't sure that was a bad thing. He was living in his grandmother's house and taking care of his grandmother's dog. He didn't need his grandmother choosing the women he dated too.

He wasn't up for dating anyway. He and Von had just a few months to get The PX off the ground; that's where his focus should be.

If he tried hard enough, he could convince himself that he'd done himself a favor by turning Ashanti against him.

Without another word, she turned and marched out the way she'd come. Thad had to step on Puddin's leash to stop him from running after her. He couldn't blame the dog. Those head rubs looked pretty addicting.

He turned to Von and said, "What the fuck was that?"

"What?"

"*Maybe I can come check it out,*" Thad said, doing a purposely exaggerated imitation of Von's voice.

He shrugged. "I like dogs."

He said it with a straight face, as if he hadn't just called Thad to come and get Puddin'.

"Just because I'm not a fan of *that* dog, it doesn't mean I don't like dogs," Von said, doing that annoying mind-reading shit again. He pointed to Puddin', who still looked longingly at the door his best friend had just exited. "Speaking of that one, you should really think about bringing him back to doggy daycare during the day. He's getting in the way here, and it will only get worse once demo starts. Last thing you want is for your grandmother to disown you because a wood beam crushed her poodle's skull."

"Puddin's head is too hard to get crushed," he answered, even though he knew Von was right. He wasn't looking forward to suffering through what he now knew would be unrequited attraction every time he saw Ashanti, but he was good at masking his feelings. She would never know the difference.

"I'll think about it." Thad handed him the broom. "Let's get back to work."

9

Ashanti felt as if she were wearing leaden cross-trainers as she trudged up the steps to Barkingham Palace. Mrs. Short stood outside with her watering can, tending to the marigolds in the window boxes in front of the house. Ashanti contemplated speaking, but only for a second before deciding against it. She was not up for a confrontation, especially now that it looked as if she and this curmudgeon would be neighbors a lot longer than she was expecting.

She brought her hand to her stomach to stave off the nausea.

She could not believe she'd allowed this to happen. That house was supposed to be hers. She had already mapped out the floor plan. The pet suites were going to be three square feet larger, and there was even room to do two queen suites, big enough for families with multiple dogs or one very spoiled one.

And, just like that, it was gone. She was stuck in a building her business had outgrown. There was only one other house in this entire city that even remotely fit the bill—her dream location—and Ashanti knew she wouldn't be able to afford it even if it miraculously went up for sale. Not with twin sisters to put through college and the overhead of running this place.

She entered the daycare and stopped short. Deja, Ridley, Evie, Leslie, and Mark were all standing in the reception area, facing the door as if they expected Ed McMahon's ghost to come in with a check for five million dollars.

Mark was the first to speak. "Thank God," he said, making the sign of the cross. "You didn't get yourself arrested. Unless they allowed you to come back to get your purse. Do cops do that?"

"I did not get arrested. Don't be ridiculous," Ashanti said.

"Good. I can go back to work now." He gathered her in a hug and added an extra squeeze.

The phone rang, sending Deja running to the reception desk. Ridley and Evie continued staring at her with guarded looks, as if they were waiting for her to spontaneously combust at any moment.

Or to burst out crying. Which was highly likely.

"So, did someone really buy the house?" Evie asked.

Ashanti nodded. The sudden lump that had formed in her throat made it difficult to speak.

"I knew it," Ridley said.

"Not now, Rid," Evie said.

"Well, she's right," Ashanti said. "I didn't believe someone had bought the house even after Ridley told me. And you would never guess who bought it," she called to Deja.

The receptionist held up a finger, then after a moment hung up the phone and said, "Who?"

"Mrs. Sutherland's grandson."

"The hottie?"

"Who's a hottie?" Ridley asked.

"Girl! You should have seen him!" Deja said, rounding the reception desk and returning to where they all stood.

"Mrs. Sutherland is Puddin's owner, right?" Evie asked. "He's sweet on Duchess. They're the cutest."

"If you think *they're* cute, you should see her grandson." Deja pumped up her arm. "Muscles, face, voice. Baybee, he ain't missing none of them. Got it all, you hear me?"

"Yeah, well, now he has my house too," Ashanti said. "He and his business partner are turning my house into a sports bar!"

"Whose house?" Ridley asked.

Ashanti leveled her with a look she usually reserved for the twins to let them know she was done with their bullshit.

"I'm just saying." Ridley raised her hands. "If you had made an offer on the house when I told you to, Mr. Hottie would not have had the chance to swoop in and buy it."

"You're not helping," Evie said. She turned to Ashanti and enveloped her in a hug. "I need to get back to the practice. I'll call you later, okay?" She captured her chin in her palm and smiled. "You bounce back better than anyone I know, Shanti. Don't let this get you down."

They were used to her *always look on the bright side of things* attitude, but Ashanti couldn't summon up a bit of that right now. The most she could manage was a wan smile.

"Thanks for coming in to check on Lulu," she told Evie. "I owe you."

"Oh, don't worry. You'll get my invoice at the end of the month as usual." Evie laughed. She hugged Ridley, then gave her a playful punch on the arm. "Ease up on her. It's not about you being right all the time."

"Says who?" Ridley asked.

Evie rolled her eyes as she hefted her ever-present backpack—she'd upgraded to higher-priced designer brands since college—and left the daycare.

Exhausted, Ashanti took a handful of treats from the reception desk and started toward the back. Ridley followed.

"Will I not be allowed to mourn losing my house in peace?" Ashanti asked over her shoulder.

"Again, it is not your house. I warned you about claiming it before buying it and now look what's happened."

She usually didn't mind a good *I told you so*, but this time it grated on her still very raw nerves. Probably because that house was integral to all her plans. Without it she didn't have a place to expand the daycare or to start her bakery. Without it, the kitchen at home would have to continue working over-time to churn out doggy treats.

But how long could she sustain that? Something would have to give.

Ashanti felt the seductive pull of negative thinking creep-ing along the edges of her mind and forced herself to snap out of it. She did not have the luxury to spend time wallowing. She had too many responsibilities tugging at her from every crook and crevice of her life.

"It doesn't matter," Ashanti said. "This just means the house was not meant for me and that something better will eventually come along."

"Oh, so this is what we're doing? You spend over a month detailing all the ways you're going to turn this house into the per-fect new spot for your daycare, yet now it wasn't meant for you?"

"Evie was right, you're not helping. You harping on me won't change anything."

"First of all, I do not harp," Ridley said. "Secondly, I don't want to see you lose out on something fantastic, Shanti. You, of all people, deserve a damn break. And this could have been your big break if you had not been so hesitant to pull the trigger. Stop betting against yourself, sweetie. That's all I want for you."

She would give anything to deny Ridley's words, but her friend had just read her like the latest Brit Bennett novel. Ashanti had allowed fear to stop her from making an offer on that house. Fear that this business, which had already proven to be successful by its rapid growth over the last three years, would suddenly fall out from under her. She had been afraid that the doggy treats were just a fluke, despite now getting so many orders that she had to turn some down.

Why was she so afraid that someone would show up and tell her this was all a lie? That her accomplishments were not real, and that everything she had worked so hard for since losing her parents would be taken away from her?

She stopped at the door that led to the pet suites and turned to face Ridley.

"There's nothing I can do about any of this now, Rid." Ashanti shrugged. "All I can do is make sure I never let another opportunity like this one pass me by. *If* I ever get another opportunity," she added.

"You will," Ridley said. "And you had better believe that I will hold those petite feet to the fire." She held her arms out. "Give me a hug. I'm not going in there. You know I don't like being around those dogs."

"Yet, you're always here."

"Which should tell you how much I love your ass."

Ridley headed back to her office in the Central Business District, and Ashanti went in to check on the dogs. All were doing fine, except for her dog.

A French bulldog's smushed face could look forlorn even at the happiest of times, but it was obvious Duchess was back to missing Puddin'. She refused to play with the other dogs and ignored her favorite chew toys.

"I'm sorry, baby," Ashanti said, rubbing behind her little bat ear. "I know you miss him, but maybe we'll run into Puddin' somewhere around town."

Duchess's nubby tail began wagging the moment Ashanti mentioned the poodle. Her dog was truly missing her man. Yet another reason Thad Sims had quickly become enemy number one. Not only had he stolen her house, but he was making Duchess miserable.

"Let's go for a W-A-L-K," Ashanti said, hooking a leash onto Duchess's harness. Anyone who worked in a kennel knew to never actually say the word *walk* unless they wanted a dozen dogs scrambling to get out of their pens.

Just as she turned for the door, Kara burst through it.

"You are going to love me," she said in a singsongy voice. Duchess seemed to have forgotten that she was supposed to be melancholy. She shot toward Kara and began trying to climb her like a tree. Her sister dropped to the floor and rubbed her ears in the same way Ashanti had. Duchess ate it up.

Pleasure hound.

"Hey there, girl," Kara said. She looked up at Ashanti. "Guess what? I found a printer that can do glossy labels for a third less than the one we agreed to go with."

"Why aren't you at school?" Ashanti asked.

"It's lunch. Anyway, we will have to make sure we are absolutely in *looove* with the design, because to get that price we have to buy like twenty thousand labels."

Ashanti wasn't sure she would be able to keep making treats long enough to sell another two hundred.

She didn't want to think about this right now, but she

knew she had to. Just because she didn't feel like dealing with it, it didn't mean she could ignore her business.

"Send me your latest designs," she said. "I'll pick one."

"I sent them to you an hour ago, but ignore those because I came up with something better."

"You should have been in class an hour ago," Ashanti told her. "I don't care that you get all As, you still have to pay attention in class, Kara. And you need to stop skipping. You're only a few weeks into the new school year."

"I told you we're at lunch!" Kara said. "Oh! Oh! Oh! Did I tell you that Atilla emailed me? Can you believe that? Email, like it's the 1950s."

"What did she want?" Ashanti asked, not bothering to correct her erroneous assumptions about the history of electronic communication. "And stop calling her Atilla."

Even though their father's older sister, Anita, had rightfully earned the nickname. Who was she kidding? Attila the Hun had nothing on Anita.

"She wants to take me and Kendra to a plant show in Baton Rouge."

Ashanti frowned. "What's a plant show?"

"That was *my* question." Kara took out her phone. "I had to look it up, and it is exactly what it sounds like." She turned the phone to face Ashanti. "An event where you go to look at and buy plants." She said it in the same tone one would use to describe an event where you would go and buy body parts. "Why, Shanti? Why is that woman like this? Dad wasn't like this, was he?"

"You were ten years old when Dad died. You know he was nothing like his sister."

"Who hurt her? And why does she want to inflict us with that same pain?"

"Don't worry about Atilla—Anita," Ashanti corrected. "I'll make up an excuse for you and Kendra for the weekend. Maybe I'll tell her that you both have to help clean out the pet suites here. In fact, you can start now."

Kara looked at her phone's blank screen. "Would you look at that? It's time for my world history class. I need to be getting back." She pointed at Duchess. "This dog is suffering."

"I know," Ashanti said. She tipped her head to the door. "Come on, Kara. I'll follow you to the lobby. I need to get a longer leash."

"You have to get Puddin' back here," Kara said. "Fans of the doggy cam were so excited when he showed up for the pageant, but now they're back to wanting to riot. They miss the Duchess and Puddin' show. The public demands an explanation for why it is not happening."

"Yeah, well, you can tell the public that the Duchess and Puddin' show is over because Puddin's new owner is a complete ass," Ashanti said over her shoulder as she slid the lobby's pocket doors open.

"Is this how you talk about all your customers?"

Within seconds her entire body went from ice-cold to raging hot. She turned, fully expecting Thad Sims to be irate. Instead, she found a subtle smile pulling at the corners of his mouth. The grin was as devastating as it was irritating.

"Umm...hey, Boss Lady," Deja said. "Mr. Sims would like a word with you about Puddin'."

"That is, if you don't mind talking to a complete ass," Thad said.

As if she had a choice.

10

Thad took a moment to relish in Ashanti Wright's discomfort as she mumbled a string of apologies that were made even more entertaining by the fact that she obviously didn't mean a word of it. He got the sense that being seen as unpleasant didn't sit right with her, whereas he didn't give two shits what anyone thought about him. Except for his grandmother and his sister.

For a brief span of time, between last Monday when he first met her and a few hours ago when she'd accused him of buying her house out from under her, he'd cared what Ashanti thought of him. The bitch of it was that he kinda still cared. He should probably work on that.

"What can I do for you, Mr. Sims?" Ashanti finally asked.

"You can call me Thad," he said.

She folded her arms over her chest. "Can I help you?" she asked.

He tried not to wince.

He was willing to accept that Grams's dream match between her dog sitter and her grandson would never happen, but the fact that she couldn't bring herself to use his name stung. It's not as if he wanted her to like him; he just didn't want her to *not* like him.

Okay, that was a lie.

If he took the time to consider what he wanted from Ashanti, ambivalence was at the bottom of the list. Right there with a kick to the groin and a haircut to match Puddin's.

The current state he found himself in was comically ironic, especially when he thought back to his response to the dozen or so women who had actually *wanted* to get with him this past year. The appeal just hadn't been there.

Von accused him of punishing himself, because for some reason, his friend was convinced that Thad believed he didn't deserve joy.

Was that Ashanti's appeal? Was he so interested because he knew he had zero chance when it came to her?

And because she was cute as hell with freckles that drove him out of his mind. That was definitely part of her appeal.

He did not have time for this introspection shit right now. And he sure as hell didn't need to give Von's ridiculous assessment any more air.

"Hey, so I know I said that Puddin' wouldn't be coming to the daycare anymore, but I was hoping you hadn't given his spot away yet," Thad said.

Her dog began to bark and twirl around like a chunky ballerina the minute he said Puddin's name.

"Duchess, sit," Ashanti ordered. The dog immediately plopped its butt on the floor.

Thad should not have found her commanding tone sexy, but apparently that's where his brain wanted to take everything when it came to Ashanti Wright.

Impressive. *That's* what it was. He couldn't get Puddin' to sit on command if he promised that little asshole every dog biscuit in New Orleans.

"Are you Puddin's new owner?" asked the teenager who had followed Ashanti into the lobby. There was a resemblance between the two. It was probably stronger than it appeared, but Thad was thrown off by the teen's hot pink–tipped hair and matching hot pink eyeglasses and tennis shoes.

"Kara, get to school," Ashanti said.

"Going." She held her hands up in surrender before reaching down to pat Duchess's head. "See you later, girl." To Thad she said, "Please bring back Duchess's boyfriend. She is miserable without him." To Ashanti she said, "I'll send you some new label designs in an hour or so."

"No, you won't, because you'll be in class," Ashanti called.

The teen held her hands up again.

"Sorry, what were you saying?" Ashanti asked.

"I need to put Puddin' back in daycare. I can't cart him around with me all day, but he barks constantly if I try to leave him at the house."

"It's because he isn't used to being at home alone," Ashanti said. "Mrs. Frances has been bringing Puddin' here since he was a puppy, back when she was still running the dry cleaning business."

"Yeah, I know," Thad said. "So can he stay here?" He hooked his thumb toward the door. "I can get him out of the truck right now."

"He's outside?" Ashanti asked, aghast.

Just then, the front door opened and the teen, Kara, walked back in. "This guy has Puddin' in a truck. We don't do that around here, sir. Puddin' is royalty."

"The dog is fine," Thad said. "The truck is locked and I cracked the window open."

Kara looked him up and down in the most judgmental way possible. Then she looked to Ashanti. "Are we rescuing Puddin' or what?"

"*I'm* rescuing Puddin'. *You're* going back to school. Can you take Duchess for me, Deja?" Ashanti handed the leash to the woman behind the reception desk and held her hand, palm up, out to Thad. "Keys, please."

He sighed. "I'll go get the dog. Does this mean he can return to daycare?"

"Of course," Ashanti said. "I didn't want you to take him in the first place."

Thad went outside and, in a matter of minutes, was back with Puddin'. The moment the poodle saw the French bulldog, he ran to her and the two began frolicking around the lobby together.

"Look, I know you're upset about the house, but the owner didn't mention any other interested buyers."

She held up a hand. "Forget the house. What's the deal with Puddin'? Are you only taking care of him for Mrs. Frances, or are you considered his new owner?" Ashanti walked behind the desk without looking at him.

Thad stiffened.

He was trying to soften what he could tell was a big blow to her future plans, but she wasn't making it easy. He wouldn't have just let her have the house if he'd known she was interested in it, but maybe he would have continued their search. Von had lined up multiple properties for them to look at.

"So?" Ashanti asked.

"It's probably best to think of me as his new owner." Unfortunately.

"Then you will need to fill out this paperwork." She handed him a purple folder with the Barkingham Palace logo embossed on the front.

Thad opened the folder and took a physical step back. What the hell was all this?

"Can't you just transfer the information you already have on him? I didn't have to fill out this much shit when I retired from the Army."

"Sorry, but the primary caretaker must be on file. When you fill it out, please don't forget to include two references and two emergency contacts."

"Two references? I don't want to apply for a job, I just want you to watch the dog. Why do you need references?"

Ashanti sighed.

"I get that you're a new dog owner and probably don't understand their psychology, but dogs tend to mimic the people around them. If you're not a good person, it rubs off on your pet. Thus, the need to verify that you're a good person." She hunched her shoulders. "Of course, I don't expect that to happen with Puddin' because he has a strong personality and already gets along with the dogs here. Nevertheless, it's part of the paperwork. You don't have to fill out everything right now. You can bring it back when you come to pick him up."

Just when he thought this place was over-the-top, he learned something else about it that made it even *more* over-the-top.

"Fine," Thad said, shaking his head. "Pickup is at six p.m., right?"

"Yes. It's fifteen dollars for every half hour that you are late, up to eight p.m."

"But isn't it sixty bucks for the dog to stay overnight? It makes sense to just leave him here if I can't get to him by six p.m."

"You have to book an overnight stay three days in advance. Anything shorter is considered emergency boarding and costs ninety dollars per night."

There was no way in hell it should cost this much to watch a dog.

"Any other questions?" Ashanti asked.

Thad shook his head.

He heard a whine. It was probably one of the dogs, but could also have been his bank account.

He and Von would have some long days that would bleed into long evenings during reno, especially if The PX was going to open by Veterans Day. He would have to set an alarm to remind him to pick Puddin' up by six. It wouldn't hurt the dog to be locked up at the Bywater house for a couple of hours in one of the rooms they weren't working on.

Thad could hear his grandmother's voice in his head, cursing him out in the broken creole French she'd learned as a child just for him thinking it would be okay to leave her precious Puddin' locked in a room.

"Do I need to sign anything before leaving him right now, or is everything in here?" he asked, holding up the folder.

"That's everything. You can leave a credit card on file, or fill out paperwork so that we can do an automatic deduction from your bank account."

Yeah, right. That's all he needed, to wake up and find his account overdrawn because Puddin' wanted extra high-priced dog treats. He reached in his back pocket for his wallet. He handed the card to the woman behind the desk, his eyes narrowing as he caught the two dogs getting a little too comfortable with each other. They'd been the same way on Saturday.

"Hey, are they both fixed? Because they look like they need a room."

"All dogs must be spayed or neutered in order to board. And they're just friendly," Ashanti said. "Puddin' and Duchess have been best friends since the day they met."

"Looks a bit more than just friendly to me," Thad said. "Looks like Puddin' has a better love life than I do."

"Probably because he's more approachable," she said.

The receptionist gasped.

"Did I say that out loud?" Ashanti asked. Thad nodded. So did the receptionist. She sighed and shook her head. "I'm sorry. That was mean and inappropriate and unprofessional."

"Three things that you are not," the receptionist said. She looked to Thad. "She's actually the nicest person I know."

"I'm always nice," Ashanti said. "You're bringing out the worst in me today."

And wasn't that just his luck. Bringing out the worst in her was the exact opposite of what he wanted. But maybe it was for the best.

"It's probably because he bought the house you've coveted for your new location," offered the receptionist.

Ashanti tipped her head to the side, studying him. "That's part of it, but I disliked him even before he bought my house."

"Actually, it's my house," Thad said without thinking. She shot him an irritated look.

This is why she didn't like him.

"I'll be here to get Puddin' by six," Thad said. "I promised my grandmother I would bring him by today, even though he's only supposed to visit on the weekends. She's already sweet-talked the director into giving her special treatment. This is the second midweek visit since I got him."

"That sounds like Mrs. Frances," Ashanti said. She was smiling now. He vastly preferred that to her scowl. Although, even her scowl was cute.

"How is she doing? I'm not being nosy," she interjected. "It's just that I never got the full story about what happened to her. We sent her updates about Puddin' but didn't get any about her."

Thad didn't see the harm in sharing. She was obviously concerned, and he could tell she cared about his grandmother.

"Grams broke her hip and her ankle. Surgery repaired both, but rehab is going to take some time. We got together as a family and decided it was better that she move into an assisted living facility where she can do rehab and then transition into permanent living."

"And she was okay with that?"

He shrugged. "Her biggest issue was having to give up Puddin'. Once I agreed to move back to New Orleans and take care of the dog, she was in it one hundred percent. Honestly, I think she's been lonely in that house. She's already making friends at this new place."

"That doesn't surprise me one bit. Your grandmother is one of the sweetest people I know. Please let her know I'm praying for her."

There was no artifice in her words. She genuinely cared; Thad could see it in her expression.

"I will," he said.

"Thank you."

His reaction to her soft smile was a clear indication that he needed to get out of here. Thad turned to leave, but Ashanti's voice stopped him.

"Mr. Sims?"

He turned back to face her. "You really can call me Thad," he said.

"Thad," she amended. "Aren't you forgetting something?"

His hands immediately went to his pockets, but his wallet was there, along with his keys.

Ashanti pointed to the two dogs. "To tell Puddin' goodbye?"

She had to be fucking with him.

"This is how you develop a relationship with your pet," she said.

No, she wasn't fucking with him. She was serious.

"Bye, dog," Thad said.

Ashanti's look of disappointment rivaled the one his grandfather gave Thad when he was fifteen and came home with one ear pierced.

He practically growled as he walked over to where Puddin' and his girlfriend were still all up in each other's faces. He reached down and patted the stupid puff on top of the dog's head.

"See you later, you little asshole."

"Really?" Ashanti said.

Thad shrugged. "Best I can do."

Then he got out of there before she could hear him laugh.

11

Ashanti pushed her fingers through her microbraids, slightly tugging on them as she chewed her bottom lip. She immediately dropped her hand and reached for the dog bone–shaped stress ball she'd received from a vendor. She didn't need an early trip to the hair braider on top of the rest of these bills.

Her office door opened, and Leslie walked in carrying a familiar white paper cup with a green logo. Ashanti wanted to tackle hug her.

"Bless you," she said as she captured the salted caramel latte between her hands as if it were the Holy Grail.

"What had you so upset when I walked in?" Leslie asked. "That was the third time I've seen you frowning this week."

Ashanti took the lid off the coffee cup and lapped at the sweet whipped cream before recapping it and taking a sip.

"It's been that kind of week. The liability insurance is going up by fifteen percent—probably because of the mauling at that daycare in Philadelphia, even though it was determined that the guy had been harassing the dog. And they've discontinued the special shampoo the Martins like us to use on Baxter."

"Want me to try to find some on the black market?" Leslie asked.

"Even if you could find it, it would probably cost us an arm and a leg." Ashanti let out the sigh she had been trying to withhold all morning. Sighing made it seem as if she was giving up, but there was only so much she could take. "I'll have to tell them that they either supply it themselves, or Baxter uses the same shampoo as every other dog."

"Shelia Martin will just threaten to take Baxter to another daycare."

"Let her do it," Ashanti said. "I've had it up to my hairline with difficult pet owners."

Her phone vibrated a second before the *Stars Wars* "Imperial March" began to play. Ashanti dropped her head to her desk.

"Speaking of difficult people," she mumbled. She sat up straight, lifted her coffee and mouthed *thank you* to Leslie, and took another sip. Then she answered the phone, putting Anita on speakerphone.

"Hello, Anita, can I help you?"

Leslie backed out of the office, giving her a thumbs-up on her way out.

"I want the girls this weekend," Anita answered, not bothering with a greeting.

Ashanti dropped her head on the desk again. She was not up for this today. Or any day, for that matter. Any day that involved speaking to Anita usually ended with Ashanti indulging in a rare glass of wine.

Before she could respond, Anita started in on a monologue about the annual Plant and Garden Show and how it was an opportune time to buy exotic plants that were not native to the area.

Ashanti rolled her eyes, grateful they were not on a video call.

She had never had the best relationship with Anita, even as a young girl, but it had taken a nosedive after her parents died. Ashanti's hands still clenched into fists whenever she thought about how Anita had come to her at the repast meal following the funeral to tell her that she would be seeking custody of Kara and Kendra. The woman had not seen the twins in years, yet all of a sudden, she wanted to raise them?

When she thought about how close they'd come to that happening thanks to her ex-boyfriend's decision to drive while intoxicated, it made her want to hurl her coffee against the wall.

"I'm sorry, but I promised the girls I would take them shopping for supplies for their science project," Ashanti said.

She took another sip of coffee and made a decision she should have made a long time ago.

"Actually, that's a lie," Ashanti said. She was done pretending, and she no longer cared about keeping the peace. "The girls do not want to go to the plant show with you."

"How do you know that?" Anita said.

Because I'm psychic.

Ashanti stopped herself before she could blurt out the disrespectful reply. "Because Kara told me she doesn't want to go," she said.

"What about Kendra?"

Yeah, right. She could barely get Kendra to talk to *her*. Kendra would probably growl at Anita if she came near.

"She doesn't want to go either," Ashanti said.

"Well, you make them," Anita said.

"No. They're sixteen, not ten. The girls can decide how

they want to spend their weekend, and no one will force them to do anything they don't want to do."

"You're behind this, aren't you?" Anita hissed. "You're turning my brother's children against me."

Ashanti had heard this song too many times. She was not up for a repeat.

"Look, I have to go. You have both Kara's and Kendra's phone numbers. Call and ask if they want to go shopping for plants with you. Like I said, they're old enough to make their own decisions. There's no need for me to play the middleman."

She didn't bother saying goodbye before disconnecting the call. She would probably hear something about her rudeness, but she couldn't bring herself to care about Anita's feelings anymore. Lord knew the woman had never cared about hers.

Anita had not even been on speaking terms with her brother when he died, but no one would know that based on her attitude these past six years. She came across as a paragon of sibling love. Ashanti still wasn't sure if it was guilt or just an act. She doubted it was true grief.

Her office door burst open for the second time in twenty minutes. This time it was Kara who came rushing in, a wide smile stretched across her face. Ashanti hadn't seen when she left the house this morning, so she'd missed today's purple hair color.

Ashanti checked the time on her phone.

"Why are you not at school?" Yet another question she was tired of asking. "And I don't want to hear the excuse that you're at lunch because lunch isn't for another two hours, at least."

"No, no, I'm definitely cutting class right now," Kara said, rounding the crowded desk. "I could have texted, but I had to see your reaction when you saw this. Look!"

She stuck her phone in Ashanti's face. Ashanti took it from her and stared at the screen. She immediately recognized the setting.

"It's the doggy cam," Ashanti said.

"No shit, Sherlock."

"Hey! Language."

Kara rolled her eyes. "Just keep watching. This is footage from yesterday. Make sure you're looking at the pop-up tent in the bottom right corner."

There were twenty-four doggy cams in Barkingham Palace, including one in each of the pet suites that could be accessed through their website with a password. But there was one public webcam with a live feed that ran twenty-four hours a day. Ashanti always found it interesting—and a bit disconcerting—that people watched the feed in the dead of night, when the dogs were all in their suites and nowhere near the public camera. There had to be something better on Netflix or Hulu.

"I don't understand," Ashanti said, throwing her hands up. "What am I looking for?"

"Just wait," Kara said. "Riiiiight…there."

Mark lifted the pop-up tent and unveiled Duchess and Puddin' sharing one of Duchess Delights' signature dog treats. They were eating it *Lady and the Tramp*–style, each with an end between their teeth, their mouths nearly touching. The dogs looked up at Mark, then ran in opposite directions, like two teenagers who had been caught kissing under the bleachers.

Ashanti burst out laughing. "Okay, so maybe things *have* gotten out of hand between those two."

"Shanti, do you understand what's happening?" Kara asked, her voice frustrated.

"What?" she asked.

"Look at the number of views!" She pointed at the screen.

Ashanti squinted as she peered at the phone. "Does that say…"

"2.5 million," Kara said. "And climbing. The video was posted to this IG account this morning and it's already been shared over sixty thousand times."

"Who posted it?" she asked, searching for the Instagram handle. "What does Jinyoung4Lyfe mean?"

"They're a K-pop fan, but they're also one of our regular viewers."

"I didn't realize we had regulars."

"You know nothing about any of this, do you?" Kara asked.

"Hey, I know enough," Ashanti said. She didn't know nearly as much as she should. She left all the online stuff to Kara because she was good at it, and her labor came cheap. Basically, free.

"And that's not the best part," Kara said. Her fingers swiped across the screen. "Not only has that video blown up, so has *our* IG account. Barkingham Palace has been holding steady at eight hundred fifty-three followers for the last month. Now…?"

Ashanti gasped when Kara turned the phone to face her again. "Over fifteen thousand?"

"It's obscene," Kara said. "Of course, I've been driving people to the YouTube channel all day in our Stories. I'm going to search through archived livestream footage and make some Reels to post to IG."

Ashanti avoided social media as much as one could in this day and age. The thought of posting every aspect of her life on the Internet for strangers—even for friends—made her break out in hives. But she couldn't expect Kara to handle this on her own.

"This means I will have to use Instagram more often, doesn't it?" Ashanti asked.

"Yes, unless you want me to drop out of high school to become Barkingham Palace's full-time social media manager. I think that's the route we should go, to be honest."

"I think we can manage between me and Deja," Ashanti said.

"We can manage what?" Deja asked, sticking her head into the opened office door.

"Social media?" Ashanti said.

"I can do some TikTok dances," Deja said. She shimmied her shoulders.

"Or maybe not," Kara said.

Deja hooked a thumb toward the front of the building. "Umm, I don't know what's going on, but the phones have been ringing nonstop for the past two hours. I just had a woman call from Jackson, Mississippi, wanting to bring her Chihuahua down to spend a day at the daycare. Not because she wants to explore New Orleans. Coming to the daycare is the entire point of her trip."

"And it starts," Kara said. "We are officially a destination." She plopped down in the office's lone other chair, folded her hands behind her head, and propped her feet up on Ashanti's desk.

"If you don't get these shoes off my desk," Ashanti said, shoving her purple tennis shoes away.

"Can someone explain to me what's going on?" Deja asked.

"Puddin' and Duchess were caught canoodling on the doggy cam and it went viral," Kara said.

"No way!" Deja came farther into the office.

"Yep!" Kara shoved the phone at her. Ashanti could tell the moment the canoodling was revealed by Deja's delighted squeal.

"If you asked me, you should make a silhouette of this shot the label for Duchess Delights," Deja said.

"Yes! Oh em gee, that is genius!" Kara hopped out of the chair. She covered her eyes with her fingers, opening and closing them like she was playing peekaboo. "Wait, no. No, I don't...Yeah, I can see it. Yes, I love that idea."

Ashanti rolled her eyes at her sister's dramatics.

"Get back to school," she told her.

"Do you really expect me to be able to concentrate on calculus when the Duchess and Puddin' Show has just hit the mainstream?"

"Yes, I do," Ashanti said. "And tell your sister that I expect her to be home for dinner. It's po' boy night."

"Fried catfish with no lettuce and extra pickles for me," Kara said, as if she had not been ordering the same po' boy every week for the past six years. "And Kendra has cheerleading practice, even though she is the grouchiest cheerleader I have ever seen."

"What's going on with her?" Ashanti asked.

Kara hunched her shoulders. "I would say PMS, but that doesn't last weeks." She picked up her backpack and pulled the strap over her shoulder. "Don't worry about Kendra. She'll snap out of whatever is going on with her." She held up her cell phone. "If I were you, I'd get to making more treats—specifically the I Woof You chew sticks. People are already blowing up our DMs asking where they can buy them."

"How many?" Ashanti asked, but Kara had already left the room. Ashanti picked up her phone and clicked on the Instagram app. She tried to sign in but she couldn't access the daycare's account.

She hopped up from her desk and rushed out of the office, catching Kara in the lobby.

"Hey, what's going on with the Barkingham Palace Instagram account?" Ashanti asked.

"Oh, I changed the password. Can't have you doing rogue IG lives the way you did the other morning."

"What is the password, Kara?"

"Sorry, calculus awaits," her sister said in the singsongy voice she used when she wanted to annoy Ashanti. It was working.

"Kara!"

"Fine," she said. She took Ashanti's phone and started typing on it. "I'll let you in, but don't touch anything. And, by all means, do *not* post or reply to anyone."

"You do realize this is *my* business, right?"

"Oh yeah? Log into your YouTube channel," Kara said.

Ashanti snatched the phone from her hand. "Get back to school."

12

Thad added a tablespoon of dried basil to the ground turkey crumbles sizzling in the skillet his grandmother had owned since before he was born. The fact that he was using this skillet to cook a poodle's breakfast made him roll his eyes. There was probably someone Dumpster diving in this city at this very moment, yet here he was using high-quality ingredients because Puddin' had a sensitive stomach. When had his grandmother lost her good sense?

"Probably when you came to live with her," he said to Puddin', who stood watch next to him. Judging his cooking skills, no doubt.

"You'd better be glad I love that woman, because you would be eating table scraps if it were up to me."

Thad could only imagine the uproar it would cause if he even uttered those words in his grandmother's presence, or around Ashanti Wright. She treated Puddin' as if he were *her* dog.

Thad glanced down at him. "She ever kiss you on the mouth?"

It was probably for the best that Puddin' couldn't answer. For one thing, he was grossed out by people who kissed dogs on the mouth. For another, he was jealous enough of this poodle. He didn't need yet another reason to hate him.

Thad measured out a half cup of the ground turkey, brown rice, and sweet potato mixture and dumped it in Puddin's Burberry dog bowl. He still regretted Googling the price of it. He would never view his grandmother in the same way knowing she'd spent that kind of money on a dog bowl.

Puddin' looked down at the food and then back up at him.

"What?" Thad asked. Then he remembered. "Sorry, I forgot to add your kibble, your royal highness."

He grabbed the high-priced specialty dog food from the pantry and added some to the bowl. Then he topped off Puddin's water before bringing a cup of coffee into the dining room where he'd set up his laptop. He needed to check his bank account before heading to the Bywater house.

Call him old-fashioned, but Thad still couldn't bring himself to download banking apps onto his phone. He didn't fully trust checking his account on the home computer either, but at least he'd added an extra layer of encryption to the house's Wi-Fi.

He checked off the bills that had come through overnight using a pen and notepad he kept specifically for tracking his finances—another relic of times gone by. Just as he logged out of the bank's website, an email notification popped up in the monitor's right-hand corner.

He clicked on the icon. It was from the genealogy website Nadia had pestered him into sending a DNA sample to. It had started when a Tee Ball teammate of one of his nieces was diagnosed with a hereditary heart condition. Nadia became obsessed with learning about their father's medical history. Since they wouldn't know where to find the asshole who had left their mother months after Thad was born, going the 23andMe route seemed like the best course of action.

But what had started out as something to protect her girls' health had turned into an obsession for his sister. She was determined to learn everything there was to know about both sides of their family.

Thad had no idea how this stuff worked, but apparently there was information that could only be found on the Y-chromosome, and now that he was the last remaining male on the Sutherland side, mailing off his spit was the only way to dig deeper into the histories his sister so desperately wanted to learn.

A waste of time and money, in his opinion, but if anyone could bother him until he was willing to do anything to make it stop—including sharing his DNA—it was Nadia.

Thad knew there were people who shied away from using genealogy services because they didn't want the government to be able to access it, but that wasn't an issue for him. Uncle Sam had owned his DNA since he was eighteen.

He clicked the email and then the link that brought him to the website's direct message page. Thad frowned in confusion, but it soon turned to irritation as he read through the message.

"What kind of bullshit is this?" He clicked on the sender's icon. He had never seen this woman before in his life, yet she was claiming they shared the same grandfather? As if he was supposed to just believe that screenshot she'd attached was legit. Anyone with a smartphone could manipulate a photo.

"Of course, you'd love to meet your family in Louisiana," Thad said with a grunt.

And how long after she met them would she try to shake his grandmother down for money? The woman had probably run across the profile from the local paper on Grams after she sold Sutherland Dry Cleaning, and figured an old widow with money in the bank would welcome her with open arms. Never mind the fact that her long-lost relative bit was essentially accusing that widow's husband of having bastard children floating around out there. She probably hadn't even considered that.

Thad reached over, intending to delete the message, but the longer he stared at it, the more it pissed him off. His grandfather was the most upstanding man he had ever met. Taking in his daughter and her two children after her husband bailed. Raising those two children as his own so his daughter could return to college and make a life for herself. Becoming a pillar of the community who had literally given the shirt off his back to those in need, or at least the shirts that had been abandoned by customers.

And *that's* the man this woman had decided to disparage?

Thad began typing a response. He wanted to see how far this scammer would go.

"Dude, what's going on?"

"What the fuck!" Thad yelled, jumping up from the dining room chair and slamming the laptop closed. "What are you doing sneaking up on people, Von?"

"I texted you that I was coming in. I knocked, but you didn't answer. So I used the key you gave me."

"That's for emergencies. So unless something's on fire I'm kicking your ass."

"This is an emergency," Von said. "Actually, it isn't." He gestured to the computer. "I caught you looking at porn, didn't I?"

"Shut up," Thad said. "As if I give two shits whether you see me watching porn. I'm a grown man. I can watch porn if I want to."

"You would watch porn in your grandparents' house? What kind of sick monster are you?"

Thad was two seconds away from tossing his best friend out on his ass. He would do it with a smile.

"Wait, you weren't on one of those message boards again, were you? We talked about this, Thad."

"I wasn't on a military message board. Did you come here for a reason?"

"Yeah." Von pulled out a rolled sheaf of papers from his back pocket. "I got the estimate back from the contractor. It's up there, man. No way can we afford to use this guy."

Thad snatched the papers from his hands. His eyes widened at the number in bold at the bottom of the page.

"Damn. Maybe we're going into the wrong business. What does it take to become a contractor?"

"I thought the same thing." Von laughed. "The shitty part is, based on what I've found online, his prices are reasonable." He turned around one of the dining room chairs and straddled it. "We were already planning to do most of the work ourselves. My suggestion is that we only use the contractor for the heavy stuff, like electrical and plumbing, and figure out a way to conquer the rest on our own. We can probably find a few more vets in need of work. It will still cost us less than what this guy is charging."

"Yeah, but even with hiring more men, this still means

putting in a lot more time than we first thought," Thad pointed out.

"You got something better to do with your time? Other than hang out with this dog?" He hooked a thumb at Puddin', who had joined them in the dining room.

"Don't remind me about this dog," Thad said. It occurred to him why Puddin' was standing at attention. "Shit. I forgot his vitamins."

He grabbed the bag of multivitamins disguised as chicken-flavored dog treats from the kitchen counter and tossed two toward Puddin'. The poodle caught them midair.

"Impressive," Von said. "You two should take your act on the road." He grabbed a handful of walnuts from the bowl Thad kept on the dining room table.

For as long as he could remember, his grandfather had kept a wooden bowl filled with unshelled pecans, walnuts, and Brazil nuts, along with a nutcracker, on the dining room table. He'd been surprised when he got here and realized that his grandmother had gotten rid of Granddad's nut bowl. It was probably Nadia's idea, because the wooden bowl no longer matched the color scheme.

"You're bringing him back to daycare today, right?" Von asked.

"Yeah," Thad said. Then he cursed as something else occurred to him.

"What's wrong?" Von asked.

"Putting in longer hours at The PX means I'll have to leave Puddin' at the damn doggy daycare until eight most nights of the week," Thad answered. "That's an extra sixty dollars a day, on top of the regular daily fee."

"Damn!" Von looked as if he'd swallowed the walnut whole. "We *are* getting into the wrong business."

Thad ran a hand down his face. "Maybe I can cut a deal with the daycare owner."

"Are we talking about the same daycare owner who came to the Bywater house looking like she wanted to strangle you? That daycare owner?"

"Yeah, that's her," Thad said.

"Maybe I should ask her. She seems to like me better than she likes you."

Thad refrained from responding because anything he said would reveal too much and he wasn't in the mood to hear Von's mouth. He was grateful that, for once, Von hadn't been able to read his mind.

"Let me refill my coffee and pack up the dog's food. I'll meet you at The PX in about thirty."

Von followed him into the kitchen and stood to the side while Thad grabbed a travel mug from the kitchen cabinet. His grandmother had at least a half dozen of them, all with logos from various companies that sold dry cleaning supplies. The moment Thad filled the cup, Von took it from his hand.

"Pour yourself another. I'll see you at the site."

"Asshole," Thad mumbled under his breath. He grabbed another travel mug.

After fixing his coffee, he packed enough food for Puddin's dinner, then stored the rest in the refrigerator. He was running late. He'd decided yesterday that if he was going to pay for this dog to go to daycare, then Puddin' would be at Barkingham Palace as soon as the doors opened.

He stopped at the dining room table and stared at the

closed laptop. He had not downloaded the genealogy site's app onto his phone yet, but now he was thinking maybe he should.

No, he shouldn't. He wasn't wasting any more time today on that scammer. He whistled for Puddin' to follow him.

Even though the daycare was only a few miles from his grandmother's house, it still took twenty minutes to get there. If people would stop checking their cell phones while stopped at traffic lights it would cut his travel time in half. He'd had to blow his horn at every single light.

The moment Thad walked through the doors of Barkingham Palace, he sensed that something was different. The space hummed with excitement. Three women occupied the lobby, along with four dogs.

"I'm sorry, but we're full for today," the receptionist was telling a woman who held a brown fur ball against her chest.

"Is there a waitlist?" the woman asked.

The receptionist—Deja, if he remembered correctly— nodded. "You can access it through our website."

Another woman in line turned to look over her shoulder and gasped. "That's him!" she said.

Thad took a step back as the women in the lobby converged on him.

Wait. It wasn't *him* they were after. They all hunched down and crowded around Puddin'.

"Watch it, ladies," Deja called from behind the desk. "He's taken."

"Where's his girlfriend?" asked a woman trying to wrestle two medium-size dogs on leashes.

"In the back with her mama," Deja answered. "Let me call her to come get Puddin'."

Deja summoned Ashanti through the intercom system.

A minute later, the door leading to the back of the daycare opened and Ashanti walked in, holding a leash with her French bulldog on the other end of it.

Thad fully acknowledged the heat that spread throughout his chest at the sight of her. She glanced his way, and it was as if she'd looked straight through him.

Damn, this one-sided attraction thing was brutal.

He had to remind himself that it was for the best that Ashanti Wright thought he was an asshole.

"There's my boy," Ashanti said. She knelt on one knee and rubbed Puddin' behind the ear. "Aht, aht," she said, turning her face away when the dog's snout got too close. "You know I don't play that."

Thank you, sweet baby Jesus. She didn't kiss dogs on the mouth. His attraction to her grew exponentially.

Puddin' turned his attention to Duchess. The two performed their usual greeting, sniffing each other's butts, then Puddin' leaned forward so Duchess could snuggle against his neck.

"Oh, my word! They are just too precious together," one of the women said.

"Aren't they?" Ashanti said. She tugged on Puddin's leash and glanced at Thad. "I'll take him. You can leave his food with Deja." Then she addressed the others in the lobby. "I'm sorry we don't have room. We are trying to secure a bigger location. I almost had one, but..." She looked directly at Thad this time. "It fell through."

"Oh no," the woman with the brown fur ball said. "I hope you can find a new one soon. Betty Boop would love it here."

Thad shook his head. He was convinced if any of these

dogs could talk, they would curse their owners out over these stupid-ass names.

"You can still watch the Barkingham Palace webcam," Ashanti said. "We're going to have two streams open to the public soon, the one we have now and one that showcases our outdoor space."

With that, Ashanti left the lobby without so much as another glance his way. Thad managed to hide his disappointment.

Betty Boop's mom walked up to him. "Are you Puddin's owner?"

"Um, I guess you can say that," Thad said.

"He is the cutest. You must be so proud."

Of what? That Puddin' had only spent ten minutes licking his own balls this morning instead of twenty?

"Uh, sure," Thad said.

He waited until the women left the daycare before approaching Deja. He nodded toward the door as she set Puddin's food on the counter.

"What was that all about?" he asked.

"You don't know about the viral livestream video?" she asked. She picked up a cell phone and, after a few swipes at the screen, turned it to face Thad. He snorted a laugh when the guy on the video lifted the tent and discovered the two dogs together.

"Damn, Puddin' really is getting more action than I am," Thad said. He shrugged. "I guess I should try to find those dog biscuits."

Deja stooped down and came up with a basket of cellophane-wrapped treats.

"They're sold out everywhere, but Ashanti makes sure we

always have some available for our clients." She set two treats on the desk. "But we have to limit the amount you can buy until she's able to bake more inventory. We're getting orders from around the world. The last twenty-four hours have been unreal."

"She makes these herself?" Thad asked.

Deja nodded. "I'll add these two to Puddin's bill. Remember, pickup is at six."

"How could I forget," Thad said.

13

Ashanti added a cup of pureed pumpkin to the stand-alone mixer's bowl, locked the flat beater into place, and started it on a slow mix. She checked on the treats baking in the oven before filling a piping bag with icing and finishing up those that had already cooled.

"Only five hundred more to go," she said.

When their website had crashed this weekend from being inundated with people inquiring about the doggy treats Duchess and Puddin' were caught sharing, Ashanti's first instinct had been to panic. She swiftly rearranged her thinking, choosing instead to count her blessings.

This is what she wanted, right? For everyone to clamor for Duchess Delights. National brands paid tens of thousands of dollars for the free marketing she'd gotten from that viral video.

For months she'd questioned whether pet owners would be interested in a full-size pet bakery. Well, she had her answer. What she needed now was inventory. And a bigger place for her business.

The doorbell chimed.

"One minute," Ashanti called, setting the piping bag on the table. "Scoot, Duchess," she told her dog. The cute little booger would try to escape in a heartbeat if given half a chance.

Ashanti opened the door and smiled in relief.

"At your service," Evie said.

"Thank you." Ashanti enveloped her in a hug. She stepped back and held up her hands. "And before you ask, yes, I've already put out feelers for a second baker. I know better than to even *try* to keep up this pace on my own. But, until I can find someone, I need as much help as I can get." She motioned for Evie to follow her to the kitchen and pointed to the cookie sheets stacked up on the counter. "Let me get the set that's baking out of the oven, and I'll help you bring those to the car."

"It's three hundred fifty degrees for twelve minutes, right?"

"Yes. Not a minute longer," Ashanti said.

"The only time I've taken advantage of the double ovens in my house is the year I hosted Thanksgiving. You'd better be grateful I haven't had time to do the kitchen reno I've been wanting to do, because that double oven would be gone. Actually, thank Cameron for that. He's the one who keeps putting it off."

"Give your fiancé this kiss from me," Ashanti said. She kissed Evie on the cheek before carrying the treats she'd just taken from the oven to the dining room table.

She heard the front door open a second before seeing a green-and-white jacket pass through the room in a blur.

"Was that Kendra?" Evie asked.

"Yes," Ashanti said with a sigh. "I need to talk to her, but I'm not up for a fight right now."

"Teenagers." Evie shook her shoulders in an exaggerated shudder. "I want no part of it."

"Yeah, well, I didn't really have a choice," Ashanti said. "It was me or Atilla."

Evie shuddered again. "Those girls need to thank you every day of their lives. Speaking of thanking you, why aren't they in here *helping* you?"

"One of them doesn't even talk to me most days," Ashanti said, gesturing to the stairs. "And Kara has volleyball practice." She tried her best to shake off the disquiet that filled her regarding Kendra these days. She had to figure out what was going on with that one. "I'll help you get these in the car."

It took two trips to cart all the cookie sheets and plastic containers filled with unbaked treats out to Evie's SUV. Ashanti was about to put another two dozen in the oven, but thought better of it. She needed to check in on Kendra first, and if by some miracle she could get her sister to give her more than a few monosyllabic responses, she didn't want to have to stop their conversation so that she could get dog biscuits out of the oven.

Before she could go upstairs, Kendra came back down. She had changed into the tracksuit she wore over her cheerleader uniform and carried a green-and-white duffle on one shoulder.

"Where are you going?" Ashanti asked.

"To the volleyball match," she answered.

"You mean volleyball *practice*," Ashanti said.

"No, I mean the volleyball match," she said. "They're playing Country Day Academy."

"No," Ashanti said, covering her face with her hands. "Please, don't tell me that match is today."

"Yes, it is. And, yes, Kara is starting at setter. I gotta go."

Ashanti's stomach dropped. Country Day was the girls' volleyball team's biggest rival. She had promised Kara she would be there.

"Kendra, we need to talk. Soon," Ashanti said.

"We really don't. I'm fine."

"You don't seem fine."

Kendra released an overly exaggerated sigh. "Do you really want to do this now? How do you think Kara will feel if *neither* of her sisters are there to see her first match as a starter?"

"Go," Ashanti said. "But we *are* going to talk. And tell Kara I'm sorry I have to miss the match. I just have too many orders to fill."

Kendra's only response was to tell Duchess to get back as she left through the front door.

"Come here, girl," Ashanti called. She reached into her mother's blasphemous ceramic cookie jar of the cat from Alice in Wonderland and slipped Duchess one of the mini treats she'd made last week. Ashanti thought they would be a good addition to her offerings, but she would have to table that idea for now. This was not the time to experiment with new products.

She did a mental tally of how many dozens she still needed to make, and tried to figure out how long she would have to stay up baking tonight if she were to stop for a while and go to Kara's match.

There was just no way. Even with Evie taking over some of the baking, she still had to decorate and bake at least another ten dozen before tomorrow. She would be lucky if she carried herself to bed before two a.m.

Her bottom lip began to tremble, but Ashanti closed her eyes and pulled in a deep breath before things could get out of hand.

"You're doing as best you can." She whispered the words to herself a couple times more, until she felt a sense of calm come over her.

"Okay, now get back to work," she said.

She was in the middle of adding edible sugar pearls to the crown-shape treats when her phone rang. Not recognizing the number, she let it go to voicemail. Two minutes later, the phone rang again. It was the same number. Ashanti frowned at the phone. The caller had left a voicemail, yet had called right back?

She waited for them to hang up, then immediately listened to the first voicemail.

"Oh my God!" Ashanti screamed.

Duchess came running in on her short legs.

"Oh my God! Oh my God! Oh my God!" She rushed over to the junk drawer and pulled out a pen and notepad, then she put the phone on speaker and played back the voicemail so that she could write down the number.

"Okay, okay, calm down," Ashanti ordered herself. She looked down at Duchess. "We got this. We're professionals."

She called the number.

"Hello," Ashanti said the minute the man on the other end of the line answered. "This is Ashanti Wright, owner of Barkingham Palace."

The words rushed out of her mouth.

Calm down.

She could barely contain her smile as the man repeated the same message he'd left on her voicemail, that he was a producer from one of the local television stations and that they were interested in doing a story about the daycare.

The minute Ashanti was done with the call, she Face-Timed Ridley and Evie.

"Don't tell me, you got into a fistfight with Kendra," Evie said.

"Yes, I would totally fist fight my sixteen-year-old sister," Ashanti said. "No! I just got a call from Channel 6! They want to do a story about Barkingham Palace tomorrow for the morning news."

"Get the hell outta here," Ridley said. "I told you Duchess was going to put you on the map one day."

She'd told her no such thing.

"This livestream video is blowing up way more than I could have ever expected," Ashanti said. "I need to send that K-pop Instagrammer a gift basket for posting it."

"Does the news station want you in the studio?" Ridley asked.

"No, they're coming to the daycare."

"I'll be at your house tomorrow morning at five," Ridley said.

"Why?"

"To do your makeup," Ridley and Evie said at the same time.

"I can do—"

"Girl, don't even try to go there," Evie said. "You cannot be trusted to fix your own face."

"Hey, I know how to put on makeup. I just don't," Ashanti said. The minuscule amount of makeup she owned was at least three years old.

"Okay, so maybe I can use a little help," Ashanti said. "Be here at four thirty. They asked me to meet them at the daycare for six."

"Four thirty? Now I'm sorry I offered," Ridley said.

"I love you too," Ashanti said. "I'll talk to you both later. I need to make a call. Evie, I'll swing by to pick the treats up in a couple of hours."

"I can bring them," she said. "You've got enough on your plate."

"You're the one I *really* love, Ev," Ashanti said.

She laughed at Ridley's obscenity-laced goodbye. She could not buy better friends with all the gold in the world.

Ashanti's grin quickly turned into a frown as she considered the call she desperately needed to make.

"Just remember, you're a professional," she said. Although, there was nothing professional about what she was getting ready to do. She shrugged. It couldn't be helped.

She used the remote access on her laptop to log in to Barkingham Palace's system and pulled up Puddin's account. Later, she would examine the ethics of using the customer database to get a client's personal cell phone number for nonemergency purposes.

She called Thad before she could talk herself out of doing it.

"Sims," he answered.

No hello. Just Sims.

"Um, hi," Ashanti said, actively ignoring her body's reaction to his voice. My goodness, she could feel the texture of his smooth, deep tone on her skin. "This is Ashanti Wright from Barkingham Palace."

"Puddin' is right here with me," he said, a hint of leeriness in his voice. "On my damn lap, as a matter of fact."

"Yes, I know," she said. "I didn't know he was on your lap, of course. I'm not peeking through your window or anything."

Oh my God! Shut up!

"Look, I need a really big favor," Ashanti said. She would need wine after this call.

"From me?" Thad asked.

No, from the ice cream man. Who did he think?

"Yes, from you," Ashanti said. "I was contacted by one of the local television stations. They want to do a story about Puddin' and Duchess going viral on the livestream."

He paused for a long, uncomfortable moment. "Okay," he finally said.

A man of so few words.

"They're meeting me at the daycare at six tomorrow morning. And, well, since it *is* a story about Duchess *and* Puddin' they kinda expect…"

Another pause. "You are not asking me to bring this poodle to the daycare at six in the morning, are you?"

"Five thirty, actually. Just to be on the safe side."

He groaned. Even that sounded nicer than it should. Low and husky and resonant.

"I know it's asking a lot," Ashanti said. "But…" Should she go there? Yes, of course she should go there. "But you bought my building out from under me, so you owe me one."

She regretted the words the moment she said them. The only person responsible for her not getting her hands on that building was her. Thad had no idea she'd had her heart set on buying it, and even if he did, he was under no obligation to just sit back and let her have that gorgeous house when he wanted it for his business. He didn't owe her anything.

Yet, instead of calling her on her outrageous take, he said, "Okay."

"Really?" Ashanti was ready to do a backflip.

"For a price," he added.

Nix on the backflip. She should have known it wouldn't be this easy.

She was almost afraid to ask. "What's the price?"

She could hear him shifting a moment before mumbling, "Move, dog."

"You know, he may respond to you better if you used his name."

"I hate his name," Thad said. "And I do use it sometimes. It doesn't make a difference. This dog is hardheaded, and he doesn't listen. Now, about my price," he continued. "I'm gonna have to put in some long hours at the Bywater house over the next couple of months to get it renovated in time for our grand opening. I want a week of free—what do you call it when you have to keep the dogs after six p.m.?"

"After-care," she answered.

"That's it. A week's worth of free after-care. Take it or leave it."

She did quick math. "So you're charging me three hundred dollars to bring Puddin' to the daycare a couple of hours early tomorrow?"

"Take it or leave it," Thad said again. She heard the amusement in his response and hated how much she *didn't* hate the sound of it. It added another layer to that already decadent voice.

"I'll take it," Ashanti said, as if she had a choice. Puddin' was the other half of the story.

"I'll make sure his rhinestone collar is nice and shiny," Thad said. "See you in the morning."

He disconnected the call before she could, which irritated her even more. The least he could have done was given her the satisfaction of hanging up on him.

She wished she was in the position to throw his offer back in his face, but Thad held all the cards here. She counted herself lucky he hadn't demanded a month of free after-care. She would have agreed to it.

"He's so annoying," she said, setting the phone on the counter. Ashanti caught herself grinning and immediately stopped. There was no space in her life for grinning like a schoolgirl because she had just talked to Mrs. Frances's exasperating, yet outrageously fine, grandson.

So maybe she should stop grinning and get back to baking.

14

If this interview didn't end soon Ashanti was going to sweat through her shirt. She'd already dropped Duchess's leash twice because her hands began shaking uncontrollably the moment the camera started rolling.

At least her voice no longer shook.

As much.

"How has Puddin' and Duchess's newfound fame affected Barkingham Palace?" asked the reporter, who was much shorter in person than he looked on TV.

"It's been amazing. We've been getting calls from people from all over the country wanting to board their dogs," Ashanti said. "I wish we could take them all, but there's only so much room here at the daycare."

Kara stood a few feet behind and to the right of the cameraman. She was making a motion for Ashanti to smile.

Ashanti was going to strangle her once this interview was over.

The segment producer had called just before six this morning to tell her that the reporter was being pulled off her story to cover a fire near the industrial canal, but that they would try to fit her in during the noon broadcast. So not only had she suffered through wearing makeup all morning, but she now had to live up to her bargain with Thad, even though it would have been just fine if he had brought Puddin' at his normal time.

He had been here at five thirty, just as she'd asked. And looking way too good in worn jeans and a fitted T-shirt for such an obscene time of the morning. He'd looked like someone who'd gotten ten hours of sleep followed by a facial. It was unfair.

"I read in your LinkedIn profile that you attended vet school at LSU," the reporter asked. "How did you go from wanting to be a veterinarian to running a doggy daycare?"

First, she had forgotten all about that LinkedIn profile. And second, rude.

It was a legitimate question, but the way he framed it made it seem as if she should feel ashamed. As if she had settled. Or, worse, that she couldn't cut it. Neither was true. Well, not entirely true.

"I went through a major life event that compelled me to change course." Ashanti hunched her shoulders and dialed up her smile. Kara gave her a thumbs-up. "It was just one of the curveballs that life tends to throw at you. But I've always prided myself on being nimble."

"It seems you turned that curveball into a home run," the reporter said.

Goodness, where was a bottle of Mylanta when she needed one?

The reporter turned his $20,000 smile back to the camera and wrapped up the segment with a reminder that Barkingham

Palace had a waitlist. He told viewers they would share the local boutiques that sold Duchess Delights on the station's website, then threw it back to the anchors at the news desk.

"That's a wrap," he told the cameraman. He turned to Ashanti and stuck out his hand. "My producer apologizes again for this morning."

"I get it," Ashanti said. "Remember what I said about being nimble?"

He made pistol fingers at her and she legit thought she would barf. What a cheeseball.

"Good job," Kara said.

"What are you doing here?" Ashanti asked, shrugging out of the cardigan she'd worn over her Barkingham Palace long-sleeved T-shirt. She thought it would dress it up a bit, make her more presentable. She should have stuck with only the T-shirt.

"Did you honestly think I would miss your big television debut?" Kara asked.

"If I get called down to that school because of your skipping, there will be hell to pay, Kara."

"But I'm skipping with permission this time. Mrs. Calloway knows I'm here. I told her you needed moral support because you tend to get nervous when you talk about yourself. I was right."

"I wasn't nervous," Ashanti lied.

"Of course you were." Kara waved her off. "By the way, Mrs. Calloway wants to know if you have any treats she can buy for her Yorkie because she can't find them anywhere. I told her I would bring her one. On the house."

"So now you're bargaining with your teachers to get time away from class?"

"I'm a businesswoman," Kara said. She pinched Ashanti's cheek. "I learned from the best."

"Get back to school. You're not allowed to skip another day for the rest of the semester," Ashanti said. "If you do, I'm turning you in to the front office myself."

"You'll lose cool points."

"I don't care about cool points."

It was a lie. She totally cared about cool points. But balancing being the cool older sister and the responsible guardian was something she was still working on six years into this role that had been thrust upon her. Responsible guardian won out this time.

Kara took Duchess's leash from her and, with Ashanti and Puddin' following behind, entered the daycare.

"You did great," Deja said from behind the desk, where she had been streaming the noon broadcast on the computer.

"Could you tell how nervous I was?" Ashanti asked, rounding the desk and getting one of the treats from the private stash. She handed it to Kara in exchange for Duchess's leash. "Now get back to school."

Kara rolled her eyes and left.

"That girl is going to fail eleventh grade if she skips any more school," Deja said.

"I don't understand how she does it and still gets to play volleyball."

"Sweet talk," Deja said. "She got twenty bucks and my Netflix password out of me the other day."

"Deja," Ashanti said. "No Netflix was part of her punishment for skipping last week."

Deja shrugged. "She's a good manipulator." She handed Ashanti a pink sticky note. "Mrs. Frances called halfway through the segment. Apparently, her grandson didn't think to mention that her dog had become a celebrity."

"I meant to tell her about the interview," Ashanti said, feeling like a big bag of dog poop. "Thad should have. He knows his grandmother would get a kick out of this."

"At least she still caught the segment," Deja said.

"I'll give her a call as soon as I get Duchess and Puddin' settled in the back."

Ashanti brought the dogs to the backyard exercise pen. When she learned that her story was being moved to the noon broadcast, she'd taken advantage of the extra time to bathe and groom both Duchess and Puddin'. As a result, they had missed their morning exercise.

"How did it go?" Colleen asked from the other side of the Rover Jump Over.

"Nerve-racking," Ashanti said. "But it'll be good for business."

Colleen walked over to her. "I know this seems counter-productive, but business is a little too good already," she said. "In case you haven't noticed, we're bursting at the seams." She picked up a tennis ball and tossed it to Sunshine, the Dumases' golden retriever. Sunshine took off like a rocket. "The point is," Colleen continued, "without a bigger facility, all the free publicity in the world won't do us any good."

"I know," Ashanti said. She'd told herself she wouldn't bemoan Thad buying her house again, but she deserved at least a few more days to mourn. "It's just hard to find the perfect spot, and other than that two-story in the Lower Garden District across from Coliseum Square Park, there is no place better than the house in the Bywater."

"Ever think of moving out to Metairie?" Colleen asked.

"Absolutely not!" Ashanti's answer was immediate.

Colleen took the ball out of Sunshine's mouth and held her hands up in mock surrender.

"Okay, okay. Don't shoot me for asking," she said.

Ashanti's cell phone rang. She pulled it from her back pocket and rolled her eyes.

"It's Ridley," Ashanti said as she turned back toward the daycare. She answered the phone with an overly dramatic sigh. "What did I do wrong during the interview?" she asked.

"Is that how you answer a phone?"

"It's how *you* would."

"Touché," her friend said. "And I have no idea what you did wrong. I've been in a meeting Uptown all day. I haven't seen the segment. I did, however, just see something that will make your entire year. Move, asswipe!" Ridley yelled.

"I'm gonna assume you're driving," Ashanti said.

"I've got another meeting at my office downtown. I swear, you would think with all we've learned about telecommuting these past few years that these people wouldn't insist on holding in-person meetings. As if stale muffins and bitter-ass coffee is supposed to make up for being stuck in traffic."

"So what is supposed to make my year?" Ashanti asked.

"I'm getting there," Ridley said. "You ready?"

Ashanti made a *get on with it* gesture, even though Ridley couldn't see her.

"I just saw a FOR SALE sign on the house you want."

Ashanti's stomach immediately dropped. Had Thad backed out of the sale? She should be ecstatic yet couldn't deny a pinch of sadness that he wouldn't be a few blocks away.

But then she remembered that Ridley said she was driving from *Uptown*.

"Wait," Ashanti said, her hand on the screen door's handle. "Which house?"

"Which one do you think? The Greek Revival on the corner of Terpsichore and Camp Streets."

Her heart stopped. It literally stopped for at least three seconds. "Ridley, I swear, if this is some kind of joke—"

"When do I ever joke?"

Good point.

"I took a picture of the sign," Ridley continued. "I'll text it to you as soon as I'm stopped at a red light. You had better call the real estate agent to make an offer ASAP, because this house will not last long on the market. I wouldn't be surprised if they've gotten offers already. Call them as soon as I send the number, okay?"

"Uh—" Ashanti had hesitated for only a second before Ridley started yelling through the phone.

"Ashanti Jacinta Wright, if you miss out on this house, we are taking it to the fucking streets, you hear me? I swear, girl. Don't play with me. I *will* fight you."

"I don't even know what they're asking for it," Ashanti pointed out.

"I don't care what they're asking for it! You've got orders for those dog cookies coming out of your ass. And I can promise you there will be even more orders after this spot on the news today. You can't afford *not* to get this house. Don't mess this up, Shanti. I swear I will never speak to you again if you do."

Ridley had been threatening never to speak to her again since the first time they went shopping at Claire's and Ashanti wavered on a pair of half-dollar-size gold hoop earrings. She contended to this day that those earrings were too big for her head.

This house, however, was perfect for her. Ridley was right. She deserved to have her ass kicked in the streets if she allowed it to pass her by.

"Send the info," Ashanti said.

15

As she studied the number Ridley had texted, Ashanti's heartbeat went from normal to climax scene in a *Friday the 13th* movie, but she refused to let that have any effect on her decision-making. She could not allow anxiety or fear to get in the way of this opportunity.

This was a test of faith. She'd told herself that Thad swooping in and buying the house meant that there was something bigger and better on the horizon for her. Well, bigger and better had just dropped into her lap.

She had been willing to settle for the place in the Bywater, but there was not a single property in New Orleans better suited for what she envisioned for Barkingham Palace than that beautiful two-story house in the Lower Garden District. The bed-and-breakfast/café that occupied it for years had closed during the thick of the pandemic and had remained empty all this time. Even as she set her sights on the house in the Bywater, Ashanti had prayed this one would become available.

Her prayers had been answered. So why was she waiting to call?

"Because you know it will be outside of your price range," she said with a sigh.

The Lower Garden District was one of the city's most expensive neighborhoods. When Ridley was house-hunting for a new condo, there was not a two-bedroom for under a half million. And that was for only one condo. Ashanti's stomach turned at the thought of what an entire building would cost, especially one in such a prime location.

The house was also more than twice the size of Barkingham Palace's current location, with a huge fenced-in backyard. There would be ample room for the bakery, a kitchen, and a bigger daycare.

She called the number.

A woman answered on the first ring. Ashanti didn't even have to tell her which property she was interested in; the real estate agent said they had been getting calls all day about the place on Terpsichore. She went through the basics: size, number of rooms—all things Ashanti had already learned through her numerous searches on various real estate sites.

"What is the asking price?" Ashanti asked.

"One point six million," the woman answered. "But I have a feeling this one will go over the asking price. In fact, we've already had an offer for more than what they're asking for it."

Ashanti massaged her forehead. "I'm not surprised," she murmured.

"We start taking official bids on Monday," the real estate agent said.

Ashanti thanked her for her time and tried not to feel defeated as she disconnected the call.

Back when she was a little girl, whenever she asked for something, her mother would ask if she thought money grew on trees. She'd vowed to one day find a money-growing tree to prove that they existed.

Ashanti looked up at the ceiling. "I need to find one of those trees, Mama."

Even with the boost the daycare had received from that viral livestream, there was no way she could afford that house, especially when she was looking at another three- to four-hundred thousand to renovate and outfit it for boarding and a bakery.

She needed to hug her dog.

Ashanti pushed back from the desk and nearly had a heart attack as Ridley came bursting through the door.

"Did you call?" she asked.

"What the heck, Rid?" Ashanti yelled, splaying her hand to her chest. "What are you doing here? I thought you had a meeting?"

"I canceled it," she said. "This is more important."

"Yes, I called."

"And?"

"And." Ashanti braced herself for Ridley's inevitable reaction. "I can't afford it."

In a stunning turn of events, her melodramatic friend did not go into an immediate meltdown. Ridley quietly rounded the chair that faced Ashanti's desk and sat. Hanging her arms on either side of the chair, she manspreaded as wide as her pencil skirt would allow and began to sink to the floor.

Ah, there were the theatrics.

"Get up," Ashanti said, walking over to the chair. She hooked her arm in the crook of Ridley's elbow and lifted her.

"No. Just let me go. You insist on killing me, so just let me go."

"They're asking for a million, six hundred thousand, Rid."

"That's all?"

"That's all?" Ashanti laughed.

"That house can easily go for two million."

"And you think I can afford to pay that kind of money?"

Ridley stood. She took the bottle of conditioning shampoo out of Ashanti's hands and tossed it on the desk. "I am not allowing you to do this, Shanti," Ridley said.

"Do what?"

"Give up!" Ridley jabbed a finger at Ashanti's Meghan and Harry pencil holder. "You deserve this. And I will not stop pushing until I know you've exhausted every single avenue. Now, when was the last time you had an evaluation done on Barkingham Palace?"

She'd known Ridley long enough to tell when she wasn't going to let something go. This was one of those times.

"Never," Ashanti answered.

"So you have no idea how much this business is worth? Let me clue you in on something, Shanti. You've got a fucking gold mine here. You can get a loan like that." She snapped her fingers. "Add in that viral video and the plans for a bakery, and you can have your pick of lenders."

"A bank is not going to loan me two million dollars because a video of Duchess and Puddin' sharing a doggy treat went viral. I would need collateral. And even if I could get a loan, I can't afford to take on that kind of debt."

"First of all, you live in a house that's worth three times as much as it was back when your parents bought it," Ridley said. "There's your collateral right there."

Ashanti's head reared back as if one of her best friends in the world had just slapped her clear across the mouth. "First of all, you know I would never put my parents' home up for collateral. I can't believe you would even suggest it."

"People do it all the time, Shanti."

"Not this person," she said. "And in case you have forgotten, the twins will be off to college soon. I can't saddle myself with millions in loans when I have to pay for the girls to go to school."

"Another thing people do all the time? They take out student loans," Ridley said.

Ashanti was already shaking her head. "My parents paid for me to go to college and vet school so that I could begin my career debt-free. They would want the same for Kara and Kendra. And as their legal guardian, it's up to me to make sure that happens."

She folded her arms across her chest and took a couple of steps back, leaning against the wall next to the portrait of Duchess dressed up as Angelica Schuyler from *Hamilton* the musical.

"You're forgetting another thing," Ashanti said. "Think for one minute, Rid. Just imagine for a millisecond the shitstorm that would ensue if Anita found out I put her dear baby brother's house up for collateral for my business."

"Fuck Atilla," Ridley said. "You don't owe her an accounting of your finances. What you do is none of her business."

"Maybe you should tell her that the next time she comes around," Ashanti said.

"Girl, just call me. Please! I can be in the middle of getting my back blown out by my fine-ass doorman, and I'd leave him hanging just so I can curse Atilla out to her face."

Only Ridley could make her go from wanting to cry to laughing until her side hurt in the span of two minutes. They both had to wipe tears from their eyes.

"You know it pisses me off whenever you bring up that woman's name," Ridley said.

"She has that effect on people," Ashanti said, still dabbing at tears.

"I'm serious about this, Shanti. You have sacrificed everything for your sisters. You put your entire life on hold and then took a complete detour from all the plans you'd made. That bitch doesn't get to tell you anything, especially when it comes to Kara, Kendra, or that house. If her baby brother wanted her involved in any way, he would have made sure it was known. He didn't, so..."

Ridley dusted her hands, as if the matter was done.

Ashanti wished it was that easy, but she'd been dealing with Anita for six years.

"Rid, I know your heart and your head are both in the right place, but the house is off-limits. I would maybe consider talking to the bank about a loan, but the thought of taking on that kind of debt scares the crap out of me." She unfolded her hands and ran them through her braids, which she'd unbounded from her hair tie hours ago. "The real estate agent said they will begin accepting bids on Monday. I'll keep thinking and maybe I can figure something out by then."

There was nothing to figure out. She couldn't afford the house. But this would, at least, get Ridley off her case for the time being.

"You know I'm not going to drop this, right?" Ridley said.

Or, maybe not.

Ridley stepped up to her with arms wide open, enveloping her in a hug. She added an extra squeeze, which Ashanti appreciated. It was all love between them, even when they didn't see eye to eye.

"I'm going to watch the news segment when I get back to my office. I'll let you know everything you did wrong."

"Thanks." Ashanti huffed out a laugh.

She waited until Ridley left the office, then slumped down in her chair and dropped her head onto the desk. But she didn't get the mere five minutes of refuge she so desperately needed to clear her head, because within two minutes Colleen came into her office looking like she'd swallowed a gallon of raw seaweed.

"I think it's something I ate at lunch," she said. "Pro tip: If you're not sure how long your leftover sushi has been in the fridge, don't eat it."

"Ew," Ashanti said. "Go home. I'll Instacart you some ginger ale and saltine crackers."

"Why?"

She shrugged. "It's what my mom always fed me when I was sick." She flicked her fingers at her. "Now go."

Not even twenty minutes after Colleen left, Mark went home, taken down by the same suspect sushi. Their absence highlighted another vulnerability Ashanti was well aware of: She needed more staff. She had been lucky to find a group of such dedicated, hardworking, dog-loving people, but there was only so much the five of them could do. And when two of those five went down with apparent food poisoning?

Yeah, she needed help, but there was nothing she could do about it now.

Ashanti spent the rest of the afternoon and evening exercising the smaller dogs, taking care of the afternoon feedings, and manning the reception area whenever Deja needed a break—the number of calls they were now getting was seriously ridiculous. Ashanti hadn't worked this much since those early days of the daycare, when it was only the three of them. Back then, Kara and Kendra used to spend their afternoons helping out with the dogs. She missed those days.

Except for the work. She didn't miss that level of mind-numbing exhaustion at all.

There were only three dogs that required after-care hours, and surprisingly, no overnight boarders, but Leslie had remained. She found Ashanti cleaning the suite where they kept Mrs. LeBlanc's geriatric toy poodle, Muffin Top. Muffin Top was eighteen years old and peed in her suite more than she did outside.

"Are you sure you don't want me to stay?" Leslie asked.

"I got it," Ashanti said. She looked up. "Has Puddin' been picked up yet?"

"Not yet. I tried calling Thad Sims again, but the phone went to voicemail."

Ashanti glanced at her watch. It was ten minutes past eight.

Her first instinct was to curse him out for taking advantage of their agreement, but she had been sole guardian of her sisters for too long not to feel a pinch of worry that maybe something had happened to him.

"Go on," she told Leslie. "I'll continue trying to contact him."

Ashanti leaned the mop handle against the wall and scrolled through her recent calls. She spotted Thad's number easy enough, it was the only number that didn't have a 504 area code in her most recent calls.

She called the number, but it went to voicemail. She got a jolt when she heard his deep voice on the voicemail greeting instead of a modulated robotic one. She hadn't pegged him as the type to record his own greeting.

"This is Ashanti Wright at Barkingham Palace. It is—" She checked her watch again. "Eight thirteen. After-care hours ended at eight p.m., so I'm assuming you want Puddin' to be boarded for the night. And because you did not pre-book the overnight stay, the ninety-dollar emergency overnight boarding fee will be charged to your account. Have a good evening," she ended.

A minute later her phone buzzed with a text.

Very sorry. Be there in 10.

He made it in five.

Ashanti stood in the daycare entrance with her arms crossed over her chest. It was her *you're in trouble* pose. She hoped it worked on him better than it did on the twins.

"I'm sorry," Thad said, holding his hands up as he climbed the steps. "I swear, I didn't do this on purpose. I left my phone in my glove box and lost track of time."

She was probably foolish to believe him. Then again, why would he lie? His white T-shirt and the well-worn jeans that fit his body to perfection were both caked with dust and grime, indicating a long and brutal workday.

"I promise, it's the truth," he said. "Please, don't charge me ninety dollars."

Ashanti stepped out of the way so that he could enter.

"Where's the dog?" he asked.

"Who?" She cupped her palm behind her ear.

"Puddin'," he amended. "Where's Puddin'?"

"He's in the back with Duchess. I'll get them." He started

to follow, but she stopped him. "I'm not saying you're a serial rapist ax murderer, but I don't know that you're *not* a serial rapist ax murderer. So I'm gonna need you to stay in the lobby."

"That's fair," he said. He held his hands out and waved them around. "But I don't have an ax, so that takes care of that one. And I can only tell you that I'm not a rapist of any kind, but it's up to you to believe me. I was raised, in part, by Frances Sutherland, if that holds any weight."

Ashanti tried her best to hold her composure as she looked him up and down. If she laughed it would only encourage him.

"It does," she finally said and motioned for him to follow her.

"Yes." He did a celebratory fist pump. "Grams for the win."

She lost the battle, laughing as they made their way to the back.

They entered the small dog play area and Ashanti headed straight for the ball pit. It was Puddin' and Duchess's favorite. Colorful plastic balls popped up in the air like kernels in a popcorn maker as the two frolicked around the pool.

"These two are probably the only ones who aren't upset that you're late, but I can tell you who *is* upset with you."

"Besides you?"

"Besides me," she said. She looked over at him. "Your grandmother is pissed. How could you not call to let her know Puddin' would be making his television debut?"

Thad threw his head back and let out a sigh. "I should have," he said.

"Did you even watch the news segment?"

"I was planning to watch the replay on the evening broadcast."

She wasn't buying that for a minute. She was raising teen-agers; she knew fake earnestness when she saw it.

"You are so lying right now," Ashanti said.

A slow grin played across his lips. It did things to her. Adult things. Very specific, very indecent adult things.

Lord, save me from fine men with nice smiles.

"Okay, no, I wasn't planning on watching it," Thad admitted. His grin turned sheepish. "You're judging me right now, aren't you?"

"Harshly," Ashanti said. She walked over to the right side of the room and grabbed the dog leashes from the wall pegs, keeping her back turned so that he couldn't see her smiling. "Do you know how ironic it is that everyone in the country loves Puddin' except for the person blessed with the opportunity to care for him?"

She turned back to find Thad rubbing both dogs underneath their chins. Her heart melted then and there.

This was *so* not good.

"In my defense, I was busy all day," Thad said.

Ashanti held up a hand. "Please, spare me. I can't handle hearing about whatever it is you're doing to my house."

"Still calling it your house, huh?" He took the leash from her and fastened it to Puddin's collar.

"I did promise myself I would stop thinking of it that way," Ashanti admitted, hooking Duchess to her leash.

"That sounds like a healthier way to cope."

She rolled her eyes. "Thanks for the tip." She turned out the light in the play area, and she and Thad made their way back to the lobby. "You'd better have your apology ready for your grandmother," Ashanti said as she gave the reception area a final once-over.

Thad held the front door open for her. "I know how to win over Grams," he said. "But I guess I need to watch the news story, just in case she asks me about it."

"I'll text you a link to the segment." Ashanti stopped with her hand on the door. "That is, if you don't mind me texting. I don't make a habit of sending personal texts to clients. I usually only contact clients in cases of emergency, but I figured since—"

"Ashanti." He cut her off.

She met his eyes. "Yeah?"

"I don't mind getting texts from you," Thad said.

She sucked in a breath and begged herself to stop staring at his deep brown eyes.

"Okay."

God, why did her voice sound like she'd just hiked a mile through mud?

She locked the front door and Thad gestured for her to go ahead of him down the stairs. At first, Ashanti thought it was his truck parked at the curb in front of Mrs. Short's house, but the closer she got to it she realized that truck was dark green, not black.

She turned to Thad to tell him that he didn't have to walk her to her car, but they were already there.

"This yours?" he asked.

She nodded.

Several beats passed before Thad said, "So you getting in?"

She nodded again. Why could she not use words?

Thad continued staring at her, and it wasn't until Duchess barked that Ashanti remembered what she should have been doing.

"I'm sorry," she said, shaking her head as she used her key fob to unlock her SUV. "It's been a long day."

"I apologize again for making it longer," he said.

She opened the back door and helped Duchess climb up and into her booster seat, strapping her in. She turned and noticed that Thad had moved several feet back. The streetlight illuminated him from above, highlighting every inviting feature. This man was an amazing physical specimen. Thank goodness his personality—at least what she knew of it—rubbed her the wrong way.

At least it *used* to rub her the wrong way. It had started rubbing her a different way lately.

"Thanks for walking me to my car," Ashanti said.

"Thanks for not charging me ninety bucks because I was late," he said.

She grinned. "You haven't gotten your bill yet. Besides, after-care is on me this week, remember?"

"Ah, yes!" He pitched his head back and chuckled up at the sky. "Thank you. I promise to pick the dog up on time tomorrow."

"Who are you picking up on time?" Ashanti asked as she climbed into the SUV.

He frowned, then laughed. "Puddin'. I promise to pick Puddin' up on time tomorrow."

She nodded. "See that you do."

She waved at Puddin' before closing the door and pulling away from the curb. She glanced in her rearview mirror several times, finding Thad in the same spot on the sidewalk, watching her drive away.

16

"Why did I let you drag me out here?" Thad yelled.

"What?" Von yelled back.

Of course Von hadn't heard him. The combination of noise from the twenty flat screens tuned to the same Thursday Night Football game, the deejay playing nineties R&B from a dais in the corner, and the crush of people packed into the Frenchmen Street bar made it hard for Thad to hear his own thoughts.

"What'd you say?" Von asked, so close to his ear Thad felt spit. He shoved him away.

"I said I'm kicking your ass for dragging me here tonight!"

"Hey, man. We gotta check out the competition." Von gestured to the crowd with his glass of Crown and Coke. "We need to figure out how to get people to fill up The PX like this once we open."

Von's head turned like a slow-moving sprinkler as a woman in painted-on jeans and a shirt so tight it looked as if she was giving herself chest compressions with every breath walked past them.

Thad side-eyed him. "Yeah, it's the competition you're checking out."

"Have the women in this city always looked like this? How did you bear to leave?" Von finished his drink in a giant gulp, then set the glass on the bar. "Be right back."

Thad rolled his eyes as he settled both elbows on the bar and took stock of the scene before him. He couldn't deny that this place was lit, especially for a weeknight. They didn't have any type of gimmick like fifty-cent wings or open mic night either. The bartender told him this was typical, and that if they *really* wanted to see a crowd, they should come back this Sunday for the Saints home opener against the Atlanta Falcons.

Thad was tempted to come back just to see how they managed to fit in more people without violating the fire codes. There wasn't an unoccupied seat in the entire bar.

He took a pull on his beer and mistakenly made eye contact with the woman he'd been trying to avoid three spots down. She had done a piss-poor job of being subtle for the past half hour, shooting him a smile every time he glanced to his left.

A year ago, Thad would have been right there with Von, happy to oblige one of the numerous women who hit on him in places like this. But, unlike his friend, he wasn't in the mood. Hadn't been for a while.

Should he play dumb and pretend he hadn't seen her?

Too late. She'd slid off her barstool and was walking toward him.

Shit.

"Can I buy you another?" the woman asked as she approached. She stuck her hand out. "I'm Desiree, by the way."

"Thad," he said, shaking her hand. A childhood spent with Frances Sutherland drumming the importance of proper manners into his head wouldn't allow him to leave her hanging.

"About that drink...?" Desiree asked.

He waited half a second to see if there was the tiniest spark of interest, but there wasn't even a flicker. Thad pasted on a *thanks, but no thanks* smile and said, "Sorry, but I'm the designated driver tonight."

She wedged herself between him and the guy with dreads sitting on the stool to Thad's left.

"I'll cover an Uber for you and your friend. Or, better yet, I can bring you back to get your car in the morning."

Well, damn. Guess she was done being subtle.

"I appreciate the offer—both of them," Thad said. "But I still have to decline."

She hunched her shoulders in a casual shrug and slipped away. Thad glanced just long enough to make sure she had taken the hint when he caught another woman staring in his direction. She started toward him, but he held his hand up and shook his head.

He was going to fucking murder Von.

"You handled that well," Thad heard from over his shoulder.

He turned around to find the bartender changing the stainless-steel pour spout on a bottle of Jack Daniel's. Thad held up his near-empty beer bottle and the bartender nodded.

He and Von were, in fact, smart enough to have come by ride-share. Though Thad didn't plan on having more than two beers tonight. After all, this was supposed to be a recon mission.

"I think she would have had a better chance with your

friend," the bartender said as he popped the cap off Thad's Abita lager.

His friend, the asshole. Thad glanced around, but didn't spot him. Knowing Von, he'd taken chest compression girl back to his place without telling Thad.

He turned around and faced the bar.

"If you don't mind my saying, you don't look like the bar type," the bartender said.

"I guess I need to change the way I look," Thad said. The bartender's brows lifted in curiosity. "My friend and I are opening a place in the Bywater," he clarified. "That's why we're here tonight. He says we're scoping out the competition, but there's competition on every corner here."

"Yeah, if there's one thing New Orleans can handle with ease, it's adding another bar. Where in the Bywater?"

He told the bartender the address and the man nodded.

Thad caught sight of what looked like an anchor peeking from the hem of his shirtsleeve. He took a sip from his bottle, then pointed it at the bartender's arm.

"You serve?"

The bartender glanced down at where Thad had pointed. "Did my twenty years," he said.

Thad held his hand out. "I made it to fifteen." They shook and Thad automatically felt more at ease.

He had been cautioned upon leaving the military that it would be too easy to fall into the routine of associating only with like-minded people. Von had accused him of falling into that trap—it was one of the reasons he harped on Thad about spending so much time on the military message boards.

But he couldn't help it. This was where he felt the most comfortable. It was why he was itching to get The PX up and running, and his own self-serving reason for making sure they employed and catered specifically to military. He loved his family, but this was different. He missed the camaraderie he'd found with his fellow brothers- and sisters-in-arms.

"The bar we're planning to open, it's specifically so those in the military will have a place they can feel at home," Thad said.

He spent the next half hour explaining the concept of The PX to the bartender, who'd introduced himself as Rob, and talking about his time in the service, pausing only when Rob had to step away to grab bottles from the back shelf.

"You know, I make a good living here, but if you need someone behind the bar, I'm willing to help you guys out," Rob said. "I like the sound of what you're doing. There's a lot of those I served with who could benefit from it too."

"That's the whole point," Thad said. "We want to create a place where vets and active duty can have a good time, but also feel safe enough to reach out to people who understand what they're going through. It's been nearly a year for me, and I'm still having a hard time adjusting."

"It's been five years since I left. I'm not sure that feeling ever goes away," Rob said. He wiped his hand on a towel and stuck it out to Thad. "I'm pulling for you guys. And I meant what I said about helping you out. Hit me up when you're ready to open."

Thad shook his hand again. "Thanks, man."

This is what he had been missing. That warm, feel-good rush that washed over him. He didn't want to say that he needed this to feel whole, but...

He needed this to feel whole.

"You still here?" Von said, coming back to where Thad

sat. "I thought you said you wanted to be home by ten? I fig-ured you'd left."

Thad looked over at him and narrowed his eyes. "Did you even get her name?"

Von's shit-eating grin was all the answer he needed.

Thad could only shake his head.

"Hey, she didn't ask for my name either. Didn't stop either of us from having a good time. You ready to bounce?"

Their Uber driver was waiting when they exited the bar. Von had left his car parked at Thad's since Thad's house was closer.

"That bar was okay, but I wasn't impressed with the vibe," Von said as they settled into the back seat. "I don't want the kind of place where you can fuck in the restroom and no one notices. Excuse the language," Von said to the Uber driver.

"No problem, dawg," the guy replied. "Sounds like I need to check out that bar." He reached back and fist-bumped Von.

Thad wanted to throw them both out of the car.

He clicked into his messages. Nadia had sent a bunch of fuming-face emojis with a promise to pluck Thad in the mid-dle of his forehead the next time she saw him for not telling their grandmother about Puddin's television debut.

She followed the threat with a video of his nieces' reactions when they discovered that the dog in the viral video everyone at their school was talking about was Puddin'. She said they'd watched the twenty-second clip at least a hundred times.

He replied that she needed to do a better job monitoring their time online.

Thad clicked over to his email. His jaw tightened the moment he saw the first one.

"What's up?" Von asked.

Thad glanced at him. "Nothing."

"I don't think so," Von said. "I can tell something's wrong."

This clairvoyant motherfucker over here.

They arrived at his house just in time to avoid Von's questioning. But, of course, there was no avoiding Von's questioning. He picked it back up the moment the Uber driver pulled away.

"What's going on?" Von asked. "I know you aren't pissed that you didn't get any at the bar, because you had the opportunity. You still do." He retrieved a folded napkin from his pocket. "One chick slipped me her number to give to you."

"Still not interested," Thad said.

"Such a waste." Von shook his head as he stuck the napkin back into his pocket. "So, what's up with you?" he asked as he followed Thad into the house. Puddin' greeted them with a bark, then gave them his bare ass as he snuggled back into his doggy bed.

"Wait. Before you tell me, is it the kind of news I have to sit down for?" Von asked. "Did you lose all your money shooting dice or something?"

"When have you known me to shoot dice?"

Von shrugged. "I never pegged you as the type to put a sweater on a dog either."

"My grandmother made me put that sweater on him," Thad groused.

He considered his options. He could try to continue evading Von, or he could broker world peace. Both would require the same amount of effort.

"I got an email from this woman in Alabama saying she's a long-lost family member," Thad said. World peace would have to wait.

"Hmm, according to my emails, all my long-lost family members are broke princes from Nigeria who need me to send them some cash."

"Yeah, that's usually the case with these schemes, but this woman is just a few states away. *If* she's really in Alabama."

"Who cares, man. Don't waste your time on some rando claiming to be family."

"*I* care. It pisses me off when grifters like this try to take advantage of vulnerable people. It scares me too. What if I wasn't here and this woman approached my grandmother?"

Von nodded. "Yeah, when you put it that way, it is scary. So, what are you going to do about it?"

"I was going to ignore her message, but now I think I'm going to answer. I'll string her along, wait for her to ask for money, and then turn it over to whatever agency handles this kind of stuff."

"You do know that most people just delete the email, right?" Von asked.

"And that's why these scammers continue to do it. I'm here to protect Grams, but the next target may not have someone to help."

"You should tell her the Sutherlands have a family reunion coming up and invite her to join in. See how she reacts to that," Von said. "I'm gonna grab a water from the fridge, then jet."

Thad toed his shoes off and put them in the small closet next to the door, then he checked Puddin's water bowl to make sure it was full.

"I'm meeting Delonte Johnson and Micah Samuels at the Bywater house in the morning," Von called from the kitchen. A couple of seconds later he came back into the living room with two bottles of water and a bag of Doritos. "Delonte and Micah were both working for a contractor in Gretna, but the job just ended. They said they have a few other guys they can bring in on the demo. All vets."

"That sounds good." Thad nodded at his hands. "You know there are several convenience stores between this house and your apartment, right?"

"Yeah, but then I'd have to pay for this stuff. Nothing convenient about that."

Asshole.

"See you tomorrow," Von said.

Thad locked up and headed straight for his bedroom. He hadn't even considered moving into his grandparents' room, even though it was bigger.

For one, there was always the possibility of his grand-mother spending the occasional night in her house, especially when Nadia and her girls came to visit. But Thad was more comfortable in the room he'd grown up in. The familiarity of it had helped him to adjust during the first few nights he'd been back.

He undressed, tossing the dirty shirt, jeans, and socks in the rattan hamper in the corner. Then, wearing only his boxer briefs, fell back onto the mattress. He stared up at the ceiling, pushing thoughts of that email out of his mind. He'd figure out the best way to catch that scammer in her lie later.

He closed his eyes and Ashanti Wright's face immediately appeared. Thad groaned. His night out with Von had been tortuous enough, he didn't need reminders of what he wanted but would never have adding to it.

Thad heard the pitter-patter of paws a few seconds before

his bed shook with the weight of a fifty-pound poodle jumping into it.

"Out of the bed, dog." He opened his eyes to find Puddin's elongated nose two inches from his. "Move!"

The dog walked in a circle three times, then plopped onto the pillow on the right side of the bed.

"This ain't cool, Puddin'. That's my side."

The pom-pom at the end of Puddin's tail began to swish back and forth.

Thad was too tired for this shit. He folded the other pillow in half and slipped under the covers.

"Stupid-ass dog," he muttered before using the remote on the fancy ceiling fan and light combo that had been installed—no doubt his sister's doing—and going to bed.

17

Ashanti balanced her cell phone between her shoulder and ear as she piped icing around the edges of the scepter-shaped cookies—her newest design courtesy of Evie's late-night cookie-cutter Etsy shopping spree.

She listened with half an ear as the reporter from some small town in Illinois droned on about the summer she volunteered at their local animal shelter back when she was in high school. Ashanti now understood what Ridley meant when she told her to be selective regarding the media interviews. Nothing about this story would benefit her or Barkingham Palace.

She'd thought the hoopla over the viral livestream video would have died down by now, but it had been shared by the host of a popular TV show on the Animal Planet network over the weekend, restarting the madness and kicking it up several notches. Deja had called a half hour ago, threatening to quit.

So now they forwarded incoming calls to the overnight answering service and sent texts to all clients with pets being boarded today with instructions to call Ashanti's office line if they needed to get in touch.

Ashanti had promised to join her staff at the daycare as soon as she could, but orders for Duchess Delights had gone through the roof. She'd farmed out some work to her next-door neighbor's son, Bernard—a six-year senior at the University of New Orleans who spent more time playing video games on his mom's couch than in class. He was currently bagging treats and would make deliveries later today.

Thanks to Duchess Delights' newfound fame, Ashanti's inbox was filled with job applicants for the daycare. She felt even more confident about the decision she'd made yesterday to put a bid in on the house in the Lower Garden District. It was no longer a question that she would need the extra space.

She'd sweet-talked Leslie, Deja, and Colleen with promises of pizza and wine if they would stay late to review resumes. Ashanti trusted them to weed out candidates, but the final decision on who they hired would be hers.

If she could find time to conduct interviews.

She heard the front door open and looked up from the dining room table, expecting to see Kara walk in from the foyer. Instead, it was Kendra.

"Hey," her sister said.

When she realized Kendra wasn't making a mad dash up the stairs to her bedroom, Ashanti abruptly ended the interview and set the phone down.

"Hey," she said. "No cheerleader practice today?"

Kendra shook her head. Defying all of Ashanti's expectations, she walked farther into the dining room and poked around at the doggy treat–making paraphernalia littering the table. She picked up the scepter cookie cutter.

"Why are you making penis cookies?"

"It's a scepter," Ashanti said. Her chest felt uncomfortably tight as a string of awkward seconds passed with neither of them speaking.

"Do you…uh…want to talk?" Ashanti asked.

"There's nothing to talk about, Shanti. I told you already, I'm fine."

She was not fine, but Ashanti knew better than to push. The fact that Kendra was even speaking to her was a gift.

She still couldn't believe she'd allowed things to get to this point, where it felt like a victory to have her sixteen-year-old sister speak more than two nonhostile words to her.

"Do you want to help me out with these?" she asked, holding up the piping bag. "I can use it."

Ashanti held her breath. She released it, along with more of the tension she'd been holding, when Kendra dropped the backpack she'd still had hanging on her shoulder and sat down at the table.

"Those are ready to be packaged." Ashanti nodded toward the decorated cookies on a silicon drying mat.

"It looks as if that viral video has been good for business," Kendra said as she closed the cellophane bag with a label.

"I have so many orders that I hired Mrs. Willis's son from next door to help package them."

"Ugh." Kendra scrunched up her nose. "Bernard Willis is gross. The other day he offered to let me 'experiment on him' to see if I'm really gay."

"What?" Ashanti pitched the piping bag into the bowl of icing. "That little bastard! I'm gonna kill him!"

"Don't bother," Kendra said. "I threatened to sic Duchess on him if he comes near me. Bernard is terrified of your dog."

He should be terrified of *her*. Ashanti picked up her phone and sent him a text, telling him to put the treats on his front step and to never so much as look at either of her sisters again.

"I'll be right back," she told Kendra.

"Shanti, don't go there starting mess. It's not worth it," her sister called.

She stopped in the kitchen to wash the icing off her hands and put another batch of treats in the oven. When she opened her front door, the box of cookies, labels, and cellophane bags were waiting on her front steps.

Kendra came up behind her. "What did you tell him?"

"He was gone by the time I opened the door," Ashanti said. She carried the box into the dining room and set it on the table. "The next time I see that son of a bitch, he's getting an earful."

"Oh, Bernard had better watch out because you *mad* mad right now." Kendra reclaimed her seat. "I can't remember the last time I heard you use two swear words in a single day. You just used 'bastard' and 'bitch' in less than ten minutes."

"Kendra." Ashanti shot her a warning look.

"Sorry," she said, those eyes that looked so much like their mother's glittering with amusement.

Ashanti could do nothing but laugh, but then she sobered. "Tell me if he bothers you again. I mean it."

"I will, but he won't," Kendra said. "Don't blow this out of proportion, Shanti. You know how you can get."

It was no secret that she became the very definition of a mama bear when it came to the twins, but that was her job. Protecting her sisters was her only priority. The daycare, the house, her very life; they all came second.

Ashanti could admit that she had gone overboard when Kendra came out to her two years ago. She immediately bought a rainbow flag to hang in the front window and a WE DO NOT

TOLERATE HATE sign for the yard. Kendra had asked her to pump the brakes on her allyship, which she reluctantly did.

But there was no way in hell she would allow Bernard Willis to get away with what he'd said to her baby sister. She would take care of him later.

"So how have things been going so far this school year?" she asked. "Has the Literary Club started working on the first issue of this year's magazine?"

Kendra's demeanor shifted. Her shoulders stiffened and her back went ramrod straight.

"It's fine," she muttered. She gathered the cellophane bags and the tray of cookies. "I'll do these in my room and bring them down when I'm done."

"Ken—" Ashanti called to her, but she'd already started up the stairs.

What was that about?

Just then, the front door opened, and Kara came bursting through.

"Don't be mad at me," she said.

Ashanti threw down the piping bag she'd just picked up again. "What did you do?"

"Nothing! I mean, nothing bad. This is a good thing, I promise."

"Before you tell me what you did," Ashanti started, then she lowered her voice to a whisper and motioned for Kara to come closer. "Did Kendra mention something happening with the Literary Club? We were having a nice conversation for once, but when I asked her about the magazine she clammed up and raced off to her room."

"I don't know." Kara hunched her shoulders. "She hasn't told me anything. I swear, I would tell you if she had."

Ashanti wasn't sure if she believed her, but she couldn't force either of the girls to share what they weren't willing to share. She'd learned at least that much over these last six years.

"Okay, so what is this good thing that I'm not supposed to be mad about?" she asked.

"It's not just a good thing, it's an *amazing* thing. And the only reason you may be a little upset is because it'll add extra work to your plate."

"Really, Kara? Because two hours of sleep is too much for me?"

"I know, but this is amazing, remember?" Kara said. "So I was playing around online during Life Skills one day—"

"I thought you couldn't use your phone during class?"

"It's an elective. It's not even a real class," she said. "Like I was saying, I was playing around and ran across this site for Black entrepreneurs, specifically Black women entrepreneurs. They're all about uplifting worthy small business owners, and we all know who *my* favorite small business owner is."

"Kara, come out with it."

"You're messing up my big build-up," she said. "Anyway, I nominated Barkingham Palace and you were picked as a finalist!"

"Nominated it for what?"

"It's like a scholarship or something. I didn't read everything, but I know that the grand prize is two hundred and fifty thousand dollars and mentorship by some bigwig business person."

Ashanti set down the cookie she had been decorating. "Two hundred and fifty thousand dollars?"

"Yes! You also get an ad in several magazines across the country and other online promotion. It is a huge deal!" She started typing on her phone. "It's a good thing Atilla sent that email the other day. I would have missed their response. Check your phone, I just sent it to you."

She needed to get back to this order, but it would have to wait. Ashanti opened her email app and stopped cold.

"What is…?" Kara asked.

Ashanti read over the email that had come to her inbox a half hour ago. She brought her hand up to her mouth.

"Oh. My. God," Ashanti said.

"What?" Kara asked, running to her. She tried to grab Ashanti's phone, but she pulled it out of her reach. "Step back, Kara."

"What's going on? Is it the contest?"

Ashanti read through the short email twice before looking up at her sister. "*Up Early with Leah and Luke!* wants Duchess and Puddin' on their show!"

"What! Ohmigod!" Kara screamed. "Ohmigod! Ohmigod! Let me see!"

Kendra came running down the stairs. "Who died?" she asked.

"No one died," Ashanti said. "Everybody, calm down. Let me read over the email again." The oven timer buzzed. "Shit! Kara, go get the treats out of the oven."

"That's three curse words from you in less than an hour," Kendra said.

"No shit?" Kara said.

Ashanti ignored them and escaped to her bedroom. She closed the door and sat on the bed, reading over the email for the third time. Then she sent a text to Ridley and Evie.

Get here quick.

❧

An hour later, Ashanti, Kara, Evie, and Ridley all sat around the living room, packaging Duchess Delights dog biscuits and hammering out what Ashanti would need for her national television debut. Kendra had returned to her room, once again a passenger on the surly teen train.

Unsure what Ashanti's admittedly vague text was about, Ridley had arrived with wine, whiskey, and chocolate—the trio to cure all that ails, in her friend's opinion. They'd tabled the alcohol for now so they could remain focused. The chocolates, however, had proved to be the fuel Ashanti needed.

"When do they want the dogs there?" Ridley asked. She stood in front of a poster board that had been tacked to the wall, a Sharpie poised in her hand.

"Friday morning," Ashanti said, rubbing the spot on Duchess's head that made her dog's right hind leg shake.

Ridley turned to Kara. "I know you're used to running point on marketing and promo for the daycare, but this is above your skill set, sugarplum."

Kara held up her hands. "And above my pay grade. I know when to step back."

"Good. Now, I have a friend who works in PR who owes me a favor," Ridley said. "I'm going to bring Dom in on this. She is kickass at this kind of stuff. She'll have an entire media blitz set up in less than a day."

"How much does this Dom cost?" Ashanti asked.

"Stop worrying about what things cost," Ridley said.

"Yeah, whatever it costs, it's worth spending," Evie said. "You have to capitalize on this, Shanti. Strike while the iron is hot and all that good stuff."

"What about what's his face." Ridley snapped her fingers. "Come on, what's Puddin's fine-ass owner's name?"

"Thad," Ashanti said. "He's required to sign a release for Puddin' to appear on the show, but the producer asked if I thought he would also be willing to make the trip. I told them I would ask, but he's never going to go for this," Ashanti said. "He hates Puddin'."

"That's too bad for him, because he has to be there. There is absolutely no way around it." Ridley made a gimme motion to Ashanti. "Do you have his number in your phone?"

She considered what it would be like to unleash Ridley on an unsuspecting Thad, and decided he didn't deserve it. Yet.

Ashanti checked the time on her phone. It was a quarter to seven, after business hours.

"I'll ask him first thing in the morning," she said.

"No. Tonight," Ridley said. "I'm about to call Dom right now. By tomorrow morning you're going to have your boarding passes for your flight to JFK."

"The producer said they would fly me up there on Thursday."

"That's because the producer is thinking about *his* show. You have got to think of every other outlet that will allow you to keep this story going." She counted them off on her fingers. "Radio, podcasts, other local New York affiliates. Think of this as the media junket for the Duchess and Puddin' Show."

"That's what I call it too," Kara said.

Ridley winked at her. "You're going to give Dom a run for her money soon." She returned her attention to Ashanti. "Call him, or I will."

"You don't have his number."

"I have my ways," Ridley said.

Ashanti scooted Duchess into Kara's lap and pushed herself up from the sofa. "I'll be right back."

She walked outside, took a seat on the front step, and pulled up Thad's number, calling him before she could talk herself out of it.

"Hello," he answered, his voice a bit unsure, yet still capable of doing…*things* to her.

"Um, hi. This is Ashanti."

"I know," he answered. "I saved your number the last time you called."

That bit of information should not have sent a shock of heat straight through her body, and yet here she was, burning up.

"Is everything okay?" Thad asked.

"Yes. Sort of," Ashanti said. "This is a very strange request, but—"

"I'm sorry. One sec." He cut her off. Then she heard, "A second pry bar was delivered with the other supplies we got today. Check out back."

"Are you still at the house in the Bywater?" Ashanti asked. She hadn't referred to it as *her* house. Kara would call that hashtag growth.

"There's a lot of work to be done," was Thad's reply.

Yet another reason he wouldn't be able to fly up to New York on a moment's notice. He'd told her that he was working on a tight timeline to get the house renovated. He wasn't about to miss out on several days' work to join her on a morning television show.

Unless…

"How long will you be there?" Ashanti asked.

18

Holding on to the end of the heavy tarp opposite Delonte Johnson, Thad helped him crab walk the load of plaster to the Dumpster that had been delivered earlier today. He'd figured they would need at least two loads hauled away during the course of the demo, but based on the rot they were finding as they sledgehammered the walls, he wouldn't be surprised if they didn't fill it up twice that many times.

"Didn't take long to reach the halfway point of this Dumpster," Delonte commented.

"It means we got some good work done today," Thad said. And that the inspector had missed a shit load of issues during his tour of the house. The structure was solid, but they had encountered several snags that could endanger their plans for opening by Veterans Day. Thad wasn't willing to call this place a money pit yet, but it was getting close.

"You and Micah didn't come to play around," Thad continued. "I appreciate the hard work."

Delonte and Micah's approach to demo had been the unexpected highlight of his day. The two young soldiers required very little direction, and because they had been doing this kind of work longer than both Von and Thad, they'd offered advice that had saved them time and materials.

"Von mentioned you've been cutting hair on the side," Thad said. "That true?"

"Nah, I've been doing construction work on the side," Delonte said. "I've got a hundred apprenticeship hours to go before I can take the state licensing exam to be a barber. And you better believe The PX will be the first place I put in an application."

"You'll have a job waiting for you," Thad said. He gestured toward the house. "Tell Micah that the two of you can head home. Von and I can handle the rest for the night."

"You sure?" Delonte asked.

Thad nodded.

"At least let me help with the tarp."

"I've got this," Thad said. "I'll see you tomorrow."

As he watched the kid jog toward the house, Thad couldn't help thinking about how that could have been him if he'd decided to leave the Army after putting in his four years. Yet, the more he thought about it, the more he realized that *wouldn't* have been him, because he would not have had the option of going back to school to learn a trade. It was either the Army or joining his grandfather's dry cleaning business.

Nothing illustrated just how much he'd hated the thought of becoming part of the Sutherland Dry Cleaning empire more than the fact that, when given the choice, he went with the option that could get him taken out by enemy fire. Thad had loved his grandfather more than just about any human being on the planet, and appreciated all he'd sacrificed, but he'd known the dry cleaning biz wasn't for him from the first

Saturday he'd spent behind the counter his junior year of high school.

Thankfully, Gramps had been more than okay with his career choice. Thad could still remember the pride on his grandfather's face when he told him that he wanted to join the Army.

Thad had just finished folding up the tarp when Ashanti's SUV pulled up in front of the house. He tucked the heavy plastic under his arm and braced himself for the impact of seeing her.

Denying that she affected him was pointless. Was it inconvenient? Fuck yes! But that's where things stood. No use pretending her face didn't pop up in his head a hundred times a day.

The worst game ever was the one he now played religiously, where he debated if things would be different between them if he'd never driven past this house. He'd earned the first mark against him by being a brash, ornery asshole the first time he'd met her, but Thad had gotten a sense that they were moving past that the day of the dog pageant. Buying this house had put the proverbial nail in the coffin of anything possibly happening between them.

Even so, she'd started to soften toward him over the past week, enough for him to believe that they could at least be friends. Maybe they could partner together for some type of function for military kids, like Grams had suggested.

The problem was he didn't want to be just a friend to her.

Thad frowned as he watched her through the driver's side window. She gripped the steering wheel tightly with both hands. It looked as though she was having an animated conversation, most likely with herself.

He usually found quirky shit like that to be annoying as hell. Why was it so fucking attractive on her?

She had been vague on the phone, only sharing that she needed to speak to him as soon as possible and that it would be better if she did so in person. He'd immediately checked in with his grandmother. Even though he was listed as her emergency contact, he wouldn't have put it past her to reach out to her dog sitter before she called him. She and Ashanti shared a closer relationship than he first assumed.

But all was well with Grams. Well, other than the fact that she chewed him out for not bringing Puddin' to see her on Sunday, and demanded he bring him tomorrow.

Ashanti finally got out of her SUV and, just as he had anticipated, Thad's pulse started hammering on his carotid like Phil Collins pounding out the "In the Air Tonight" drum solo. But, as she approached, he noticed her smile was more apprehensive than friendly. It put him on edge.

"Hi," she said.

"Evening," Thad said. He tilted his head to the side. "What's wrong?"

"Nothing's wrong. I just—" She looked past him, and her smile grew a bit warmer.

Thad looked over his shoulder to see Von sidling up the stone walkway. He shot him a menacing look, which his business partner promptly ignored.

"Well, hey there, friend," Von greeted.

Thad shoved the tarp at him before he could even think of reaching for Ashanti's hand.

"Take care of this for me," he said. "Ashanti and I have private business to discuss."

"No, no, he can stay," Ashanti said. "This affects him too. Well, in a way."

"Really?" Von asked. "You looking to partner up with us, aren't you?" He winked. "I've been thinking about ways we can work together. I told you I used to train dogs in the military, right?"

"Yes, you told her that," Thad said. He turned his shoulders so that he was partially blocking Von. "Why did you need to see me so urgently?"

She took a deep breath, as if steadying herself. Thad braced for whatever she was about to throw his way.

"I received an interesting email today with a *very* interesting request. Do either of you watch morning news shows?"

"No." Thad frowned.

"I'm usually running in the morning," Von said. "I've had to add two miles to my daily run to combat all the great food I've been eating since moving to New Orleans." He patted his flat stomach. "Gotta keep up this physique."

"Why do you ask?" Thad directed at Ashanti.

"A producer from *Up Early with Leah and Luke!* contacted me this afternoon."

"Whaaa?" Von said. "My mom loves Leah and Luke."

"Everyone loves Leah and Luke. They have the highest-rated morning show in the country. They saw Puddin' and Duchess's viral video and want them on their show."

"No shit!" Von said. "Those little dogs are making a name for themselves, huh? That's crazy."

"It's absolutely bananas. The phones at Barkingham Palace have not stopped ringing since that video went viral. Someone even tagged our Instagram page with a Duchess and

Puddin' tattoo. We later found out it was only a temporary tattoo, but still, bananas right?"

Just then, Thad felt a couple of raindrops. He looked up at the dark sky. "Looks like that rain that's been threatening to fall all day is finally here. Let's take this inside."

He wanted to send Von straight to his car, but Ashanti said this affected him too. Although Thad still wasn't sure how.

They piled into the parlor. It was now just a hollowed-out space with several wall studs that would need to be replaced.

"Wow," Ashanti said. "You all are making quick work of gutting my—this house," she said.

"It turns out walls are easy to take down when they're mostly rotted." Thad grabbed several bottles of water from the ice chest they kept on the site. He offered her one, but she shook her head.

"No, thank you."

"I'll take one," Von said.

He credited years of strict discipline drilled into him by the United States Army with stopping him from launching the bottle at Von's head with the force of an FGM-148 Javelin missile.

Puddin' started barking from the back room; he must have smelled Ashanti in the house. Their moldy, dusty surroundings couldn't mask that slightly floral, slightly peachy scent that wreaked the most delicious havoc on Thad's senses.

"Where's Puddin'?" Ashanti asked, heading in the direction of the barking.

"He's fine," Thad said. "We keep him locked up to keep him safe."

She opened the door to the downstairs bathroom that was just off to the right of the parlor. Puddin' charged at her.

"Hey there, boy," Ashanti said, rubbing the top of the dog's poofy head. "I missed you today." She looked up at Thad and Von, her expression both irritated and mournful. "I was at home making doggy treats all day. I didn't get a chance to visit the daycare."

She patted Puddin' on the head, then ordered him back to the mound of blankets Thad had fashioned into a make-shift dog bed. Her choosing to leave Puddin' in the bath-room was a clear indication of how important she deemed this conversation.

"Looks like the rain has stopped already," she said, tipping her head toward the opened front door as she returned to the parlor. She clasped her hands in front of her. "So, about *Up Early with Leah and Luke!*"

"What time do you need me to bring the dog to the day-care?" Thad asked.

She shook her head. "They want Duchess and Puddin' in their studio. In New York."

He choked on the water he'd just sipped. "You want to bring my grandmother's dog to New York?"

"Noooo." Ashanti dragged out the word. "I want *you* to bring your grandmother's dog to New York."

Thad just stared at her. She had to be kidding.

Von was the one who spoke up. "When?"

"We would leave tomorrow."

"Damn, you don't play around do you?" Von said.

"Please," Ashanti said. "I know it's a lot to ask, but the Luke and Leah show is an amazing opportunity. This would benefit *both* of our businesses. The story is about Duchess and

Puddin', but this would also be a way for you to introduce your new bar to potential customers. On a *national* stage."

"We won't open for another month and a half. If we're lucky," Thad tacked on. "The country will have moved on to the next stupid pet video by then. You think people will remember me mentioning The PX in a five-minute spot on some morning show two months from now?"

"Yes, the country will very likely have moved on, which is why we need to capitalize on this now." She grimaced. "Goodness, I sound like Ridley. But now I see that she's right."

"Who's Ridley?" Von asked.

Thad turned to him. "I'm handling this, Von. You can pack up for today."

"No, I can't, because this affects me too. Partner," Von added, his voice void of his usual affability.

Thad held his hands up, conceding the point. Maybe it was because The PX had been his initial idea and he'd brought Von in on it, but Thad recognized that he needed to respect Von as a full partner and deserved to be called out when he didn't.

"I'm sorry," Thad said. He motioned to Ashanti. "You were saying?"

She looked between the two of them. It was obvious she thought Von would be the easier sell, but concluded that Thad was the one she needed to convince.

"This could be your jump-off point," she said. "While Duchess and Puddin' are being their delightful selves on the show, you can talk about your new business and encourage viewers to follow your social media." She held her hands up. "Hold on a minute. Have you ever thought about documenting the renovations via social media?"

"I'm not big on social media," Von said. "I have the personality for it, of course, but it just seems like too much work."

"I get it," Ashanti said. "But you don't have a choice these days, especially if you're trying to attract people to your business. Having a social media presence now, in these early stages, is genius. People can follow along with the transformation of this gorgeous house into a bar."

"The bar will be gorgeous too," Von said. "But I get what you're saying." He turned to Thad. "I like the sound of this. It would get people invested in The PX before we ever open the doors."

"And, best of all, it's free advertising," Ashanti said.

"It isn't free. It's costing me time away from the reno, the cost of flying up to New York—"

"The show is paying for our flights and two nights of lodging," Ashanti said. "We're flying up a day early because my friend Ridley is setting up a number of media spots while we're there. She's talking with a public relations specialist right now."

"Wait, they contacted you this afternoon and you already have a PR person on this? I see why that little daycare you got there is doing so well," Von said. "You ever think of doing PR for a sports bar-slash-barbershop-slash-cigar bar-slash-hangout spot?"

"I am not your person when it comes to PR," she said with a laugh. "Believe it or not, my sixteen-year-old sister handles most of the social media and marketing for Barkingham Palace."

"You sound pretty good at it to me," Von said.

Thad was done with this one and his flirting.

"Give me tonight to think it over. I'll get in touch with you in the morning," Thad said.

"I need to know now. We need to book the flights as soon as possible and the PR rep needs to set up the additional media interviews."

"He'll do it," Von said.

Thad whipped around. "You can't make this decision for me."

"You heard her, man. This is genius marketing. And it's better to hop on the social media train with Puddin's star power while the dog still has it. We drag our feet too long and we'll both be out here doing TikTok dances to entice people to come to The PX."

"Honestly, you may still have to do a few TikTok dances," Ashanti said with an infectious grin. It made her freckles sparkle like rubies.

The ache that settled in Thad's chest was as delicious as it was painful. He couldn't remember the last time he'd been this attracted to someone.

"I think I have the solution to our problem," Von said with a wink in Ashanti's direction. "Thad, why don't we call your grandmother and ask her what she thinks?"

"You're such an asshole," Thad said. "But you just reminded me of another reason why I can't fly to New York tomorrow. I have to bring Puddin' over to Grams'."

"You're going to see Mrs. Frances? Can I join you?" Ashanti asked. "I've been wanting to visit her, but things have been so busy at work. This is the perfect opportunity. We can go together, and then head to the airport."

"It *is* perfect," Von said. "There's something about the way your brain works that's just…I don't know…thrilling."

There was no way in hell Thad would make it to the grand opening of The PX without causing his partner bodily harm. He should just get it out of the way and kick Von's ass right now.

He brought his hand up to the base of his neck and rubbed at the spot rock hard with tension. He honestly could not think of a single thing he loathed more than the thought of being on some morning talk show, sitting across from a couple of perky hosts with alliterative names. But Ashanti had made excellent point after excellent point, especially about documenting the renovations. It was a great way to start creating early buzz.

And what could be bigger than introducing The PX to the world via a national morning broadcast?

"Fine, I'll do it," Thad said.

"You will?" Her eyes grew wide before the brightest smile he'd ever seen lit up her face. His reaction to it was instant and intense. For a brief moment, if she'd asked, he would have gladly handed over his every possession to see that unrestrained smile again.

He was *so* fucked.

Thad cleared his throat. "I'll text you the info you need to book the airline ticket," he said.

"What time were you planning to visit Mrs. Frances? I can meet you there."

He shrugged. "I guess I'll go as early as possible if we have to catch a flight to New York."

"I swear, this will be worth it," Ashanti promised. "And painless. It will be worth it and painless."

"And fun," Von said. "You forgot fun."

"That too," she said with a laugh. She blew out a relieved

breath and hunched her shoulders. "Okay, I guess I'll see you in the morning."

Thad and Von both started to walk her out at the same time, but she held up her hand. "I can see my way out. Get back to doing the work you were doing so you can get Puddin' home."

"See you tomorrow," Thad called, leaning against the stud opposite the one Von leaned against. He glanced over at him and frowned.

"Hey, stop looking at her ass," Thad warned the moment Ashanti was out of earshot.

"*You're* looking at her ass."

"I—" Thad swallowed the words he was about to say, along with water from the bottle he still held.

Von walked over to him and crossed his arms over his chest. Thad's skin felt hot under his partner's assessing gaze.

"Now, is it that you don't want me to look at her ass because you want to be the *only* one looking at her ass? Because, if that's the case, I can find another ass to look at."

Thad took another drink, then mumbled, "Just don't look at her ass."

"Why not?"

If he could get away with knocking that shit-eating grin off Von's face he would do it in a heartbeat.

"Because I want to be the only one looking at her ass, okay?" Thad confessed. "Shut up," he said before Von could respond.

Von held up both hands. "That's all you had to say, man. I do have one question for you, though."

"What?"

"Did you consider what it's going to be like to be up there

in New York with her when all you want to do is look at her ass?"

Thad ran a hand down his face. Of course he had considered it. He just hadn't taken the time to fully process it. This was why he hated making important decisions on the fly. He needed time to consider all angles, weigh the cost and benefit, and ponder the consequences.

He already saw one consequence he would be forced to wrestle with in New York: a persistent case of blue balls. It wasn't as if he didn't have to deal with that in New Orleans, but at least he wasn't constantly around Ashanti when he was here. That wouldn't be the case in New York.

"This had better be worth it," Thad muttered.

19

Ashanti spotted Thad's pickup parked at the curb in front of Chateau Esplanade Senior Living Facility. She glanced at the time on her dashboard.

7:53 a.m.

She wasn't surprised. He struck her as one of those *you're on time if you're five minutes early* types.

She crept around the block, searching for a parking spot. She didn't like her chances. Between the seniors' facility, a middle school, and several restaurants, finding a place to park in this area would be like winning the lottery. When she turned the corner at Esplanade and Burgundy, she found Thad standing in an open spot behind his truck, waving her to come his way. Had he been sitting behind the wheel when she passed by the first time?

There was another pickup truck—this one white with rusty ladder racks mounted on the truck bed—idling parallel to Thad's. A tattooed arm waved out of the driver's side window, its owner gesturing irately.

"Find another spot," Thad called out to the guy.

The driver had apparently laid claim to this one and didn't seem inclined to continue his search. The door to the white pickup truck opened and a man big enough to play The Rock's stunt double climbed out.

"Oh, good Lord," Ashanti said. She could find another parking spot. She pulled up closer to tell Thad just that, but it was too late.

Ashanti's breath caught as the man marched over to Thad and pointed a finger in his face. Thad didn't respond. He braced his feet apart, crossed his arms over his chest, and smirked.

If there was bloodshed over a parking spot, she would kill them both.

The man yelled a half-dozen four-letter words in Thad's face, then stomped back to his truck and took off. Thad simply turned as if nothing had happened and continued to direct her into the parking spot.

It took her four tries before she was finally able to maneuver into the spot. She blamed nerves. And a lifetime of bad driving. She'd had Evie teach the twins before enrolling them both in driver's ed.

Ashanti jumped out of her SUV and rounded the front where Thad was standing, that smirk now directed at her.

"Are you insane?" she yelled at him.

"Good morning to you too," he said. "Not the best at parallel parking, are you?"

"That man could have murdered you over a parking spot," Ashanti said, ignoring his warranted dig at her driving skills.

"A random stranger can murder me at the grocery store, doesn't mean I'll stop shopping for grapes."

She threw her hands up. "That makes no sense."

He shrugged. "You're right, it doesn't. Guess I'm lucky that guy wasn't in the mood for murder. Probably because he didn't want to lose his job."

Thad gestured to something over her shoulder and Ashanti turned to find the guy from the white truck walking up the sidewalk, balancing a ladder over one shoulder. His truck was now parked on the other side of the street.

"Asshole," the guy called, giving Thad the finger.

Thad replied with a proper army salute. "Nice day to you too."

Ashanti rolled her eyes at the ridiculousness of both men.

"Thanks for saving the parking spot for me, but please do not take chances like this once we get to New York," she told Thad.

"Can't make any promises. Have you ever met a New Yorker?" He shook his head. "Give me a minute to get Puddin', then we can go see Grams."

She followed him to his truck and was pleasantly surprised to find that he'd bought Puddin' a proper car harness. He reached behind the seat.

"Can you hold this for a minute?" he asked, handing her a blue-and-white box with CANDIES FROM AROUND THE WORLD printed all over it.

"What's this?" she asked.

"It's for my grandmother." He hooked the leash onto Puddin's collar and helped the poodle alight from the passenger side seat. "Back when I was in the Army, I would ship candies to her from wherever I was deployed. I signed up for this subscription box now that I'm permanently stateside. This way she doesn't have to miss out on her sweets."

If one's heart truly could melt, hers would be a puddle in the middle of the sidewalk right now. Was he for real?

Thad took the box from her and handed her Puddin's leash. They started up said sidewalk, toward the metal gate.

"I already told Grams we can't stay long," Thad said.

"Does she know about New York?"

"She knows we're going, but I didn't tell her why, exactly." He glanced at her. "I figured you can do that. She'll get a kick out of it."

"She's going to explode," Ashanti said.

"Let's hope not. I wasn't planning to change out of these clothes before the flight."

She paused for a moment before she burst out laughing. "Did the UPS driver deliver a better sense of humor along with this box of candy, or have you purposely been hiding it from me all this time?"

His charming grin was heart-stopping. "I'll leave you guessing."

Ashanti took a step back and concentrated on taking deep breaths as Thad pressed the button on the speaker attached to the gate. She did a quick mental rundown of the reasons she should not allow this man and his alluring smile—and this sense of humor that had come from out of nowhere! Umm... hello!—affect her.

She refused to backtrack on her vow to swear off dating until the girls were off to college. Even though she could already tell that Thad was a thousand times more responsible than her ex-boyfriend, Simon, she wasn't about to give Anita fodder for another custody battle.

But that wasn't the only reason. She was on the precipice of taking her business to a level she could not have fathomed reaching. Distractions were kryptonite. And Thaddeus Sims was the very definition of a distraction.

Thad explained to the person on the other side of the speaker why they were visiting, and a moment later, the lock clicked. He held the gate open for her.

Frances Sutherland was waiting next to a column in front of the facility's entrance.

"Mrs. Frances," Ashanti called, hastening her steps.

As usual, the older woman looked as if she were on her way to a Saks Fifth Avenue catalog photo shoot, despite the early hour. Her pressed caramel-colored slacks, burgundy, navy-blue, and brown striped silk shirt, and designer navy ballet flats fit like they were custom made. Even the wooden cane she held—a new addition to her wardrobe—was fashionable.

"It's all my favorites," Mrs. Frances said. She gathered Ashanti in a hug, gave Thad a quick peck on the cheek, and then lavished her attention on Puddin'.

The reunion between the two brought tears to Ashanti's eyes. She hated being away from Duchess for just a few hours—yet another reason she resented being stuck at home baking instead of at the daycare. She could only imagine how difficult it had been for Mrs. Frances to have to give up Puddin'.

"The rocking chairs are free," Mrs. Frances said. "Let's sit before one of these old folks comes out here and snatches one up."

They climbed the steps to the facility's wraparound porch and walked over to a set of rocking chairs that faced Esplanade Avenue. Thad propped himself against the wooden porch railing while the women sat.

In total disregard of her fancy attire, Mrs. Frances allowed the poodle to put his dusty paws in her lap.

"How are you doing today, my baby?" she asked, pressing

a kiss against Puddin's head. "Thaddeus isn't being mean to you, is he?"

"You don't hear him complaining, do you?" Thad asked.

Puddin' barked and growled at him.

"Lies," Thad said.

Ashanti laughed. She had no idea where this sense of humor had come from, but it was dangerous on him. She found him attractive enough when he was being a surly curmudgeon. She would not be able to handle funny and charming. And gorgeous. She couldn't forget gorgeous.

Mrs. Frances spent the next ten minutes regaling them with the juicy gossip floating around the assisted living facility. Ashanti was both intrigued and disturbed by the coding system residents used to indicate who were swingers. She would never look at Mardi Gras beads in the same way again.

"Now, tell me about this trip to New York?" Mrs. Frances said. "It will be Puddin's first time on an airplane. I think you should give him an edible just in case he gets anxious."

"I'm not feeding your dog edibles," Thad said.

"Why not? They're calming."

"Grams, you're not up in here eating edibles, are you?"

Mrs. Frances stuck her nose in the air. "I'm seventy-eight years old, Thaddeus. I do what I want."

"Grams."

She leveled him with what Kara called the Grown-Ass, Unbothered, Black Woman Face and turned to Ashanti. "So," she said. "About New York."

"Grams!" Thad said.

Ashanti looked back and forth between the two of them, unsure if she should speak.

"Ashanti," Mrs. Frances said, dismissing her grandson.

Thad dropped his head back and muttered toward the sky. Was he a fan of the Serenity Prayer too?

"About New York," Mrs. Frances pressed.

"Um, we have pretty exciting news," Ashanti said. "Puddin' will be on *Up Early with Leah and Luke!*"

Mrs. Frances clasped her hands against her chest. "That cute brother and sister duo? I love them! I knew it was only a matter of time before Duchess and Puddin' became stars. You could not find two more precious dogs." She gave Puddin's head another kiss and hugged him.

"Now," Mrs. Frances continued, "will you and Thaddeus be sharing a room while you're in New York?"

"Grams," Thad said.

"What? I don't know how these things work. They're flying you up there together, aren't they?"

"You know the network doesn't expect us to share a room."

"Maybe they should," she said.

Ashanti's face felt as if she were standing next to a wood-burning pizza oven. "Uh, no. That would be inappropriate," she said.

Her phone vibrated against her thigh. She pulled it out and read a text from Ridley, commanding both Ashanti and Thad come to her condo ASAP to meet with the public relations specialist.

Ashanti held up her phone. "Thad, we're being summoned."

"Go. Go," Mrs. Frances said. "Show my baby New York City and then you come right back here so you can tell me about the trip. What day will you be on the show?"

"Friday morning," Ashanti said. "I'll text you before we're about to go on. Just remember that New York is an hour ahead of us."

"I finally learned how to use the DVR in my unit. I'm not missing a single moment of that show." She pointed a manicured finger at Thad. "Remember what I said about the edibles."

"Forget the edibles," Thad said, giving her a kiss on her forehead.

"I'll have Barkingham Palace's veterinarian prescribe something for anxiety for both dogs," Ashanti promised her.

Puddin' was not happy to leave and made his dissatisfaction known by planting his butt on the porch and refusing to move. Ashanti had to entice him with a Cheetos-type snack from Australia that Mrs. Frances grabbed from the box of snacks Thad had brought for her.

Once they finally got Puddin' to move, Ashanti and Thad started down the walkway toward the gate.

"Is there any question as to why your grandmother is one of my favorite people on earth?" Ashanti asked. "I love that woman."

"She's a troublemaker," Thad said.

"But she does it with such dignity and grace," Ashanti said with a laugh. She bit the side of her lip as Thad once again opened the gate for her. "Although, it sounds as if she was trying to make more than just trouble. She's not very subtle with her matchmaking, is she?"

"Frances Sutherland and subtle should never be mentioned in the same sentence," Thad said. "I'm sorry about that. I'm used to her matchmaking. Don't let her make you uncomfortable."

"It didn't," she lied. "I just don't want you to feel awkward. I mean, we *are* flying up to New York together. And, according to Kara, there has already been chatter online about the two of us."

He stopped short. "What kind of chatter?"

"That we're a couple." The heat was back, but not just on her face. Every part of her body warmed as Thad's gaze drifted over her. "You know how people are," Ashanti continued. "Our dogs were caught necking and they automatically project the same onto the owners."

"But how does anyone even know I'm Puddin's owner? I didn't do that midday newscast with you."

"Remember the night you were late picking him up and you followed me to the playroom? There's a twenty-four-seven livestream camera in there."

Thad shook his head. "People really need to find a life outside of the Internet. Who sits around watching a doggy cam at eight o'clock at night?"

"You'd be surprised," Ashanti said. She hunched her shoulders. "Like I said, I just don't want either of us to feel awkward or pressured or anything like that. We both know that the thought of the two of us together is laughable."

Her ego wanted to believe it was disappointment she'd glimpsed in his eyes, but it was probably just dust.

Still, she felt the need to clarify. "Not that there's anything wrong with you. It's just that you're not at all my type."

"Well, damn. Just come on out and call me ugly," Thad said, an amused grin pulling at one corner of his mouth.

"I didn't say you were ugly!" Ashanti protested. "My type loves dogs."

They came upon her car and Ashanti used her key fob to unlock it. Thad reached for the door handle before she could and opened the car door for her.

"Thank you," she said, sliding in behind the wheel.

He started to close the door, but then stopped. He leaned

forward, resting his arm against the door frame. "So are you saying that if I learned to like dogs—" He stood up straight and shook his head. "Never mind. Forget I said anything."

Her phone vibrated again. Ashanti fumbled trying to pull it from her pocket. She had to be the color of a fire hydrant at this point.

"That's Ridley," she said. "We need to get to her place before she gets in her car and comes looking for us."

Thad blew out a breath. "Okay."

"Um, I'll text you the address, but you can also just follow me. She's less than ten minutes away."

"Text me the address, just in case I lose you in traffic," he said. Then he closed her door and went to his truck.

Ashanti squeezed the steering wheel so tight she was surprised she didn't bend it.

"Good Lord," she whispered.

Was he about to ask her what she *thought* he was about to ask her? She'd had exactly two long-term boyfriends, and had not been on a single date since she broke up with Simon. Her ability to read between the lines when it came to men was a negative five hundred.

It was a *really* good thing Thad wasn't her type. Now if only she didn't have to keep reminding herself of that.

20

Thad managed to keep up with her in traffic after all, due to running at least one red light and cutting off a delivery truck. Ashanti had called Ridley to let her know that they would be arriving at her place within ten minutes so she could put their names on her condo's visitors' list.

She pulled just beyond the parking gate after being let into the condo building's garage and idled while the attendant checked Thad's credentials. She waited until the arm of the gate rose before she drove forward and made a right, parking in one of the open visitors' slots.

She stood next to Thad's back bumper as he hooked Puddin' to his leash and guided him out of the truck, keeping her eyes averted as he approached, praying he wouldn't revive his aborted question from just before they left his grandmother. She wasn't sure how she would answer—how she would *want* to answer—if he did.

Okay, so she knew how she wanted to answer. But what she wanted and what was best for where she was in this stage

of her life were on opposite ends of a very long, very complicated spectrum.

"This way," Ashanti said, gesturing to the smoke-gray
glass door that led to the building's lobby. She had only visited Ridley's condo a couple of times since she'd moved here,
mainly because they were all so used to hanging out at the
daycare and at her house since she'd started baking the Duchess Delights treats.

They walked up to a podium just to the right of a bank of
elevators.

"Afternoon," the doorman said.

Ashanti couldn't help but wonder if this was the doorman
who had spent time blowing Ridley's back out. Goodness, she
hoped not. He couldn't be more than twenty-three years old.

"We're here to see Ridley King in 1210."

His ears and neck immediately became flushed.

Good Lord, he was the one.

"She's expecting us," Ashanti said.

As they waited for the doorman to confirm their arrival,
Thad looked around the sleek lobby. Everything was glass and
chrome, a departure from most of the structures around here,
which leaned into the city's old-world French architecture.

"What exactly does your friend do for a living?" he asked.
"A one-bedroom in a place like this must run four thousand a
month."

"She's tried to explain it, but I honestly have no idea what
Ridley does for a living," Ashanti said. "She has a doctoral
degree in marketing from Wharton and a huge corner office
that overlooks the Mississippi River, if that helps."

"Explains a lot," Thad said.

"You can go up now," the doorman said.

"Dogs are allowed, right?" Thad asked, pointing to Puddin'.

"Of course," the doorman said. "Wait. Is that——?"

"The poodle from the viral video," Ashanti said. "Yes."

He looked over his shoulder. "Do you mind if I take a photo?"

She had to stifle a laugh at the look of repugnance on Thad's face as he watched the doorman snap a selfie with Puddin'. He then directed them to an elevator and pressed the button. It took mere seconds to reach the twelfth floor. Ridley's two-bedroom condo was at the end of the hallway. She opened the door before Ashanti could knock.

"Finally," Ridley said. She pointed at Puddin'. "What's this?"

"Standard poodle," Thad said. "I'm Thad, by the way."

"I don't do dogs."

"Me neither."

"Cute," she said. She blew out an exasperated breath and opened the door wider. "I'll make an exception this time, but keep him away from me and the furniture."

Puddin' barked at her as they entered the condo.

Ridley jabbed her finger at him. "I will turn you into a rug."

The dog whimpered and snuck between Thad's legs.

"I like you," Thad said.

"Everyone likes me," Ridley replied. "Dominique had to get something out of her car. She'll be back up in a few minutes. Your flight boards at twelve fifteen p.m., so you'll need to head for the airport no later than eleven. You know how traffic can get."

Evie came out of the kitchen. "Ah, Puddin's here! Hi sweetheart."

Puddin' dashed from between Thad's legs and darted toward Evie, clipping Ridley along the way.

"He touches me again and he goes out in the hallway," Ridley said.

"Puddin' deserves special treatment," Evie said. "He's part of the reason we're here."

"What are *you* doing here?" Ashanti asked her. "Don't you have patients this morning?"

She waved that off before giving Ashanti a hug. "Cameron can man the practice for a few hours. This is all too exciting to miss. You two ready to hit the Big Apple?"

"We don't really have a choice," Ashanti said.

"No, you don't," Ridley said. "Just wait until you hear all the spots Dom was able to line up. By this time on Friday, anyone who didn't know about Puddin' and Duchess getting it on will definitely know."

The PR specialist returned and they all sat around the living room with its floor-to-ceiling windows that afforded a view of both the Crescent City Connection bridge and the downtown high-rises.

Ridley's colleague Dominique was a petite biracial Black and Vietnamese woman with a cute pixie haircut and the physique of a gymnast. She forwarded the itinerary to Ridley with instructions to distribute it electronically to everyone around the table.

"You arrive this afternoon and head straight for a podcast in Hell's Kitchen," Dominique started. "It shouldn't last more than an hour, and it isn't too far from your hotel. On Thursday, you have a live in-studio TikTok interview with Casey, the Dog Whisper. Once you're done there, you have another podcast in Brooklyn. Friday morning is Leah and Luke, of course."

"Is it really worth going up there a day early just to talk to someone on TikTok?" Thad asked.

"Casey, the Dog Whisper, has over twelve million followers," Dominique said. "A couple from Kansas with a new self-care line for dogs moved more product after going on her show than they did when they appeared on *Shark Tank*."

"I could have gone my entire life without knowing that people spend money on self-care products for dogs," Thad said.

"Says the man whose poodle wears a rhinestone collar?" Ridley said.

"My grandmother bought the collar."

"Back to the itinerary," Dominique said. Ashanti now saw why she and Ridley were good friends. They had the same personality. "I'm still trying to line up a radio interview with a guy who has the most popular evening drive talk show in New York's tri-state area, so more to come there." She huddled over her laptop. "The second PDF that I will send contains talking points and basic tips for dealing with the media: how to keep your cool during an interview, how to keep your responses to under twelve seconds—the longer you ramble, the more likely you're going to say something the interviewer can use against you."

"Is that something we need to worry about?" Ashanti asked. "These interviews are supposed to be friendly, right?"

"Every interview is an opportunity for a gotcha moment," Dom replied. "It's my job to make sure you're prepared for them." She glanced at her watch. "Are there any other questions?"

"I have one," Thad said. He gestured at his phone. "Who's paying for all of this? Who's paying you?"

"I'm fronting you both the money for everything the morning show doesn't cover," Ridley answered. "I do, however, expect to be paid back."

"Don't you think I should have been consulted before all these plans were made if I have to shell out money for it?" Thad asked.

"Do you know anything about marketing or public relations?" Ridley asked. "No," she said before Thad could answer. "You have no idea how valuable these next three days will be for your business. Consider it an investment."

He held up his hands, as if giving up his argument. It was probably for the best. Ridley never backed down, even when it was an argument she was losing. That wasn't the case here. Thad may still be unsure, but Ashanti had full confidence that this time in New York would be worth it.

"And you and Kara are going to handle the social media posts for the contest, right?" Ashanti asked.

Dominique swiped across her phone's touchscreen and turned it to face Ashanti. "Already have the first one ready to go."

The contest Kara had signed her up for turned out to be a much bigger deal than Ashanti had first realized. It was actually a sponsorship backed by a venture capitalist firm dedicated to helping minority businesses. And that $250,000 prize was only the first component of a five-year commitment.

In addition to the money, a nationwide marketing campaign, and the mentorship, the winner would also be given an opportunity to borrow up to two million dollars from the investment firm. Their flexible payback model, which would be based on revenue and not a set monthly payment, was one of the most generous terms Ashanti had ever seen.

Winning this contest would negate the need for a traditional loan. As much as she abhorred the thought of taking on such enormous debt, knowing she wouldn't have to start paying it back until her business showed a profit made it easier to swallow.

She *had* to win this contest.

However, in order to win it, she had to convince people to vote for Duchess Delights utilizing the nationwide online voting method the contest had set up. She was up against four other Black women-owned businesses, including a natural hair care line that was already gaining popularity and the country's first Black woman-owned microbrewery.

But there was one thing she had that none of those other contestants did: the chance to get her name out there on a national stage. This contest and the segment on Leah and Luke's show truly could not have come at a better time. Ashanti had no choice but to believe it was kismet.

"That's all I have for now," Dominique said. She handed Ashanti and Thad a square black card with a QR code on one side and in bold letters DOM. on the other. "I will text you both daily. Many of these parts are still moving, so you will need to be agile."

With that she told Ridley she would see her at some mixer next week and left the condo.

Evie hooked a thumb toward the door. "You cannot tell me that Dom is not short for dominatrix. I was afraid to breathe around her."

"Even I'll admit Dom is a bit scary, and I'm not afraid of anything," Ridley said. "But she is one of the best in the business and there are a bunch of people who are jealous of you both right now because you got the chance to work with her." She pointed at Ashanti and Thad. "Do not blow this. It's rare to get this kind of opportunity."

Thad pushed back from the table. "I'll do my best," he said. "I still need to pack, so I should get going."

"You haven't packed yet?" Ridley said. She dropped her head on the table in one of her signature overly dramatic Ridley moves. Her head popped up. "Weren't you in the Army? Isn't your slogan 'Be Prepared'?"

"That's the Boy Scouts," Thad said. He snapped his fingers and Puddin' came to stand next to him.

"You got him to follow a command," Ashanti said. "You're making progress."

"Don't get too excited. We still hate each other," Thad said. "Nice meeting you," he said to Evie. To Ashanti he asked, "Do you have a ride to the airport?"

"Puddin' will need a travel crate," Ashanti said. "I have extra at the daycare." She looked at Evie. "Maybe you could bring us in the van?" Evie had a van that she used for making house calls to her clients. "Meet us at Barkingham Palace in an hour?"

"You got it, babe," Evie said.

Thad left and Ashanti started gathering her things as well. She didn't want to admit to Ridley that she had not yet packed either. This was all moving so quickly, she barely had time to breathe since getting that email from the show producer yesterday.

"Don't be nervous, Shanti," Evie said.

"I'm not—"

"Your hands are shaking," Ridley said.

She blew out a breath. "This is just…a lot. Podcasts, radio, live on TikTok? And I just realized this is the first time I've ever taken Duchess on an airplane. The farthest I've traveled with her is the Alabama Gulf Coast for that beach vacation the girls and I took a couple of summers ago."

Evie walked up to her and captured her shoulders in her hands. "You will be fine. Duchess will be fine. It will all be *fine*, Shanti."

Ashanti nodded and tried to swallow past the lump in her throat. It didn't feel fine. It felt slightly chaotic. Couple that with the fact that she had to do all of this alongside Thad and his gorgeousness, and she would need Evie to prescribe *her* some anxiety meds before the plane ever started taxiing down the runway.

"Trust me," Evie said. "Everything is going to go wonderfully." She looked Ashanti in the eyes. "But I do have one request, and it's an important one."

"What?" Ashanti asked, alarmed by the seriousness in her tone.

Evie took her by the hands and squeezed them tight. "Promise me that you will spend at least one night in New York letting that man do the filthiest shit imaginable to you."

"Preach!" Ridley said, throwing both palms up in the air like she'd just caught the Holy Ghost.

"Evie, stop it," Ashanti said, wrenching her hands away.

"Promise me, Shanti."

"I expect stuff like that from this one." She nodded toward Ridley. "Not you."

"Girl, there is nothing wrong with a fling," Ridley said. "I have them all the time."

"We know," Ashanti and Evie said in unison.

"Keeps you young," Ridley said, taking a sip from her iced tea and letting out an *ahhhh* sound.

"This is a business trip," Ashanti reminded them.

"Business during the day, orgasms throughout the night. What could be better than that?" Ridley shrugged. "Just make sure to double up on protection, because that man looks like he can get you pregnant just by breathing on you."

"Just by *looking* at you," Evie said. "I'm stopping at CVS for a pregnancy test on the way home."

They all burst out laughing.

"There will be none of that going on in New York," Ashanti said. "Thad is not my type, and vice versa."

His unfinished question from this morning popped into her mind. When he'd leaned into her car and asked if he learned to like dogs...What? Would that make him her type? It was the only logical follow-through she could think of, but she didn't want to think about it at all, not when she was spending the next three days in New York with him.

And now Evie and Ridley had put the thought of orgasms in her head.

"I need to get going," Ashanti said, pulling her purse strap over her shoulder. "I'll meet you at the daycare, Evie." She gave Ridley a hug. "Thanks for setting all this up."

"Do me proud, girl," Ridley said, squeezing her tight.

Ashanti returned her squeeze. "That's a promise I'm willing to make and keep."

21

Thad was in the middle of packing when his cell phone rang.

"Sims," Thad answered.

"Sims-Williams," his sister replied.

"What's up?" Thad asked.

"When were you going to tell me that you were on your way to New York for *Up Early with Leah and Luke!*" Nadia yelled so loud Thad was sure the neighbors across the street heard her.

"I'm on my way to New York for *Up Early with Leah and Luke!*," Thad said. "There you go. Just told you."

"You get on my very last nerve sometimes," Nadia said. "Grams said you'll be on the show Friday morning? I'm going to let the girls stay home to watch it live."

"It's not that serious. Definitely doesn't warrant the girls skipping school. Hey, I can wear jeans and a T-shirt to a podcast, right? Those aren't on camera or anything."

"People wear jeans and T-shirts on nationally televised award shows, so I think you're safe. Just don't say anything that will make people question whether you're a real human," she said.

Thad pulled the phone from his ear and looked at it, even though they weren't on a video call.

"What is that supposed to mean?"

"I say this with love, Thad, but you can come across as a bit of a robot sometimes. It's not your fault; you've been conditioned not to have feelings."

"Was that not supposed to sting as much because it was said with love?" he asked.

"Everything stings less when said with love. Oh, and don't forget about Ree's wedding in a couple of weeks," his sister said. "I added a plus-one for you just in case you want to bring Von."

It wasn't unusual for Von to join him as his plus-one, but this time the thought settled in Thad's stomach like a sour oyster. Maybe if he wasn't such an unfeeling robot, he would have a better chance of bringing a plus-one who wouldn't leave him at the first sight of a pretty woman in a tight dress.

Thad closed the lid on the carry-on with more force than necessary. The thing couldn't hold nearly as much as his military rucksack.

Hadn't he already decided this wasn't the right time to get involved with anyone? That he needed to get settled and find his footing in New Orleans? If that's what he was going with, he needed to stick to it. Especially after learning the only woman he was even remotely interested in had determined he wasn't her type.

His grip tightened on the luggage handle. This was going to be the most frustrating three days of his life, without question.

Nadia started in on her friend Reshonda's bachelorette party, which she was hosting in Sedona.

"I'm trying to convince her to take a road trip to Vegas, but Ree said she would rather go to the Grand Canyon! The Grand freaking Canyon. This is why I'm glad I got married in my twenties."

"You can have a rocking good time at the Grand Canyon," Thad said.

"Just for that joke, you're getting a second pluck in the middle of the forehead the next time I see you. Now, before I go, you're not keeping anything else from me, are you?"

Thad froze. What did Nadia know? Had the scammer tried to contact her? "Why would you ask that?" he asked.

"Uh, hello! Because you didn't tell me about New York!" she said. "What is up with you?"

The tension ebbed from his shoulders.

"Nothing," Thad said.

For a minute he considered telling her about the messages he'd been getting from the woman in Alabama. There had been three, so far, including the one he'd gotten today. She'd shared that she, too, was a budding entrepreneur, and that's when he'd figured out her angle. She was going to ask for money to help get whatever business she had off the ground.

He'd shot back a quick reply, praising his grandfather's business savvy and asking about her endeavors. He fully expected her to go in for the kill in her next message.

Thad checked his watch. He had twenty-seven minutes to meet Ashanti at the daycare. If he mentioned the scammer to Nadia right now, she would have him on the phone for at least an hour. He'd wait to tell her face-to-face. It would be more enjoyable that way.

"Nothing else to report," Thad said, answering her question. "I need to finish up some stuff here, Nadia," Thad said.

"I'll shoot you a text once I'm in New York and have more information about the TV show."

"Sure you will," his sister said. "Love you, Big Head."

"Love you too. Kiss my nieces for me. And send them to school on Friday. You can record the show."

"Nope. Bye," Nadia said.

"Nad—" But she had already ended the call.

Thad wheeled his luggage from the bedroom and grabbed Puddin's leash by the front door.

"You ready for this?" he asked the dog.

Puddin' turned away from him and settled into his bed.

"Well, it's too bad if you're not," Thad said, clipping the leash to his collar. "You and your girlfriend are the ones who got us into this."

Just before walking out the door, Thad picked up Puddin's alligator and stuffed it in the carry-on's front compartment with his deodorant. He couldn't chance Puddin' chewing up everything in New York.

22

Ashanti stood next to the curbside check-in kiosk outside Louis Armstrong International Airport, attempting with decreasing degrees of success not to worry that Thad had decided to pull out of this whole thing at the last minute.

She texted Deja to find out if he'd stopped in for the travel crate. She responded that he'd come by not even ten minutes after Ashanti and Evie left.

If he'd picked up the crate, he was at least still planning to travel with Puddin'. But he should have been here by now.

Just as she was about to text him, his black pickup pulled up to the curb. The passenger door swung open, and Thad hopped out before the truck had a chance to come to a complete stop.

"Wasn't my fault," he said, quickly lifting the travel crate from the truck bed. He set it, along with a rolling carry-on suitcase, next to Duchess's crate. "Three semi-trucks were clogging up I-10. We were stuck going fifty miles per hour on the interstate."

"We're still good," Ashanti said, checking her watch to

make sure she wasn't telling a lie. The ticketing agent had told her all was well as long as they got Puddin' and Duchess checked in at least forty-five minutes before departure.

"Hey, friend," Von called from behind the wheel. "Keep that one out of trouble for me."

Ashanti brought two fingers to her forehead in salute. "You got it," she said with a laugh.

"Ignore him," Thad said. He got Puddin' out of the back seat. "Thanks for the ride," he told Von as he shut the door.

The passenger side window lowered. "Remember, the keyword is *fun*," Von said.

"You have a house to demo, right?" Thad asked.

"And TikTok videos to post." Von gave him a thumbs-up before winking at Ashanti and pulling off.

She laughed again. "Don't get me wrong, I'm still upset that you're turning the Bywater house into a bar, but it helps to know that Von will make sure there's never a dull moment there."

"I guess that's a selling point," Thad said. "Can we check the dogs curbside?"

"The ticketing agent inside told me to come straight to her once you arrived. She'll let us bypass the line."

They started for the terminal, Ashanti carrying Duchess's much smaller crate in her right hand and rolling the hard-case carry-on she'd borrowed from Evie with her left. It had been so long since she'd taken a vacation that she hadn't realized she didn't have a proper suitcase until she went to pack.

She glanced over her shoulder as they walked through the parting automatic doors. "I'll be honest, I thought you were standing me up."

"I would never do that," Thad said. He stopped her,

catching her by the arm. "Really, if I say I'm going to do something, I follow through. I'm sorry again for making you wait."

His earnestness softened any hard feelings his tardiness
had caused. She could tell how much it bothered him to have
her think he'd gone back on his word.

"You're here now," Ashanti said. "That's what matters,
right? Come on, let's do this."

They checked the dogs in with the ticketing agent and
headed for security. Even though he had TSA PreCheck desig-
nation, which had a much shorter wait, Thad joined her in the
regular security line.

"It's not as if I'll get on the plane without you," he told
Ashanti when she tried to get him to go through the shorter
checkpoint. He nodded toward the front of the line. "It's moving fast. We're good."

It took them less than ten minutes to get through the
line, leaving enough time for Ashanti to stop at her favorite candy store in the airport. She loaded up on overpriced
chocolate-covered Swedish Fish and Hot Tamales.

"You sure you don't want any?" she called to Thad, who
stood just outside the store with his arms crossed, as if he was
a bodyguard on a detail.

"I'm good. Thanks," he said.

Ashanti paid for her candy and walked up to him. "I forget that you're a former soldier. You probably haven't eaten
sugar in a decade."

One corner of his mouth angled up in a grin as they
started for the B concourse.

"What?" Ashanti asked.

"If you only knew how much junk food I have in my grandmother's pantry," Thad said. "I'm addicted to Tootsie Rolls."

"Seriously? How can you be addicted to junk food and still have a body like that?" Her steps came to an abrupt stop. "Not that I've spent too much time studying your body or anything," Ashanti said. "I just figured…"

Goodness, girl! Shut up!

It would be challenging enough to get through this trip without it being awkward between them, especially after his grandmother's comment about the two of them sharing a room. One way to ensure the awkwardness joined them in New York like a giant third wheel was to let the man know that thoughts of what his body must look like naked flashed through her mind at least a thousand times a day.

Please, God. Don't let her mention his naked body.

"You haven't spent *too* much time? Which means you've spent some?" Thad asked.

Ashanti's head shot up at the amusement she heard in his voice. She didn't need a mirror to know that her freckles were the color of the Hot Tamales she'd just bought.

"Excuse us," a woman said as she cut between them. Three young children—all pulling Mickey Mouse suitcases—trailed her.

"We're in the way," Ashanti said. She looked around, searching for some place they could have this extremely important discussion before they got on that plane. "Come with me." Her face still burned as she led Thad to an alcove near the restrooms.

Ashanti released a deep breath.

"Okay, so do you remember when you asked me to forget that thing you said earlier when we were outside Mrs. Frances's place?"

He nodded.

"Well, I'm asking you to do the same now."

"What am I forgetting?"

"That I just admitted to spending time thinking about your body," she said. God, she needed an ice bath. "Forget I said that."

He stuffed his hands in his front pockets. "So does this mean we're going to keep demanding the other person develop a case of selective amnesia when we say what we really feel?"

"Yes," she answered quickly. "Yes, that's exactly what we will do. I just can't do..." She waved a hand between them. "This. For numerous reasons, I can't do this right now. It's best if we do the selective amnesia thing."

"Is it realistic?" Thad asked.

Not even a little bit. But...

"It has to be," Ashanti said.

This time, his grin didn't hold much humor. There was disappointment there, and maybe a smidge of resignation.

"If that's what you want," he finally said.

Want?

No, it wasn't even remotely close to what she wanted. But it was, without a doubt, the best course of action here.

A relationship of any kind was off the table, even that fling Ridley had suggested. She wasn't even thinking about Anita and her threat to petition the courts; Ashanti simply didn't have the bandwidth to handle any emotional entanglements. Her life was currently broken up into twelve-minute segments—the time it took to bake a batch of Duchess Delights treats.

And she had a feeling when Thad got down to business he needed way more than twelve minutes.

That was *not* where she needed her mind to go right now.

"This *is* what you want, right?" Thad asked.

"It's what we both want," Ashanti said. "Isn't that why you asked me to forget what you said when we were leaving the assisted living facility?"

He blew out a breath and ran a hand down his face. "Not really," he mumbled. "But you're right."

"Okay," Ashanti said with a nod, pretending she hadn't heard the first half of his answer. "So now that we've gotten that out of the way, we can just enjoy New York without any more awkwardness. And if I slip and say something like that again, you can ignore me."

"Just so I'm clear, how many times am I supposed to ignore you before acknowledging that those slipups are how you really feel?"

One hundred? Two, maybe?

"I won't slip up again," Ashanti said.

His shrug said he didn't believe her. He was probably right.

It was going to be a long three days.

They headed for their gate, which turned out to be just a few yards down the concourse. The moment they arrived, Ashanti could tell something was off. The whispers and murmurs were low at first, but within two minutes of her taking her seat, the questions started.

The woman sitting directly across from her leaned over and asked, "Excuse me, but are you Duchess and Puddin's two owners?"

"Yes, they are," answered a younger girl with braids and a Southeastern Louisiana University sweatshirt. She held her phone up to the woman who'd initially asked the question, then turned it to face Ashanti. It was a screenshot of her and Thad in the playroom at Barkingham Palace.

"My suite mates are going to be so mad they flew out on an earlier flight," the girl said. "We are all obsessed with Puddin' and Duchess. Where are they?"

"Um, they're flying cargo," Ashanti said. "They're both too big for the main cabin."

"It's so sweet that you two take them on vacation with you," the first woman said.

"Oh no, we're not going on va—"

But then Ashanti remembered that they were told to keep their appearance on *Up Early with Leah and Luke!* hush-hush until it was announced in a teaser this afternoon. She had no idea what time the commercial was supposed to run.

Thankfully, she was saved from having to explain their trip by the gate agent, who announced that the first boarding group was welcome to board.

Thad put her suitcase in the overhead compartment before heading for his seat. Because their flight had been booked so late, they were in different rows; he in 26A and her in 13B. Ashanti hoped this wasn't an omen of things to come. Not only was she in a center seat but unlucky number thirteen.

After buckling her seat belt, she stuffed her mouth with a handful of Swedish Fish and leaned her head back. Exhaustion took care of the rest. She was sleeping before they reached 10,000 feet and didn't awaken until the plane landed at JFK.

She insisted they go to the holding area where the dogs would be brought out the moment they were allowed to deplane. It was probably best that she'd slept through the flight because otherwise she would have spent all her time worrying about Duchess in the cargo area.

"Hey, baby." She stuck her finger through the grate and

wiggled it. Duchess licked at her, then settled back down, seeming no worse for wear.

"We have the podcast first, right?" Thad asked.

Ashanti nodded, fighting back the anxiety that threatened to claw its way into her psyche. She had been nervous enough talking to the reporter from their local TV station. That was small potatoes compared to what she was about to embark upon. Much of this media campaign would be seen by a nationwide audience.

What was she thinking? *Everything* had a national audience these days—a worldwide audience, in fact. Her segment from that noon broadcast had been viewed over 500,000 times on YouTube.

She had way too much riding on these next few days to allow nerves to take her down. She would employ Dom's media tips and face those interviewers with the same confidence she displayed when she stood before a mirror and pretended to accept a Grammy, or an Oscar, or a Tony Award back when she was a kid. Couldn't no one tell her that she couldn't sing, dance, or act.

While they were in the air, Dom had sent a message saying that their appearance on *Up Early with Leah and Luke!* had been moved up to the next morning instead of Friday, but that Ashanti and Thad shouldn't panic because she had already rescheduled their other meetings.

She had also sent over a file with the addresses of every stop on their whirlwind media tour. All Ashanti had to do was plug the address into her Uber app.

"Okay, so Dom really is the best at her job," she said. "I don't know what she charges, but I have a feeling it'll be worth it."

"I'll wait until after I see her invoice before I decide that," Thad said.

Because their flight had landed early and traffic was, in their Uber driver's words "mad light, yo" on their ride into Manhattan, they had time to drop off their bags and the dog crates at their hotel in midtown. Puddin' and Duchess were both recognized the moment they walked into the lobby.

For a town known to treat movie stars as regular people, it seemed those unwritten rules went away when it came to celebrities of the canine variety. Ashanti took a step back as multiple guests who had been in line to check-in converged on them. People were either snapping pictures, recording video, or going live on their social media accounts. It was wild.

"Please, stand back," the concierge said as he escorted them out of the lobby to their waiting cab.

"Did that really just happen?" Ashanti asked as she settled in the car.

"You mean these two dogs getting treated like Meghan and Harry?"

She pointed at him. "I knew you secretly loved the royals! I can tell a fellow royal watcher."

"I only know their names because you have it under their picture at the daycare," Thad said. He patted Puddin's topknot. "Don't let this go to your head. Be humble."

"I know you won't admit it, but he's growing on you," Ashanti said.

"Like a rash on my ass."

She threw her head against the seatback and laughed. "You really should stop hating on Puddin'."

"But I won't."

"Why not?"

"Because he's spoiled."

"That isn't his fault. Blame Mrs. Frances for that."

"Oh, I do," Thad said. "I can both blame her *for* him being spoiled and continue to dislike him *because* he's spoiled." He shrugged. "Though, he's not half bad when it comes to watching sports on TV. Doesn't crowd me. Eats the kettle corn when it falls to the floor. So I guess he has some redeeming qualities."

"He's also going to bring more attention to your new business than you could have ever imagined," she reminded him.

"The jury is still out on that, but if you're right, I'll upgrade that collar to cubic zirconia."

Ashanti was still laughing by the time they pulled up to a nondescript building two blocks from the Hudson River.

"No need to get out," she told the cab driver when he opened his door.

He got out of the cab anyway, phone in hand. "Can I get a selfie with Puddin' and Duchess?" he asked.

"You gotta be kidding me," Thad muttered.

"Of course," Ashanti said.

After their impromptu photo shoot—the cabbie turned out to be one of those people who took a dozen selfies before he was satisfied that he'd gotten the perfect shot—they entered the building and took the elevator to the third floor. Ashanti was disappointed that there wasn't a view of the river, but she was determined to make her way to one of the piers before she left New York.

They were led into the podcast studio and introduced to their hosts, Beth and Seth. Ashanti was excited to learn that the husband and wife duo had started the podcast to help people with a fear of dogs overcome their phobia.

"I've held events at my daycare to help kids with phobias,"

she said. "Duchess has the perfect temperament for it, but Puddin'—" She wiggled her hand. "He can be a bit high-strung at times."

The poodle immediately illustrated her point by jumping two feet when Seth pulled the microphones into place.

"Calm down, Puddin'," Thad said, dropping to one knee and rubbing under the dog's chin.

It wasn't until Thad mouthed *close your mouth* that Ashanti realized her jaw had gone slack. What had gotten into him?

Thad stood and whispered to her, "I figured I should at least pretend that I like the dog."

"You like the dog," she whispered back. "Just admit it."

"Are we ready to get started?" Beth asked.

"No, I don't," he said against her ear as he pulled her chair out for her. Awareness shot down her spine.

Ashanti's nerves ratcheted up even more when they were informed that today's episode would be livestreamed on the podcast's YouTube channel.

"We could not have Puddin' and Duchess in studio and not stream it live," Seth said. "Our audience would show up with pitchforks."

"Well, if there's one thing Duchess and Puddin' are used to, it's being livestreamed for all the world to see," Ashanti said.

"Our eight million subscribers are ready!" Beth said.

Ashanti's knees nearly gave out. "Eight million?" she asked. "Really?"

"You'll do fine," Thad said, covering her hand with his own. Ashanti looked down at their hands and then at him. She nodded.

It turned out that was right. Once the podcast started, her anxiety began to melt away. It helped to have Duchess in her lap. Puddin' stood between her and Thad's chairs with his chin on Ashanti's leg. According to Beth, the YouTube channel's chat box went berserk whenever Puddin' and Duchess rubbed noses.

The conversation was funny and lighthearted, though heavy on the dog puns. She cringed every time Seth asked for another "round of a-paws" as they went into a commercial break. But at least she tried to hide her low-key embarrassment for their corny host.

Thad, on the other hand, was as transparent as fine vellum. He barely cracked a smile.

"So *howl* is business going, Thad?" Seth asked with a dorky laugh. Ashanti winced.

"It hasn't opened yet," Thad answered with the enthusiasm of a wet slug.

"But you can follow Thad and his business partner's journey as they renovate a beautiful home in one of New Orleans's quirkiest neighborhoods. You may even see Puddin' helping with demolition, right Thad?" Ashanti asked, trying to signal to him to lighten up.

"Uh, yeah," Thad said.

Despite his continued aloofness and Seth trying way too hard to crack said aloofness, she thought the podcast was a great start to their media junket.

Beth and Seth ended the broadcast with promises to keep in touch, then immediately ushered Ashanti, Thad, and the dogs out of their tiny studio. Apparently there was some kind of podcaster gala in New Jersey tonight that was a must-do.

Thad turned to her on the sidewalk as they waited for their Uber to arrive.

"Be straight with me, are the Leah and Luke folks like that?"

"Not at all," Ashanti said with a laugh. "Leah and Luke have much more chill."

"Thank God."

"You could have been a little more chill yourself," she said. "Poor Seth was trying so hard to be your friend."

"I would rather go through a year of basic training than be friends with Seth," he said.

Ashanti burst out laughing.

Their Uber pulled up and Thad opened the door and motioned for her to get in, followed by Duchess and Puddin'.

"We don't have their harnesses, so please drive carefully," Ashanti told the driver. She hadn't thought about how they would get around Manhattan. She hated riding with Duchess not strapped into her little doggy seat belt.

Her phone rang just as the driver was pulling away.

"It's Ridley," she said to Thad, rolling her eyes as she answered. "Hey, Rid."

"Put the phone on speaker so soldier boy can hear me," Ridley said.

This wasn't good. Ashanti bit the side of her lip.

"Um, she wants to talk to you," Ashanti said. She switched the call to speaker. "You're on speaker."

"Thaddeus?" Ridley asked.

"I'm here."

"Loosen the fuck up."

Thad jerked his head back. "Excuse me?"

"You looked and sounded like you were in pain during that podcast. Lighten up. You are too fucking hot to be so uptight."

"I don't think that was supposed to be a compliment," Thad said.

"It wasn't a compliment. It was an order. I told you both before you left New Orleans not to blow this chance. You have twelve hours to learn how to be charismatic. Do not go on that show tomorrow looking like you just ate a bowl of stewed prunes, okay?"

"Yes, ma'am," Thad answered.

"Shanti, you were amazing. Hell, even Duchess and Puddin' were amazing with their little doggy kisses. Carry that same energy over to the studio tomorrow. I gotta go. I'll call you later tonight."

Ridley disconnected the call.

Silence filled the car, until the Uber driver broke it with a low whistle. "Wow," he said.

"Yeah," Thad said, rubbing the back of his neck.

"Ridley means well," Ashanti said. "She's just a bit… blunt."

"A bit?" Thad asked. "Hey, my man," he called up to the Uber driver. "Any chance they sell charisma at Macy's?"

"I think you have more than enough," Ashanti said with a light laugh. "You just need to learn how to use it."

He turned that grin on her, the one that made her heart do a two-step. "Guess I know what I'll be doing tonight. Maybe I can find some videos on YouTube that'll teach me how to be charismatic."

"You can learn everything else on there," the driver said.

23

Thad leaned against a door in the hallway opposite Ashanti's room, which shared a wall with *his* room. Lord, help him.

He'd planned to get Thai food delivered for his dinner—a ritual whenever he visited New York—then fall to sleep watching season three of *The Wire*. But when Ashanti shared that this was her first time in New York, and that she had her heart set on seeing some of the city, his plans changed.

Thad pitched his head back against the door and pulled in a steadying breath. There was no need for him to feel this on edge. He had been with her all day, from their visit to his grandmother's, which felt like a lifetime ago, to their appearance on that podcast. Why did it suddenly feel different—more significant—now that they would be together after the sun had gone down?

Maybe because he now knew this attraction wasn't as one-sided as he'd first thought.

Whether what she felt was purely physical or something deeper didn't matter. Knowing she wasn't indifferent to him—that she felt *some*thing—made him ache to push this thing between them in another direction. A non-platonic direction.

Was he even ready for that?

Things were finally starting to fall into place with The PX, but it felt as if, when it came to the rest of his life, he was still trying to find steady ground. He wanted the kind of relationship his grandparents shared. A bond built on trust and respect and an unbreakable commitment. But Thad knew that didn't just happen; it required work. Was he prepared to put in that kind of effort?

He ran a hand down his face.

He was getting *way* ahead of himself. He'd offered to show Ashanti around town so that she could get a little taste of New York, and that's all that would be happening tonight. Period.

The door to Ashanti's room opened, and Thad stood up straight.

"Sorry," she said. "I know we said eight o'clock, but Duchess is being a bit fussy. She's a creature of habit and this is a strange place."

"Should I bring Puddin' over? Would it be better if they kept each other company while we're out?"

She tilted her head to the side and tapped her finger against her chin.

"Those two together? Unsupervised? I'm not sure about that." She laughed that laugh that Thad felt on his skin. Every single time. "She'll be fine. I left *SpongeBob* playing on the TV. He always calms her."

Thad huffed out a laugh, shaking his head. "The way you all spoil these dogs."

They started for the elevator, but then he stopped. "One

minute. I forgot my wallet," he lied, patting his pockets for emphasis.

He used his phone to unlock the door, and found Puddin' curled up on the bed, his head on the pillow Thad had planned to sleep with. It was a good thing there were four. He picked up the remote, turned on the TV, and searched until he found ESPN.

"For the record, I am not spoiling you," Thad said. "I just don't want you disturbing the people in the next room with your barking when you get bored."

Puddin' released one of his whimpering sighs and turned so he faced the television.

Thad shook his head as he grabbed a chicken-flavored homemade biscuit from the container Ashanti had given him and threw it on the pillow. Two weeks ago he would have ordered this poodle into the bathroom and left him there with a bowl of water until he returned. When in the hell had he turned into one of *those* people? A dog person.

"I am not a dog person," he told Puddin'. "I'll see you when I get back."

And now he was talking to the damn dog as if he understood a word he said. Just like a dog person.

"Did you have trouble finding your wallet?" Ashanti asked when he returned.

He patted his back pocket. "I had it the entire time. Not sure how I missed it."

They took the elevator down and exited the lobby with little fanfare now that the superstars were tucked in bed. The sidewalk outside their Eighth Avenue hotel was buzzing with people running late for Broadway shows or heading for dinner at one of the hundreds of restaurants in the area.

"So what do you want to see first?" Thad asked. "Times Square, the Statue of Liberty, the Empire State Building? According to Google, the Empire State Building closes for tours at eleven, so it makes sense to hit that one up first. The Staten Island Ferry runs twenty-four seven, and Times Square is always busy, no matter what time of the day or night."

"Actually," Ashanti said, taking her phone out of her pocket and swiping across the screen. "There's a food truck at Forty-Ninth and Sixth Avenue, across from Rockefeller Center. I've been wanting to try it for forever."

"A food truck?"

"Yes! And there's a cupcake shop, another that sells this donut and croissant mashup thing, and, of course, I have to get a New York bagel."

"So you basically came here to eat?"

She nodded. "The Food Network is my background noise when I'm baking. I've been making a list of foods I must try if I'm ever in New York."

Thad chuckled. "Whatever you want," he said. "Let's get a taste of New York. Literally."

Even though it was only one stop, they took the subway so Ashanti could have the experience. Then they walked the two giant avenue blocks to Fiftieth and Sixth. The line for the food truck, which Thad learned sold Greek food, stretched halfway to Seventh Avenue, but the cooks made quick work of getting food to the hungry patrons.

They took their gyros—lamb for her, chicken for him—along with seasoned French fries, and started down Sixth Avenue. After less than a block, Ashanti stopped and pointed across the street.

"That's the cupcake place. They're legendary."

"Exactly what must a cupcake do to attain legend status?" Thad asked as he stuffed three fries in his mouth.

"Probably get someone like Dom to create a PR campaign for it." She shrugged. "I don't care. I still have to try it. They're on my must-have list."

She gestured to their right, where a huge fountain in front of a Chase Bank gently gurgled. A marble ledge that was more than wide enough to sit on surrounded the fountain's base.

"Let's sit here and eat," Ashanti said. "And then I can get the cupcake for dessert."

"There's no way you're going to be able to eat all the food you want to try tonight," Thad said.

"Watch me," she said.

He laughed as he took a seat. "I do love a woman who loves food." He sat up straight and turned to her. "I didn't mean—" *Shit.* "You know what I meant."

Ashanti tipped her head back and sighed up at the clear September night sky.

"This is ridiculous," she said. "We are going to lose our minds if we spend the next two days apologizing for every little thing we say that *might* get misinterpreted. We're ignoring slipups, remember?"

The ridiculous part was them trying to ignore this attraction between them, but hadn't he just convinced himself it was for the best?

"That's what we agreed to do," Thad answered.

He would pretend to ignore it. He would also mentally obsess over anything that even remotely hinted that her interest in him was shifting into something different. Because, apparently, torturing himself was now on *his* list of must-do's.

"Just for the record," Thad continued. "I really do love

when a person can enjoy a good meal without being self-conscious about it."

"Why would I be self-conscious? A girl's gotta eat. And while in New York, this girl is going to eat everything." She nudged her chin toward the pita in his hand. "You better get going on that. I don't want the cupcake place to close on me. In fact..." She took out her phone. "Oh, good. They're open until ten. We've got time."

Thad took two big bites out of his gyro, which was, admittedly, one of the best he'd had outside of Mykonos.

"So is New York everything you thought it would be?" he asked.

"Pretty much," Ashanti said. "Tall buildings, lots of people, good food. The selfie-obsessed cab driver threw me, but I guess that just goes to show how much star power Duchess and Puddin' have."

"I still don't get it," Thad said.

"Have you ever watched the video that went viral?" Ashanti asked. "It is the very definition of adorable."

"I guess I just find it weird how some people can treat pets better than they treat actual people," he said. "Case in point." He nodded toward the woman walking a medium-size dog. Its pristine white fur was trimmed to perfection and it had on a hot pink coat with matching hot pink boots. "She probably paid more for that dog's outfit than some people pay for their entire wardrobe."

"Not unless it's couture," Ashanti said. "I'm kidding." Then she shook her head. "I take that back. I've seen some dresses that run in the four figures."

"Anyone paying four figures for a dog's dress needs to have their credit card taken away," Thad said. He looked over at her, not sure if he wanted to know the answer to his next question. "Please tell me Duchess doesn't have clothes that cost a thousand dollars?"

Her easy laugh melded with the sounds of the city traffic.

"There is no way I would spend over forty dollars for any piece of clothing for my dog." She held up a finger. "And just to be clear, I've only spent forty dollars once, to support a client who has a doggy clothing shop on Etsy. I have my own business to grow and twin sisters who will be starting college in a couple of years. I have to watch my money."

"Twins? You mean there's a clone of the one who wanted to chop off my head for leaving Puddin' locked in my truck?"

"Sure is. Kara and Kendra. They're identical twins, but their personalities could not be further apart. Kendra would have walked past your truck and shrugged at the sight of Puddin' in there."

It was none of his business, but he still asked, "And you're raising them on your own?"

She nodded, slipping another fry in her mouth. After taking a sip from the bottle of water she'd brought with her from the hotel, she said, "My parents died six years ago."

Thad winced. "I'm sorry. Car accident?"

That was usually the case when a couple died together. That, or a fire. Or a murder suicide. Shit, he hoped it wasn't a murder suicide.

"I wish it was that simple," Ashanti said. She glanced over at him. "It's kind of a long story. Actually, it's not that long, just...complex."

Definitely murder suicide. Damn.

"You see, my dad *did* die in a car accident," she said. "On the same day that we lost my mom."

"But not together?"

"Nope." She wrapped up the other half of her gyro and set it next to her on the fountain ledge. Then she rubbed her balled-up fists against her thighs and stared straight ahead, to the cars rolling along Sixth Avenue.

Her face was impassive, but Thad could sense the unease emanating from her. Her shoulders had gone rigid with a tension he could suddenly feel in his own muscles.

"You don't have to talk about this if you don't want to," he said.

"No, no. I'm good," Ashanti said. "Okay, I'll never be good when it comes to talking about losing my parents, but it has gotten better with time."

Thad remained silent, giving her the time she needed to get comfortable with what she was preparing to share.

"My mom was a mail carrier for the postal service," Ashanti started. "She was almost at the end of her route when she passed out in the lobby of a building downtown. Turns out she'd had an aneurysm. There was an ambulance just a couple of blocks away, but she was gone before they got her to the hospital."

"Damn, Ashanti. I'm sorry," he said again.

Was there another set of words in the English language that sounded more inadequate? But Thad couldn't think of anything else to say. It took every ounce of restraint he possessed not to reach for her. A hand on her arm, on her shoulder? Would she reject the gesture, or lean into it?

"What about your dad?" he asked, deciding to keep his hands to himself.

She sucked in a deep, shaky breath. He was about to retract his question, when she continued.

"When he got the call about what had happened from Mom's supervisor, he dropped everything and went to the hospital."

She kneaded her thighs again, dragging the heels of her palms up and down. When she spoke, her voice was so soft Thad could barely hear it above the traffic.

"He ran a red light on his way home from the hospital, and there was an accident," she said. "No one else was hurt, but the medics said my dad died instantly."

Fuck.

Life could be cruel and then it could be downright savage. But he knew that better than most. He'd witnessed children become orphans, their entire family taken out by high-capacity artillery projectiles strong enough to destroy a city block. He was an instrument of life's brutality.

"That was bad enough," Ashanti continued. "Seriously, it was unlike anything I ever imagined living through. But then the life insurance company made it a thousand times worse." She looked over at him again. The taut lines pulling down the corners of her mouth told him he wasn't going to like where her next words landed. "They tried to get out of honoring his policy by saying that my dad ran the red light on purpose—that he died by suicide."

"What the fuck? Excuse my language," Thad said. "But that is fucked up."

"It was awful. It wasn't even a huge policy, just enough to pay off the house and cover the funerals." She pulled her bottom lip between her teeth. When she spoke again, her voice was weak. Thready. "Thing is, I'm not sure if the insurance company wasn't right."

"Ashanti," he whispered, barely able to get her name past the lump in his throat.

"In my heart I know Dad wouldn't leave me and the girls alone on purpose, but my mom was his entire world. It isn't out of the realm of possibility that the thought of facing life without her was too much for him to bear.

"They met when I was seven years old, and it was love at first sight for all three of us, me, dad, and my mom. My biological dad died when I was still a baby. He had a rare form of cancer that took him within months of his diagnosis." She shrugged. "Lincoln Wright was the only dad I ever knew, and he was perfect."

Her smile at the memory told Thad all he needed to know about her stepdad—her dad.

"Even after the twins were born, he never once treated me as anything other than his own," she said. "I was so broken the day we lost them. If not for Evie and Ridley at my side, and knowing that I had to be there for Kara and Kendra, I'm not sure if I would have made it through that night."

"Yet you've made it through six years. And grown a business. And raised twin teenagers. I should nominate you for a Medal of Honor, or whatever is the civilian equivalent."

Her smile broadened. "I don't deserve any medals. Believe me. I constantly fall down on the job, and there have been times…" She shook her head. "Let's just say it hasn't been the easiest road to travel. The year the girls turned twelve there were at least a half-dozen instances when I considered changing my name and running away from home."

"Ouch," Thad said.

"Yeah, that was the year of Kara's Ramona Flowers phase. She discovered the movie *Scott Pilgrim vs. the World* and decided that being a sulky, sarcastic preteen who changed her hair color on a regular basis was the only way to be. She's dialed

back on the sarcasm—a little—but stuck with the hair dye."
She huffed out a laugh. "Now it's Kendra who's the sulky one."

"Was there no one who could help with raising them? No
family members you could call on?"

"My dad has an older sister, but I don't even want to go
there. She was *not* an option."

The hostility that entered her voice piqued his interest,
but he wouldn't ask her to wade into anything she wasn't up to
discussing. At the same time, he didn't want her to stop.

Given how challenging it had been for him to adjust after
the void leaving the Army had created, Thad was awed by
her ability to overcome the life-altering loss she'd suffered.
How had she managed to surmount that kind of pain at such
a young age, let alone guide twin teenagers through it?

"So, what stopped you from changing your name and running away?" he asked.

This time her smile was genuine. And achingly beautiful.

"Duchess," she answered.

Thad chuckled. "Why am I not surprised?"

"Her powers go far beyond starring in viral videos,"
Ashanti said. "She really was a lifesaver. It wasn't until about
two years after my parents died that I finally conceded that we
needed to talk to a therapist. He was the one who suggested
bringing a pet into the home. I took the girls to a local shelter,
and we all fell in love with Duchess the moment we saw her."

She paused as a double-decker tour bus rolled by, then
continued. "It's funny, because I had avoided getting another
dog for years." She glanced over at him. "My dad bought me
a golden retriever, Toby, the year he and Mom got married.
I had him through grade school, up to my freshman year

of college. I wanted to wait until after I finished veterinary school before I got another dog."

"You were in vet school?"

She nodded. "I was in my final year when Mom and Dad died," she said. "And before you ask, yes, it was a huge blow to have to quit before I earned my degree. And, yes, I do think about going back, although I don't like to admit it."

She turned to him then, pulling one foot up on the ledge and resting her chin against her bent knee.

"You know what I realized not too long ago? I don't think about it all that often anymore. I would have been a great veterinarian, but I got the idea to open Barkingham Palace after boarding Duchess at another facility. My biological dad left a small trust that was turned over to me when I turned twenty-five. I used that money to start the daycare, and I don't regret it. I learned that sometimes the hand you're dealt is better than the one you'd originally planned to play."

Her optimism in the face of such tragic circumstances floored him. If anyone had the right to whine, it was her.

"Yeah, well, even a good hand can have a couple of shitty cards," Thad said. "It sounds like you were dealt more than your share."

"No argument there," she said with a rueful chuckle. Thad had to fight the urge to brush back several of her braids that had fallen out of place.

"I wouldn't wish what happened to my family on anyone," Ashanti continued. "But things have gotten better with time."

"Was Duchess the inspiration for the daycare? Is she the reason behind the theme, because her name was Duchess?"

"Her name was originally Jelly Bean," she said.

"Ah! So *this* is why she worships you. You rescued her from both a shelter and a stupid name."

"Stop it," she said, tapping his arm with a playful punch. The innocent touch stirred a prickle of awareness that penetrated through the layers of his shirt and jacket.

"My mom is the inspiration behind both Duchess's name and the Buckingham Palace theme," she said, blithely unaware of the havoc she was wreaking in him. "Her obsession with the royals makes Beyoncé's BeyHive look like child's play."

"I hope this doesn't make you think less of me, but I have no idea what Beyonce's beehive is. Is it a line of flavored honey?"

Her laugh was rich and undiluted and without a single thought for his feelings. Thad joined her so that she would be laughing *with* him and not *at* him.

"Not well-versed in pop culture, huh?" Ashanti asked when she finally came up for air. "It's the *Bey*Hive, not beehive. And it's what her fanbase calls itself. Come to think of it, my mom would have fit right in with them. She loved Beyoncé. She even learned the 'Single Ladies' dance with Kara and Kendra.

"But her love of the royals topped anything I've ever seen. She thought Princess Diana was the ultimate lady, and that Fergie, the Duchess of York, was the most badass woman in the world. I was going to name Duchess Fergie, but I thought people would assume she was named after the singer from the Black Eyed Peas."

"I do know who they are," Thad was quick to say.

"I wouldn't have judged you either way," she said. A winsome smile drew across her lips. "You know, the first time I ever saw my mother cry was during Princess Diana's funeral.

I was maybe five or six at the time and had no idea what was going on. I just remember climbing onto her lap with this dirty little stuffed lamb that I used to carry everywhere. I put my head on her chest and watched the procession on TV."

This time, Thad didn't fight the urge to touch her. He reached over and tapped the toes of her simple canvas tennis shoes.

"I'll bet it was quite the scene in heaven when your mom finally got the chance to meet Princess Diana."

Her face instantly lit up with a smile so bright it outshone all the lights in the city. His vow to remain unaffected by her was no match for that smile. It was fast on its way to being broken.

"I can only imagine," Ashanti said. She lifted his hand from her foot and squeezed it. "Thank you for that. I still have those days when the grief hits me out of nowhere, but it will make things easier to think about Mom up there with the woman she idolized so much. Seriously, thank you."

She started to let go of his hand, but Thad wouldn't let her. He slightly twisted his so that they were palm against palm, then he rubbed his thumb back and forth across her smooth skin, feeling a nick along the ridge of her knuckle. He wanted to ask how she got it, and how she managed to keep a smile on her face when she had suffered through such tragedy, and how she'd managed to keep her head above water while shouldering more responsibilities than any single person should have to shoulder. He wanted to know a thousand and one things about her.

But he couldn't ask her any of that. That wasn't the type of relationship they had.

Relationship?

They didn't have a relationship. He doubted Ashanti would call what they had a friendship. He was one of her customers.

Thad didn't know how to classify the sharp ache that hit him in the chest. Regret? Frustration? A combination of both?

He finally dropped her hand and asked the only question that truly needed answering.

"Ready for that cupcake?"

24

"Who's the better dancer, you or Von?"

For the past half hour, Ashanti had intentionally stuck to lighthearted topics, trying to banish the lingering heavy weight of discussing her parents' deaths.

She and Thad had started back for their hotel after buying a half-dozen cupcakes from Magnolia Bakery, deciding to walk instead of taking the subway so that she could see Times Square and other midtown Manhattan sites.

He'd rolled his eyes when she made him double back so she could walk through the mini plexiglass waterfall tunnel between Forty-Eighth and Forty-Ninth Streets and take pictures with the bronze Paparazzi Dogman and Paparazzi Rabbitgirl sculptures that shared a terrace with it. But when she told him the significance behind the art piece and its connection to Princess Diana—how the dog represented the media that literally hunted down the princess, leading to her death—he not only brought her back but stepped in as her photographer.

"Well?" Ashanti now prompted him as they turned the

corner onto Seventh Avenue. "Which of you is the better dancer? You or Von?"

"I don't dance," Thad answered.

"Oh, come on. You at least do the Electric Slide at cookouts."

He shook his head. "Nope."

"Seriously?" Ashanti held out her hand. "That's an unforgivable offense. Give me your Black card."

"Hey, no relinquishing of the Black card." He laughed. "I'm usually the one manning the grill at the cookout, so I get a pass."

She gave him a suspicious look before dropping her hand. "Okay, you're forgiven. It's still no excuse for never dancing."

"I didn't say I *never* dance. I can't tell you how many Army balls I've had to attend over the last decade."

"That doesn't count. You can't do any real dancing in those starched uniforms." She took a bite of her vanilla cupcake with strawberry frosting and released a moan. "I swear, if I'd known how good these cupcakes really were, I would have bought a dozen."

"Agreed," Thad said. "They're definitely worth a trip back to that bakery before we leave New York."

"You mentioned your sweet tooth at the airport, but to see it in action is another thing entirely." She bumped him on the arm with her elbow. "I would have thought a soldier would have more discipline when it came to sugar."

He held his hands up. "I'm not saying I would have divulged state secrets for a box of Little Debbies, but it's a good thing I was never put to the test."

There was that humor again. He could not possibly know how, of any of the characteristics a person could possess, having the ability to make her laugh was the one she cherished above all.

She blamed Ridley. She was the one who'd ordered him to be more charismatic. He had turned the charm up several notches tonight and Ashanti was *not* okay. It made it even harder to fight these growing feelings she didn't even want to acknowledge she had for him.

"So why the Army?" she asked as they stood under the massive curved electronic billboard above the Hershey's Chocolate World store, waiting for the light to change.

Thad hitched a shoulder. "Because I didn't want to become a dry cleaner."

Her head jerked back at his unexpected answer. "Were those your only options?"

"It felt that way at the time." He licked frosting off his knuckle, and Ashanti almost forgot how to breathe. She forced herself to look away so he couldn't glean what that innocent act had done to her.

"This is a sidewalk, not a parking lot," a woman pulling a wheeled trolley bag said as she edged past them.

"Yikes," Ashanti said. "That was a good one, though. I might have to use that the next time I'm stuck behind a bunch of tourists in the French Quarter."

When they crossed the street, Thad pointed to the red TKTS bleachers in the middle of the pedestrian area. "Let's grab a seat. You can take in Times Square for a few minutes."

They climbed about a dozen rows and settled in the center of the bleachers. Ashanti set the cupcake bag between them, then looked up at the buildings stretching skyward. Their stories-tall LCD screens advertised everything from perfume to tennis shoes. She was tempted to take her phone out and snap pictures, but she could find a million photos of these buildings on Google in a matter of seconds. She wanted to live in this moment. To soak it in so she could remember how it felt.

"I can't believe I'm finally here. And I can't believe my dog is the reason behind my visit," she said. "I've wanted to come to New York ever since seeing that movie *Weekend at Bernie's*."

"Doesn't most of that movie take place in the Hamptons?"

"Yes, but there's a scene where Larry and Richard are on a rooftop and the New York skyline is all around them. That was enough for me to decide that I had to visit this place one day."

She nudged his shoulder.

"Back to you and this decision to enter the Army," she said. "Let me guess. You were a troublemaker and your grandfather gave you an ultimatum after high school, either join the family business where he could keep an eye on you, or enter the military where Uncle Sam could do the watching?"

"Umm..." He wiggled his hand. "You're kind of on the right track. Actually, no you're not," he laughed. "I was never a troublemaker, and my grandfather never gave me any kind of ultimatum. But it felt as if joining the military was the only profession I could choose outside of Sutherland Dry Cleaning that wouldn't disappoint him. His older brothers were all in the Army, so nothing was more noble than entering the service."

He put both feet up on the bleacher below and rested his elbows on his raised knees.

"The initial plan was for me to do my four years, earn my degree, and then gently break it to Gramps that I wanted a job that required a suit and tie—that's how he referred to corporate jobs. But I fell in love with military life." He folded his hands and rested his chin on them. "And since my entire reason for becoming a soldier was to make my grandfather proud, I decided to stick with it."

"So your grandfather was still proud, even though you never joined the family business?"

"Of course," he said, as if that was never a question. "Just ask any of his customers. According to Grams, no one could drop off or pick up their dry cleaning without having to suffer through a story about whatever it was I was doing at the time. I would send pictures during my deployment, and he would print them, along with information about the country I was in, and tape them to the counter so customers could read about it while they waited."

Ashanti slapped her hand against her chest. "That's so sweet. He sounds like an amazing man. Of course, he would have to be amazing to catch a woman like Mrs. Frances."

"Yeah, Gramps was a good one. Best man I've ever known." Thad's expression sobered and she realized it must hurt for him to talk about his grandfather in the past tense. She knew that feeling intimately.

"I'm sure he would still be very proud of your post-military career, as well," she offered. "Despite my opposition to what you are doing to the house in the Bywater, I will admit that I am impressed by your business model. In a city that has more bars than pharmacies, you came up with an idea that is unique. That's quite an achievement."

"I'm glad you approve." His eyes sparkled with his grin.

"Not that you *need* my approval," Ashanti said, bumping him with her shoulder again. "But yes, I approve."

"I may not need it, but I like having it all the same."

The amusement in his eyes was coupled with a sincerity she had never before heard in his voice. It compelled Ashanti to believe that he truly did value her opinion. The thought sent a ribbon of deliciously warm feelings twisting through her.

Why was this man turning out to be nothing like she first assumed?

"You know," Ashanti said. "You're not as much of a curmudgeon as I thought you were."

"Yes, I am," he said with a laugh. "But I'm trying to get better at not being such a hard ass."

They drifted into a comfortable silence as they people-watched from their perch on the bleachers. Ashanti's entire being hummed with the urge to thread her arm through Thad's and rest her head on his shoulder. She abruptly stood before she could give in to the impulse.

"It's getting late, and we have a long day ahead of us tomorrow," she said.

She wobbled as she started down the steps, and Thad caught her by the waist. His fingers brushed against the skin at the small of her back, where her sweatshirt had ridden up, igniting her body like a sparkler on New Year's Eve.

"Take it easy," Thad said. "You okay?"

Ashanti pulled in a steadying breath and nodded. She took a second to glance in his direction and immediately recognized her error. Looking at him gave him the chance to see what she was desperately trying to hide, the wanting she knew was evident in her eyes.

When he spoke, his voice was so soft she was surprised she even heard it above the fray of the busy square.

"Ashanti—" Thad said.

She felt his whisper on her skin; the longing in that simple utterance reaching deep inside her. It tugged on emotions she'd vowed she wouldn't give in to.

Once she was back home, she would share a bottle of wine with Evie and Ridley, and lament over Anita's long-ago threat continuing to cockblock her. That's the way things had to be for the next two years. Nothing was worth jeopardizing her guardianship of the girls.

"We should go," Ashanti said. She divested from his hold and made her way down the bleachers.

Thad was at her side within seconds, but he blessedly withheld any comment about what had transpired a minute ago. He stuck his hands in his pockets and gestured with his head. "Our hotel is this way."

The crisp New York night provided welcome relief from the heat that continued to consume her from the inside out. Ashanti remained ferociously cognizant of where she was in proximity to Thad for their somewhat awkward, yet still surprisingly pleasant, walk back to the hotel.

They entered the lobby and were immediately recognized by two young women who looked to be in their late teens or early twenties.

"Oh, snap, you're Puddin' and Duchess!" exclaimed the one wearing a Philadelphia Flyers sweatshirt.

"Um, actually, we're their owners," Ashanti said. "Puddin' and Duchess are the dogs."

"Sure, sure," the girl said. "That's what I meant."

"You two are the cutest couple," her companion said. "Almost as cute as Puddin' and Duchess. You know what, you two should re-create their video! But instead of the dog treat you can share like a hot dog or a churro or something like that. How cute would that be?"

"For real, for real," the other girl said. "My timeline would blow up after seeing a video like that."

"We'll take that into consideration," Thad said, gently capturing Ashanti by the elbow and ushering her to the bank of elevators. One opened just as they were walking up to it.

"A churro?" Ashanti asked once they were ensconced in the ascending elevator.

"I guess it could work," he said with a shrug.

They got off on the eleventh floor and negotiated the network of short hallways that brought them to their rooms. The brief reprieve from the awkwardness that the comical encounter in the lobby offered evaporated as they approached her door.

Ashanti turned to face him.

"Uh, thanks for going out with me. This was fun. Hey, maybe you should call Von tonight and tell him. He kept stressing how much he wanted you to have fun."

Thad didn't respond to her rambling. He just stared at her.

Words, Ashanti realized, were unnecessary. His eyes said it all.

She could scarcely breathe as she absorbed all that his intense gaze conveyed: the heat, the longing, the disquieting way it called bullshit on every excuse she could even think to throw at him.

"We can't keep pretending," Thad finally said.

"Yes, we can." She nodded like a bobblehead doll. "We absolutely can."

He stuffed his hands in his pockets and backed up against the wall opposite her door. Regarding her with a look that was equal parts frustration and need. "I've tried not to want this—to want you. I told myself that I wasn't ready for it, that it wasn't the right time, that I need to concentrate on getting The PX off the ground before I jumped into anything serious." He shook his head. "None of it's working."

"Try harder," she said.

"People already think we're together," he pointed out. "Why don't we just…I don't know…see what happens?"

"No."

"Why not?"

She barked out a shaky laugh. "Because."

She hated that it was the only thing she could think to say. She never let the twins get away with answering *because* when she asked them a question.

The door next to Thad's opened and a middle-aged man with perfectly coiffed silver hair like a dad from an early nineties sitcom came out carrying an ice bucket.

"Oh, excuse me," he said, walking between them. He stopped, turned, and pointed at Ashanti. "You're Duchess and Puddin's mom. I've almost convinced my wife to get a Frenchie because of you."

Ashanti flashed him a faint smile. "Good luck with that."

Once he'd continued his trek to the ice machine, she grabbed Thad by the arm, used the keycard to open the door to her room, and pulled him inside.

Duchess immediately scampered over to her, her stubby tail wiggling at 100 mph. Ashanti tossed her keycard and the bag of cupcakes on the extra-long TV stand/dresser combo and scooped her up. She pressed a kiss to the top of her head and deposited her on the bed where she burrowed under the covers.

Ashanti turned to face Thad.

"Look, I will admit that I am extremely attracted to you."

She covered her face in her hands. "I can't believe I just said that out loud."

"It wasn't really a secret," Thad said.

She dropped her hands. "Really?"

"I'm just saying." He shrugged. "It's not a secret that I'm extremely attracted to you too. *Beyond* extremely."

Ashanti brought her hand to her throat to massage the lump of desire lodged in it.

"I can't," she said. "Things are just too complicated with the twins, and I'm trying to buy another house—my dream location—for the daycare. And you've got all kinds of stuff going on." She let out a sigh. "I can't do a relationship right now, and I don't do casual sex."

The air in the room grew dense with the arousal, frustration, and yearning that pulsed between them.

"Maybe we can find an in-between," he said. Thad took a step forward, and added, "For now."

He took another step toward her, and her feet refused to take a step back. Instead, they moved forward, until she was standing close enough to touch him.

Then she did.

Ashanti hooked her hands behind his neck, pulled his head down, and pressed her lips to his. She was struck by how soft they felt. Never could she have imagined a hardened Army veteran would have lips that felt like brushed velvet; soft and supple and pliant.

But then she realized she must have caught him off guard, because after a moment those gentle lips turned forceful, advancing with purpose as his hands came up to cradle her face. He parted her lips with his tongue and swept it inside her mouth, his tasting like the sugary cupcakes they'd eaten.

It had been so long since she'd felt this, the intense rush of intimately connecting with another human being. Of allowing herself to be vulnerable enough to share something so deep, so personal. She hadn't even been tempted to share this with anyone in such a long time.

Until this man.

His tongue explored with a fervency that stole her breath, weakened her knees, set her entire being ablaze. His hands slid from her cheeks to her waist.

And then common sense returned to her brain.

"Okay, stop," Ashanti said. She took several steps back and braced her hand against the dresser. "We can't do this."

"Ashanti—"

"We agreed—"

"It's not working," he said, cutting her off. "We can't just ignore this pull between us. And there's not a case of amnesia severe enough to make me forget the way your tongue felt against mine a minute ago."

"I can't," she whispered. The words hurt—physically hurt—as they moved past her lips.

He backed away, holding up his hands. "I'm not going to push you to do anything you don't want. But I think you want this as much as I do."

I do. Goodness, I do want this.

Ashanti folded her arms across her chest and mourned the absence of his strong muscles against her. She sucked in a deep breath.

"We have a long day tomorrow," she said.

He dropped his head forward and silently shook it.

"Okay," he whispered. Then he said it again, louder this time. "Okay. You call the shots here. I'll see you in the morning."

She waited until the door clicked before turning to the bed and falling facedown on it.

Her phone immediately buzzed in her back pocket. She expected to see Thad's name, but it was from Kara.

> You up?

Ashanti groaned and twisted onto her back. She texted back.

> Yes.

She refrained from tacking on *Why are you still up?* It was almost midnight back home, and the urge to tell Kara she should be sleeping was strong, but one did not give sixteen-year-olds bedtimes.

You and the Carol's Daughter wannabe are neck and neck, came Kara's next text.

She followed it with a screenshot of the vote tally for the finalists in the Young Black Woman Entrepreneur contest. The voting would be open for another five days.

A rush of excitement raced across Ashanti's skin at how close she was to winning such a life-changing prize. It was the reminder she'd needed. She'd come to New York with one goal, to use Duchess and Puddin's fifteen minutes of fame to her best advantage. Everything else was just noise.

Thanks for the update, Ashanti texted back. Wish me luck for tomorrow.

The luck you wish for is granted, she texted back. Followed by the genie emoji.

Now go to sleep, Ashanti couldn't help adding.

She needed to take her own advice, but the chances of getting any rest tonight were as slim as stealing back any of the covers from Duchess.

She pushed up from the bed and headed for the dresser. The two things she wanted most right now—sex and sleep—would not be happening anytime soon. A cupcake would have to do.

25

What in the entire fuck, Puddin'!"

Thad stood in the bathroom doorway, praying he was mistaken about what those dark brown blobs dotting the floor were, but knowing he wasn't. Mainly because it was the smell of liquid dog shit that had woken him from the piss-poor sleep he'd been struggling to get.

It was just after four a.m. A car was scheduled to pick them up at six thirty to get them to the studio in plenty of time before their spot in the morning show's nine o'clock hour.

"A half hour," Thad said. "All I wanted was another half hour of sleep."

Puddin' let out a mournful wail and began turning in a circle. Then he hunched down on his skinny legs.

"No," Thad said, but it was too late. Fuck! The bathroom floor looked like a dalmatian.

For a moment, Thad just stood there, paralyzed. What was he supposed to do with this? He didn't want to use the hotel's towels to pick it up, but he didn't want to call house-keeping to take care of it either. There wasn't a tip he could

leave that would be large enough to compensate a room attendant having to clean up this mess.

But before he took care of the bathroom, he had to see
about this dog.

"You *would* decide to get sick when you're hundreds of
miles away from your vet," Thad said.

His vet may not be close, but the next best thing was just
a door away.

He hated to wake Ashanti this early, but he knew she'd be
angrier if he let her sleep and risked Puddin's health. Seeing
as she was raising twin sixteen-year-olds, he doubted she had
her text messages silenced during overnight hours, so he took
a chance and sent a text.

Within one minute there was a knock on the door that
connected their two rooms.

"What's wrong with him?" she asked as soon as Thad
opened his side of the double doors.

He took a second to process her attire. The faded, thread-
bare New Orleans Saints T-shirt and cut-off sweats confirmed
everything he already knew. She was his perfect woman. He
had never been one for lacy lingerie—that shit was itchy, not
sexy. Give him soft, warm, and comfortable.

She looked *so* soft, warm, and comfortable.

"Thad, what's going on with Puddin'?" she asked.

He jerked to attention and shook his head.

"Uh, I don't know," he said, stepping out of the way so she
could enter the room. "He has the shits. The bathroom is a
disaster zone."

"Puddin' Pop," she called. "What's the matter?"

Why did Thad suddenly want a cute, stupid nickname?
He hated himself right now.

He started to close the door just as Duchess came wad-dling into the room on her stout little legs, following Ashanti to the bathroom. He joined them.

Ashanti looked up from the floor, where she was already attacking a liquid shit pile with toilet tissue.

"This isn't that bad," she said.

"Isn't bad?" What in the hell was it, if not bad?

"No. He's probably just nervous because he's in a strange environment. It tends to happen to some dogs. I have loper-amide in my bag because I was afraid Duchess would need some." She threw the wad of tissue in the toilet and flushed. Then she rubbed Puddin' on the head. "A little of that and a tummy rub should do the trick, huh, boy," Ashanti said.

She reached for more tissue.

"You don't have to do that, Ashanti. I'll clean this up," Thad said.

She shot him a grin. "I'm used to it."

"How does anyone get used to this?" Thad said, bringing his T-shirt up to cover his nose and mouth.

"Oh, don't worry, you'll get used to it soon too. Give me a sec."

She washed her hands, then went back to her room. After a couple of minutes she returned with a purple-and-white box, along with a bag of treats. She handed both to him.

"These cookies have a soft center. Take one pill and hide it in the soft part. Then give Duchess an unmedicated treat, because she'll be jealous if she's left out."

She returned to the bathroom while he sat on the edge of the bed and did as Ashanti had instructed. Once both dogs had eaten their treats, he scooted down onto the floor, pulled Puddin' to him, and started rubbing his belly. Duchess immediately walked over to his other hand and nudged it with her head.

"Really?" Thad asked.

Another nudge.

"Come here," he said, fighting back a grin as the Frenchie snuggled in next to him.

He closed his eyes, leaned his head back against the mattress, and wondered if he could make it as a doggy massage therapist if The PX didn't work out.

"You do not play fair."

Thad's head popped up. "Huh?"

Ashanti stood in front of him, hands on her hips. "I tell you that I can't get into any kind of involvement with you and then I catch you doing the absolute *most* to win me over? Not fair, Thad."

He grinned as he continued to rub the dogs. "I was a Ranger for eight years. It's not in my DNA to give up after the first try."

Duchess abandoned the head rub and waddled over to Ashanti. Puddin' was quick to join them.

"Well, I guess these hands aren't as magical as I thought," Thad said.

"I doubt that," Ashanti said. She looked at him, her eyes going wide.

"Yes, you said that out loud, but according to our agreement I'm supposed to ignore it."

She blew out a sigh. "I still have—" She looked at her watch. "Twenty more minutes before my alarm goes off. I'm going back to bed." She snapped her fingers. "Come Duchess. You too, Puddin'."

The three of them went into her room and she closed

the connecting door. It was hard for him not to feel left out, but it wasn't as if he had expected an invite when she'd just reminded him that she was against the two of them getting involved.

Remaining on the floor with his head against the bed, Thad closed his eyes and utilized those power-napping skills he'd honed during deployments.

Three hours later, as he downed his second cup of coffee in the greenroom at *Up Early with Leah and Luke!*, he was forced to acknowledge that his power-napping skills didn't have the same effect as they used to. He would have to count on caffeine and adrenaline to take up the slack.

Thad had convinced himself that Puddin's early-morning shit show portended how the rest of the day would progress, but he was cautiously optimistic that all was not headed for the outhouse. In a way, he was grateful for Puddin' and his weak stomach. The incident had smoothed the edges of tension he feared would show up between him and Ashanti after the way they'd left things last night. When he'd met her in the hallway a couple of hours after she'd returned to her room with the dogs, it was as if that kiss between them, and any uneasiness it may have ushered in, had never happened.

He wasn't sure how he felt about that part. He was still working out the steps forward in his head.

Ashanti stood at the buffet, adding flavored creamer to a cup of coffee. The dogs were in another holding room because, as it had been explained to them, the guest for the segment just before theirs was allergic to pet dander. A bonus and a raise for whoever had come up with this morning's schedule.

Thad walked up to Ashanti and snagged a mini croissant from the table.

"You nervous?" he asked.

"Tell me I'm hiding it well, even if you have to lie to me."

He laughed. "Actually, you are. That's why I asked."

"Are *you* nervous?"

"Not as much as I thought I'd be. I felt a lot better after that production assistant said the segment will only be four minutes and twenty seconds. We were on that podcast for an hour yesterday. Less than five minutes today should be a breeze."

An old Bruce Springsteen song sounded throughout the studio, a teaser to the story that was right after theirs on the lineup about some charity event the legend was headlining in his home state of New Jersey. The PA came into the greenroom.

"You're up," she said. "Puddin' and Duchess are being brought in now."

They were led to a living room setup with a cream-colored couch that had to have been custom made—at least eight people could fit on that thing—along with two upholstered chairs.

The hosts simultaneously rose from the anchor desk adjacent to the set and started for them. They were both taller than Thad had expected. And they were undeniably twins. If Leah wore her hair slicked back instead of in a crown of coily natural curls, Thad wouldn't be able to tell them apart.

"Thanks so much for coming to the show, and for bringing

the dogs all the way to New York," she greeted. "I'm handling this segment, but Luke wanted to meet the pair."

"And the two of you," Luke called from where he crouched before the dogs.

"Thanks so much for the invitation," Ashanti said. "I'm such a big fan. I still can't believe I'm here."

"Coming in," someone called from the shadowed part of the studio. He, Ashanti, and Leah took their places on the couch and Luke hauled ass.

"We have a real treat for you all this morning," Leah opened. "And it all started with a dog biscuit."

A short clip of Duchess and Puddin' getting caught with the Duchess Delights treat ran, followed by ten seconds of people's online reactions to the video.

"I think it's safe to say the country is obsessed with Puddin' and Duchess," Leah said once the montage ended. "What has this been like for the two of you and, more importantly, for the dogs?"

Thad sat back and watched as Ashanti gave a spirited account of all that had transpired in the past week without any hint of the nerves she'd feared. She was masterful, getting in mentions of both the daycare and Duchess Delights.

"And how about you, Thaddeus? How does it feel to know your poodle is one of the most beloved dogs in the world?"

Ashanti's eyes widened with apprehension. Thad flashed her a smile before focusing on Leah.

"Makes me feel like the luckiest man alive. Everyone loves Puddin', but I'm the one who gets to play fetch with him every day."

He couldn't be certain, but he was pretty sure he heard Ashanti squeak. He glanced at her and had to cover his laugh with a cough. How could she look to be on the verge of exploding yet look so damn good at the same time?

"Excuse me. What was that, Leah?" Thad asked.

"I asked about your venture, The PX, that will soon open in New Orleans. I absolutely love the story behind it."

Thad knew their time was running short, so he gave a brief overview of the mission behind The PX and their push to get it up and running by Veterans Day.

"I know what's about to become my new social media obsession," Leah said, after Thad mentioned following the progress of their build on The PX's Instagram account. She pivoted back to Ashanti. "Ashanti, are Duchess Delights available online?"

She cleared her throat. "Not yet, but we plan to launch an online storefront soon. Along with a bakery once we're at our new location."

"Well, I'm sure I speak for every pet owner in the country when I say that I cannot wait to order. And can people contact Barkingham Palace if they want their fur baby to be treated like royalty for the day?"

"Of course," she answered.

"There you have it, folks," Leah said. "Stick around. Just after the break we'll tell you how to score your chance at seeing The Boss live in concert while supporting a worthy cause."

"That was amazing," Leah said once they'd gone to commercial. "We went over our allotted time, but the interview was going so well that the producer told me to just roll with it."

"Thanks again for having us," Ashanti said.

Leah leaned in closer and said in a slightly lower voice, "I have to say, you two make such a lovely couple." She winked. "The chemistry pops."

Thad was about to tell her that he thought the same, but then the production assistant ushered them back to the greenroom.

"Hang here for just a minute," the PA said, then was gone yet again.

"Oh my God, why did I say that?" Ashanti asked, clamping both hands to her head.

"What?"

"That people can call the daycare. Deja is going to murder me. Or she's going to quit." She dropped her hands and punched Thad on the arm. "And what about you? 'I get to play fetch with him every day.' I almost lost it."

"I noticed," Thad said with an unrepentant grin. "I thought that was pretty good."

"Be honest, you were part of some clandestine counterterrorism unit or something," she said.

"Why would you think that?"

"Because that lie came out much too easily for someone not used to doing it."

"You don't know if it's a lie. Puddin' and I may play fetch every morning, and he just doesn't tell you."

Her freckles seemed to dance with her grin. "You are full of that stuff I cleaned up in your bathroom this morning."

One of her braids fell from the updo she wore and he brought his hand up, pausing a moment before pushing it behind her ear.

"You did good out there to say you were nervous," he said. He let his fingers linger a second longer than necessary, reluctant to leave behind the feel of her soft skin.

"So did you," she said, her voice restrained as she stared up at him. "I...I think Ridley will be pleased with the amount of charisma you found between yesterday and this morning."

"It had been staring back at me in the bathroom mirror this entire time. Shocked the hell out of me."

Her laugh was gentle. "Well, keep it going. This media circus is just getting started."

26

The production assistant returned and guided them to another area of the building filled with people wearing headsets and carrying electronic tablets. Ashanti had never been one to be impressed by celebrity, but she was disappointed that, aside from Leah and Luke, Puddin' and Duchess seemed to be the biggest celebrities in the building this morning. Why wasn't Kerry Washington or Octavia Spencer out promoting a new movie?

"Wait here and Eliza will be in to start the interview," the PA said.

"Eliza?" Thad asked.

"Cunningham?" Ashanti added. "She's the correspondent who does the stories on struggling mom-and-pop restaurants, isn't she?"

"She also handles the fluff pieces for content on our all-day streaming channel," the production assistant said before leaving them yet again.

Thad hooked a thumb over his shoulder. "She called us a fluff piece. I think I'm insulted."

"Don't be. The world needs more fluff," Ashanti said. "But what is this second interview about? This is the first I'm hearing of it."

It turned out there was much more to their visit than those five minutes on-screen with Leah and Luke. For the next two hours, Thad, Ashanti, Puddin', and Duchess were paraded around the studio, having their pictures taken for the show's social media channels, and shooting short video clips of them playing with the dogs. Puddin' refused to go after the Frisbee Thad threw, proving his early crack about playing fetch was, indeed, a lie.

They were then subjected to two additional interviews, which they were told may or may not make it to the network's website later today, depending on the amount of breaking news. By the time they were done, it was time for lunch and a nap.

"I wish we could skip that podcast. I just want to eat and sleep," Ashanti said to Thad as they gathered their belongings. They were told a car would pick them up in twenty minutes to bring them back to their hotel.

"Didn't you get the text from Dom?" Thad asked.

"What text?" She pulled out her phone.

There was a text from Dominique and one from Ridley. She quickly read Dom's, which—*thank you, thank you, thank you*—said the podcaster needed to push their interview back by a day. Dom had already switched them to a later flight for tomorrow. She honestly deserved every single cent she charged. Whatever she charged.

Ashanti pulled up Ridley's text next.

DID YOU FUCK THAT MAN LAST NIGHT?

That text had been followed twenty minutes later by another.

BITCH, CALL ME.

Ashanti closed the app and looked over her shoulder to make sure Thad hadn't seen it. He was attaching Puddin' to his leash.

"I need to make a quick call," she told him, then walked a few yards away so that she could call Ridley.

"What took you so damn long?" Ridley answered. "I texted you an hour ago."

"Woman, what is *wrong* with you?" Ashanti hissed.

"What?" Ridley asked, the epitome of innocence, as if she hadn't sent those all-caps texts.

"Uh, the texts you sent?" Ashanti asked. "What was that about?"

"Oh, *that* was about you eye-fucking soldier boy the entire time you two were on camera," Ridley said.

"I was not!"

Please, say I was not.

"Girl, please. I'm surprised that man didn't need a cigarette after that interview. So did you screw him last night?" Ridley asked.

"No!" Ashanti said.

Did she think about it? All night long. But she would falsely confess to robbing a bank before admitting to the thoughts she'd had of Thad while she lay in bed last night. And in the shower this morning.

"So, what did you think of the interview?" Ashanti asked,

steering the conversation away from the subject of Thad and how much she did, indeed, want to screw him.

"It was perfection!" Ridley said. "You were both witty and charming and everything you were supposed to be. Wait, no. It wasn't perfect because you forgot to bring up the Black entrepreneur contest, but I think you'll still get a heap of votes because of Luke and Leah."

"I considered mentioning it, but then I thought it would sound too desperate, like those musicians who plug their upcoming albums when presenting awards at the Grammy's."

"That's what showbiz is all about," Ridley said. "Oh, and I know the podcast was postponed, but Dom set up this other thing for you all this afternoon. She's going to email instructions in a minute."

Ashanti threw her head back and rubbed the space between her eyes. She had been *so* close to getting that nap.

"Another podcast?" Ashanti asked.

"No, a photo shoot. One of the biggest dog charities in New York is putting together their calendar for next year, and when they found out the country's most famous dogs were in town they, of course, requested Duchess and Puddin' be in it."

"I don't know about this one, Rid. Will a calendar that comes out *next* year really be worth the trouble?"

"Hey, it's not what you thought you would be doing up there, but it's still all good. Trust Dom. She wouldn't have set it up if she didn't think it would help your overall PR goals. And shag soldier boy tonight."

"Bye, Ridley," Ashanti said.

Just as she was about to tuck her phone back into her bag, she got a text from Kara.

> Just watched You on L & L. You and Thad
> look like ur banging each other. You did
> good tho.

Good God. Exactly what did she do during that segment? She was almost afraid to watch it. She didn't *feel* as if she had been eye-fucking Thad. Then again, can one tell when they're eye-fucking someone?

I am not banging anyone. And thanks, Ashanti texted back. You should be in class.

> Going.

Three dots appeared, indicating that Kara was sending another text. They disappeared, then reappeared.

What? Ashanti texted.

> Didn't want to worry you but Ken didn't show
> up at school today.

Ashanti's heart stopped beating. Kara sent three texts back-to-back-to-back.

> I talked to her. She's not hurt.

> Well not physically.

> Don't text her. Just let her be. Will check on
> her at lunch.

A fourth text.

Gotta go.

Ashanti didn't consider for even a minute not contacting Kendra, but instead of texting, she called. The phone rang until voicemail picked up. She called again, with the same result.

This time she texted:

Pick up or I'm sending the police over to do a wellness check.

Before she could call again, her phone rang. The picture of Kendra on the carousel at City Park during her and Kara's eighth birthday party popped up on her screen.

"What's wrong?" Ashanti asked.

"Besides my twin sister being a narc?" she asked.

"Kendra, what is going on? Are you sick?"

"I'm okay," she said. "I'm not sick. I was just feeling… blah. Kara skips school all the time. I figured I deserved a day."

Ashanti rested her palm against her forehead and pulled in a deep, relieved breath.

"Ken, I…I don't know what is going on with you, but we are *very* close to needing a come-to-Jesus moment."

Her sister paused for a bit, then said, "Maybe we can talk when you get back home."

Ashanti's breath caught in her throat. "Yes," she said. She began to pace. "Please, that's all I want. Whatever is wrong we will handle it—or you will. I won't try to swoop in and fix anything for you if that's not what you're looking for from me. I'll just listen. But I need to know what's going on."

"Okay," Kendra said. "I promise. We'll talk when you get home. Now go back to doing your little *Puddin' and Duchess Take Manhattan* thing. I watched the Luke and Leah show this morning. You did good. Just try not to get pregnant while you're out there."

"Kendra!" Ashanti said.

"Bye."

Ashanti rubbed between her eyes again. The entire country probably thought she and Thad were sleeping together. She was surprised Evie hadn't said anything.

And, just like that, a text popped up from Evie.

> Great show this morning. Puddin' and
> Duchess are rock stars. I can tell you and
> Thad got it on. Get it, girl!

It was followed by the gif of a twerking Tina Belcher from *Bob's Burgers*.

"Everything okay?"

Ashanti yelped, clamping her hand to her chest and spinning around to find Thad just a few inches away.

"Whoa, whoa," he said, steadying her with his hands on her shoulders. "No more coffee for you." He frowned, his eyes narrowing as they zeroed in on her. "Are you sure you're okay?"

"I'm fine," Ashanti said. She shook her head and blew out a calming breath. "It's fine. I thought there was a mini disaster happening with one of the twins, but all seems to be okay."

He nodded. "Good. Well, our car is here," he said. "I don't know if you've had the chance to check your email—"

"Ridley told me about the photo shoot," she said. She glanced up at him. "Are you on board with this?"

"Do I have a choice?"

"Of course. All choices come with consequences, though."

"Yeah, I'm not about to face the wrath of Ridley or Dominique."

"Forget about them. Can you imagine what Mrs. Frances would say if she found out Puddin' had the chance to be Dog of the Month in some big, fancy calendar and you turned it down?"

Thad closed his eyes and shook his shoulders in a pretend shiver. Ashanti laughed.

"Let's go," he said. "I've already talked to the driver. He's going to bring us straight to where the photo shoot is taking place. Oh, and here's a bonus. It's only two blocks from the Empire State Building. We won't be able to go up there with the dogs, but at least you'll get to see it up close. Maybe we can snap a few pictures of them walking around Manhattan for Barkingham Palace's social media."

"Watch out there," she said with a grin. "You're starting to sound like a dog person."

27

Thad wedged his finger between the bow tie and his neck while he silently cursed whoever had come up with the idea that dogs deserved to be on calendars.

Why had he agreed to do this photo shoot?

He felt like every kind of fool known to man, standing under these hot-as-hell lights dressed in a top hat and bow tie. His only consolation was that Puddin' was stuck wearing the same, and he didn't seem to be enjoying himself either.

Ashanti, on the other hand, was living this up, snapping pictures with her phone and shouting out words of encouragement to Puddin'. Seeing the smile on her face as he and the dog were instructed to strike pose after ridiculous pose was the only reason Thad hadn't thrown this stupid hat and tie in the trash and hauled ass out of here.

And his grandmother, of course. He couldn't help but think about how much Grams would love these pictures when they were done. She would probably buy a calendar for every resident of the assisted living facility.

"Smile, Thad," Ashanti called out to him. "Not everyone

gets to be the very first month in the calendar. You should feel like a rock star."

"Every rock star I've ever seen has had sweat dripping down their faces like a waterfall, so in a way, you're right."

"Just a few more shots," the photographer said. "I want you to hold up Puddin's paw so that it looks as if you two are high-fiving."

Thad barely managed to hold in his groan.

Of course, Puddin' didn't cooperate. It took another ten minutes before the photographer was able to get the shot she wanted.

"We're done with January," the woman called. "Now it's time for *my* birthday month: May! Ashanti, your costumes are behind the curtain. You and Duchess can get ready while I replace the backdrop and props."

Ten minutes later, Thad's attitude about today's photo shoot had taken a complete one-eighty.

He stood to the side, arms crossed over his chest as he watched Ashanti pose in an airy, soft peach dress with a crown of colorful flowers propped on her head. Duchess looked as if she had been made for the camera in her matching peach tutu. Even a non–dog lover like him couldn't deny that she was cute with her flower crown askew on her head and her stubby tail wagging like a flag in a windstorm.

"I have to stop snapping, but I can't," the photographer said. "These are just too adorable."

"Well, if you don't stop soon both me and Duchess will probably have an accident," Ashanti said.

"Okay, okay." The photographer lowered her camera. "Both dogs probably need a potty break, but I would like to get a few shots with both of them together before we wrap up."

Thad took Duchess and Puddin' out to the tiny six-by-eight patio that was conveniently equipped with a couple of squares of landscaping sod for the dogs to use to relieve themselves. He returned to find the photographer up on a ladder, unclipping the spring meadow backdrop from the rod that held it up. Ashanti was scrolling through her phone, a smile brightening her face.

"What has you smiling?" Thad asked.

"Instagram." She took only a second to glance up at him before returning to her phone. "Kara or Dom added still shots of our interview and people are losing their minds over how cute Duchess and Puddin' were this morning." She pulled her bottom lip between her teeth. "Unfortunately, those rumors seem to be spreading." She looked up at him again. "Everyone thinks we're a couple."

Thad hunched his shoulders. "I usually don't care what everyone thinks, but in this instance..."

Ashanti sent him what she probably thought was a mean glare. All Thad could think about was how cute she looked when her freckles deepened with her blush.

"I'm pretty sure you're going to approve of this last backdrop," the photographer said. She hooked the grommets through two hooks then let the backdrop unfurl with a flourish. It was a portrait of Buckingham Palace.

"Ah!" Ashanti squealed. "I love it!"

"Aaaaand," the photographer said, drawing the word out as she darted to the boxes of props. She pulled out a tiara and crown. "Accessories worthy of a duchess and her duke."

They were nearing the two-and-a-half-hour mark of what was supposed to be a two-hour photo shoot, but Thad knew better than to say anything. Other than that stupid bow tie that had tried to choke him, the afternoon had not been all that painful.

But he was still relieved when, ten minutes later, the photographer wrapped up the photo shoot. They left shortly after.

"We are totally having picture day at Barkingham Palace," Ashanti said. "I'm ordering one of those backdrops as soon as we're back home."

"I could have predicted that the moment that backdrop fluttered to the floor. Your eyes lit up."

"It's so adorable! This is also a genius fundraising tool. I'll probably buy three dozen of those calendars for holiday gifts."

They spent the next hour playing tourists, snapping pictures in front of Penn Station, the Garden, Macy's and, of course, the Empire State Building. Thad found out the Flatiron Building was on her list of must-sees, so they headed south.

They ended up at Madison Square Park. Puddin' and Duchess were both recognized, of course, and after taking pictures with fellow dogs, Thad unclipped both their leashes and let them run free in the smaller, enclosed dog park.

"What an afternoon," Ashanti said as she plopped down on a bench. "I needed this."

"I could tell," Thad said without thinking.

She frowned. "What do you mean?"

Shit. If he'd just messed up the lighthearted mood of their afternoon, he would assign fifty push-ups to his damn self.

"I wasn't going to say anything, but earlier, when we were still at the Luke and Leah show, you seemed upset," Thad said. "You always have such a positive vibe about you. Even when you were chewing me out for buying the Bywater house out from under you, it was the politest chewing out I've ever seen."

She laughed. "And here I thought I was being too mean to you," she said.

"My sister has given me more attitude when wishing me a happy birthday, Ashanti. You are seriously the most upbeat person I've ever met. Seeing you upset earlier threw me a little. You said all was okay with your sisters, but..." He shrugged. "It still threw me."

"Everything is okay," she said. Then added, "For the most part."

"And the other part?" he asked.

This time her laugh held very little humor. "You know that saying 'smile to keep from crying'?"

He didn't like the sound of that. Thad settled his elbows on his thighs and looked over at her. "You want to talk about it?"

She sent him a wan smile. "Thanks, but you didn't come to New York to be my therapist, Thad. I'm not unloading all of my shi—crap on you."

"First, it's okay to say the word *shit* around me. I promise I won't judge you, because I will likely say much worse without even realizing it. Second, I would never suggest that I'm capable of being anyone's therapist. I've been seen by enough therapists to know that I could never do the work they do.

"Yes," Thad said at the sight of her arched brows. "I have no problem admitting that I've been to therapy. Some mandated by the US Army and a couple of times just on my own. I've got shit I've had to work out. I could probably do with a few more sessions. My point is that I'm not trying to be your therapist. Just a friend," he said.

"And as your friend, I want you to feel comfortable enough to share what's bothering you. I'm pretty good at listening to people get things off their chests. It was a requirement of my job for a long time."

"That sounds like a therapist."

Thad laughed as he realized she was right. "I guess a commanding officer does have a few things in common with a therapist." He nudged her with his elbow. "What's going on, Ashanti?"

She tilted her head back and pinched her eyes shut.

"It's Kendra, the twin you haven't met. She's been so sullen and moody lately—far beyond typical teenage moodiness. Kara is pulling the twin sister code of silence on me, so I can't get anything out of her." She released a deep sigh, running her fingers through the skinny braids she'd unbound after they left the photo shoot. "The thing is, I'm not sure Kara knows what's going on either, and that worries me more than anything. I've gotten the silent treatment before—Kendra didn't speak to me for a week after I wouldn't allow her to go to a school dance last year—but freezing out Kara is different."

"Do you think it's boy trouble?"

"That would be girl trouble if you're talking about Kendra—she came out two years ago." She shook her head. "But it's not that. She and her girlfriend broke up last year, but they're still good friends. Zalia doesn't know what's going on with her either."

She hunched her shoulders. "The good thing is, today Kendra told me that she's ready to talk. Or, at least, she will be ready to talk once I get back home."

Ashanti rubbed her eyes with the heels of her hands.

"I just...it's so hard to figure out if I'm doing the right thing with them. Sometimes, every decision seems like the wrong one."

"Yeah, I've been there," Thad said. "I got off on somewhat of a rocky start as a commanding officer. Von said it's because I wanted to be more friend than CO, but that wasn't it. Some of those kids needed a father figure and I wanted to do for them what my grandfather did for me." He shrugged. "But, of course, some tried to take advantage of my benevolence."

"Because teenagers will always try you," she laughed.

Damn, but he loved her laugh. He wasn't sure he had ever even taken note of another woman's laugh before.

Thad glanced out at the park to make sure Duchess and Puddin' weren't getting into anything dangerous, then angled toward Ashanti. "What makes you think you're messing up with your sisters?"

"I don't know. With the daycare and now Duchess Delights, it feels as if I'm not devoting enough time to them. Yet, when I ask if they want to hang out, they say no. Especially Kendra."

"They're teenagers."

"I know. I just...I wonder if they wouldn't have been better off with my dad's older sister." She immediately shook her head. "That's not true. If there is one thing I *do* know, it's that they are better off with me than with Anita. The girls call her Atilla, as in the Hun."

"Damn," Thad said.

"Yes, she's *that* bad," Ashanti said. She pulled her lip between her teeth. "It's just...I have to look on the bright side of everything, because if I allow myself to wallow in all that bad—the shitty stuff—I'm afraid I'll drown."

"I've met your friends, Ashanti. They wouldn't let you drown."

He wanted to touch her so badly. To reach out and take

her hand in his and bring it to his lips. And then bring his lips to hers. He wanted to kiss that sad smile from her face.

But that wasn't what she wanted from him.

"That's true," she said. "Evie and Ridley are amazing."

"And now you have this *new* friend in your life who doesn't mind listening to you rant about insufferable teenagers."

She looked over at him, her eyes glinting with amusement and something else. Something more. Something that made him wonder if he was wrong about how she would react to him kissing her again.

"That's true," she repeated, her voice as soft as her gaze as she regarded him with an awareness Thad had never seen from her before. As if she was only now recognizing what he had been feeling since that first day he walked into her daycare.

But then she tore her gaze away from his, focusing on the stand of trees on the opposite side of the park.

"Um, I think I owe you an explanation," she said.

He frowned. "For what?"

"For why I keep insisting that we ignore what we both know is happening between us," she said. She glanced at him, then at the trees, and then finally back at him. "Like I said, it's complicated."

"I can handle complicated," Thad said.

"Even though my parents specified in their will that I be granted custody of Kendra and Kara if anything were to happen to them, Anita petitioned the court for legal custody. She said I was too young to raise them, and that my workload as a fourth-year veterinary school student would be too much for me to handle."

"So you quit school," Thad said.

She shook her head. "I tried to make it work for a while.

The judge decided it was unfair to assume I would not be able to take care of the girls while also pursing my degree. Everything was going okay until one night when I got caught up at a study group." She massaged her right temple with her thumb. "Kendra and Kara were at day camp, so I asked my boyfriend at the time to pick them up. I didn't realize he'd spent the day out at the Lakefront drinking with his buddies."

"Don't tell me..."

She nodded. "Thankfully, he got stopped for a DUI *before* he picked up the girls, but he told the arresting officer that he had been on his way to get them. It was all the ammunition Anita needed."

"Shit," Thad whispered.

"Anita tried to convince the courts that I was unfit because of Simon's actions." Her bottom lip trembled, a clear indication the accusation still affected her. "*That's* when I quit school. It's also when I decided that putting dating off for a few years wasn't a big sacrifice if it meant not jeopardizing my guardianship of the girls."

"But you quit veterinary school in your final year. Wasn't that enough of a sacrifice?"

"When it comes to Kendra and Kara, there is nothing that I will not do to ensure that Anita never gains custody." She cut her eyes at him, though a grin tugged at her lips. "I was doing just fine until you came along with your cute smile and that sexy tattoo on your arm that keeps playing peekaboo."

Thad wanted to laugh, but the steadfastness he heard in her voice as she explained her rationale for not dating wrecked him. Her aunt's unreasonable expectations were straight up bullshit.

"You didn't ask for my opinion, and yeah, my motives

are selfish," Thad admitted. "But this is just wrong. You were young, and your boyfriend, though an asshole, was also young. It's unfair that your aunt can continue to hold something that happened years ago against you."

"Tell that to her," Ashanti said with a humorless laugh. "This isn't solely about her though," she continued. "The incident with Simon reminded me why I need to be careful about who I bring around the girls. I'm raising impressionable teenagers. There's a responsibility that comes with that and I refuse to take it lightly."

How could he argue with that?

"I get it," Thad said.

He didn't like it. He fucking hated it, to be honest, but he understood and respected her stance.

Duchess came waddling over to the bench, with Puddin' not far behind. Ashanti leaned over and rubbed the Frenchie's head and Thad automatically did the same to Puddin'. He didn't even hesitate.

"Thank you," Ashanti said. "For listening. For…all of this. If you'd told me a few weeks ago that *you* would be one of the friends I shared anything with, I would never have believed you. But life is funny. It has a way of moving in directions you could have never imagined."

She nudged her head toward Puddin'. "It looks as if you two are finally starting to get along."

"See what I mean?" Thad said. "You're eternally hopeful, even when it's a lost cause."

She laughed. "Nothing is ever a lost cause," she said.

"Maybe you're right," he said.

He was counting on it.

28

"Are your eyes still closed?"

A mixture of arousal and anticipation skirted down Ashanti's spine at the sound of Thad's gruff whisper, his breath warm against her ear. Arousal was the last thing she should be feeling when surrounded by dozens of New Yorkers, but with her eyes closed, the rest of her senses were heightened, amplifying Thad's every word. His every touch.

His fingertips against the small of her back caused her skin to burn as he guided her to what he assured her was one of the most unique views of the city.

"Yes, my eyes are still closed," she answered. "I'm putting a lot of trust in you, so this had better be worth it."

"It will be," he said. His hands moved to her shoulders as he positioned her against some sort of railing. "Now, tip your head back and open your eyes."

Ashanti did as he instructed and released a gasp.

"Told you," Thad said, a satisfied smugness lacing his voice. He earned the right to be smug.

"This is breathtaking," Ashanti said as she looked up

at the inky sky, the tips of several skyscrapers skirting the periphery of the view from the Vessel.

She had never even heard of the Vessel before Thad told her about it. The spiral staircase in Manhattan's Hudson Yards area looked like a cross between a honeycomb and a hornet's nest, and the view looking up from on the ground on the inside was just as remarkable.

"The structure is beautiful from the outside, but you were right about this vantage point," Ashanti admitted.

Dominique had called while they were still at Madison Square Park with news that the Gen Z-er behind the Dog Whisper TikTok account could fit them in for a quick interview, but they would have to get there within a half hour if they wanted to be on the live show. Thankfully, the interview was in Gramercy Park, just a few blocks from where they were at the time.

After the TikTok Live, they'd brought the dogs back to the hotel and headed out with the intention of fitting in as many of the food spots that remained on Ashanti's list. That's when Thad had mentioned the one other tourist site she had to see.

"It's too bad we can't go to the upper landings," Ashanti said. "I can only imagine how beautiful the view is from up there."

"I was able to go to the top before they shut that down. It's nice, but you can see that view from dozens of buildings around Manhattan. There's something about this view when you're looking up. The sky looks different."

"Gorgeous," Ashanti said.

She wobbled and caught his arm to steady herself. Before she knew what she was doing, she squeezed his bicep, marveling at the tautness.

"Goodness, you're solid," Ashanti said. It shouldn't have caught her off guard, yet it did. So much about him surprised her.

"Oh, wait!" Ashanti said as something occurred to her. "Am I doing it now?"

"Doing what?" Thad asked.

She took out her phone and opened the camera app. Her eyes didn't look any different than they usually did.

She blew out an exasperated breath. "I still can't tell."

"Ashanti?" His voice was cautious, as if he was afraid of startling her. "What are you talking about?"

"Apparently, during our segment on *Leah and Luke*, I was...well..."

"You were?" Thad encouraged.

Was she really about to say this?

"Eye-fucking you," she said. She covered her face in her hands and groaned. "I cannot believe I just said that."

Thad's deep chuckle made her face heat even more. "I wasn't going to bring it up until later," he said. "But, yes, you were."

"Oh, God." She groaned again. "Why didn't you say anything?"

"What was I supposed to say? Thank you?"

If the FDNY happened to drive past them right now they would hose her down. She peeked at him through her fingers. His grin was both sexy and understanding, which, for some reason made this even worse.

"You already know the drill," Ashanti said. "Just ignore it."

"Yeah, about that," he said. "No."

She dropped her hands and jerked her head back. "What?"

"No," he repeated. "I've decided that the only thing I'm

ignoring from now on is that agreement we made. This?" He gestured between the two of them. "I'm done ignoring it. No more acting. No more pretending I don't want you."

"Thad, don't."

"Don't what? What don't you want me to do, Ashanti? Acknowledge that you're the first person I have been even remotely interested in since longer than I can remember? You're smart. You're funny. And you made me sort of like my grandmother's dog, which means you probably have magical powers or something."

She laughed despite not wanting to encourage him. Ashanti shook her head, wishing things could be different.

She ached with the desire to admit that she felt the same way about him, but then she heard Anita's voice in her head and remembered why she couldn't.

"Why are you doing this?" she asked.

"Because I've seen too much bad shit in my life to pass up something I believe can be amazing. I have to at least try to see if it could turn into something deeper."

"But you don't get to decide that on your own," she said.

"No, you need to be a willing participant. I'm just letting you know that I'm no longer playing this game where we ignore that we're into each other," he said. "I didn't want to risk messing up our time together in New York, but after last night it's a risk I'm willing to take, because I don't want to return to New Orleans and have things be the way they were when we left. I want you to be more to me than just the person who watches my grandmother's dog."

"Thad," she whispered. "I told you already, I can't be in a relationship with you right now."

"There is no set way for a relationship to operate," he said.

"We can go slow. At a sloth's pace, if that's what you need right now. It doesn't have to be all or nothing, Ashanti."

She swallowed hard. "I—" she started, but he cut her off.

"Can I show you?" he asked.

"Show me what?"

"This." He captured her chin between his fingers and tipped her head up. "What I'm about to show you right now? This is how slow we can take it."

He dipped his head and brushed his lips so softly against hers that she barely felt them. He applied slightly more pressure, but not enough to open her mouth. So Ashanti did it for him, passing her tongue along the seam of his lips as her hand snaked up his back to cradle his head.

He opened his mouth and sucked her tongue inside, and Ashanti nearly forgot where she was.

She was quickly reminded when she heard a child giggling, followed by an irritated voice.

"That's what hotel rooms are for," a woman said.

Ashanti and Thad broke apart like two teenagers caught kissing underneath the bleachers. She had no doubt her freckles were the color of chili peppers. Her face felt just as hot.

"You're going to get us arrested for indecent exposure," she told Thad.

"You're the one who added tongue. We were supposed to go slow, remember?"

She flashed him a mean look, then remembered that her mean look was milquetoast.

"Come on," Thad said. "You said you wanted to go to that brownie place in Chelsea Market."

They made their way there via the High Line, the parkway that stretched between Hudson Yard and the Chelsea neighborhood. Ashanti bought so much stuff that she was certain she would need to buy another bag in order to get it all home.

By the time they made it back to their hotel, it was nearing midnight. Yet her body was still so wired from that kiss that she knew she would not be falling asleep anytime soon.

Once again, Thad walked her to her door, even though it was only steps away from his.

They stood in the hallway, which hummed with enough electricity to light up every building on this island of millions. Evie's and Ridley's advice popped into her head, but Ashanti immediately batted it away. She was not sleeping with this man tonight. Maybe not ever.

No. She wouldn't say that. She knew better than to try to predict the future, and she loved herself too much to dismiss the idea of ever being with Thad. Would he be willing to wait two years, until losing custody of her sisters was no longer a threat? She couldn't predict that either.

What she did know was that she was not ready to sleep with him tonight.

Lies.

So maybe her body was ready, but she had never been one to allow her baser needs to call the shots.

"Well, goodnight," Ashanti said. "The podcast isn't until the afternoon, so we can take our time in the morning. It's been a while since I've been able to sleep in."

She stared at a tiny stain on the wallpaper because just the thought of looking into Thad's eyes at the moment made her feel as if she would catch fire. She let herself into the room and closed the door, pressing the back of her head against it like the lead actress in a sappy rom-com.

Maybe that's what she could do tonight. Take a shower, get into her pjs and watch *The Proposal* or *Two Can Play That Game*. At least a dogwalker had taken the pups out.

After giving Duchess the attention she demanded, she showered and threw on her LSU softball T-shirt and a pair of jogger cutoffs and got in bed. But when she reached for the remote, her hand stopped midair.

Ashanti stared at the door that connected her room to Thad's.

"You are not seriously considering this," she whispered.

Yes, she was.

She was more than a thousand miles away from home. A thousand miles away from Anita, the daycare, the twins. A thousand miles away from all the other responsibilities that ran her life. She could push them out of her mind for this one night, couldn't she?

She sucked her bottom lip between her teeth, remembering the way Thad's muscle had felt under her hand. Was his entire body that solid? She already knew the answer to that; she could tell just by looking at him.

She peeled away the bedding covering her lower half and scooted off the mattress. Ashanti felt as if she were having an out-of-body experience, as if she were hovering above the room, watching herself walk to the connecting door.

She was sure her heart would bruise her rib cage with the way it pounded against her chest. She gave one last valiant attempt at reminding herself of all the reasons she shouldn't do this, but her mind wouldn't allow any of those arguments to take up space. All she could think about was how much she desperately wanted this—wanted *him*.

If there were any regrets, she would deal with them in the morning. Right now, she was going for what she wanted.

She knocked on the connecting door.

She could hear Thad shuffling just beyond it, as if he was hopping off the bed. A second later, the door opened.

His gray ARMY T-shirt and matching sweatpants had both seen better days, but on him they looked perfect.

"You needed something?" he asked.

"Um, yeah." She licked her lips. "Duchess was feeling lonely. I think she wants to spend the night. And, uh, I think I want to join her."

He stared at her and, just like that, Ashanti understood what it meant to be eye-fucked.

He stepped aside and she entered his room.

The moment she crossed the threshold, Thad scooped her into his arms and propped her against the wall.

She knew he would be strong, but not *this* strong. Ashanti looped one arm around his neck and braced her other hand against his firm chest. It felt like a concrete wall underneath her fingers.

She pulled at his T-shirt, needing it off. She wanted to feel him without the barrier, because while his muscles were hard, she suspected his skin would be soft and silky. She needed to know if her suspicions were accurate.

Thad pinned her against the wall with his pelvis, wedging his hips between her thighs to hold her in place while he used one hand to tug his T-shirt up. Ashanti handled the rest, pulling it over his head.

Better. So, so much better.

He gripped her hips and thrust his tongue into her mouth.

His erection was rigid, pressing into her belly and setting her entire body on fire.

"This up-against-the-wall thing looks great in the movies, but I need you on the bed," Ashanti said.

"I think I can wait that long," Thad said. "Maybe." He cradled her bottom with one arm and her back with the other, then turned and carried her the seven or so feet to the bed.

"Made it," he said. Then he dove for her mouth, plunging his tongue inside and stroking like the Army gave out medals for it. Ashanti remembered their time at the Vessel tonight and closed her eyes so that she could heighten the sensation of his body against hers.

Their mouths remained fused together as she pulled off her shorts. Thad pushed up her shirt and the sports bra she wore to bed—why hadn't she thought to get rid of it—both bunching at her neck as he roughly explored her nipples with his teeth and tongue.

"We're one hundred percent certain about this, right?" he asked as he trailed his lips up her neck and along her shoulder, peeling her shirt and bra off the rest of the way.

"One thousand percent."

"Thank God," he said, the words leaving his lips in a desperate prayer.

He reached for his wallet on the nightstand and, within moments, had a condom open and rolled onto his intimidatingly thick erection.

Ashanti ground the back of her head into the pillow as Thad splayed his fingers across her thighs and opened them wide. Her back bowed off the bed when he entered her, the shock of sensations she hadn't felt in so long sending her soaring. She lifted her hips to meet him, thrusting up as he plunged down, her body craving every delicious inch of his.

He returned to her breast, lapping at her nipple and closing his mouth over it as he sank deeper inside of her.

"This is so much better than watching a rom-com," Ashanti said.

Thad's head popped up. "What?"

"Ignore me," she said. "Please, just…just…"

"Say it," he taunted. He lowered his head and trailed his tongue along her collarbone and up her neck. "Just what?" he whispered against her skin.

"Fuck me," Ashanti pushed out on an urgent breath. "Please. Just fuck me until I say stop."

"As long as you promise you won't say stop for a very long time."

She locked her hands behind his head and reached up for a kiss, sealing her lips against his.

"Not until the sun comes up."

She gasped as he pumped his hips.

"Too soon," Thad said. "Checkout isn't until eleven."

29

The effort it took to calm his body down so that he could prolong his time with Ashanti was unlike any Thad had ever had to exert. The connection between his brain and his dick must have been broken, because no matter how much he told himself to take this slow, his body refused to listen.

Ashanti's pleasurable gasps and mewls weren't making it any easier. Every sexy little whimper was like an injection of fuel, accelerating his need to draw out that response from her over and over again. He wanted to make her cry out in pleasure, to make it so good that she wouldn't even think about limiting this to a one-time thing.

Thad hooked his arms under the bend of her knees and angled her hips upward, his own limbs growing weak at the ecstasy the shift in position produced. He immersed himself in her, not just her body but her entire essence. He could feel himself becoming more enthralled with every delicious thrust. She intoxicated him. Captivated him, body, soul, and everything in between.

"This first time won't last until morning," Thad breathed

against her neck. "But I promise if you stay in this bed, I'm going to make it worth your while."

"I'm not leaving," she said. "Please...just."

She didn't have to say more. Thad licked two fingers and shoved his hand between their bodies, finding her clit and stroking it as his dick drove in and out, his hips pumping with increasing speed. The familiar sensation started at the base of his spine and quickly rushed to his front, his balls growing heavy with the need to come.

He felt Ashanti coming undone underneath him only a few seconds before the orgasm swept through him. His entire body shook with the force of it, leaving him gulping for breaths.

His pleasure was instantly replaced with panic at the thought that what he'd felt was *not* Ashanti coming. But when he looked down, there was no mistaking the cause of the unmitigated bliss blanketing her face.

"Thank God," Thad said before collapsing on top of her, relief and the aftereffects of his orgasm sapping what little strength still remained in his bones. Thad forced himself to get up so he could dispose of the condom. In under a minute, he was back in the bed, stretching alongside Ashanti.

He rolled onto his back and caught her by the hips, pulling her on top of him. He needed to feel her against him even though he was no longer inside of her. For now.

"That was nice. And necessary," she said. "Evie and Ridley would be proud."

Thad peered at her. "Do I even want to know?"

She shook her head, her chin rubbing against his breastbone. She turned her head and rested her cheek on him, emitting a satisfied sigh. His dick twitched at the sound. His recovery time would be even shorter than he'd first thought.

"This will come as no shock," Ashanti said. "But it has been a long time since I did this. I forgot how much I miss out on when it's just me and my vibrator." Her head popped up, the sprinkling of freckles across her nose deepening to a rich crimson. "Why did I just tell you that?"

"Because my ego can use every boost it can get?" Thad said. "I'm not sure if this will shock you or not, but it's been a long time since I did this too."

"That absolutely shocks me," she said. "You are so lying right now."

"I'm not," he said. "I told you earlier that you're the first woman in a very long time that I've been interested in."

"Yeah, but you don't have to be interested in someone to, you know, do what we just did."

"You're confusing me with Von," Thad said "It's not that I've never done the casual thing, but it just doesn't appeal to me anymore. And, please, when you talk about what we just did, say that we fucked. Because the hottest thing I have ever heard in my life is the word fuck coming out of your mouth."

Her sharp laugh sounded around the room.

He nudged her, lifting his hips. "Come on. Say it."

"Thad."

"Say it," he goaded.

One corner of her mouth tilted up in a grin. She rolled her eyes, but then, in a voice so sultry it nearly killed him, she said, "Fuck."

Thad threw his head back against the mattress and groaned.

"You're so silly." She laughed. "*That's* what surprises me. Well, that's the *other* thing that surprises me. I never would have expected you to have this sense of humor, not based on my first impression of you."

"To be fair—" he started, then stopped. "Wait a minute." He wrapped an arm around her waist and lifted her, then pushed himself up so that his back was against the headboard. "That's better," he said. "As I was saying, to be fair, I was not at my best on the day we first met. I was still salty that I'd been roped into looking after Puddin'."

At the sound of his name, Puddin' came running. He jumped onto the bed and sniffed Thad's face.

"Down," Ashanti said.

The dog immediately jumped off the bed and stood at attention beside it.

"That's sexy too. The way you get them to obey your commands like that?" He struck the mattress with his fists. "It turns me the fuck on, Ashanti."

"That is…strange," she finished, the soft rumble of her laugh feeling like heaven against his chest. She scooted off the bed.

"Where are you going?" Thad asked.

"I love these two, but they're going to have to hang out on their own for a while."

He stared at her exquisite body, loving the way her braids swished back and forth just above her ass as she guided the dogs into her room. She came back and climbed in the bed, twisting around so that her back was to his front. He fully acknowledged that she could ask anything of him right now and he would give it to her, provided her naked ass remained in his lap.

"Now," she said, pulling the sheet up over her and totally

ruining his view, "You really want me to believe that you were this surly grouch because of Puddin'?"

"Ouch. Was I that bad?"

"Yes," she answered with an emphatic nod.

"It wasn't just Puddin'," Thad was willing to concede. "Although he did account for a lot of it." He shrugged. "Honestly, I've been in a pretty fucked-up mood since I left the military."

She looked back at him over her bare shoulder. "You weren't ready to leave, were you?"

He swallowed hard and decided to go with the truth.

"No." Then he thought better of it. "Actually, that's not true. It was time. It was past time for me to leave. I just thought I would have been better prepared. Mentally," he added. "I spent the first six months wandering around like a kid lost in a big department store. Just...floundering."

"Is that when you came up with the idea for The PX?"

"I had the idea for The PX well before I left the military. Von and I had already shored up our plans before we filed the paperwork for retirement. That's the thing, I knew what I *should* be doing, but I couldn't seem to get my ass in gear to actually do it. It felt as if I'd left things...I don't know... unfinished."

How had he allowed the conversation to veer so far to the left? It was as if he was trying to guarantee that they were one and done when it came to sex tonight.

"Maybe it isn't meant to be finished," she said. "What you're trying to do with The PX seems like an extension of your service."

He had thought about it in the same way, yet he was still stunned by the effect her words had on him.

"I'm pulling for you and Von," she continued. "If Barkingham Palace can't make use of that beautiful house in the Bywater, I'm glad that you are. Your mission is a good one." She pressed her finger to the center of his chest. "*You're* a good one."

Thad captured her hand and brought it to his mouth, placing a kiss in the center of her palm. This moment was the most at peace he'd felt since leaving Colorado.

He didn't want to scare her off by sharing anything too deep, but deep was the only way to describe how profoundly he was falling for her.

He was falling so, so, *so* fucking deep.

30

Ashanti sat as close as she could to the armrest of the black pleather couch, holding her body so still that she was unsure she would be able to stand once they were finally called in for this final podcast of their media junket. For all the lazy, relaxed hours she'd spent snuggled up with Thad last night, reality had set in this morning, bringing along a self-consciousness she could not shake.

"Stop freaking out," Thad said.

Ashanti jumped, stiffening her shoulders and holding her head erect. "I'm not freaking out," she rebutted.

"You are," he said. "You're edgy as hell. You've been this way since we left the hotel."

"I'm not—" she started, but then realized it made no sense to lie when he clearly could see what she thought she had been hiding so well. "Okay, maybe I'm freaking out a little."

"Don't. Remember, we're taking this slow. Keep this up and you're going to have me developing performance anxiety."

"What?" Her head jerked back for another reason entirely.

"You should be *less* stressed after last night. All this anxiety coming from you has me questioning by abilities."

Just like that, some of the tension released from her shoulders. Ashanti threw the wadded-up napkin she'd used while eating her bagel at him.

"Shut up," she said. "For the record, your performance exceeded expectations. And I expected a lot from you."

His grin was devilish. "My ego thanks you."

She rolled her eyes.

"Oh, and here's a plus." He leaned over and, in a lowered voice, said, "This podcast won't be video streamed, so at least no one will notice you eye-fucking me this time."

"Stop it." Ashanti pushed him away.

The door across from them opened and the podcast producer came in to greet them.

Dominique hadn't explained much about this podcast, so both Ashanti and Thad were surprised to learn that it was geared toward the military, the podcasters were a husband and wife duo who tailored their show to those recently out of military life. It wouldn't be video streamed, but it was another special live broadcast.

The fact that they'd been told they could leave the dogs at the hotel should have been a clue that this podcast would be different.

If Dom were here right now, Ashanti would kiss her for giving Thad this opportunity. She had been feeling guilty because so much of what they'd done in New York had benefitted her business and her standing in that online contest. This balanced things out, at least a little.

She left most of the discussion to Thad, adding a comment

here and there, but only when asked. This was his chance to shine a light on the subjects closest to his heart—his military family and The PX—and she wasn't about to get in his way. His enthusiasm was infectious as he gave a rundown of everything his bar would include. By the time they were done, Ashanti was ready to drop in and have a drink at The PX herself.

"I have never seen you more animated," Ashanti said as they left the studio. "I think you've finally fulfilled Von's request to have fun."

"Last night covered that," he said. "But I'll agree that I had a good time during that podcast."

"So are you finally willing to admit that Dom is worth whatever she charges?"

"I'll admit it," he conceded. He pulled out his phone and swiped across the screen. "How much do you think she charges to run an Instagram account? I felt the notifications going off in my pocket the entire time we were on the air."

"I don't know Dom's prices yet, but I can already tell you it's too much to pay just for someone to run your social media. It sounds like you need to brush up on your hashtag knowledge."

"What about your sister? Maybe she could run Barkingham Palace and The PX."

"That girl has trouble enough staying in class. Don't even think about it," Ashanti said.

They returned to the hotel to scoop up the dogs, then headed to JFK for their late-evening flight. That unsettling sensation from earlier began crawling over Ashanti once more, an awareness that their time in New York was coming to an end and they were returning to reality.

"You're doing it again," Thad said as they waited at the gate. "Stop freaking out."

She wasn't going to deny it. Instead, she didn't say anything. Just sat in her increasingly uncomfortable seat at the gate, bouncing her knee up and down until her boarding group was called.

Once again, she and Thad were seated in different rows. Ashanti put her head back and closed her eyes as soon as the plane began to taxi the runway.

About twenty minutes into their flight, she felt the man in the middle seat get up. She'd heard him asking the flight attendant about using the restroom before they took off. He returned moments later, wedging himself back in the seat. Then he took her hand.

Ashanti jerked her hand away, her eyes popping open.

"You can go back to sleep," Thad said, recapturing her hand.

"Did you switch seats with that guy?"

He nodded.

"You gave up the aisle for a middle seat? To be closer to me?"

He nodded again, then looked over at her. "This means we're going steady."

She couldn't help but laugh at his cute, antiquated term and the seriousness in how he said it.

"Is that how this works?" she asked.

"As far as I'm concerned."

He entwined their fingers and put his head back. They sat that way for the remainder of the flight, her anxiety flowing away like the clouds they passed in the sky.

But the tension returned the moment Ashanti took her

phone out of Airplane Mode after touching down at Louis Armstrong International. There was a string of text messages from Kara.

> Mayday! Mayday! Mayday!
>
> Ken has locked herself in her room.
>
> Don't think she's coming out.

She followed it with a meme of a woman muttering "drama, drama, drama."

It was followed by another string of texts:

> Real emergency this time. You're getting your a$$ kicked. Raw Beauty brought out the big guns.

Ashanti frowned. What did that even mean?

She recognized Raw Beauty as one of the contestants in the Black Woman Entrepreneur contest, but what did Kara mean by big guns? And why was Ashanti getting her butt kicked? She was winning by 18 percent when she checked the polls before leaving the hotel.

"Something wrong?" Thad asked.

"Everything is wrong, according to Kara. I'm not sure exactly what's going on, except for Kendra having a meltdown."

"It was nice being off big-sister duty for a few days, wasn't it?"

He had no idea.

The pilot announced that another plane was at their gate so they would have to hang back for a few minutes.

Ashanti tried calling Kendra, even though she knew her sister wouldn't answer. She didn't, but she immediately texted back.

Ignore Kara. I'm fine.

Don't want to talk tonight. We can talk tomorrow.

Just after Ashanti sent Kendra a thumbs-up emoji, Ridley called.

"Can you believe this shit?" Ridley said the moment Ashanti answered. "After all the work we put into this New York trip, it all goes to shit because of one damn Instagram post."

"Rid, what happened?" Ashanti asked, her pulse rate skyrocketing.

"You haven't seen the post?"

"I've been in the air for the last three hours."

"Oh, shit. How did I forget that you all had to switch to a later flight. I thought you would have heard by now."

"Heard what?" She was going to strangle someone if Ridley didn't tell her what the heck was going on. "Kara sent a bunch of vague text messages but didn't say what they were about. Only that I'm getting my butt kicked in the contest. I don't understand how that can be when I was so far ahead of the entire pack just hours ago."

"I'll tell you how," Ridley said. "Because you are not cousins with one Pilar Jones."

"The singer?" Ashanti asked as the plane finally pulled into the gate area. "What does she have to do with this?"

"Turns out she and the owner of Raw Beauty Products are first cousins. Pilar just posted a video plugging the beauty line *and* the contest to her forty million Instagram followers. You can forget the contest, Shanti. Raw Beauty is running away with it."

Ashanti's heart dropped.

"Maybe there's—"

"Honey, they're up by forty-two percent," Ridley said. "Duchess and Puddin' are cute and all, but they are no Pilar Jones."

Ashanti put her head back against the headrest and closed her eyes. She wanted the $250,000 prize money, but she *needed* the loan that would be offered to the winner. She could never get those favorable terms from a bank.

She felt that house in the Lower Garden District slipping away, and it made her sick to her stomach.

"We're moving," Thad told her. People on board had started to deplane.

"Rid, I have to go."

"Call me later. I'm sorry," Ridley said before ending the call.

Thad stepped back so that Ashanti could go ahead of him. She wasn't sure how her legs were still working when she could barely feel them.

The moment they entered the concourse, Thad took her by the hand and brought her to an empty seat in the gate area. He stooped down and looked into her eyes.

"What's wrong?"

"It's nothing," Ashanti said. "We have to get the dogs."

"The dogs will be fine for a few minutes. Is someone hurt?"

She shook her head. "No, no. Nothing like that." She blew out a breath. "I've mentioned that online contest, right?" He nodded. "I thought it was a sure thing because of all the publicity Duchess and Puddin' have gotten this week, but one of the other contestants got a celebrity to endorse them and now they're running away with the votes."

"Damn," Thad said. "I'm sorry. But at least you got some good publicity out of it."

"You don't get it, Thad. *Everything* hinged on that contest," Ashanti said.

"I'm gonna assume that is hyperbole," Thad said.

She shook her head. "It's not. I made an offer on that building in the Lower Garden District because, in addition to a two-hundred-and-fifty-thousand-dollar grand prize, the winner of the contest is guaranteed a loan of up to two million. That's how I was planning to buy the building. Talk about counting your damn chickens before they hatch!"

Thad captured her hands. "It'll be okay, Ashanti. I don't know how yet, but things will work out. They just will."

She was usually the one with the perpetually positive outlook, but Ashanti couldn't summon a bit of that positivity right now. All she could think about was that location she'd coveted above all others and how close she had come to owning it.

She pushed herself up from the seat.

"Let's go. I need my dog."

❖

By the time Ashanti arrived home, all she wanted to do was lose herself in an hour-long bubble bath and a good book, but she hadn't had the chance to indulge in those kinds of luxuries in nearly three years. What she *wanted* to do didn't matter, there was one thing she *had* to do.

She filled Duchess's water bowl, gave her a treat for being such a good dog on the ride home from the airport, and set her in front of the TV with an episode of *SpongeBob*. Then she headed for the stairs.

"We've got this," Ashanti whispered to her parents' picture as she passed it on her way to Kendra's room. She rapped on the door with her knuckles.

"Ken?" Ashanti called.

Several beats of silence ticked by before the door opened.

"Hey," Kendra said.

"I know you said you didn't want to talk tonight, but it's time. No more putting this off."

Kendra waved her in, then went over to her bed and sat cross-legged on it. Ashanti settled into the faux fur desk chair. Just as she was about to speak, she heard the familiar *tap, tap, tap* of Duchess's nails a moment before her dog waddled into the room. She walked over to the edge of Kendra's bed and barked at her.

"Are you demanding to get in my bed?" Kendra asked. She scooped Duchess up and sat her between her spread-out knees. "You go to New York and come back acting like even more of a diva."

"That's a nationwide star you have in your arms there," Ashanti said. She smiled, but then sobered. "Okay, Ken, what's the deal? Why have you been in such a mood lately?"

"It's stupid, Shanti. I don't know why you're so worked up over this."

"Because you haven't been yourself, and it has me worried. Is it girlfriend trouble?"

Kendra rolled her eyes. "I don't have a girlfriend anymore," she said.

"I know that, but maybe that's the problem."

"It's not girlfriend trouble," she said. She wrapped her arms around Duchess and rested her cheek on the top of the dog's head. Duchess, of course, ate up the attention, wiggling her butt in a clear invitation for scritches. Kendra scratched her bottom.

"If it isn't girlfriend trouble, then what is it?" Ashanti asked. "Is something going on at school?"

Kendra's eyes flashed to hers before focusing on Duchess again.

"What's going on at school?" Ashanti asked. "And don't say it's nothing. It is something, and I'm not leaving this room until you tell me what it is. Now, based on your reaction when I asked about the literary magazine just before I left for New York, I think that may have something to do with it? Am I on the right track?"

Kendra blew out a heavy sigh. "That's part of it," she said.

And just like that, Ashanti knew what was wrong. "You didn't get the managing editor position, did you?"

Kendra shook her head.

"Oh, Ken." Ashanti pinched her eyes shut and released a breath. She should feel relieved that it wasn't anything more serious, but when she thought back on how worried she had been, it made her want to scream. She could not believe her sister had put her through all of this because of that school magazine. Yet, she understood why Kendra felt this way. That magazine meant everything to her.

"These things happen," Ashanti said. "I know you've been vying for that position, but you still have your senior year. That is no reason for you to be in such a funk."

"You have to admit being managing editor would be impressive on my college applications."

"I literally pointed out that you still have your senior year to make managing editor not even five seconds ago, Kendra." Why were teenagers so dramatic? "You have time."

Her sister didn't look convinced. The way she nervously bit her bottom lip was her telltale sign. Ashanti knew there were no words she could say right now that would assuage Kendra's hurt and anxiety, but her sister would eventually get past this.

"Thank you for finally opening up to me about this. You can always come to me, Kendra. You know that, right?"

She nodded. "I know." She pressed a kiss to Duchess's head, then hefted her up and held her out to Ashanti. "Now here, take your dog."

31

Thad tilted his head back and let the warm water cascade down his face and shoulders. Gone were the days of three-minute showers. After the hours he'd put in at the Bywater house today, and the dust and grime that stuck to him like a second skin, he needed a minimum of ten minutes under this spray.

He finally got out and changed into a pair of sweats and a T-shirt. Puddin' was waiting at the bathroom door, his way of telling Thad that it was time to feed him his damn dinner.

"I'm coming," he told the dog, who took off for the kitchen.

He fixed Puddin's food, then made himself a sandwich and grabbed a bag of chips from the pantry. He ate both perched against the kitchen counter, washing it all down with a bottle of beer from a microbrewery in Hattiesburg, Mississippi.

Switch the poodle out for a boxer or a Great Dane, and he would be the epitome of the bachelor cliché.

That had never bothered him before. But after several days of only seeing Ashanti when he picked Puddin' up in the

evenings—and sometimes not even then if she was busy in
the back with other dogs—Thad was more than ready to turn
in his bachelor card.

If she would have allowed it, he would have been at her
house waiting for her every single night this week, but he
understood her need to stick with a slow approach. She was
raising teenagers. He got it. He didn't like it, but he got it.

Thad finished off his beer and snapped a picture of the
label before tossing it. He wouldn't mind serving this one
at The PX. He grabbed a Little Debbie Fudge Round from
the pantry and went over to his computer. Von had emailed
a revised bid from another contractor. Time was moving at
lightning speed; if they didn't find someone who could provide an enormous crew soon they could forget opening on Veterans Day.

It wouldn't be the most devastating thing in the world to
have to push back their opening date, but he had imagined a
Veterans Day celebration filled with a crowd of former military friends from the moment he came up with the concept of
The PX. Thad was ready to do all he could to make that part
of his dream happen, even if it meant paying a contractor to
do more than just the electrical and plumbing.

One thing he could count on was the crowd. He knew
the support would be there based on the way their new social
media platforms had blown up in the days since he'd come
back from New York. His biggest problem now was that Von
was as concerned with filming content as he was with getting
the damn bar built.

Thad opened his email and immediately closed his eyes.
Shit.

Another one from the woman in Alabama was waiting in

his inbox. Thad had hoped she'd given up, but it was obvious she wouldn't stop until she got money out of her newfound family. She had yet to make her pitch, but he knew it was coming.

He opened the email and scanned it.

"Wait. What?"

Thad frowned, his eyes narrowing as he leaned forward and read the email more closely. He sat back in his chair, the sandwich he'd just eaten suddenly feeling like lead in the pit of his stomach.

"What the fuck," he whispered, dragging his hands from the back of his head and down his face, finally resting his fingers against his lips as he stared at the photo the woman had attached to the email. It looked as if he were staring at his own mother.

But it wasn't his mother. According to her email, this was *her* mother, who was one of three children her grandmother shared with her grandfather.

His grandfather.

This couldn't be real. That picture had to be the result of some kind of artificial intelligence bullshit.

But where would the scammer have gotten a picture of his mother to feed into an AI generator? The way his mom escaped the camera was a running joke in his family. She was always the one taking pictures, never in them. And she detested social media.

It was starting to seem less likely that this woman would go through so much trouble to scam his family, especially when she had yet to ask for money.

But if this wasn't about money...

Thad swallowed hard, trying to push down the knot of anger that instantly clogged his throat.

All those long trips. Dry cleaning conventions. Sales meetings.

Bullshit.

They had all been excuses so his grandfather could see another woman. Thad threw his head back and closed his eyes tight, struggling to stave off the tears that suddenly burned his eyes. He could think of a thousand other things his grandfather could have been involved in—embezzlement, underground gambling—and none would hurt as much as this.

"How could you have done this to Grams?" Thad said. He pushed the computer aside and propped his elbows on the table, then ground the heels of his hands against his eyes. His stomach clenched with the abrupt onset of nausea.

He felt like a kid who'd just found out his favorite superhero was really the villain.

Thad picked up his phone to call Nadia. He couldn't keep this from her any longer. He clicked into his favorites, then set the phone back on the table.

This wasn't the type of thing you shared over the phone. His sister would be here in less than a week for Reshonda's wedding. His conversation with Nadia could wait.

But *he* couldn't. He had to talk to *some*body.

Thad picked up the phone again and sent Ashanti a text.

> Puddin' is missing Duchess. You think she's
> up for a walk?

The fact that his mind went to Ashanti instead of Von was telling. He'd fallen far past deep when it came to this woman. He was in the Mariana Trench.

I'll meet you at Crescent Park, came Ashanti's reply.

It was just after nine p.m. when Thad pulled into the parking lot next to the crescent-shaped bridge that led to Crescent Park. He saw headlights flash in his rearview mirror a moment before Ashanti's SUV slipped into the spot next to his. Some of the ache that had settled in his chest immediately started to dissipate. She was better than aspirin.

They opened their doors at the same time. While he retrieved Puddin' from his harness, she did the same with Duchess. They met at the spot between their two front bumpers.

"Something's wrong," she said.

"Can I kiss you before we talk?" he asked. "I haven't done that in far too long."

"Is someone hurt?" she asked.

"No," Thad said, shaking his head. Just his heart.

She nodded. "Okay, you can kiss me."

He leaned forward and captured her lips in a slow, sweet kiss, like the one he had been aching to give her for days.

"That's better," Thad said once he finally released her. "Let's walk, and then we can talk."

They crossed over the bridge and into the park that ran along the bank of the river. Thad had never come here before, even as a kid. He was blown away by the beautiful view of the city skyline.

"This is nice," he said.

"I love this park. So does Duchess." She bumped him with her elbow. "My plans were to take the dogs at Barkingham Palace for walks here if I'd bought the Bywater House."

"The other one is directly across from a park, though, right?"

She sighed. "I'm not getting that house, Thad. I can't afford it."

"I told you not to count yourself out."

"I don't even want to talk about it. It depresses me. What about you?" she asked. "What's going on?"

After that kiss and this nice stroll, he hated the thought of polluting their time together with the news he'd found out. But that was the reason he'd asked her to join him in the first place.

Thad started from the beginning, with Nadia sending him the DNA test kit, then told her about the emails from the woman in Alabama.

"I thought it was a scam," Thad said. "I've been playing along, waiting for her to make her pitch for money, until the last email, when she sent an actual picture."

"What was it?"

"A photo of her mother." He looked over at Ashanti, not even bothering to hide the hurt in his eyes. He couldn't even if he'd tried. "She looks as if she could be my mom's twin."

"Oh, shit," Ashanti said.

Thad grinned at her curse, despite his somber mood.

"Yeah. Oh, shit," he said. "It looks like my grandfather has an entire second family in a little town just outside of Mobile, Alabama."

"Oh my goodness," Ashanti said. "How could he do such a thing to Mrs. Frances?"

Her gentle outrage on his grandmother's behalf sent a wave of reassuring comfort washing over him. It felt good to know he was justified in his anger. Not that he had any doubts that his rage was warranted.

But it wasn't the anger that was eating him up; it was the disappointment.

"That's the thing that keeps gnawing at me," Thad said.

"I can't believe he would do this to Grams. I was young, but I was still aware of the sacrifices she made for the business. Sutherland Dry Cleaning wouldn't exist if not for her. To now know that he was off fucking some other woman while my Grams was holding down everything at home *and* at the dry cleaners?"

Thad clenched his fists so tight Puddin's leash started to dig into the fleshy part of his palm.

"It feels as if everything I grew up admiring about my grandfather was a lie." He huffed out a laugh. "And to think he used to call my dad a cheating bastard—which he was. That asshole doesn't get a pass here. But it looks as if Gramps was just like him. And that kills me, Ashanti." Thad pressed his fist against his stomach.

"Everything that I am—every virtue, every principle—he is the foundation of it. Every significant decision I've ever made, I made it with him in mind. I would always ask myself, 'What would Gramps think about this? Would he approve? Will this make him proud?'" He shook his head. "I feel like a fool."

"Thad, you had no way of knowing. Your grandfather kept this from everyone."

He squeezed his eyes shut. "Thinking about what this will do to my grandmother kills me."

Ashanti asked the question that Thad had been asking himself for the past hour. "Do you have to tell her?"

He brought his free hand up to the back of his neck and massaged the muscles there.

"I don't know," Thad said. "My gut says no. What good would it do to devastate her like this? But then I think about his other family. What if it *does* become about money? What if they try to make some kind of claim for the house or my grandfather's estate? Grams made a good profit when she sold the dry cleaning business. Are they entitled to any of that? I don't know how this shit works."

"I don't know either," Ashanti said.

She took Puddin's leash from him and wrapped it around the hand where she held Duchess's. Then she took his hand and entwined their fingers.

Thad closed his eyes again and welcomed the peace her touch brought him.

"Come home with me," he said. He didn't know where the words had come from and cursed them the moment they left his mouth. She'd told him about her aunt's threats. He knew she wouldn't risk losing her sisters, even if those threats were bullshit in his view. It wasn't fair to put her in this position.

Yet, instead of apologizing, he added, "Please."

It felt as if a thousand years passed before she made him believe that not everything in his world was lost with one softly spoken word.

"Okay."

32

They didn't even pretend that they had come back to his house for any reason other than this one thing.

The moment they crossed the threshold, clothes began flying. Thad didn't think about where the dogs were or if his grandmother's nosy-ass neighbor was looking through the window, seeing him toss his T-shirt across the living room. His sole focus was getting Ashanti in his bed and getting inside of her as quickly as possible.

"This way," he said, leading her to his room. He toed off his tennis shoes and shucked his sweats and underwear down his legs. Then he helped Ashanti with hers, peeling the jeans from her hips, traveling down with them as he made his way to the floor.

Thad brushed a kiss against her stomach, just above her belly button. He moved lower, trailing kisses along her skin, adding his tongue once he reached the spot between her legs. He groaned against her.

"Sit down," Thad whispered.

When she did, he pulled her to the edge of the mattress

and lifted both her legs, placing her thighs on his shoulders. Then he dipped his head and spread her open with his tongue.

She gasped, and the sound sent a jolt of sensation straight to his dick.

Fuck!

He knew she would taste good, but this was so much better than good.

He stroked her with his tongue, dragging slow, firm licks from her clit on down, and then back up again. Ashanti lifted her hips, grinding against his mouth as he continued to lap at her.

Her cries filled the room, hesitant as they were. Thad wanted to tell her to let go, to just give in and not hold back. But he didn't want to stop what he was doing long enough to speak.

He caught her by the waist and held her down while he wedged his tongue inside her, driving in and out. Her legs moved restlessly against his shoulders, as if she didn't know what to do with herself. He tried to make out what she was saying between her breathy pants and realized it was his name. She was calling his name over and over again.

Thad had never heard anything sexier in his entire life. It drove him to keep going until he felt her legs shake and tense.

She came against his tongue. But instead of stopping, he ramped up the intensity, closing his mouth over her clit and sucking until she came again and again and again.

Her body was limp by the time he lifted her legs and set them back on the bed. He stood. As he stared down at Ashanti completely spent on his mattress, Thad realized his ego would never need stroking again.

"Are you okay?" he asked her.

"I'm a puddle," she said. "Don't ask me to move, because I can't."

Nope. No ego stroking necessary for the newly crowned king of cunnilingus.

He went around to the side of the bed and lifted her up, placing her head on one of his pillows. The picture she created made his chest grow tight. It was so perfect, so right seeing her relaxed and satiated in his bed. Thad slipped in beside her, doing his best to tamp down the need throbbing in his dick. She was too weak to do anything right now.

"We're not finished, are we?" she asked, as if she'd just read his mind.

"Hell no," Thad said. "But you look as if you can use some recovery time."

"Please." She turned into him, resting her head against his chest. "Just a few minutes."

Thank God. Because that's about all the wait he had in him. The need to be inside of her was so immense, it took his breath away.

When had he ever experienced anything like this?

"So," Ashanti said. "If I tell you something, will you promise not to judge?"

Shit. He hated questions like that, especially during situations like this.

"Do I want to hear this?" Thad asked.

She hunched her shoulders, then looked up at him, pulling her bottom lip between her teeth.

No, he probably didn't want to hear this, but he asked anyway. "Okay, what is it?"

"That was the first time anyone has ever, you know, performed oral sex on me."

He jerked his head back. "What?"

"You said you wouldn't judge me!"

"I'm not judging *you*. I'm judging the assholes you've slept with. What the hell, Ashanti?"

"Well, there haven't been *that* many," she said. "And they weren't very adventurous."

He looked down at her. "For the record, if given the chance, I will eat you out every single day for the rest of my life. First thing in the morning. You would be my breakfast."

Her face turned so red that it had to be hot to the touch.

"That doesn't sound very nutritious, but I wouldn't be opposed to it," she said with a laugh. "Uh, I'm ready to do it the regular way now. Grab a condom."

Thad held up a finger. "Wait exactly one minute," he said before climbing out of the bed and making his way across the hall to the bathroom where he'd stashed the box of condoms he'd picked up when he got back from New York. He needed to get a nightstand with a drawer. That little side table next to the bed wouldn't cut it.

When he returned to his room, he found Ashanti lying on her back, the covers pulled up to just above her breasts.

He thought about what she'd just told him, about her other boyfriends—the sad sacks of shit they were—not being adventurous.

Thad ripped open a condom wrapper and rolled one on, then he grabbed the edge of the covers and jerked them off the bed.

"Thad!" she screeched. "What are you doing?"

"It's time for some adventure," he said. "Roll over."

Her eyes narrowed, then brightened as understanding set in. She scrambled onto all fours, then looked back over her shoulder. "Before you even ask, no I've never done it this way either."

"Assholes," Thad muttered. "But that's enough talk about your old boyfriends. I promise you won't remember their names after tonight."

By the time they were done, they were both too weak to move. The most strength Thad could muster was reaching over and picking the covers up from the floor.

"What time is it?" Ashanti asked.

He summoned enough energy to reach over to the side table and grab a phone. A picture of Duchess and a text message notification popped up when he touched the screen. He couldn't help but read the **Where R U** text from Kara.

"It's just after eleven," Thad said, already anticipating and dreading what her reaction would be.

"Oh, shoot! I have to go."

Shit. He knew she would say that. He handed her the phone.

"There's a text from your sister," he said.

She took the phone from him and sat up, her thumbs flying across the screen. It dinged with two back-to-back text messages moments after she finished typing.

"These girls. I swear," Ashanti said.

"What?"

"I told them not to worry about me, that I was on my way home. These are the replies I got." She turned the phone to face him.

The first one was from Kara: **If ur with Thad stay the night.**

The other was labeled Ken: **The week. You need it.**

"Sounds to me like you and Duchess are staying awhile," Thad said.

She rolled her eyes, but then—thank you, God—she

reached across him and set her phone back on the table. She once again settled against his chest like it was the most natural thing in the world.

"This feels weird," she said.

Or, maybe not the most natural thing.

"Simon was the last person I was with, and once I ended things with him, I didn't even consider bringing another man around my sisters," she continued. "For them to know where I am *and* what we're doing?"

"Actually, they encouraged you to do what we're doing."

Thad debated saying more, recognizing that he was probably crossing a line. But she needed to hear this. In just the short time he'd known her, it had become more than obvious that she put herself dead last.

"Maybe the twins realize their big sister deserves to have a life outside of her work and the job of raising them," Thad said. "It's too bad your aunt doesn't see that."

"Anita isn't my aunt," she said. "Lincoln was my dad in every way that counts, but that woman was never an aunt to me. And if you can find me another five hours in the day, then maybe I can think about having a life outside of the daycare, baking dog biscuits, and raising the girls," Ashanti said. "Or, give me a couple of years, once Kara and Kendra are off to college. I'll get a life then."

Thad clenched his teeth in frustration, hating what he was about to do. He had to remind himself that the fact that she had come home with him was a gift she hadn't even considered giving to any other man in years.

"Look, Ashanti, as much as I want you to, you don't have to stay if it will cause trouble."

"Well, since the girls already figured it out and seem to be okay with it, I guess one night won't hurt. It's not as if they will run and tell Anita." She paused and frowned, then reached for her phone. "I'm texting them, just in case, because I can totally see Kara casually letting it slip just for the shock factor."

Once she was done texting her sisters, she settled more securely against Thad's chest and brought his arm across her waist. He pressed a kiss to her bare shoulder because it was right there, looking as delicious as a piece of candy.

"Have I thanked you yet for taking my mind off that email?" Thad asked.

"It was my pleasure. Literally," she answered. "Actually, you did the same for me. I got one of those kinds of emails myself this week."

"Wait. What?"

"Not someone saying that my stepdad had another family stashed away somewhere," she clarified. "I mean one of those emails with the potential to knock your world off kilter."

Thad repositioned them, laying alongside her and perching himself up on his elbow.

"What are you talking about?" he asked.

She closed her eyes and blew out a weary breath. "One of the country's largest pet food companies contacted me. They want to buy Duchess Delights."

That wasn't what he had been expecting.

"Um, how do you feel about that?"

"About as confused as I have ever felt about anything," she said. "It's wild because Duchess Delights wasn't even a thing a year ago, and now the thought of selling it makes my chest hurt." She peered up at him. "Did I ever tell you that your grandmother is the reason behind why I started selling them commercially?"

"No. But I'm not surprised." Thad chuckled. "That woman has a mind for business."

"She is as sharp as anyone I have ever met. And she is the best cheerleader. She put it in my head that I could make an actual business out of this. I only started making the treats for Duchess because the brand I used to give her changed their ingredients. It was never supposed to grow into anything. Now look at it."

"Is their offer worth entertaining?"

"They didn't provide any numbers. It was only the initial email, stating their interest. I told them I would get back to them." She expelled another weighty breath. "I'm not sure if I want to entertain any offers. It's too much to even think about right now.

"What about you and *your* email?" She brought her hand up to his cheek and stroked it. Her simple, gentle gesture caused a lump to form in his throat. "What are you going to do?"

"It's not my decision to make alone," Thad said. "My sister will be in town next week for her best friend's wedding. I'll tell her then and we'll decide what to do about it."

Before he could give himself a chance to talk himself out of it, Thad asked, "Would you like to join me at the wedding?"

Her shoulders stiffened in surprise.

"It's at the Four Seasons," Thad added, hoping to entice her with fancy food. "I'm not sure if there will be an open bar or not, but—"

"Thad," she cut him off. Her eyes softened, the corners tipping up with her smile. "I would love to join you."

33

Ashanti sprayed a mixture of peppermint and clove oil on the terrycloth blanket that she'd hung on the back fence at Barkingham Palace. After saturating it, she added it to the pile of others. She had done the same with every piece of bedding she'd taken from the suite where one of their new clients, an Afghan hound, had spent the night. All would have to be scalded, washed twice, and bleached before they could be used again.

The owner had obviously lied about her dog being on flea prevention, because when Colleen went in for the morning feeding, the enclosed suite was overwhelmed with fleas. Which meant every suite in that section of the daycare would need to be treated.

This was why they'd vetted their clients so thoroughly in the early days, and why they needed to get back to being more selective when deciding which pets to keep. The influx of people wanting to board their dogs was nice and all, but it had come with its own issues. She was not about to compromise the integrity she'd built into this place over the last three years just to make a quick buck.

Ashanti had ordered that all dogs be given free baths before leaving today. Barkingham Palace's reputation wouldn't be worth anything if one of their dogs brought home fleas.

Yet, despite a morning consumed with ridding the daycare of a potential infestation, Ashanti could not stop this stupid smile from spreading across her face. It was just one of the outcomes of waking up in Thad's arms. Another was the R-rated movie that continued to play in her mind with scenes from everything that had taken place in his bed last night.

She had to stop this. If any of her staff came out here right now, they would know exactly what she was thinking about. Her freckles would give her away.

Her phone rang. She pulled it out and frowned in confusion at the sight of the daycare's number.

"Deja?" she answered.

"Boss Lady, I tried to call you on the intercom, but you didn't answer."

"I'm still outside spraying down the bedding from the Frogmore Suite," she said.

"Anita is on her way back there. And she is pissed."

Just then, the back door opened and her "guest" came marching down the steps. Ashanti finally found something that would remove the smile from her face.

"Hi, Anita," she said flatly. She refused to even pretend she was excited to see her. "Do you need something?"

"As a matter of fact, I do." Anita crossed her bony arms over her chest and thrust her right hip forward. "I need to know who is taking care of my nieces while you're living it up in New York City with some man *and* staying in the same hotel with him."

"Excuse me?" Ashanti set the spray bottle on the ground. "That was a work trip."

"It doesn't matter. I've seen the type of men you deem acceptable, and I don't want *any* of them around my nieces."

And, just like that, Ashanti decided she was done.

She had allowed this woman and her threats to control her life for long enough. The girls were sixteen, not twelve, and that incident with Simon had nothing to do with her life today. The chance of a judge revoking her guardianship simply because she was in a relationship was so slight that it barely registered. She had been so afraid of losing Kara and Kendra that she had been unwilling to take any chances, but she was done giving Anita such power over her life.

And if she *did* take Ashanti to court, there was no way a judge would look at Thad—an upstanding Army veteran and future business owner—and think that he posed a potential danger to her sisters.

"Even if it wasn't a work trip, it's none of your business where I go or who I spend time with," Ashanti told her.

"It is when you're the person who is supposed to be taking care of my brother's children."

"If my dad wanted you to raise the girls, he would have made that known. But he didn't, did he?"

"It was a mistake that I'm sure has him turning over in his grave." Anita huffed. "Going off to New York, and leaving those girls in that house all by themselves last night."

Ashanti felt her face grow hot. "What did you say?"

"Yes, I called last night when I didn't see your car there," Anita continued. "That one with the smart mouth said you were spending the night with your boyfriend."

Dammit, Kara.

Knowing her sister, she'd shared that with the sole purpose of getting under Anita's skin, even though Ashanti had specifically told them not to tell anyone. All she did was give her aunt more ammunition.

"What are you doing snooping around my house?" she asked Anita.

"Someone needs to be concerned about those girls."

"Kara and Kendra know that I am only a phone call away."

"Would you even answer the phone if you're laid up under some man?"

Line. Crossed.

Ashanti closed the distance between them, until she was barely a foot way. "Apparently, you didn't hear me the first time," she said. "Who I fuck is none of your business."

Anita gasped, her head snapping back. Her mouth opened and closed but no words came out.

"I should petition the courts!" she finally screeched. "Get those girls away from you."

"Try it," Ashanti said.

"You shouldn't be raising my brother's children!"

"I am tired of your bullshit, Anita. You hadn't talked to your 'beloved' brother for over three years before he died. I know my dad tried to contact you, and you ignored him."

"He was not your father!"

"Fuck you! He *is* my father. He loved me and treated me like his own flesh and blood. You, on the other hand, who actually *was* his flesh and blood, didn't want anything to do with him until he was buried in the ground. And all because he took your mother's dishes."

"It was her wedding china and it was mine!" Anita said. "And it has nothing to do with you."

"No, it doesn't. I don't care why you cut your own brother out of your life. What I *do* care about are my sisters. You talk about wanting to raise Kara and Kendra? You live an hour away and saw them five times in the first ten years of their lives.

"I know what this is, it's guilt," Ashanti continued. "But you don't get to alleviate the shame and regret you feel at the way you treated your own brother by making my sisters' lives hell."

Ashanti took several steps back. Her chest rose and fell with the deep breaths she pulled in and blew out. When she could finally speak, she issued a warning: "Unless you have a dog to board, you're trespassing. Leave my place of business or I'm calling the police."

Anita's nostrils flared, but she didn't say another word. She turned and marched away, leaving the stench of indignation in her wake.

Ashanti walked over to the wooden fence and leaned her forehead against it, flexing her fingers to relieve the rage still flooding her senses.

Let Anita try to take her to court. She was ready for her.

Her phone rang. It was the daycare's number again.

Ashanti closed her eyes. Whatever it was, she didn't want to know.

But she couldn't ignore the call.

"Yes, Deja?" she answered.

"Uh, Boss Lady?" Deja asked in a cautious voice. "I know

this is probably a bad time, based on the way Atilla the Hun stomped out of here a minute ago, but you said you would handle reception while I bring P. J.'s cookie cake to school."

"Yes, of course," Ashanti said. She'd encouraged Deja to take the day off to celebrate her eight-year-old's birthday. She was now grateful her receptionist had turned down the offer, choosing to bring a cookie cake to school to share with the class instead. "I'll be up there in just a minute."

Ashanti made the decision then and there to put Anita and her threats out of her mind. Whether they were empty or not, she would deal with it later.

She had a business to run.

34

Once again, Ashanti found herself in awe of Deja's ability to handle the madness that had become Barkingham Palace's reception area. She'd been trying to place a supply order for the last twenty minutes, but every time she so much as looked away from the phone, it rang.

And she thought she wouldn't be able to get Anita's visit off her mind. She barely had time to take a breath, let alone devote brain function to Anita and her threats.

The front door opened and a woman walked in with a gorgeous brindled Akita Inu on the end of a leash.

"Welcome to Barkingham Palace," Ashanti greeted. "Can I help you?"

"Yes. This is Sano. We have a reservation for three nights of boarding."

Ashanti skimmed through the reservations for today. "Found him," she said. "It looks as if Sano had his observation day a week ago."

She had been in New York at the time. That would explain why she didn't recognize this stunning dog.

"Let me make sure all is set with your reservation, and I'll bring Sano in the back."

As she pulled up the client software on the computer, her eye caught an email notification as it popped up on her phone. She noticed the sender shared the last name with a local grocery store chain and couldn't fight off her curiosity long enough to get through checking in the dog.

She used one hand to pull up her email on her phone while using the other to scroll through the client list on the desktop, and wondered for the millionth time why humans had yet to perfect cloning.

"Here we are," Ashanti said. "Oh, Sano is booked for the Sandringham Suite. Great choice. That will give him a lot of extra room to roam around."

She opened the email from the local grocer and scrolled. Her pulse quickened. They wanted to carry Duchess Delights. A grocery store?

"That suite called to him," the woman said. "It was very busy the day we came in for the observation, so we were only in for about an hour. But that was long enough for Sano to get a feel for the place."

"We've been extremely busy," Ashanti said.

"I'm not sure I mentioned it when we came for his observation day, but Sano doesn't tolerate other dogs well. I've already prepaid for one-on-one playtime for him, separate from the other dogs."

"I'll make a note of it," Ashanti said, pulling a Post-it from the dispenser near the computer mouse.

She skimmed the email, her eyes widening as they ran across the number of treats the grocery store chain was requesting. Her heart started pounding against her rib cage like it wanted to escape. Or dance. Maybe her heart *was* dancing. That's what she felt like doing.

"Um, can you give me just a moment?" Ashanti asked.

"I have a plane to catch," the woman said.

Damn it. Ashanti set down her phone. Barkingham Palace was her bread and butter; it had to be her focus. Although, if she'd read that email correctly, there was a whole lot of butter in her future.

If she could fill such a giant order.

She could and she would, because she had spent the past week working on a backup plan.

She finished checking Sano in for his boarding, then brought the dog to one of their largest suites. She poked her head into the small dog playroom to get an update on the Sanchezes' Pomeranians and check in on Duchess. By the time she returned to the lobby, Deja had made it back from her son's school.

"Thank God," Ashanti said. "You're getting a bonus and a raise as soon as I can afford one."

"I graciously accept," Deja said.

"I'll be in my office," Ashanti told her.

Once behind her desk, she sifted through the papers cluttering it, looking for the number she'd jotted down earlier this week. She'd come up with the idea to rent out professional kitchen space as a temporary solution to her small kitchen. And it's a good thing she'd started looking, because there was no way her little oven could handle this, even if she recruited Evie to help with the baking again.

Ashanti called the number and—thank you, God!—discovered the kitchen was still available. The woman offered to meet her there in a half hour to tour the space.

"I'm only a few minutes away," Ashanti said.

The kitchen was on the river side of St. Claude Avenue, not too far from the Bywater house.

The house in the Lower Garden District wasn't hers yet, but it would be. It was just a matter of time and red tape. At Ridley's urging—nagging—she had set up a meeting with her bank to talk financing. And, even though it made her stomach roil, had decided to put her parents' house up for collateral if it came to that.

But she didn't have the time to look for kitchen space in the Garden District. According to the email, the grocery store chain wanted to line up the order with a huge pet adoption day event they were hosting in partnership with the local SPCA. She needed to get those ovens going.

Ashanti grabbed her keys and headed back to the lobby.

"Deja, I'll be back in a couple of hours." She didn't want to jinx things, but had to share. "Guess who wants to carry Duchess Delights?"

Deja screamed when she told her, giving Ashanti a high five.

"Tell me you hired bakers from the list we gave you," Deja said.

Ashanti had been reviewing the résumés they'd forwarded to her, but hadn't contacted anyone yet. The time for her to do that was yesterday.

"Not yet, but I will," Ashanti said.

She got in the car and turned left onto St. Claude, heading for the commissary kitchen. She glanced down Clouet as she passed it and had to stop herself from stomping on the brake at the sight of fire trucks blocking the street.

"That can't be..." Ashanti murmured as she quickly drove

to the next street that would allow her to turn into the Bywater neighborhood. She kept telling herself that her judgment was off when it came to distance, even though she knew darn well it wasn't. She'd had her eyes on that house for so long, she knew exactly where it was in proximity to every area of this city.

She turned onto Burgundy Street, her stomach pulling tight as she approached the fire engine parked in front of the Bywater house. She spotted Thad and Von standing on the front lawn with another man. Several more men, all wearing fluorescent orange vests and hard hats, stood closer to the house.

Ashanti parked one house down from them. She hurried out of her car and rushed over to Thad.

"What happened?" she asked as she approached.

He spun around, his expression turning from concerned to sunny in a matter of seconds.

"Hey," he said. "What are you doing here?"

"How's it going, friend?" Von said.

Ashanti pointed to the fire truck. "What happened?" she asked again.

Von waved a hand at the house. "It was just a teeny, tiny fire. Nothing to get worked up about. It was confined to one part of that front room upstairs."

Relief washed over her. She looked up to the window of the room that she had toured both in-person and virtually multiple times.

"My office," she said. "That's what I'd planned to make that room."

"It's going to be part of our cigar bar," Von said. "Hey, at least we now know it can handle smoke."

"Always with the jokes." Thad rolled his eyes. "It really wasn't much of anything," he told Ashanti. "We'd actually put the fire out before the fire truck even arrived. A neighbor called them, so the firefighters decided to check things out just to make sure the integrity of the room hasn't been compromised."

"That fire took out a wall that had to come down any-way," the other man said. He wore starchily pressed jeans and a button-down shirt with MILLER CONTRACTORS embroidered on the pocket.

"So, you see, you don't have to worry about your house," Von said. "I told you we're going to take care of it."

"I wasn't worried about the house," Ashanti said, and real-ized it was true. The initial jolt of fear had been for Thad, not the house. "I'm just glad you all are okay."

"How did you know about the fire?" Thad asked.

"I didn't. I just happened to look this way while on my way to see an industrial kitchen that's available for rent." She told him about the huge order she'd received. "I have to make sure the space will work before I can say yes to the order," Ashanti said. "Do you, uh, want to come check it out with me? It's not too far from here."

"Take him," Von said. "Please."

Thad cut his eyes at Von before following Ashanti to her car.

"I'm getting the sense that something is going on between you and Von," Ashanti said as she drove past the house and turned right again, heading back to St. Claude Avenue.

"He thought the fire would make me want to back out of going into business together. He's convinced I'm going to come out of retirement."

Her head whipped around as she pulled up to a red light.

"I'm not," Thad said before she could voice her question. He leaned over and kissed her. "Even if I had entertained thoughts of going back to Colorado—which I hadn't—there's no way I'm leaving New Orleans now." He kissed her again. "Now, tell me about this order. You think you can handle it?"

His question set off a surge of anxiety in her belly.

She had been asking herself that same question from the moment she first read the email. Once again, things were happening way too quickly. She needed to pause, to think things over and make sure she wasn't biting off more than she could chew.

But she could also make the case for striking while the iron was hot. How much would it hurt Duchess Delights were she to turn down her largest order yet, an order that could get the treats into the hands of thousands? It would be ideal if she could gradually scale up her business, but sometimes it didn't work out that way. Sometimes, you just had to go for it and trust that the path you've chosen is for the best.

She looked over at Thad and tried to keep the apprehension from showing on her face.

"I guess we'll find out," Ashanti said.

The manager of the commissary kitchen was waiting for them. As they toured it, Ashanti had no problem picturing herself working here. The counter space alone was enough to make her weep with joy.

"So do you think this will work for you?" the manager asked.

"It would change everything," Ashanti said. She looked to the manager. "What do I have to do?"

"Tenants must sign a six-month lease with a minimum of twenty hours of use per month, at forty dollars per hour."

Ashanti did the quick math. Eight hundred dollars. Although she would need the kitchen way more than just five hours per week. She should probably double that number.

"And that includes the use of *all* the kitchen equipment?" she asked.

"Everything you see here," the woman said. "Linens as well, but I don't think that applies to your needs."

"The ovens and the shelf space are all I need," she said.

But did she want to commit to six months in a kitchen in this neighborhood if Barkingham Palace was moving to the Lower Garden District? It would take at least twenty minutes to make the trek, and that was during non-rush-hour times.

Did she have a choice?

If she was going to accept that order, she would have to get to baking as soon as possible. She didn't have time to seek out another kitchen and hope it had availability. Besides, it wasn't as if the house on the corner of Terpsichore and Camp Street was move-in ready anyway. It would take at least six months, if not longer, to renovate.

She could not waffle on making this decision, because something else had occurred to her soon after she read that email.

The deal with the local grocery store chain was how she would get her hands on that house in the Lower Garden District. She wouldn't have to put her parents' house up for collateral; all she had to do was show the bank the purchase order.

Sure, her days would be spread even thinner than they were now, but that's what it took to build a business. She had to go for it.

She turned to the commissary's manager.

"Where do I sign?"

35

Thad perched against the stainless-steel kitchen counter, observing Ashanti as she counted the sheet pans stacked on the worktable opposite where he stood. The commissary kitchen manager had left them to explore the kitchens while she showed the adjacent space to potential tenants.

"I can easily fit two dozen of the scepter treats on these," Ashanti said. "And I can get six pans in the oven at a time. I can't believe I waited so long to rent this space. Do you know how much time this will save me?"

"I'm guessing a lot by the smile on your face," Thad answered.

After the morning he'd had with the fire that turned out to be nothing, but that scared the hell out of him all the same, seeing that smile was exactly what he needed. And yet, it was unnerving to realize the effect her presence could have on his mood. So much of his happiness—his feeling of worth—had been tied to the Army; it was unsettling to think that he was replacing that with something else. Or, in this case, some*one* else.

Still, Thad couldn't deny that she made him happy. Despite the fact that, in most regards, they were polar opposites. She was sweet where he was surly, optimistic where he was always looking to spot where things could go wrong. She loved dogs where he...well, that was changing. He had her to thank—or rather, blame—for that too.

Ashanti looked over her shoulder. "You don't have to stay," she told him. "I know you didn't expect to be stuck here while I inspect every corner of these kitchens."

"Do you hear me complaining?" Thad asked.

She grinned. "Well, if that's the case, go over there and check those hood vents for me."

He pushed away from the counter and walked over to the six-burner stove. Ashanti explained that most of the work would be done by the huge commercial ovens, but some of the ingredients had to be cooked and cooled before being added to the batter.

"Cooked pumpkin, butternut squash, and carrots are the key to super-soft doggy treats," she said.

"I'll take your word for it," Thad said, laughing at her eye roll. He resumed his perched position against the counter. "So now that you've examined every piece of equipment in the kitchen, what do you think?"

"I think it's perfect," she said. She shifted her gaze to the three-section sink and pulled her bottom lip between her teeth. Then she looked back at him and smiled an overly bright smile. "It's exactly what I need."

Thad tilted his head, studying her face. "Then why do you look nervous?" he asked.

She huffed out a humorless laugh. "And this is why I can never play poker."

"What's wrong, Ashanti?"

She came over to where he stood and assumed his position, folding her arms across her chest.

"This is a huge step," she said. "The kind that can make or break Duchess Delights. And..."

"And you're afraid you'll ruin your business if you can't deliver?" he asked.

"I guess that's it," she said. "A part of me doesn't know *how* to feel. Everything has happened so quickly. I went from baking a few dozen doggy treats in my home kitchen to now renting out something like this so that I can fulfill an order for twenty thousand?" She shook her head. "I should be more excited, but instead I feel like drinking Pepto Bismol straight from the bottle."

"Is there any other way to drink it?"

That got a laugh out of her. A real one this time.

"You reserve the right to feel overwhelmed. But don't let it get in the way of your dream."

"I think that's what has me so uneasy." She pulled her bottom lip between her teeth again and stared out at the kitchen. "You see, this *wasn't* my dream. It was never part of my original plan. Now it seems as if my little side hustle has taken over."

Thad pushed away from the counter and came to stand in front of her. "Are you saying you don't want to continue with Duchess Delights?"

"No. I would be a fool to give it up."

"Not if it isn't something you want to do."

"I *do* want it," she said. "I just don't want to feel so

overwhelmed by it all. Maybe once I hire more people I'll feel better about this. Speaking of, I need to finally go through the list of candidates my staff suggested and start making some job offers. I need bakers in this kitchen tomorrow."

In a show of impeccable timing, the manager returned and collected the information she needed from Ashanti to complete the contract. Thad watched her closely, ready to step in and offer reassurance if that's what she needed. But she handled it well.

As they started for the car, it hit him that she would drive him to the Bywater house and in less than ten minutes their time together would be done. The thought caused a physical ache to settle in his chest.

He strived for nonchalance when he asked, "Do you have time for a late lunch? There's a little Jamaican place a couple of blocks away that's pretty good."

"I don't have time, but that sounds so much better than the ham sandwich waiting for me at the daycare. Do they serve alcohol with their jerk chicken?"

"Does the thought of signing that contract make you *that* nervous?"

"It's not the contract," she said with a sigh. They arrived at her car, but neither made a move to get in.

"What is it?" Thad asked.

"Anita came to the daycare this morning, threatening to take me to court over the girls because I spent the night at your house."

"The fuck?" His anger was instant.

Ashanti waved him off. "Don't bother getting worked up over it." A mischievous grin pulled at one corner of her mouth.

"I threatened to call the cops on her if she didn't leave the daycare. It was amazing."

"Next time don't just threaten. Do it," Thad said.

"Maybe I will," she said, her smile widening. She tipped her head to the side. "You know what, I think I deserve that lunch. I have a feeling it will be a long time before I'm able to sit and enjoy a good meal once I start this big order."

They'd just headed north on Lesseps Street when Ashanti's phone rang.

"I'm tempted to not answer it," she said, pulling the phone from her back pocket. She held it up. "As I suspected, Deja probably calling with my next headache of the day." She answered the phone. "Hey, Deja. What's up?"

She stopped walking. "Oh my God," she whispered.

Panic gripped Thad's chest.

"Oh my God! I'm on my way!" Ashanti started running back to her car before Thad could question her.

"Ashanti," he called, catching up to her in just a couple of strides. "What's going on?"

She was shaking so badly that her hand slipped as she tried to open the SUV's door.

"Ashanti!" Thad said.

"It's Duchess," she said. "She was attacked by another dog."

Thad jutted his chin toward the passenger side. "Get in. I'll drive."

36

Ashanti couldn't stop shivering.

In the five minutes since they'd left the commissary kitchen on their way to the daycare, five million scenarios had played out in her head, all ending with her sweet baby bloody and in pain.

Thad tried to calm her, rubbing his thumb across her hand as he held it and telling her that everything would be okay, but the awfulness crowding her brain wouldn't allow his words to seep in. She needed to see her Duchess for herself.

"Let me out right here," Ashanti said the moment they arrived at the daycare.

He didn't even make a case for parking; just stopped the car in the middle of the street so she could exit.

Ashanti shot up the stairs and into the lobby. Once inside, she shouted, "Where is she? Where's Duchess?"

Leslie was standing just off to the right of the door, as if she had been waiting for her.

"In back. Evie's with her," she said.

Ashanti took off for the intake room, her heart slamming into her chest when she got there.

"We're okay, Mama," Evie said, not looking up from where Duchess was stretched out on the table. "No need to panic. She's going to be fine."

"Oh, baby," Ashanti said. Duchess's stubby tail started wagging and Ashanti burst into tears.

"You're going to upset her," Evie said. "Either stop the crying or get out of here."

She was right. Ashanti sucked in a breath and pulled herself together. She walked up to the table and gently rubbed Duchess's head while Evie tended to her wounds.

"I'm going to bring her to the clinic for X-rays and stitches, but it isn't as bad as it could have been," Evie said. She looked up at Ashanti. "I am saying this with all the love in the world, please stay your ass here until I call for you."

"No way." Ashanti shook her head.

"I mean it, Shanti. I don't need you losing your shit all over my waiting room. She'll be sedated and won't be ready to come home for at least four hours. There's no reason for you to be there. I'll call when I'm done." She hitched her chin toward the door. "Now, go get her travel crate so we can get to the clinic."

"It's right here," Colleen said, coming into the room. "I'm going to take Mark to urgent care. He'll probably need a few stitches."

"Mark's hurt too?" Ashanti asked.

It hadn't even crossed her mind to inquire about anyone else. What had happened here?

"Yeah, he wrestled Duchess away from Sano," Colleen said, answering her unvoiced question.

Sano.

Ashanti's stomach dropped.

"Duchess shouldn't have been near Sano," she said. "No dog should have. Sano is supposed to be kept separate. I made—"

She stopped.

She hadn't made a note. She was supposed to. She'd grabbed a Post-it to jot it down, but she hadn't because she had been preoccupied with that email from the grocery chain.

Ashanti covered her face with her hands and began to sob.

"Oh, shit," she heard Evie say.

Thad came into the already crowded room and quickly wrapped her up in a hug, cradling her head against his chest and running his hand up and down her arm.

"How is Duchess?" he asked.

The complete silence following his question caused Ashanti to look up.

Evie, Colleen, and now Leslie, who'd walked in behind Thad, all stared at them.

"Uh, *hello*," Colleen said.

"Duchess?" Thad asked again. "How is she?"

"She's going to be fine," Evie said. "A few stitches, but that's likely the extent of it."

Thad looked down at Ashanti and drew his finger along her cheek. "That doesn't sound so bad."

Ashanti heard Leslie's swift intake of breath. She started to step away from Thad, but it felt too good nestled here in his arms. There was no walking this back at this point, so why should she even bother.

"I'll get Duchess to the clinic," Evie said, lifting the crate. "And then we are talking. Oh, bitch, we are *talking*, do you hear me? I'll tell Rid to join us."

"Can I join too?" Leslie asked. "I'll bring wine."

"Me too," Colleen said. "I've got snacks. I make a mean roasted beet hummus."

"You get Mark to urgent care," Evie said. She looked at Thad and Ashanti. "You get her to her office. Who has an extra Xanax she can take?"

"I do," Leslie and Colleen said at the same time.

"Me," Mark called from just outside the door to the exam room.

"I'm fine. I don't need Xanax," Ashanti said. "I just need a few minutes to calm down. And I need *you* to get my dog to the clinic," she said to Evie.

Evie held up her free hand. "We're going."

They all filed out of the exam room. Ashanti ignored Evie's protest as she followed her out to her van. Then she stood in the middle of the sidewalk and watched, heart in her throat, as they drove away.

"She's going to be okay," Thad said, cupping her elbow in his palm.

"I know Evie will take care of her. She's one of the best." Ashanti bit her trembling lip. "But I hate this. She could have been killed."

"But she wasn't," Thad said. He gently tugged her arm. "Come on. Let's go to your office."

She wordlessly followed him back inside. Mark and Colleen were getting ready to head to urgent care.

"Oh, Mark," Ashanti said when she noticed the six-inch gash on his forearm. Guilt had her unable to look him in the eye. "Should I come with you?"

"That's okay," Mark said.

"I've got him," Colleen said at the same time.

"Boss Lady, you need to get to your office and settle down for a minute," Deja said. "If you don't want a Xanax, at least have yourself a drink."

Thad arched his eyebrows. "That's not a bad idea," he said.

Ashanti blew out an exhausted breath. "I'll be in my office." She looked to Thad. "I know you have to get back to the—"

"No, I don't," he said before she could even finish. He started for her and Ashanti's chest expanded with gratitude. Not caring that her staff was staring at them like guppies in a fishbowl, she took the hand Thad offered and guided him to her office.

Ashanti went straight for her chair and plopped down in it.

"It's not even a Monday," she said.

"Shitty days aren't limited to Mondays," Thad said. "Ask me how I know." He walked over to her desk and perched himself against it. "Duchess is going to be okay, Ashanti. I need *you* to be okay."

"I am."

"You're shaking."

Ashanti tried to still her hands, but they continued to tremble.

"Maybe I *should* have that drink," she said.

"You can still have it," Thad said. "We can get delivery. One of the best things about New Orleans is go-cups. You can have any drink you want, just say the word."

"Thank you," she said, trying her best to smile. She shook her head. "I won't be able to eat until I know for sure Duchess is okay. And no one wants me to drink alcohol on an empty stomach. Happened once in undergrad. It wasn't pretty."

"First of all, Duchess *is* okay. I thought we already established that. She was smiling when she left. I didn't even know dogs *could* smile."

Ashanti laughed, for real this time. "She's a happy dog," she said. "She smiles all the time." She put a hand to her stomach as her eyes filled with tears "It's my fault this happened. That dog could have killed her."

"Why are you taking the blame for this?" Thad asked. He hunched down and cradled her face in his hands. "You weren't even here, Ashanti. How is it your fault?"

"Because I never wrote that damn note about the Akita not tolerating other dogs. His owner specifically asked me to do it, she even paid for private play time to protect the other dogs from him. And I forgot to make the notation in the file. I was too busy worrying about that big order for the dog treats."

She shook her head. The emotion welling up in her throat made it hard to swallow.

"I knew something like this would eventually happen," Ashanti said. "This is what happens when you have a million things going on all at once. Balls get dropped. I've been so afraid that I would mess things up with Kendra or Kara. I didn't even consider causing my dog to get maimed."

"Stop blaming yourself," Thad said.

She looked up at him. "I can't help but think about how much worse it will be if Duchess Delights continues to grow. It's all been too fast. I can't handle it. What happened today proves it. I should just call and tell the grocery store that I'll have to pass on that order."

"Don't," Thad said. "You're too agitated to make decisions about this at the moment. In fact, I don't want you to think about any of this stuff right now, just concentrate on relaxing."

Ashanti knew he was only trying to save her from suffering further anguish, but that wasn't going to happen.

How could she *not* think about the potential tragedy they had so narrowly avoided? Her dog could have been killed because Ashanti was stretched too thin and couldn't keep her focus. Someone *else's* dog could have been killed.

Ashanti's breath caught in her throat.

What if another of the dogs had been attacked?

Sure, she had liability insurance to cover financial damages, but nothing would cover the damage to Barkingham Palace's reputation. Never mind her own guilt. She wouldn't trust herself to run this business were something like this to happen again. She barely trusted herself now.

She leaned forward and rested her head against Thad's shoulder. She had some hard decisions to make.

37

You lied to me, Thaddeus Sims."

Thad looked down at Ashanti's upturned face, his eyes narrowing at the smile that played across lips he would give anything to kiss right now.

"When did I lie?"

"You told me you didn't dance," she said.

He swayed with her from side to side while gliding his feet in a slow circle.

"Actually, I told you I danced all the time at functions just like this one." He looked around the tastefully decorated ballroom teeming with elegantly dressed people in various stages of drunkenness. "Except the various military balls I've attended didn't have quite this much free-flowing alcohol."

She laughed. "It's a New Orleans wedding. Free-flowing alcohol is as mandatory as the preacher." She tipped her head to the side. "Come to think of it, one can be married by the justice of the peace, but to be married without hurricanes or Crown Royal and Coke? Blasphemous."

The band brought the slow ballad to a close. Moments later, the unmistakable opening notes of the "Electric Slide" started.

"That's my cue," Thad said, turning on his heel.

"Oh, no you don't." Ashanti caught him by the wrist. "*This* is the kind of dancing I want to see you do."

He closed his eyes and groaned, but then took two steps to the right, joining in with the dozens of others who had rushed to the dance floor. And, since he was here, he decided to play it up, getting some shoulder action in and adding some oomph to the kick.

He probably looked like a fool, but seeing the sheer delight on Ashanti's face made it worth it.

Thad had been unsure whether she would still be up for attending the wedding after the tumultuous week she'd had. He'd barely seen her between her taking care of Duchess—who, thankfully, had fully recovered from the Akita attack—hiring two bakers and setting up the kitchen for that big grocery store order, and dealing with her sisters.

He'd been surprised when she'd texted him early this morning to find out if the wedding had a certain color theme—apparently, that was something people did these days—and mentioned how much she was looking forward to a night out.

Knowing that he could take a little of her anxiety away, even if just for a few hours, made the satisfaction in his chest expand like helium filling a balloon.

The dance ended and Ashanti pleaded they stop for a

breather. Not because she'd tired herself out from dancing, but rather from laughing. At him.

Thad grabbed two bottles of water from the bar and joined her at their table. The moment he sat down, someone hooked an arm around his neck and kissed his cheek.

"I don't know what kind of magic spell you've weaved around my brother, but I like it," his sister said to Ashanti.

Thad rolled his eyes at Nadia's intrusion, but he couldn't fault her for being surprised. He would be surprised as hell if he were in her shoes too. The last time he'd danced like this was probably a family reunion when he was twelve.

"Ree Ree plans to throw the bouquet soon. Let me know if you want it and it's yours," Nadia said with a wink.

"Enough with the matchmaking, Frances," Thad said. She was as bad as his grandmother.

"Speaking of, Grams said that somebody had better bring her wedding cake first thing in the morning. She wants it for breakfast."

"Of course she does," Thad said, his good mood dulling at the thought of his grandmother and what he'd promised himself he would do when his sister came to town.

"You're thinking about that ancestry thing, aren't you?" Ashanti asked as soon as Nadia left the table.

"I guess my poker face needs some work too," he said.

"You haven't talked to your sister about it?"

He shook his head. "She's been looking forward to Reshonda's wedding. I didn't want to ruin it for her. But she knows something's up. She's got a sixth sense for shit like this. The moment she walked into the house, she asked me what I was hiding from her."

Ashanti fiddled with the cloth napkin at her place setting. "When do you plan to tell her?"

"Tonight," Thad said. "She's flying home tomorrow afternoon."

She reached across the table and covered his hand with hers. "This won't be easy for either of you. I'm sorry."

He would give anything to have Ashanti be the one coming home with him tonight. Maybe he could offer to put Nadia up in one of the hotels in the French Quarter. The benefits would be twofold, he could put off telling her about their philandering grandfather until the morning and finally wake up with Ashanti in his bed again.

Thad scratched the idea.

He owed Nadia more than just a few hours to process this kind of news before she had to fly home to her husband and daughters. He would have to tell her tonight so that they could decide together what to do about it.

The wedding reception ended sooner than Thad had hoped. After following the bride and groom in a second-line parade along the riverfront, he, Ashanti, and Nadia piled into Von's car. He'd borrowed it, figuring it was more appropriate for the occasion than his truck.

Nadia and Ashanti chatted the entire drive to Ashanti's house, with his sister dropping more poorly veiled hints about Thad and Ashanti taking their relationship to the next level.

Thad walked Ashanti to her door—and not just because his sister had demanded it—before heading home. Nadia continued with the relationship talk for the remainder of their drive home, balking when Thad told her that he wasn't sure if he and Ashanti were even in a relationship yet.

"Bullshit," Nadia said as she unsnapped her seat belt. "You

and Ashanti had more chemistry than Reshonda and Michael. You two should have been the ones getting married tonight."

"Please, don't do this," Thad said, thanking God that she hadn't said this while Ashanti was still in the car.

"You need to settle down, and she is perfect for you. Like, ridiculously perfect for you. And why are you in such a pissy mood tonight?" his sister asked, shoving him in the back as they climbed the steps of their grandparents' house. "You just spent the evening with one of *the* loveliest people I've ever met. You should be floating."

"How does one float?" Thad asked.

"How did your grumpy ass ever manage to talk that amazing woman into going out with you in the first place?"

"I'm charming when I'm not around you," Thad said.

She shoved him again as he let them into the house.

Nadia took off for her grandparents' old room, which she'd claimed after telling Thad he was a fool for choosing to sleep in his old, much smaller bedroom.

He kicked off his shoes, hung up his jacket, and loosened his tie, but he didn't change out of his clothes. The longer he stalled, the more likely he was to come up with an excuse for why he should hold off from telling her about their newfound family in Alabama.

Thad walked over to his grandparents' room and rapped on the door with his knuckle.

"Nadia, can you come in the dining room for a minute once you're done?"

He grabbed a beer from the fridge, and not one of those flavored IPAs he'd been sampling for the bar. He needed something with meat for the conversation he was about to engage in. Tonight called for a dark, malty lager.

"You finally ready to tell me why you've been moodier than usual?" Nadia asked as she entered the dining room. She'd changed into a Bruno Mars T-shirt and purple sweats. Her face still had makeup from the wedding, but she'd taken out the pins holding up her hair.

"You may want to sit for this," Thad told her.

Her smile disappeared.

"You're dying," she said. "Grams is dying!"

"No one is dying," Thad said.

His grandfather was already dead, so his sister wouldn't be able to kill him when she found out what he'd done.

She sat at the table and Thad pushed the laptop in front of her.

He started with the first email, and methodically went through each subsequent correspondence, ending with the picture of the woman's mother.

Nadia looked shell-shocked as she stared at the screen, her mouth agape. After several heavy moments ticked by, she looked up at him and said, "That son of a bitch."

Thad grimaced. "Normally, I would say it's disrespectful to speak of your grandfather in that way, but this time I think it's warranted."

"This had to have been going on for decades," Nadia said.

Thad nodded. "According to what she shared, there's sixteen years between her mom, the oldest, and her youngest uncle, who is only a few years older than you are, by the way."

"That son of a bitch!" Nadia grabbed his beer from his hand and took a long drink. "You know if he was still alive I would be charging into that room with a butcher knife, right?"

"Again, warranted," Thad said.

"What does she want?" Nadia asked.

"I thought she was after money, but it appears she just wants to get to know her relatives," he said.

"Goodness." Nadia rubbed her temples. "What are we gonna do?" She held her hands up. "What am I talking about? There's only one thing we *can* do. We have to tell Grams. You haven't said anything to her, have you?"

"No."

"I didn't think so," she said, rising from the table. "She would have called me."

Thad worried his bottom lip with his teeth, regarding his sister as she paced the length of the room while calling his grandfather everything but a child of God. He gave her the space she needed to vent. He'd had time to digest this news; she hadn't.

"Nadia, are you sure about this?" Thad asked when she finally calmed.

"Am I sure that the man I thought was a saint was actually the devil?" she asked. She pointed at the computer. "That picture tells the story."

"Not that," Thad said. "Are you sure about telling Grams? Does she really need to know about this?"

His sister looked at him as if his head had flown off his body and set itself on the table.

"Are you out of your mind? Of course we have to tell her. You want to talk about disrespect? Disrespect is letting my grandmother go on thinking that her husband was this upstanding paragon, when he was actually a lying, cheating bastard." She slapped her palm to her forehead. "I cannot believe this. I cannot believe we're talking about Gramps."

Her voice broke on the last word.

"I know," Thad said, his voice raspy with the same hurt and disappointment he could tell his sister was feeling. He rubbed the back of his neck. "If you think we should tell Grams, then that's what we'll do. She has a right to know."

When he awoke the next morning, Thad had a hard time remembering another task he'd dreaded as much as the one that lay before him today.

Nadia packed her luggage so that he could bring her straight to the airport following the visit with their grandmother. Thad picked up the piece of foiled-covered wedding cake—Grams had texted twice already this morning—and added water to Puddin's bowl before leaving the house. He was actually getting better at being home alone if Thad only left him for a few hours.

His grandmother would be upset that he hadn't brought her dog, but it would only last for a minute. She had other things to upset her this time around.

With traffic as light as it was on Sunday mornings, they made it to the assisted living facility in a matter of minutes. Grams was in her unit, which was nicer than some of the studio apartments that rented for ridiculous amounts in this city.

"I hate that you have to go back home so soon," Grams said as she wrapped Nadia in a hug. She pinched her on the arm. "That's for not bringing my great-granddaughters with you."

"I already told you that we're coming back for Thanksgiving," Nadia said.

"That's too long to wait." She looked to Thad. "Where's my cake? And why didn't you bring Puddin'?"

"I have to bring Nadia straight to the airport. Puddin'

would have just gotten in the way." Thad swallowed. "Grams, we need to tell you something."

Grams looked from him to Nadia. "Who's dead?"

"Nobody died," Thad said. What was with the women in his family? "But I...uh...I recently got some disturbing news about Gramps."

Her brows arched. "Well, he's dead, so it can't be too disturbing."

Thad looked to his sister, who nodded.

"This is hard to say, Grams, and I swear I debated the whole drive over whether or not we should even share this with you—"

"Boy, would you say whatever it is you've got to say so I can eat my cake," his grandmother prompted.

Thad sucked in a deep breath. Then, before he lost his nerve, said, "Someone contacted me a few weeks ago, claiming to be Gramps's granddaughter. I haven't confirmed her story, but we have a strong feeling that it's true. He was having an affair, Grams. For a long time."

She stared at him for a moment, then her lips tipped up in an amused, sardonic grin.

"You're talking about Sybil Jackson in Mobile?" she asked.

Thad and Nadia both looked at each other, their mouths falling open at the exact same time.

"Grams." Nadia was the first to find her voice. Thad was still searching for his. "You *know* her?"

"Do you children think I'm stupid? Do you know how long I've been on this earth?" his grandmother asked. "I knew he was up to something from early on. There aren't *that* many damn dry cleaning conventions in a single year."

"But...but..." Nadia stuttered. "You knew about it and you didn't say anything?"

"I didn't say anything to *y'all*. Why would I tell my grandchildren what's going on in my marriage? That wasn't nobody's business but mine and your grandfather's. And Sybil Jackson's, I guess."

Nadia brought her palm to her forehead, her eyes still wide with shock. "But how did you just let him get away with this without doing anything about it?"

"Let him get away with it? How do you think I got that man to put both his house *and* his business in my name?"

"Holy shit," Thad whispered.

His grandmother wiggled her fingers toward the kitchenette. "Grab me a fork so I can try this cake. I hope it doesn't have that waxy fondant icing. I hate that kind."

"Grams!" Nadia said. "You can't drop this bomb on us and then eat cake."

"I'm not letting my cake get stale." She shrugged. "And what else is there to say?"

"How did you stomach it for all those years?" Nadia asked.

"Thank goodness they went with buttercream," his grandmother said as she peeled back the foil. She set both the cake and fork on the coffee table and addressed Nadia.

"Look, times were different back then. Your grandfather was a deacon in the church and a pillar in the community. If word got out about his second family in Mobile, that status would have been lost. Never mind what it would have done to the business. I wasn't about to sully my good name or mess up my money because he wanted a little something extra on the side."

Holy *shit*. His grandmother was savage.

"I hope you children haven't spent any time getting worked up over this. There are more important things to be concerned about, like why Thaddeus is dragging his feet when it comes to Ashanti."

Thad dropped his head back and sighed up at the ceiling. "Nadia, isn't it time for you to get to the airport?"

"No, I've got time," his sister said. "And I agree, Grams. I met her last night and I love her already. We gotta figure out how to get those two together, permanently."

God, save him from the women in his family.

38

You have got to be kidding me," Ashanti said. She held up a hand. "Nope. I take that back. You're not kidding, because I can totally see Mrs. Frances pulling a move like that."

"Straight up gangsta," Thad said. He picked up a rock and pitched it into the Mississippi River. "Grams had her mind on her money and her money on her mind."

Despite how busy she had been all morning, Ashanti hadn't hesitated to drop everything and meet Thad back at Crescent Park when he'd texted. He'd contacted her while still at the airport after dropping Nadia off for her flight home. Ashanti was waiting for him when he pulled into the same parking lot they'd parked in the last time.

She had been prepared for a somber retelling of his morning with his grandmother, full of hurt and pain. What she *hadn't* expected was Mrs. Frances to turn out to be an extortionist.

"Does it help, knowing that your grandmother was okay with what your grandfather did?" Ashanti asked.

He shrugged. "In a way."

He switched Puddin's leash to his other hand and captured hers, entwining their fingers. They continued walking upriver, the sun reflecting off the buildings of the New Orleans skyline.

"I don't think anything will ever take away my disappointment," Thad said. "I truly believed that my grandfather could do no wrong. It hurts to know that he was living this lie, even if my grandmother was okay with it—which I still think isn't entirely the case. Can a woman really be okay with her husband fathering three children with someone else while they're still married?"

"Couldn't be me," Ashanti said.

"Yeah." He shrugged again. "Like Grams said, it was a different time, and he had a reputation in the community to uphold."

"And she got a house and a successful business out of it," Ashanti said. "Some women get nothing but heartache."

"She held it together well, because I never would have suspected that there was anything but love between them. They weren't the most affectionate couple, but who wants to see their grandparents being overly affectionate? But there was love there, you know? I never once thought that they didn't love each other."

"Maybe she *did* love him. Love is complicated." She lifted both shoulders in a shrug. "Again, that couldn't be me. But I'm sure your grandmother had her reasons for tolerating his behavior for all those years. What about your mother?"

Ashanti asked. "Mrs. Frances talked about her before. She's in California, right?"

"Henderson, Nevada," Thad said. "She moved a few months ago."

"Do you think she knew about it?"

"I doubt it," Thad said. "Unlike my grandmother, I'm pretty sure my mom would have told me and Nadia. She never held anything back about my dad's cheating and I just can't see her doing it for Gramps. She would have been straight with us."

They reached the end of the park's walkway. Thad hunched down and rubbed Puddin's head.

"The big question is what to do about all our new Alabama cousins. Nadia isn't ready to talk about it. She regrets ever starting that genealogy project."

"Do *you* regret it?"

He waited several beats before he finally answered.

"I don't know. Ignorance is bliss, but being ignorant about something isn't always for the best. My mind always goes to the most practical issues, like what if one of my nieces needed a kidney or something. It's good to know we have family out there that could possibly help, right?"

"Um, I guess that's one way to look at it."

"It's selfish," Thad said with a gruff laugh. "But I'm trying to find the positives in this. Maybe I just need more time to process it."

Ashanti stooped next to him and ran her fingers along his jaw. "One positive is that it wasn't the devastating blow to your grandmother that you thought it would be. This could have been so much worse."

He smiled. "You do have a knack for always finding the

bright side of a situation. I love that about you." His expression sobered as his focus settled on her. He cupped her jaw. "I don't want to scare you, Ashanti, but there are a lot of things that I love about you. Like, enough to fill the Superdome."

"It doesn't scare me," she said as she leaned over, capturing his lips in a slow, sweet kiss that she wished could last all day.

But it couldn't. Because she had forty-eight hours of work to fit into the next ten hours.

They spent the return journey discussing the additional candidates Ashanti had spent her morning reviewing. She still experienced a pinch of anxiety in her chest when she thought about accepting that huge order, but decided if she called it nervous excitement instead anxiety it would make it easier to cope.

"I need to get back home," she said once they reached their cars. She looked over at Thad and asked, "Do you want to come over?"

His brows arched. "Are your sisters there?"

"Yes. Are you up to meeting them? Officially?"

He pulled in a deep breath, glanced at the bridge, and then back at her. "Does meeting your sisters mean what I think it means?"

Ashanti nodded. "It does."

There was no mistaking it now, what flowed through her veins was pure anxiety. They both knew the significance of her offer. She'd told him before that she would not introduce him to the girls if she wasn't ready to go all in.

She was inviting him into her life. Fully. Completely. No turning back.

"Are you okay with that?" Ashanti asked.

The lion's share of her anxiety melted away at his smile.

"I am exceedingly okay with that," Thad said. He stepped up to her and wrapped his arms around her. "I am so, *so* okay with that."

Ashanti looked up at him. "I have to warn you, they can be a bit much. You've kinda met Kara already, and I'm sure she made an impression in just those few minutes."

"She is the reason I will never even think of leaving Puddin' in my truck unattended."

Ashanti laughed, remembering that conversation. It seemed like ages ago.

"Kendra, on the other hand, is quiet and reserved, even though she's the cheerleader." She shook her head. "Their personalities don't fit their personas at all. I think they do it purposely."

"Do you think they'll like me?" Thad asked. It was the most unsure Ashanti had ever seen him, and she could not deny how adorable it looked on him.

"Only one way to find out," Ashanti said.

Thad followed in his truck. Based on the smell of charcoal and the dozen extra cars parked along the street, someone in the neighborhood was having a cookout. She had to park five houses down from hers, with Thad having to park even farther.

She had yet to run into Bernard Willis. The little creep had been avoiding her, but Ashanti hadn't forgotten about the verbal beatdown she owed him.

Duchess went into a frenzy at the realization that Puddin' was joining her at her home.

"Look at those two," Ashanti said. "They look like two friends getting ready to have a sleepover." She held a hand up to Thad. "I'm not ready for that yet. And it's not because of Anita and her threats."

"You're raising impressionable teenagers. I get it, Ashanti. We're still moving slow and I am fine with that," Thad said. "But being introduced to your sisters as your boyfriend is a giant step forward. And it is fucking crazy how ready I am to take that step."

She smiled. "I'm ready for it too."

Her phone rang as they started walking toward her house. It was Kara.

"Hey, Kara, I'm outside. I'll be there in a—"

"Get in here now," Kara said. "Kendra is so upset that even I'm scared."

Ashanti's heart dropped to her stomach. "I'm on my way," she said, already starting to run.

"What's wrong?" Thad asked.

"It's Kendra," she called. She stopped and handed him Duchess's leash. "Can you take her for me?"

At the base of the steps, Ashanti turned to him and said, "Don't leave. I just need to—"

"I'm not going anywhere," Thad interrupted. He hitched his chin toward the door. "Go."

Kara opened the front door. "She's in her room."

Ashanti ran past her and up the stairs. She could hear Kendra's crying from the other side of the door. She turned the knob and was surprised to find it unlocked.

Her heart broke the moment she walked into the room. Kendra was draped across the bed, her body shaking with sobs. Ashanti took a chance and sat on the edge of the mattress.

"Ken." She ran her hand along her arm. "Ken, what's wrong? Please, talk to me."

Her sister turned and looked up at her. Her face was swollen from crying, the tears still streaming from her red eyes down her cheeks. Ashanti's throat ached with her own tears. There was nothing she hated more than to see her sisters in pain.

"Kendra?" Ashanti prompted. "Did something happen at school?"

She nodded and sat up in the bed.

"What's this about, Ken? And don't tell me it's because you didn't make managing editor of the magazine, because I won't believe you. I don't care how badly you wanted that position; you wouldn't be crying like this just because it went to someone else. Now tell me, what is going on?"

"It's..." She hiccupped. "It's Mr. Williamson."

Ashanti's back went ramrod straight. Mr. Williamson was the literary magazine's faculty sponsor, and without a doubt, Kendra's favorite teacher.

"What about him?" she asked. "Did he kick you off the magazine? Is that why you've been so upset?"

She prayed Kendra would say yes. When her sister shook her head, Ashanti's stomach dropped, along with her voice. "What did he do?" she gritted between clenched teeth.

Kendra's eyes widened. "No!" she said. "Nothing like what you're thinking."

Ashanti pressed her hand to her stomach as relief swept through her. "Then what, Kendra? And I want the truth this time."

"Mr. Williamson didn't kick me off the magazine." She sucked in a shaky breath, then said, "He's been selling grades."

Ashanti's head snapped back. "What?"

"You remember Michelle Miles, right? She's on the cheerleading squad with me." Ashanti nodded. "She was put on academic probation at the end of last year because of her grade in English. She almost lost her place on the squad. So, during cheer camp over the summer, I offered to tutor her.

"Just after the start of this school year, I asked her how things were going in English and if she maybe wanted to study together. She said no, because she already knew she would get a passing grade." Kendra sniffed and wiped at her nose with her wrist. "That's when she told me that she paid Mr. Williamson a thousand dollars to cover her grades for the semester."

Ashanti had to steady herself on the mattress. It felt as if the wind had been knocked out of her.

"Are you serious?" she asked.

Kendra nodded. "He has an entire network, Shanti. Nearly everyone who works on the magazine is in on it. They're selling term papers, taking online tests for people, everything. And not just at our school."

Ashanti brought both hands to her mouth. She could not believe this. Mr. Williamson had won her over during the very first parent-teacher night during the girls' freshman year. They'd discussed Kendra's love of reading and he'd told Ashanti about the literary magazine. She was the one who had encouraged Kendra to join the staff.

"I went straight to Mr. Williamson," Kendra continued. "I thought Michelle was lying on him, that she was trying to get him in trouble or something."

"And what did he say?"

"He asked if I wanted to join in on their little cheating circle," Kendra said, wiping at her eyes with the heels of both hands. "He said that he'd never invited me because he assumed I was too much of a goody two-shoes to come over to the dark side. He laughed, like it was a joke or something.

"When I told him I wouldn't...it was like...like his face changed before my eyes, Shanti. His eyes were so cold and just...scary. He said he would tell Principal Keller that I was the mastermind behind the whole thing, and he said that everyone who works on the magazine would back him up."

"That son of a bitch," Ashanti said.

"I didn't think they would take Mr. Williamson's side. These are my friends! Paulina Dugas, Kimberly Jackson—I've known them since middle school. But the day after I confronted Mr. Williamson, they cornered me in the restroom and said they would start spreading rumors about me, and you, and Kara if I didn't keep my mouth shut. Awful rumors," she said. "Rumors that could ruin your business."

"Oh, Ken," Ashanti said.

"So I didn't say anything, because I couldn't risk it. But I can't take it anymore," she said. "I quit the magazine."

Ashanti wrapped her arms around her, squeezing tighter than she should but unable to stop herself.

"Baby, I am so, so sorry."

The words hurt as they pushed past the knot of emotion lodged in Ashanti's throat. She'd been so frustrated with Kendra's attitude, and all the while her sister had been facing those little terrorists alone, all for the sake of protecting Ashanti. It should have been the other way around. She was the one who was supposed to protect Kendra.

And Mr. Williamson. That bastard had better be ready, because her wrath would be unlike anything he had ever suffered.

"I will be in Mrs. Keller's office Monday morning," Ashanti said.

"No!" Kendra wrestled herself out of Ashanti's hold. "Shanti, please. It's not worth it."

Bullshit.

There was no way she would let that grown-ass man get away with threatening her little sister. He was going down. They all were.

"This can't be the end of it, Kendra. What they are doing is wrong—it is illegal. Whether or not you want to work on the magazine is no longer the issue. Mr. Williamson cannot be allowed to continue teaching."

She took Kendra by the shoulders and held her so that she could look her in the eyes.

"You know this, don't you? You knew from the moment you decided to tell me the truth that this would be the outcome. Because I will *not* let him get away with this."

She nodded. "Yes, I knew," she said. She hiccupped. "I'm just...I'm so hurt, Shanti."

"Oh, baby, I know." She wiped the fresh tears that had started to stream down Kendra's face.

"I feel stupid even saying this, but Mr. Williamson felt like a dad to me these past two years." Her eyes went wide. "Not that I don't appreciate everything you do, Shanti! I just mean—"

"Shhh, it's okay, Ken. I know what you mean," she said, wrapping her up in her arms again.

Ashanti rubbed between her shoulders, gently rocking her back and forth. It reminded her so much of those nights just after their parents died, when she would have one girl on either side of her, comforting them as they all cried themselves to sleep.

She sat up straight and took Kendra's chin in her hand.

"You have a right to feel everything that you are feeling. Mr. Williamson is—was like a dad to you. He's the reason you want to go into journalism. It's okay to be hurt and disappointed that someone you looked up to turned out to be so horrible."

Ashanti tilted her head to the side as something occurred to her.

"Ken, are you up for meeting someone?"

"Who? Your new boyfriend?"

"He's not—yes," Ashanti said. "I'm talking about my new boyfriend, Thad."

"It's about time you got a new boyfriend. I don't know how you've gone this long without—"

Ashanti held up a hand. "Don't finish that statement." Relief swelled in her chest at the sight of Kendra's smile. It was the first genuine one she had seen on her face in a long time. "I don't want to spring Thad on you if you're not up for it," Ashanti continued. "But I think this would be a good time—the perfect time—for you two to meet."

She nodded. "Yeah, I'm up for meeting him."

"I'll go downstairs and get him."

"You left him downstairs with Kara? You don't plan on having him for a boyfriend for very long, do you?"

She grimaced. "Let's hope she hasn't run him away."

Ashanti pressed a kiss to Kendra's forehead. She went downstairs and found Thad and Kara sitting at the dining room table, attaching labels to Duchess Delights packaging. Duchess and Puddin' sat at the foot of Thad's chair, waiting for a treat to drop to the floor.

"Is Kendra okay?" Kara asked the moment she spotted Ashanti.

Thad immediately rose from the table and came to stand next to her.

"You two officially meet?" Ashanti asked.

"Yeah, we met," Kara said. "He's much better with Puddin' now, so I have no objections to him." She brought her palms together and bowed. "You have my blessings."

Ashanti rolled her eyes.

"Can you watch the dogs?" she asked Kara. "I need to talk to Thad."

Kara eyed her suspiciously. "Did something really bad happen and you're just not telling me?"

"Everything is going to be okay," Ashanti said. "It's just that Thad recently experienced something that's very similar to the situation Kendra is going through." She looked up at him. "I think you may be able to help her."

His brow furrowed, but he didn't question her.

Ashanti took him by the hand and started for the stairs. She stopped midway, right next to her parents' picture, and in a lowered voice gave him a summary of what Kendra had shared.

"That motherfucker needs to go down," Thad said.

"My sentiments exactly," Ashanti said. "But that's on the agenda for Monday. Right now, all I care about is Kendra, and making sure she's okay. It's a lot to ask of you, but as someone who knows what it's like to have a father figure you thought hung the moon turn out not to be the person you thought they were, I thought it would help to have you talk to her. You don't have to tell her what happened with your grandfather, but you understand the disappointment she's feeling right now better than anyone."

He remained quiet, his expression unreadable. A knot of regret formed in her throat.

"I'm sorry for assuming that you—"

"Ashanti," he stopped her. "It's not that. It's..." He released a breath. "I know how much your sisters mean to you, and I am honored and humbled that you would trust me with something so important." He took her hand and placed a kiss in the center of her palm. "Thank you."

She grasped both his hands in hers and squeezed them tight, then pressed a quick kiss to his lips.

His left hand still clutched in her right one, she guided him up the stairs and knocked on Kendra's door, which was still slightly ajar.

"Ken?" Ashanti said, pushing the door open. She moved to the side so that Thad could enter. "This is Thad Sims."

Thad gave her a wave. "Hi, Kendra," he said. "I know we're just meeting for the first time, but it turns out that you and I have something pretty unfortunate in common. You up for a chat?"

Thad could tell something was off the moment he walked into the Bywater house. Tension hummed all around him. Von stood hunched over Micah Samuels, who sat on an overturned five-gallon bucket. They were both intensely reading over the sheaf of papers Micah held.

"What's going on?" Thad asked.

Von's and Micah's heads whipped around simultaneously.

"I thought you said you would be late?" Von asked.

"I am late," he said. Although not as late as he'd thought he would be. His grandmother had called early this morning, letting him know that she was on her way to the ER.

It turned out that the new nurse at the assisted living facility had blown a tiny cut on Gram's foot way out of proportion. One butterfly bandage was all it took. When Thad left, she and several of the other residents were settling in for an all-day marathon of *The Fast and the Furious* franchise.

"This morning's crisis was averted," Thad said. "Now, what's going on? Please don't tell me even more damage was caused by the fire than we first thought?"

"So you're saying you want me to lie to you?" Von asked.

Thad closed his eyes. "Shit."

The current reconstruction permit they were operating under required that a city inspector tour the area affected by the fire. Even though the fire had been contained to one room, it had exposed just how highly combustible the original materials used to build the house were. He and Von had made the expensive, though necessary, decision to replace all the walls with fire-resistant materials.

"What is it now?" Thad asked.

"HVAC is toast," Von said. "As the inspector searched through it to make sure there was no lingering toxins or smoke damage, he discovered that most of the ducts are corroded. He said the previous owners probably didn't do any kind of maintenance, which isn't good with the level of humidity they deal with here in New Orleans."

"Did he give an estimate of what this will set us back, both financially and timewise?"

"Well, here's the bad and the good news," Von said. "It'll clean out the remainder of the contingency fund, but Micah said he has a friend whose company can get it all done in less than a week. And we wouldn't have to stop any of the work we're doing." He hunched his shoulders. "The guy isn't military, but this situation calls for an exception."

"I agree," Thad said. He took in Von's expression and didn't like what he saw. The lines around his friend's mouth remained rigid, as did his shoulders. "There's something else you're not telling me."

One side of Von's mouth tipped up in a humorless grin. He slipped his hands in his pockets and said, "So who's reading whose mind this time?"

Thad's scalp prickled with unease. "What's wrong?"

Von blew out a breath and ran a hand down his face.

"Look, Thad, I know this isn't working out the way we thought it would. All these problems that have cropped up, the added expense..."

Thad couldn't believe what he was hearing. "Are you bailing on me?"

"Me?" Von asked. He shook his head. "No. I'm giving you the chance to bail if you want to. I give you shit for it, but I know how hard it's been for you since retiring. A buddy at the VA told me about a job opening. It's a civilian position, but it's exactly the kind of—"

"Von," Thad stopped him. "I'm not looking for anything other than being co-owner of The PX with you."

"But this position—"

"I don't care about any other position," Thad said. He clamped a hand on Von's shoulder and squeezed it. "I'm in this with you." He thought about what Ashanti told him in New York and realized just how true it was. "The PX is how we will both continue to serve our military family. This thing we're doing here, it's going to benefit veterans in the same way any position I find through the VA would." He tapped Von in the center of his chest. "You don't have to worry about me going anywhere. I got you. We've got each other."

Von's relief was palpable. He chuckled, letting out a huge breath. Then he gripped Thad by the shoulder and said, "Well, let's get back to work, because we've got a shit ton of it to do."

❖

It was well past eight by the time Thad made his way to Bark-ingham Palace. Ashanti, Duchess, and Puddin' were wait-ing on the porch. Even the dogs gave him side-eye, but then Puddin' ran up to him and started jumping around like he was actually glad to see him.

"Does sorry mean anything at this hour?" Thad asked Ashanti.

"Only if it's accompanied by dinner," she said.

"In bed?" Thad added.

She grinned. "That sounds even better. Come on, Duchess."

They were at his house twenty minutes later. They had each other before their dinner arrived.

Thad pushed up from the sofa at the sound of the door-bell, surprised that he had the strength to stand. He pulled on his jeans and made his way to the door, tipping the delivery guy extra for having to wait. He returned to the living room and found Ashanti sitting up on the sofa, the blanket that was normally draped on the side chair wrapped around her.

"Do we need plates?" Thad asked.

"I'm okay eating from the carton if you are."

Thad settled in next to her and ate Chinese food bare chested in his grandparents' living room. He barely tasted the food. This was sustenance, its sole purpose to recharge his body so that he could take Ashanti to his room and go another round. Or two.

Fuck, he could go the entire night and into the morn-ing, despite having spent much of the day doing backbreaking work. She was like an elixir, capable of curing all ills.

Ashanti had eaten maybe a third of the chicken lo mein when she set the carton on the coffee table and stood.

"That's about enough of that," she said. "You ready to go again?"

"Okay, I love you," Thad said. The words slipped out before he could rein them in.

Ashanti threw her head back and laughed loud enough to wake both Duchess and Puddin' from a sleep that the smell of Chinese food hadn't been able to disturb.

He hadn't been joking, but Thad let it slide. He had the rest of his life to tell her how much he loved her. For now, he would show her.

They went through two more condoms before Thad finally admitted to himself that he was getting too old to go all night. Ashanti was in this for the long haul. He would pace himself.

He pressed a kiss to her bare shoulder before settling his chin in the soft spot between her shoulder and jaw. How could someone who'd spent their day around dogs smell this damn good?

"Now that we've gotten that out of the way," Ashanti said, turning so that she faced him. "I've got some news to share. I've had quite the interesting day."

His brows quirked. "Share away," Thad said.

"I called Fido Foods and informed them that I am willing to sell Duchess Delights."

Thad jerked his head back. His mouth opened, but no words came when he tried to speak.

"It's the right thing for me. I'm at peace with it," she said.

"Wait, wait, wait," Thad said. "When you said you had an interesting day, I thought maybe one of the dogs got out of the gate or something."

"No, thank goodness." She laughed. "This is a good thing, Thad. They can take Duchess Delights places that I could never, and I realize that I don't want to take Duchess Delights anywhere. Last night, I sat on my front stoop with my dog and a glass of wine and examined where my life is right now and where I want it to go in the future. When I took stock of everything, I came to the conclusion that my sisters, my dog, and the daycare are what's most important to me."

"Does this have to do with the situation with Kendra's teacher?"

"It has everything to do with it," she said. "I let her stay home today because Principal Keller was at the State Board of Education in Baton Rouge, but I'm going to the school with her tomorrow, and she is telling the administration everything."

"That's going to be rough," Thad said.

"This entire thing has been brutal for her, and I hate that she felt she couldn't be honest with me. Kendra and I should have had that conversation a long time ago, and maybe we would have if I didn't have so many things vying for my attention. I knew it was more than just teenage moodiness, but I had treats to bake, and kennels to clean, and a stupid online contest to win." She shook her head. "I failed her."

"You didn't, Ashanti. Come on," he said, pressing a kiss to the top of her head.

"No, I did," she said. "The same goes for Duchess getting hurt by that Akita. I haven't been able to give my full attention to the things that are most important to me, and too many have been made to suffer because of it. I'm just not willing to do it anymore."

"So where do you go from here?" Thad asked.

She smiled up at him. "To the Lower Garden District."

His brows shot up again.

"You know those meddling friends of mine?" Ashanti asked. "Well, Ridley convinced Deja to give her access to the accounting system while we were in New York. I told her I would have her arrested, but after she laid everything out for me, I forgave her."

"What did she do?"

"She called in a favor and had one of her friends do an evaluation on Duchess Delights. That same friend will also handle the negotiations with Fido Foods once we reach that stage of the acquisitions process. Ask me how much that little side hustle of mine is valued at?"

"How much?" Thad asked.

"Four point six million."

"Are you fucking serious? For dog biscuits?"

"There's big money in those little doggy treats," Ashanti said. "I will be able to buy that building in the Lower Garden District outright. Who knows, maybe I'll eventually open a full-scale doggy café on the bottom floor. Once the girls are off to college," she added.

"That's amazing, Ashanti." Thad pressed a kiss to her lips. "One word of caution, though. It's probably best if you don't tell my grandmother about the sale. You did say that she was the one who gave you the idea to turn Duchess Delights into a business. I wouldn't be surprised if she asked for a cut."

Ashanti burst out laughing. "She would deserve it."

"Actually, I think she'll be satisfied that she didn't have to do all that much matchmaking to get us together. If I know Grams, she'll say what we have here is worth more than gold."

She lifted her mouth up to his for another kiss.

"And she would be right."

EPILOGUE

Ashanti stood at the far back end of the outdoor patio at The PX, observing the crowd that had descended on the bar for the soft opening. Two supply chain snafus and a COVID-19 outbreak among the work crew had added to the already significant delays. By some miracle, they were still able to get the sports bar portion operational by today. Veterans Day.

Based on this crowd, that was enough.

Ashanti had never seen a larger collection of US military sweatshirts in her life. Every branch was well represented, and by the smiles on patrons' faces, Thad and Von would have no problem filling this place once the cigar bar and barbershop were fully up and running.

"Friend, this was a genius idea," Von said, walking up to her and wrapping an arm around her shoulders. He gestured to the scene before them. The backyard patio area was packed with people *and* dogs.

It had been Ashanti's idea to gear the soft opening toward veterans interested in dog adoption and dog training. The local VA had jumped at the idea. They'd provided trainers, along with help in getting the word out about the event through their much larger channels.

She was no Dominque, but Ashanti had to pat herself on the back for her stroke of marketing genius. She had no doubt the majority of the people here would become regulars at The PX.

And, as had become the usual scene wherever they went, Duchess and Puddin' were stealing the spotlight from everyone else. They wore their tiara and crown, with matching royal robes, and stood like the stars they both were while people lined up to take pictures with them.

"I finally understand what both you and Thad tried to tell me," Ashanti said to Von. "I can already see how much the veterans here need a spot like this. This will be so much more than just a bar."

She smiled as Thad and Ridley walked over. Evie was in work mode, having agreed to give free checkups to the dogs and answer questions on how to care for pets.

"And who is this magnificent creature," Von asked as he sidled up next to Ridley. He wiped his hand on his shirt and offered it to her. "Von Montgomery, co-proprietor of this establishment."

Ridley looked down at his hand, then to Ashanti. "This the one you were telling me about?"

"Friend!" Von said to Ashanti with fake dismay. "What have you been saying about me?"

"Only the best things," she said.

"Well, in that case." He turned and leveled a smile at Ridley that could only be described as devastating. "As I was saying, I'm Von Montgomery."

Maybe she should have warned him that whatever tactics he usually used on women wouldn't work on Ridley.

Ashanti's eyes widened at the grin that tipped up the corners of Ridley's lips. Her friend leaned forward and whispered something in Von's ear, then turned and sauntered toward the house. Von immediately took off after her.

Ashanti shook her head. "This will not end well." She looked over at Thad. "Someone should save him. Or at least warn him."

"He's grown," Thad said. He stepped in behind her, wrapped an arm around her waist, and settled his chin on her shoulder. Familiar tingles traveled down her spine when he pressed a sweet kiss to her neck.

"You still upset I took your house?" he asked.

She shook her head. "Nope, but only because the renovations on Barkingham Palace's newest location are going so well. Oh, and because you recommended Miller Construction. I can never be upset after that. They're doing a fantastic job."

"No shit. You'll probably have your official grand opening before we do."

She laughed.

"Oh, wait! I forgot to show you," Ashanti said, pulling her phone from her back pocket. She clicked on her inbox and pulled up the email from Fido Foods. "How do you like the new Duchess Delights logo?"

She turned her phone so he could see the picture she had been sent.

Ridley's friend had earned every cent of his commission with the deal he'd negotiated on her behalf. Fido Foods had agreed to pay her five million dollars, plus a 2 percent royalty. Ashanti had been thrilled when she learned they wanted to keep her and Duchess as the face of the company. She had passed along the photographer's name from the calendar shoot they did in New York, and Fido Foods had purchased the rights to use the photo of her and Duchess in their flower crowns.

"Perfection," Thad said. He leaned forward, placing the kiss directly on her lips this time. "The logo is perfect too."

Ashanti felt a blush coming on. Her freckles were definitely going to be front and center in a matter of seconds.

"I think it is," she said. "Kara suggested we carry the flower theme through to the doggy café. I wasn't sure at first, but the more I think about it, the more I like it. Maybe fashion it after the gardens at Kensington Palace. We can even get one of those flower walls with a cute neon sign. And it could double as a backdrop for pet pictures."

"I have no idea what a flower wall is, but based on how excited you are, I'd say it's the way to go," Thad said. "And speaking of Kara, will the twins make it here?"

"I doubt it," Ashanti said. "They're all going to the movies tonight. They're celebrating the literary magazine's newest managing editor's essay being selected for inclusion in that journal at LSU."

"Would that be the essay on how to move on after a crushing disappointment?"

"That would be the one," Ashanti said.

A lot had happened since Kendra had reported the cheating ring to the administration. The entire magazine staff—save Kendra—had been relieved of their duties and barred from participating in any of the school's extracurricular activities for the remainder of the school year. Mr. Williamson had been allowed to resign, but things were still up in the air regarding the threats he'd made to Kendra. Her sister was determined to take her complaint as far as possible, even if it meant jail time for her one-time father figure and favorite teacher. Ashanti could not have been prouder.

Thad looked at his watch. "It's only two in the afternoon. Why can't they come here for a bit before heading to the movies tonight?"

"Tell me you're not raising teenagers without telling me you're not raising teenagers," Ashanti said with an eye roll. "Movie *night* is an all-day affair. They must spend the hours before the movie posting on social media about what they're going to wear, where they're going to eat, and what they're going to see."

"Sounds like my nightmare, but if that's what makes the kids these days happy." He shrugged.

"What about *your* sister?" Ashanti asked. "What time is she bringing Mrs. Frances?"

"They should be here any minute," Thad said. He clamped his hands on her upper arms. "Prepare yourself for uncomfortable questions about why you don't have an engagement ring on your finger. Nadia is convinced that we are engaged and waiting to announce it here."

Ashanti nearly swallowed her tongue. "Thad, please tell me you're not planning some big, cheesy public proposal today?"

"Is that what you're expecting?"

"No!" she said. "Especially not today. We're going slow, remember?"

He tipped his head to the side. "Exactly how fast is slow?"

She smiled up at him. "Maybe by Christmas or New Year's." She grinned. "That's what you were planning, isn't it?"

"Von is the only person who can read my mind," he answered.

"Tell me!"

He winked. "Nah. I'm going to keep you guessing."

LOOK FOR EVIE'S BOOK IN SUMMER 2025!

ACKNOWLEDGMENTS

There are so many people I could thank when it comes to this particular book, but I won't thank any of them. Instead, my thanks goes to a sweet, smushy-face, bow tie–wearing French bulldog who came into our lives at just the right time and blessed it in ways I never could have fathomed.

Thank you, Winston, for being there for my niece when she needed you the most. Those months after losing her mother were some of her darkest days, but you and your smelly stuffed lamb (shout-out to Lammy) brought brightness. You gave her a reason to smile when smiles didn't come easy.

Although much of our interaction is limited to FaceTime calls, with the occasional visit here and there, I now understand the hype about Frenchies. You, Winston, have shown me just how lovable they are.

Thank you for being your sweet, friendly, inquisitive self. Thank you for taking care of my girl just as much as she has taken care of you. And thank you for being the inspiration for Duchess.

Smooches,
Auntie Farrah

ABOUT THE AUTHOR

FARRAH ROCHON is the *New York Times* and *USA Today* best-selling author of forty-plus adult romance and young adult novels, novellas, and short stories, including the popular Boyfriend Project series from Forever Romance. When she is not writing in her favorite coffee shop, Farrah spends most of her time reading, traveling the world, visiting Walt Disney World, and catching her favorite Broadway shows.

You can learn more at:

FarrahRochon.com
Instagram @FarrahRochon
Facebook.com/FarrahRochonAuthor
TikTok @FarrahRochon
X @FarrahRochon